AND MORE RAVES . . .

"Reading *The Delta Star* is like making your way through the police academy's combat shooting range. Larger-than-life characters spring up like targets, one after another, leaving the reader no time to get over the shock before the next one pops up . . . Mr. Wambaugh is a master of twists, turns and foreshadowing . . . He is the best in his field at showing—with brutal, shocking realism—what cops see and experience to make them turn out the way they do."

—*Kansas City Star*

"Wambaugh doesn't disappoint his fans . . . He's a real storyteller—a gifted one at that."

—*Cincinnati Enquirer*

"Good puzzle; lots of twists and turns; lots of page-turning delight."

—*Boston Herald American*

"Wambaugh's cops don't go gently into that good night—or anywhere else. They raise hell—defiantly, outrageously, desperately, even gloriously . . . *The Delta Star* is another ferociously comic and tough-minded book in the vein of his *The Choirboys* and *The Glitter Dome*."

—*Pittsburgh Post-Gazette*

"Wambaugh's best and funniest profile of burned out, spaced out cops in L.A."

—*Tulsa World*

AND MORE COPS . . .

JANE WAYNE—the punk Amazon of Rampart Station. A guardian in blue . . . with purple hair to match.

DILFORD AND DOLLY—"the Personality Team." The perfect partners—Dilford hates women and Dolly hates Dilford.

Bantam Books by Joseph Wambaugh

THE DELTA STAR
ECHOES IN THE DARKNESS
THE GLITTER DOME
LINES AND SHADOWS
SECRETS OF HARRY BRIGHT

THE DELTA STAR

Joseph Wambaugh

A PERIGORD PRESS BOOK

BANTAM BOOKS
TORONTO • NEW YORK • LONDON • SYDNEY • AUCKLAND

*This edition contains the complete text
of the original hardcover edition.*
NOT ONE WORD HAS BEEN OMITTED.

THE DELTA STAR
*A Bantam Book / Perigord Book / published in
association with William Morrow and Company, Inc.*

PRINTING HISTORY
*Morrow/Perigord edition published March 1983
A Literary Guild of America Selection*

*An excerpt from this book has appeared in the
February 1983 issue of* Playboy *magazine
Bantam/Perigord edition / January 1984*

ISBN 0-553-27386-8

Published simultaneously in the United States and Canada

*Bantam Books are published by Bantam Books, a division of
Bantam Doubleday Dell Publishing Group, Inc. Its trademark,
consisting of the words "Bantam Books" and the portrayal of
a rooster, is Registered in U.S. Patent and Trademark Office
and in other countries. Marca Registrada. Bantam Books,
666 Fifth Avenue, New York, New York 10103.*

PRINTED IN THE UNITED STATES OF AMERICA

KR   16 15 14 13 12 11 10 9 8 7

for Buddy and Nancy Moss

The New Centurions ★ *The Blue Knight*
The Choirboys ★ *The Black Marble*
The Onion Field ★ *The Glitter Dome*
and now . . . *The Delta Star*

THE RAVES . . .

"A page-turner . . . The characters in *The Delta Star*
are rich, human and frightening . . . *The Delta Star*
moves easily from blackmail to murder, from prostitu-
tion to intrigue and ends up with a seemingly classic
confrontation between hunter and hunted. This is a
must-read for Wambaugh fans."

—*USA Today*

"Wambaugh's world gets wilder!"

—*New York Daily News*

"Wambaugh is a great storyteller whose stories deline-
ate a world nearly too real."

—*Los Angeles Times*

"Joseph Wambaugh's characters have altered America's
view of its police."

—*Time*

"For all the raunchiness, color and humor, his story is
very moving. *The Delta Star* is another delight, a wonderful, winning book."

—*Publishers Weekly*

THE COPS . . .

MARIO VILLALOBOS—a homicide detective with a
girlfriend who's always passionate and a bottle that
always seems to be empty. This case is pushing him
too far too fast—until a crazy scientific symbol pops
up that could save his hide.

THE BAD CZECH—the biggest, meanest cop on the
force. A self-appointed judge, jury and executioner.
How'd he get the credit card of a guy who cashed in
his chips?

MORE RAVES . . .

MORE COPS . . .

HANS AND LUDWIG—a huge cop and his killer dog. Sometimes it's hard to tell one from the other.

RUMPLED RONALD—the veteran cop, just 48 hours from retirement and convinced he'll never make it.

Acknowledgments

Many thanks to the women and men of Rampart Division, Los Angeles Police Department, and the officers of Monterey Park Police Department, for the vignettes, gossip, and generally wonderful cop talk,

and

many thanks to the faculty, students, and staff of the California Institute of Technology, especially to Professor Harry B. Gray, chairman of the division of chemistry and chemical engineering, for the generous help, considerable enlightenment, and great kindness.

Prologue

In October 1981 a Soviet submarine ran aground in re-stricted Swedish waters near the naval base at Karlskrona. The Swedish foreign minister made to Moscow what were described as "unprecedented protests in the strongest language possible." The Swedish outrage cut across party lines, with the leader of the opposition calling the intrusion inconceivable.

In that the twin-engine vessel was a Whisky-class submarine, there were lots of jokes about "Whisky on the rocks." But some Swedes weren't laughing. Especially when radiation detectors outside the sub revealed the presence of uranium 238, material that is used to shield nuclear-tipped torpedoes.

In November several hundred demonstrators marched in front of the Soviet Embassy in Stockholm carrying messages such as "Keep on sleeping, Europe. Soviet missiles will wake you up."

Despite the indignant outburst, the Swedes did not call the Soviets' hand by forcibly boarding that submarine. Some pointed to Finland, the last of their neighbors to challenge the Soviets at arms, now virtually a Russian satellite.

1

Many Swedes understandably felt their anger being tempered by more sobering emotions. Within a short time some in government were looking warily across the Baltic at the Russian colossus, expressing a willingness to be better neighbors. This anxiety was not lost on many foreigners who arrived in Stockholm for the Nobel Prize ceremonies in December. It became a topic of conversation.

ONE

The House of Misery

It was Mother's Day and they were all watching The Bad Czech. Ordinarily, after three hours of well drinks and draft beer, the blinking and bruxing, staring and sighing, twitching and palpitations gave way to verbal ventilation. But this was Mother's Day, and since most of them disliked at least one mother (The Bad Czech had *three* ex-wives and didn't even like his own mother very much) the symptoms had persisted well into evening—hence, more frantic boozing.

Which pleased Leery no end. He just sucked his teeth and leered, and wiped the bar with a filthy rag and congratulated himself on being smarter than every other saloonkeeper around these parts. Leery wouldn't dream of closing on Mother's Day. He knew from years of experience that this was one of those special days when the walking wounded of the day watch *really* put it away. The seventy-year-old saloonkeeper leered as he broke open another case of Coors. A generation ago a motor cop had correctly noted that the dour tavern owner could *not* smile, nor even grin, smirk or simper. He could only leer. Ergo, the sobriquet.

Leery's Saloon, aptly dubbed The House of Misery

by the angst-ridden who gathered there, was mostly taken up by a very long bar which could accommodate perhaps sixty souls if they stood or sat hip to hip, as they did every other Wednesday (payday for the troops) and on the Friday after that Wednesday. All the rest of the time they were broke, or nearly so, but there were always a dozen or so hard-core habitués from the day watch to carry Leery profitably into the later hours, when groupies and other civilians arrived.

Leery's Saloon was very dark, as every cop's bar must be (they don't want to *see* too much when they're off duty), and had a jukebox so that they could bump and shake and grind and wiggle on the minuscule dance floor in the next room. Leery's dance floor was exactly the size of three coffins, they said. In addition to the three-coffin dance floor there was a pool table in the adjoining room where the cops often got fleeced by mediocre pool hustlers passing through.

There were inevitable markers in the tavern to let civilian tourists know it was a cops' hangout. Such as a bumper sticker over the pub mirror that said OUR COPS EAT THEIR DEAD. Or CONAN THE BARBARIAN FOR POLICE CHIEF. OR SAVE OUR COUNTRY, BOOK A DEMOCRAT. And other such messages which tended to keep out the riffraff.

But the final tip-off was the sign on the door to the women's rest room, placed there as an admonition to cops who inevitably pursued groupies with altogether too much fervor in the shank of the night. The sign on the women's room said WOMEN ONLY!

Leery's was one of those places where the boys and girls would try to name potential customers who might enjoy the sounds emanating from within when The Bad Czech read anti-cop editorials: people like Dr. Mengele, Idi Amin and the whole Spanish Inquisition.

On Mother's Day, with the off-duty cops downing them as fast as he could pour, Leery could afford to be magnanimous and play the jukebox for the boys and girls. Of course he chose a few punk and new-wave earsplitters which tended to make emotional casualties drink more.

By now The Bad Czech was *really* getting into it.

His fists were glowing white through the smoke in the saloon. He ground his teeth and gurgled, and unconsciously shredded the *Los Angeles Times* editorial page in his huge paws. The tendons rippled across his glowering jaw as he bruxed those donkey molars. Then The Bad Czech slapped himself across his broad Slavic forehead with enough force to knock an average man right off the barstool.

As though on cue, The Bad Czech's slap coincided with the sounds of The Sex Pistols crashing out of the jukebox.

"That does it!" The Bad Czech roared, loud enough to drown out a whole platoon of punkers. "She did it again! The cunt! She did it again!"

They all knew who the cunt was: it was one of the people The Bad Czech hated most in all the world. Still, playing out the familiar ritual, a rumpled cop named Ronald—who was two days from retirement and thus feared everything from traffic stops to earthquakes—said the obvious: "What did Rose Bird and The Supremes do *this* time?"

There was only one person The Bad Czech hated more than he hated the chief justice of the California Supreme Court, Rose Bird. That was Jerry Brown, the governor who had appointed her. Because of his early education in a Jesuit seminary, Governor Jerry Brown was said by the cops to be the maddest monk since Rasputin, without the sex drive.

"That scummy, filthy, rotten, puke of a . . ." Suddenly The Bad Czech started strangling on bile and spittle. Rumpled Ronald—who, with retirement so close, also feared falling bricks, toxic insect stings, and old ladies with scissors—banged The Bad Czech on the back to get him breathing again.

"You're hyperventilating, Czech," Rumpled Ronald offered. "Settle! Settle!"

Then the ten cops and three groupies who were making Leery rich on Mother's Day began composing possible bumper stickers to cheer up The Bad Czech. Such as: "Send John Hinckley a Rose Bird pinup."

The Bad Czech snatched a bottle of beer from Leery's hand, sucked it down and began taking rattling gulps of air.

Rumpled Ronald—who, these last days, feared runaway trucks and botulized burritos—had a bizarre vision of the ascetic supreme court jurist and the equally ascetic monk who was campaigning for the United States Senate. "Know what would be the world's weirdest no-action movie?" he said. "A porn flick starring Jerry Brown and Rose Bird."

"She . . . get this . . . she . . ." The Bad Czech grabbed another beer from the bar, gulped half of it, settled, and said, "The *rest* of The Supremes voted for Corky. For once they got their shit together. But not Rose. No way. She writes a twenty-two-page dissent!"

Everyone was of course used to the town crier reading the *Los Angeles Times* aloud and strangling on bile, and knew that Corky was the airport police dog who had sniffed out some dope in a suitcase and was getting his balls rapped for illegal search and seizure, just like the cops with two legs.

"Listen to this," The Bad Czech read: " 'A traveler to protect his privacy should not have to resort to an airtight suitcase or other extraordinary measures to prevent the escape of even one marijuana molecule'!" Then the monster cop tore the paper to shreds and cried, "The fuckin dog is forcin smugglers to trash their Gucci luggage. And Rose Bird says it ain't *fair!*"

Rumpled Ronald looked at his watch and marked the fifty-one hours and thirty minutes when his pension would be secure. Then he took his own pulse and thought of hypertension, aneurysm and stroke.

One of the groupies, an emaciated girl with a splayed pelvis who looked like a toilet plunger on the barstool, said, "Hey, Leery. The Czech needs some cheering up. He ain't beat up nobody for, oh, two three days now."

"Hey, Czech," another groupie giggled. "I hear you're only shooting at cans these days. Mexi-*cans*. Puerto Ri-*cans* . . ."

Well versed by the cops in the multi-ethnic makeup of Rampart Division, a third groupie said, "Naw, The Czech only shoots at knees . . . Chi-*nese* mostly."

And so forth.

The groupies were regulars in Leery's Saloon and every other cop bar from Chinatown to Hollywood. Those familiar nameless groupies were as ubiquitous as dog shit on a vice cop's shoe, as they say. When the cops were too despondent to ventilate, the girls got things going.

"Gimme a double!" cried a singsong voice from the smoke and gloom. "My throat's as parched as Jerry Brown's balls."

The voice belonged to one half of the inseparable team of Hans and Ludwig, who were shoulder to shoulder, elbows on the bar, surrounded by the three groupies.

It made The Bad Czech even meaner and madder than usual to see Hans and Ludwig getting all the attention and drinking out of the same beer bottle. But the groupies thought it was cute and adorable and they hugged Hans and Ludwig when they did it.

Even through the darkness The Bad Czech could see Ludwig's huge wet tongue slopping around on the bottle's mouth. Then Hans tipped the same bottle to his *own* mouth and, without wiping off the slobber, drank it down.

The Bad Czech longed to snatch the beer bottle from that scrawny, noodle-necked, pathetic excuse for a cop, and stick it down his throat until that whiny singsong voice of his was muffled by eight inches of bottle glass. That's what he *wanted* to do. Except that he was scared shitless of Ludwig.

Hans' partner wasn't scrawny. Ludwig was all muscle. His chest and shoulders heaved and swelled when he sucked on the beer bottle. And his eyes were nothing like the dumb little blinking eyes of his partner, Hans. Ludwig's eyes were full of yellow menace. The pupils were elongated. And along with the massive musculature, he was nearly as tall as his skinny partner.

The Bad Czech was the biggest, strongest and unarguably the *meanest* cop at Rampart Station, but he saw something in those eyes that made him gulp back his anger. Ludwig had the eyes of a *killer*. He was sapphire-black and weighed 130 pounds. He was born and raised in Hamburg, Germany, and understood no English. He was a Rottweiler, the largest dog in the K-9 Unit of the Los Angeles Police Department.

Ludwig stuck his big ugly tongue clear *inside* the beer bottle as Hans held it for him. A bleached-out groupie with fat-handles hanging over her panty girdle just *loved* it. Especially when Hans then stuck his *own* tongue in the throat of the same bottle and drank.

The Bad Czech wanted to puke.

The reason that Hans and Ludwig were at the bar on Mother's Day was sitting as far away as she could get, at the other end of the long bar. Hans beamed whenever Dolly glanced his way.

Only five feet one inch tall, Dolly was the tiniest of the new breed of female cops to be accepted by the police department after the screws were tightened by the Equal Employment Opportunity Commission. Dolly was wondering why the hell she had come to The House of Misery on this day. Wasn't life wretched enough without people tormenting themselves? Then Dolly happened to lock eyeballs with Hans. Oh God! That skinny creep of a K-9 cop even *smelled* like his big, slobbering, revolting dog. Oh God!

And then, as if Dolly wasn't depressed enough, there was her partner, Dilford, sitting on the stool right next to hers. Why the hell couldn't Dilford find some *other* place to drink, for chrissake? If she wanted to think about it, she'd probably find Dilford even more revolting than that revolting K-9 cop and his revolting dog. For two interminable months she'd been assigned as Dilford's partner, and Dilford made no secret of how much he despised working with a female officer. Even after she saved his ass.

Did Dilford thank her when she used her stick to coldcock a Cuban drag queen who, while wearing a red lamé dress and silver heels, had kicked Dilford in the

nuts, breaking the queen's ankle strap and Dilford's fighting spirit as he lay on the sidewalk holding his balls and
howling like a bloodhound? No, he didn't thank her. He
wasn't grateful. He was embarrassed. No, he was
outraged. A *female* had retrieved his burning chestnuts.
The prick!

After the drag queen incident, Dilford and Dolly
wore more or less relentless expressions of desolation as
they morosely went about their beat marking time, each
trying to avoid looking at the other's persecuted face. Everyone called them The Personality Team.

Suddenly The Bad Czech screamed: "THAT CUNT!"
causing Leery to spill four fingers of bourbon. And it
wasn't even a well drink. Leery looked sorrowfully at
maybe thirty-five cents' worth of booze dribbling away.

This time The Bad Czech was referring not to Rose
Bird but to a member of the Los Angeles City Council
who, according to the editorial page, was urging a mora-
torium on the use of the police choke hold, which closed
off the carotid artery and in recent years had resulted in
sixteen deaths of suspects, mostly blacks, at the hands of
police.

Things had really gotten out of hand when the Los
Angeles police chief committed a faux pas in public and
said that he had a hunch that "in some blacks the veins or
arteries don't open as fast as they do in normal people."
Never mind that he later said he meant "in normal fashion." *Normal* people?

The cops had lots of fun at the chief's expense, such
as referring to their black and white police cars as their
"black and normals." After the predictable hue and cry,
out the window went the baby with the bath water. No
more choke holds—which now caused The Bad Czech to
confuse genders and scream "That cunt!" when he was
referring to a male member of the city council.

"They want us to use *tasers*!" The Bad Czech thundered. "Tasers!"

The Bad Czech had eyebrows that made Leonid
Brezhnev's look plucked. Those eyebrows, when he was

cranky like this, seemed to stand on end and reach halfway up to his hairline. And at this moment he was *really*
cranky. "They want us to use taser guns," The Bad
Czech thundered. "Tasers! When you're on your belly
tryin to wrestle some mad-dog *animal* in the rat shit and
garbage? Tasers? Lasers? What the fuck is this, *Star
Trek*? How about *razors*? How about instead a chokin
their necks we jist CUT THEIR FUCKIN THROATS? Huh?
Huh?"

Everyone knew that The Bad Czech shouldn't get
this excited, but since everyone except Ludwig the
Rottweiler was scared shitless of the monster cop, nobody
tried to make him mellow. Until the door burst open and
a tall cop strode in who had the nerve to do it.

A powerful voice, very close to a baritone, said, "So
let's start shooting the assholes who wanna fight. Don't
choke em! *Smoke* em!"

The very next day there was a brand new bumper
sticker on The Bad Czech's eight-year-old pickup truck. It
said DON'T CHOKE EM. SMOKE EM!"

The cop who offered the slogan that settled The Bad
Czech right down walked boldly up behind him. This
broad-shouldered cop was over six feet tall and had good
upper-body strength and legs that could crush a beer keg,
they said. This cop was a former punker who had been a
cop for only thirteen months, who wore new-wave rouge
that couldn't be removed with a Brillo pad, but wash-
away hair dye so as not to give the lieutenant fits.

This cop put one zip-up knee boot on the bar rail
and boldly grabbed The Bad Czech by his monster eyebrows and started massaging his temples. Which made his
headache go away instantly. Her name was Jane
O'Malley. Three nights after graduation from the police
academy, she choked out a combative trucker who
thought he could drive a sixteen wheeler across the water
in MacArthur Park right onto Duckie Island. The trucker
was dusted out on PCP and it was only Jane's choke hold
that saved the life of a foot-beat cop who was nearly
beaten to death with his own stick by the duster.

After the angel dust incident, and after seeing her pumping iron on the weight machine in the men's locker room, The Bad Czech christened her Jane Wayne, and said The Duke would have been proud. And she loved the name almost as much as she loved the choke hold. Almost as much as she loved the music of The Go-Go's and Talking Heads, and new-wave clothes. In fact, she was now wearing metallic stockings and a miniskirt and patent knee boots. And Jane Wayne really loved to cellophane her brunette shag cut, which the lieutenant couldn't see at inspections but which turned purple in the sunlight. She loved all these things. But there was one thing she loved above all else: sex.

After it was learned how Jane Wayne never shrank from violence and how much she adored sex (only The Bad Czech was man enough to make it through a weekend at her apartment), she also became known as The Bionic Bitch. So while Jane Wayne, a.k.a. The Bionic Bitch, started going into heat from rubbing the enormous shoulders of The Bad Czech and whispering to him things like, "Hear there's been a run on the bank. The *sperm* bank. Wanna refill the vault?" which made everyone who was not bombed get mildly aroused, Leery decided to encourage more barroom romance.

The K-9 cop's amorous peeks at Dolly were not lost on the ever-watchful Leery. Always one to promote young love, which in turn prompted rounds of drink buying, the dour little saloonkeeper sidled up to Dolly wiggling his pinched red nose and poured her fourth Scotch and water. "Dolly, I think Hans likes you," he said. "Wanna buy him a drink?"

"Oh God!" Dolly sneered. "Stow the matchmaking, Leery. I'd sooner be fucked by Ludwig."

Ludwig by now had his head on the bar, his big black floppy ears soaking in beer puddles. He was getting sleepy. It made Dolly shiver with disgust. *Both* members of the K-9 unit were looking at her!

Leery suddenly clanged open the cash register and took out one quarter for the jukebox. He leered like a gargoyle at the gloomy barroom and played a Black Flag ditty for Jane Wayne. It was promising to be for him a *very* happy Mother's Day!

By 11:30 P.M. Leery's Saloon was more subdued but by no means deserted. A pearl-gray BMW weaved down Sunset Boulevard. It was piloted by a driver who was listening to a cassette of the late Hoagy Carmichael singing *Old Buttermilk Sky*. The driver was surprised to see the ugly pink cocktail sign blinking at Leery's Saloon. But having been a detective at Rampart Station for two years and being a twenty-year police veteran, he was well acquainted with the M.O. of the Leerys of this world. Mother's Day at a cop's wateringhole.

The BMW made an illegal U-turn, then another, and parked in a red zone outside the tavern. This way the detective could take a peek through the greasy tavern window every few minutes and make sure some gypsy wasn't ripping off his goddamn Blaupunkt radio. The BMW was the greatest luxury he had ever owned and had been mostly earned by working off-duty jobs as a security officer at Dodger Stadium. The moonlighting earned him over $13 an hour when the Dodgers were in town, but had cost him two Blaupunkts to the bands of gypsies who paid two bucks to get in the stadium parking lot, and in one night could burgle a dozen BMWs, Audis and Mercedeses for their Blaupunkts, sold easily on the street for 150 bucks a pop.

He'd spent more time at Dodger Stadium than Tommy Lasorda, earning enough to buy that goddamn car. After his second divorce, when he was left as bankrupt as Braniff Airlines, he experienced a tremendous desire to own something of value. He was pushing thirty-nine then, and a mid-life crisis on top of the divorce was making him goofy. Now his BMW wasn't brand-new anymore and he was awaiting his forty-second birthday and the mid-life crisis wasn't getting any better. All he thought of was aging. When he wasn't thinking of The Alternative.

Mario Villalobos then thought about turning around and getting back in that BMW and driving straight to his crummy West Hollywood apartment. But he had to admit it: he wanted to see someone *more* miserable than himself. This was where to find them on Mother's Day. Already a bit drunk, he staggered into the smoke and gloom.

"Happy Mother's Day, all you mothers!" he said boozily.

The only one to look up was Dilford, who was blitzed but not as blitzed as his partner Dolly, who continued her litany of grievances against Dilford, who was drunk enough to find her bad-mouthing less boring than watching Hans the K-9 cop make periodic trips into the next room to try to roust Ludwig, who had gotten sick and tired of all this human bullshit and crawled up on the pool table to go to sleep.

". . . and that's what I think a that, Dilford," Dolly yelled in her partner's ear. "And another thing—how the hell would you like it wearing a goddamn flak vest that's made for a man? I got tits, you ever noticed. And nice ones, I been told."

"So whaddaya want," Dilford sniffed, "a bulletproof vest designed by Frederick's of Hollywood? And something I don't like: do you gotta wear *double* pierced earrings? It's sickening enough after three years on the job to be working with five-foot mini-cops that wear *earrings,* let alone *two* earrings in each ear!"

Jane Wayne and The Bad Czech were doing an imitation of a slow dance on the three-coffin dance floor. One groupie was out cold on the bar and the one with fat-handles, who dressed like a thieves' market in Cairo, was trying to persuade Hans to leave the mutt and take her out to the car for a quickie, a suggestion that shocked Hans. Not the quickie, but *leaving* Ludwig. Which was why he tried unsuccessfully to arouse the Rottweiler every few minutes. Ludwig had spent many an evening sleeping in the front seat of some groupie's car while Hans was at play in the back. Not so this night.

Hans was second generation from Düsseldorf, but had never spoken German at home and knew about as much of the language as he could get from WW II movies. Still, he affected a good accent, loved dogs madly, and quickly picked up the handful of German commands he needed to con the immigrant dog into thinking he was a real kraut.

"*Fuss,* Ludwig! *Bitte,*" Hans pleaded, "wake up, baby." Kee-rist, the fat groupie was starting to look good! "*Fuss,* Ludwig! *Fuss!*"

"Why ya give him so fuckin much beer?" the groupie whined.

"Why you have to say it's so *cute* and encourage me?" Hans whined right back at her.

Which caused Jane Wayne to break the clinch of The Bad Czech, who was hanging on for all his might to keep from falling. She playfully dipped him at the conclusion of the dance, and she looked at the snoring Rottweiler sound asleep on his back, one ear hanging in the corner pocket of the pool table, lips flopping upside down baring tiger fangs, snoring louder than the groupie on the bar top.

Then, Ludwig, deep in some canine dream or fantasy, did what he often did in his sleep. He began to grow a wet, pink, pony-sized erection. Which caused a groupie staggering out of the women's room to say, "Goddamn. Just like my old man. Errol Flynn when he's asleep. Awake, Liberace. Shit!"

I'm getting out of here right now, Mario Villalobos thought. But before he could go, Leery, all business, set a double shot of vodka in front of the detective and said, "Happy Mother's Day, Mario!"

And in truth Leery was always delighted to see the detective. Straight vodka drinkers could put it away. The detective already had an $80 bar tab this week.

"Show me a straight vodka drinker, I'll show you a guy on his way out," Leery always said. And he liked to get it all before they ended up at the veterans' hospital, or Forest Lawn.

"Got all the losers of the world in one place

tonight," Mario Villalobos observed, putting the double shot down much too fast, causing the saloonkeeper to leer happily and pour him another.

"Business ain't too bad, ain't too bad," Leery said, then glanced toward the other room where Jane Wayne and The Bad Czech were waxing nostalgic and trying to boogaloo. "Wish Hans wouldn't bring that dog in here no more," he added anxiously. "Used to be Ludwig was good for business. Lapping up suds and all. Now it ain't so cute. Him sleeping on the pool table all the time. Screws up the felt. Slobber and dog hair. And what would Internal Affairs do if they caught Hans turning that dog into a alky?"

"That dog, complete with training, is probably worth several thousand dollars," Mario Villalobos said. "Which makes him more valuable to the city than every other loser in this place put together." Then, feeling malevolent, the detective added, "Which means there'd probably be a crusade on the part of the super chief himself to close down this little house of misery and send you packing to Sun City, where you oughtta be at your age with all the money you got stuffed in your mattress."

While the detective massaged his aching eyes and felt the vodka headache coming on, Leery chewed on that one. Sun City? Limping around a freaking golf course with all the other geezers? Not making any more money? Spending twenty-four hours a day with his wife Lizzy? Jesus Christ!

"Hans! Pull yourself together, goddamnit!" Leery suddenly yelled. "Get that freaking animal off the pool table! *Achtung,* Ludwig! *Achtung!*" Leery yelled.

And while Leery ran into the poolroom trying to roust the unconscious Rottweiler, with no help from Ludwig's partner, who was putting his best move on the groupie with fat-handles (who was so drunk she thought Hans was The Bad Czech, which was like comparing a dinghy to a battleship) the detective reached over the bar and poured himself half a tumbler of vodka. On the house. Which would have given Leery a heart attack had he seen it.

Rumpled Ronald looked at his watch and said, "Twelve-oh-five, Mario. I'm forty-seven hours and fifty-five minutes from owning my own pink slip!"

"Congratulations," the detective said. "You oughtta take that pension and go to Sun City with Leery. Bound to be lots of misery in a retirement community. Arthritis. Strokes. Cancer. Real need for a joint like this."

"Hope it don't rain," Rumpled Ronald said. "Looked like rain a while ago. What if it rains and I get killed in a traffic accident on wet streets? Wouldn't that be something? Forty-seven hours away. Jesus! You seen a weather report?" And the rumpled cop ran to the window looking for lightning flashes. Seeing none, he returned to his stool and tossed back a double shot of bourbon.

Then the detective started tuning in the various conversations at the bar. It meant that his loneliness was getting scary. He usually just mumbled and nodded at anything that was said so as not to offend the speaker on the next stool who was usually too drunk to give a shit anyway.

A fat cop with red hair suddenly got maudlin and tearfully announced, "My wife's screwing a nigger! Can you believe it?"

Which caused Cecil Higgins, a grizzled black beat cop, to say, "You shouldn'ta married a nigger."

"No offense, Cecil," the maudlin cop said. "I didn't see you there in the dark."

"Next time I'll click my eyeballs so's you can see me," Cecil Higgins said. Then he turned to the detective and said, "Better call the A.A. hotline, Mario. That sucker ain't gonna make it two blocks, he's drivin. Sucker's too drunk to walk, even."

The detective's eyes started to ache even more. Was it the smog? Or the ever present smoke in Leery's Saloon? The ache seemed to originate behind the eyes. He took down half the tumbler of vodka, sighed several times and massaged his temples. Then he saw The Gooned-out Vice Cop.

The vice cop was staring at his own reflection in Leery's broken bar mirror, recently shattered by The Bad

Czech, who after reading a particularly disturbing editorial in the *Los Angeles Times* folded up the newspaper and threw it across the saloon, turning the pub mirror into a spider web. Some said it was the most remarkable feat of strength ever seen in Leery's Saloon. Others said it just attested to the weight of the *Times,* which contained more ads than a Sears catalogue.

The vice cop looked at himself among the webbed cracks, and his image was fractured. The eyes didn't line up. Part of his soft blond beard was growing from where his forehead should be. The vice cop turned his head from time to time, seeming fascinated with the way the fractured image of himself moved illusively through the shards and shadows. He moved his delicate face ever so slightly. He had large black pupils. Eyes like bullet holes.

Mario Villalobos watched the bearded young vice cop, who wore a tank top and clam diggers and had a string of turquoise beads tied around one lank strip of shoulder-length sandy hair. A matching turquoise band was tied around his throat. He looked very unlike the others who, being uniform cops from Rampart day watch, dressed more conventionally in cotton shirts, jeans, and jogging shoes or cowboy boots. Virtually every male in the saloon also wore a heavy macho moustache, almost as much a part of the bluecoat's accouterment as the off-duty gun under the shirt. The L.A.P.D. owned more moustaches than the Iraqi army. Only the detective and Hans the K-9 cop were clean-shaven.

"Where's he work?" the detective asked Cecil Higgins.

And the old beat cop, who had been staring into the bottom of his empty Scotch glass, said, "Who? The Gooned-out Vice Cop? I hear he works Hollywood. Been coming in here 'bout three weeks now. Don't talk much. Likes to stare at hisself in the mirror. I think he's gooned out most a the time. On ludes or somethin. Pretty weird dude. Jist looks in that fuckin mirror. Goony. Like all the young cops comin on the job these days. I don't talk to em less I have to. I don't know why he don't go to Chinatown or Hollywood or somewheres to do his thing."

"What's his name?" the detective asked.

"Gooned-out Vice Cop is all I know him by." Cecil Higgins shrugged.

After twenty years on the department, the detective didn't like to see quiet policemen who sat and stared with eyes like bullet holes. He didn't like it one bit.

Just then Leery snapped him out of it. "*Achtung, Ludwig! Achtung!*" Leery screamed.

"Goddamnit, Leery, shut up!" The Bad Czech yelled, trying to hear David Bowie, who was singing about cat people. "You're gettin on my nerves yellin at that mutt!"

"Hans, get that dog outa here or I'm closing this joint right now!" Leery yelled to the bombed-out K-9 cop, who was being held up on the barstool by the fat groupie, who was starting to think it was going to be a long night.

"*Bitte,* Ludwig, *bitte,*" Hans mumbled as Leery warily poked the snoring Rottweiler with a pool cue and said, "*Achtung!*"

"Slap that dog upside the jibbs," said The Bad Czech, who wouldn't even have *dared* to poke Ludwig with the pool cue, so frightened was he of the huge Rottweiler, a breed of dog with such incredible jaws that its bite pressure was more than twice that of a Doberman. And theoretically could sever a human arm.

Then the detective noticed something extraordinary. The Gooned-out Vice Cop began a silent conversation with the fractured image in the mirror. At first the detective thought he was lip-syncing to David Bowie. But he wasn't. He was sitting erect on the barstool, so that the spider web of broken shards turned his face into a Picasso portrait. Part of the glow from a neon tube advertising a defunct brewery cast a ghastly green across the shards in his fractured image. The Gooned-out Vice Cop nodded very slightly and spoke to the image. At least his lips moved, and the detective, who was getting drunker by the minute, shook his head to clear it. He stared hard across the barroom and tried to see what the vice cop was saying to the mirror image.

But then all hell was about to break loose. Leery had begun to panic as he thought of what would happen if Internal Affairs Division got wind of a valuable police dog drunk on his pool table. Not to mention a saloon full of zombies, all of whom were half a fifth past the point of Leery losing a liquor license for serving them. And Leery got a flash of the chief of police himself jerking his liquor license off the wall and sending him into retirement to Sun City and twenty-four hours a day with his wife Lizzy and . . .

"That is fucking it!" Leery shrieked suddenly. "I ain't taking *this* shit! Look! Just look!"

It caused quite a stir even among those zombies who could barely lift their heads. Ludwig, deep within a canine dream or fantasy, had begun to moan, softly at first, and then with feeling.

And had begun *ejaculating*. Right on Leery's pool table, on the felt, right by the side pocket.

"Czech, you got nothing on Ludwig," said Jane Wayne admiringly.

"Like my old man. When he's *asleep!*" said the fat groupie disgustedly.

"Know why dogs lick their own balls?" said The Bad Czech profoundly. "Cause they *can*."

"*Fuss*, Ludwig! *Bitte!*" Hans cried hopelessly. "Please don't jizz on Leery's table!"

Then, pandemonium! When Leery saw the jizz he lost his temper and gave Ludwig a hell of a poke with the pool stick, right in the ass. The Rottweiler rose up with a roar that sounded like a space shuttle blast-off.

Leery dropped the pool cue and went over that bar like no man seventy years old. Jane Wayne broke down a door crashing into the men's room. The Bad Czech screamed in horror and drew down on the Rottweiler, pointing his two-inch Colt with both trembling hands. Ludwig sat upright on the pool table and roared, his huge head bumping against the hanging light and sending fearful shadows across the barroom full of terrified people.

Then, as fast as it had begun, the terrible roar subsided. Ludwig growled a bit and blinked his yellow menacing eyes, which were full of sleep and bloodshot from the smoke and booze. Then he plopped back down. In a few seconds he was snoring again.

And The Bad Czech was reholstering his gun shakily. And cops were walking, running, *crawling* out of The House of Misery.

The detective had a crazy thought when he unlocked his BMW, happy to see that no roving gypsy had ripped off his Blaupunkt. He remembered telling a professor in a police science class he once took at UCLA that police work wasn't a science. It is and always will be an *art*, he had claimed. As he watched them staggering, sliding, weaving to their cars he remembered making that observation. And he thought it over. *These?* These are *artists*?

Then the detective saw The Gooned-out Vice Cop. He wasn't getting into a car like the others. He was walking, no, *floating* down Sunset Boulevard. He seemed to be floating leisurely along the sidewalk into the darkness, his eyes like bullet holes.

Mario Villalobos' own eyes started to ache again. He needed a good night's sleep desperately. He unlocked his BMW and got in. But he wondered: what the hell did The Gooned-out Vice Cop *see* in that mirror?

The last sound the detective heard from The House of Misery was Leery's anguished cry: "*Achtung,* Ludwig! *Achtung!*"

TWO

The Hanging Wino

The Bad Czech was *really* cranky the next day. He had an awful headache. The base of his skull hurt, both temples hurt, and the top of his head, where his heavy black hair was parted by a cord of white scar (compliments of an NVA mortar fragment at Khe Sanh), hurt most of all. Even his *eyebrows* seemed to hurt. There was nothing like the central city, growling and farting and belching forth a pall of smoke and pollution, for intensifying an already brutal hangover. The Bad Czech lurched along his beat on smog-choked Alvarado Street with the old black cop Cecil Higgins, and looked like he might commit murder. Which he tried to do within the hour. And which he finally managed the next day.

But before attempting murder and finally succeeding, The Bad Czech had a rather normal morning. First order of business for the two beat cops was to stagger into Leo's Love Palace, an Alvarado bar frequented by Cubans, Puerto Ricans, Mexicans, Guatemalans, Dominicans and Salvadoreans. Leo, a Pima Indian, despised *all* the greasers even more than he despised the huge paleface and the old nigger now looking at him with agony in their

21

bloody eyes. Leo started mixing up the morning Alka-Seltzer for the beat cops without being asked.

Three Salvadoreans boogied out the back door before finishing their beers, causing Cecil Higgins, who had just removed his police hat and was massaging his aching bald head, to say, "Musta been a good hit on Sy's Clothing Store over the weekend. Those three was all wearin Calvin Kleins."

"Oh my head!" The Bad Czech moaned. "I'm feelin mainstreet pain. Don't talk too loud, Cecil."

As The Czech said it, he drank down the Alka-Seltzer, moaned again, and was licking the foam from his wiry black moustache when a black Puerto Rican came finger-popping through the door listening to station KROQ with *two* shiny new radios blaring music in his ears. He saw the two hungover blue-coats at the bar, said, "Uh oh," and highballed it back out onto Alvarado.

"Shee-it," Cecil Higgins said. "That sucker's the fifth thief I seen this morning with brand new ghetto blasters glued to his fuckin ears. Raymond's Stereo Center musta got raped over the weekend."

"I gotta get some fresh smog in my lungs or I'm gonna die, Cecil," The Bad Czech whimpered, and lurched out of Leo's Love Palace onto the busy sidewalk, the older cop following along behind, still rubbing his loose bald scalp.

"Jesus Christ on Roller Skates!" The Bad Czech suddenly cried.

"That's who it is, aw right." Cecil Higgins nodded as the two beat cops moved off the sidewalk to let Jesus Christ on Roller Skates boogie on by.

He wore an ankle-length dirty gray sari and shoulder-length dirty brown hair and a full beard and dilated blue eyes. He was about as skinny as the skateboard he was riding and could not possibly have carried the seven-foot cross made of four-by-fours if he hadn't had the ingenuity to attach a roller skate to the toe of the cross, which Cecil Higgins said proved that he might be crazy but he wasn't stupid. His mission seemed to be to stop every twenty yards or so, put the cross down and scream, "Prepare ye for my coming!" at the top of his lungs.

If that wasn't bad enough he also had a ghetto blaster strapped around *his* neck, but at least it wasn't tuned in to KROQ. He was playing a cassette of "The Old Rugged Cross."

"Wonder if Jesus Christ on Roller Skates was the chaplain for the gang that ripped off Raymond's Stereo Center?" Cecil Higgins mused.

"Maybe it's the cheap booze at Leery's," The Bad Czech groaned. "But ya know, Cecil, sometimes I ain't too sure no more what's real and what ain't."

"Huh!" Cecil Higgins grunted. "You on'y got thirteen years on the job, boy. Wait'll you got twenny-eight years like me. Some days I walk this here beat and I don't know my dick from a dumplin. Tell ya the truth, Czech, I ain't been absolutely sure what's real and what ain't for maybe twenny-two years now."

"I know that Jesus Christ on Roller Skates was real," The Bad Czech mumbled, more to himself than to Cecil Higgins, as the two blue-suited beat cops walked gingerly on their ripple soles to reduce the pain. "Only reason I know is, that screechy roller skate hurt my *head,* is how I know." Then he added, "I'm *pretty* sure that Jesus Christ on Roller Skates was real."

And while The Bad Czech was moving tenderly about his beat, Mario Villalobos, also experiencing a world-class hangover, wiped an imaginary dust spot from the roof of his BMW and headed for the back door of Rampart Station wondering how many of the locals had survived the shootings, stabbings, rapings and stranglings that undoubtedly occurred over the weekend while folks gathered to celebrate Mother's Day.

"Morning, Mario," a young voice said cheerfully. "Have a nice Mother's Day?"

"Morning," the detective answered, heading for the coffeepot.

He only glanced at Chip Muirfield and at the brand-new three-piece butter-brickle suit the young detective was wearing, and at the tanned, handsome face and sun-streaked surfer's hair. Yet somehow he had known that the young man would say "Have a nice Mother's Day?"

Chip Muirfield was the nephew of retired Deputy Chief Lorenzo Muirfield, who after retirement was appointed by the mayor to the board of police commissioners. Chip was a law-school dropout, disappointing his Uncle Lorenzo, who decided to redeem his nephew by pushing him to the top of Lorenzo's chosen profession. (When it came to nepotism the Hollywood film studios had nothing on the police department.)

Chip Muirfield was only twenty-seven years old and had been a policeman for just four years, most of it in administrative jobs. He had been temporarily assigned to Rampart Detectives on a loan to give him some "seasoning," as his uncle put it when he begged the favor. And to prepare Chip for the quick ascension up the bureaucratic ladder which was to be his destiny. This kid had *so* much topspin you couldn't keep him inside the baseline, everyone said. He'd taken to detective work with a fervor. Especially homicide, because he loved to look at dead bodies, the gorier the better. And he discovered much to his delight that Melody Waters, the only female on the homicide team, shared his fascination with mutilated corpses.

Melody was a cute-as-a-button brunette, five years older than Chip, and the only female officer on the Los Angeles Police Department with the balls to wear a shoulder holster like Clint Eastwood. Very few male detectives had the balls to wear a shoulder holster like Clint Eastwood. Chip Muirfield also wore a shoulder holster. The other cops said it was a love story: Dirty Harry meets Dirty Harriet.

Mario Villalobos sat at the homicide table and rubbed his aching eyes and looked at the two happy young hot dogs who had found each other in their shoulder holsters, and he wondered if he could afford to pull the pin when he got twenty-five years in. But he really couldn't afford to, not with the *second* divorce just final. Not with two teenaged sons to support from his first marriage. He was ever grateful that the brief second one was childless. He might have had to stay for *thirty* in order to get the maximum pension. As it was, he longed to retire at twenty-five years. Then he happened to glance down at Chip Muirfield's feet. The kid was wearing suede saddle oxfords!

It was not the same police department that Mario Villalobos had joined back in the early sixties, before the street riots and Vietnam, when dinosaurs like The Bad Czech were the rule and not the exception. Mario Villalobos III in those days had felt obliged to explain away his Spanish surname to every policeman he worked with: "No, I'm not Mexican. No, I'm not even Spanish, for chrissake. Well, I mean I had one freaking grandparent who migrated from Spain to England but *he* never spoke Spanish again. In fact, he married my grandma in Wales. I know I'm dark, but . . . no, I can't speak Welsh! Only Richard Burton can speak Welsh. And my mother was an Okie from Muskogee. If I was a Mexican I'd *admit* it!"

But even if a partner was convinced, there'd be the directed calls from communications to meet a motor cop or a traffic unit to translate for some poor wetback they were booking for drunk driving. Only to repeat: "Yes, I *know* I have a Mexican name. It's Spanish really, but I can't speak . . . Aw, shit!"

Until finally, one night while on patrol in Watts in 1965, when half the city seemed to be burning and a fire storm was lighting up the sky in the west for twenty miles, a wise old cop from San Pedro who had been moved in for riot duty said to him, "Kid, I was you I'd take advantage a my name. I mean, here you go around apologizing to everybody cause you got a name like a beaner and cause you're dark enough to pass for one. I see the department changing a lot by the time you grow up and get whiskers. If this riot means anything I think they're gonna be pushing the minorities up the totem pretty soon. I was you, I'd *be* a Mexican. Know what I mean?"

And the old cop was *almost* right. After the Civil

Rights Act and the Equal Employment Opportunities Act, the federal and state legislation tightened the screws all right. But it was the blacks, Orientals, and women of any race who finally were the beneficiaries of the pressure.

"He's a *federal* captain," the white cops might sneer when referring to a recently promoted black who otherwise (they thought) wouldn't have made it. Or, "He's another one of those *feds* we gotta accept," referring to a five-foot-three-inch mini-cop like Sunney Kee, who they said was not only a foreigner but a midget as well.

The push really began after the boat people came to Los Angeles: the Vietnamese, Cambodians, Laotians. And the Cubans. The cops just *loved* Jimmy Carter for letting in the boatloads of Cubans.

Along with the boat people came the Koreans, Thais and Chinese, and Latinos from all over Central and South America. To the center of the city, close to downtown, where they worked for minimum wage and less in restaurants, factories and sweatshops.

But Mexicans had been around *too* long for the Affirmative Action people to think about. Mario Villalobos had years ago taken the trouble to study Spanish for three years during his off-duty hours in order to be a more promotable Mexican when the time was ripe. It never was. Of course the Mexican-American cops knew he spoke *gringo* Spanish, but then so did lots of Mexican-American cops whose families were middle-class and assimilated. Mario Villalobos never claimed he *was* one. But he never said he *wasn't*. It had all taught Mario Villalobos one thing for sure: beaners usually get screwed anyway. Being a counterfeit Mexican had never helped him at all. As it turned out he should have had a Vietnamese surname.

When he got settled in his chair at the homicide table, Mario Villalobos hefted the pile of reports from the weekend and wondered if anybody was left intact in the division.

"Hey, Mario," Chip Muirfield said, "Melody and I were thinking about stopping for some brunch on the way to the coroner's. Want to join us?"

"Brunch?" Mario Villalobos said. Homicide detectives going for *brunch*? Eggs Benedict, no doubt. Maybe a glass of Chardonnay?

"No thanks," Mario Villalobos said. Then, "The coroner's? We got one being posted today?"

"Yeah, a white streetwalker from Santa Monica and Normandie. Report's on the bottom there. Looks like somebody pushed her off the roof of the Wonderland Hotel. Five floors. Probably her pimp."

Mario Villalobos said, "What're things coming to when pimps push their meal tickets off roofs?"

"I'm just guessing it was her pimp," Chip Muirfield said. "Night clerk said on the report that he saw a tall white guy he thinks is from East Hollywood. Runs girls from Santa Monica and Western."

"The night clerk's a liar or stupid," Mario Villalobos said, burning his lip with the coffee and failing to get his cigarette lit until the second try. Maybe he'd switch from vodka to Scotch? Some guys said your hands were steadier the next day.

"Why?"

"When the spades start letting a honky run girls on Santa Monica and Western, that's when Margaret Thatcher's going barhopping in Buenos Aires," Mario Villalobos said.

"Well, *some* white guy was seen going up the elevator on Saturday night about ten o'clock, just before she screamed. The postmortem begins at ten-thirty this morning."

"Anything left to post? She must look like strawberry shortcake."

"The report says she hit the roof of a panel truck. Maybe she's not busted up so bad. Is it okay if I meet you at the coroner's after I brunch with Melody?"

Mario Villalobos nodded and closed his eyes, and ran his hands through his half-combed graying hair. *Brunch* with Melody. He'd probably be at least a deputy chief like his uncle. Or a state senator like the last chief.

Already finished with their paper work because they came to work forty-five minutes early, the two young detectives gathered up their case envelopes and reports and their briefcases (Chip's wasn't plastic like Mario Villalobos', it was cowhide, handstitched) and headed for a fun-filled morning of watching dead bodies get hacked up, sawed and generally reduced into something resembling steak tartare, which they both ate for brunch.

"The prom queen and the quarterback," Mario Villalobos said, shaking his head painfully. "With shoulder holsters."

Just then a young bluecoat came charging into the squadroom, a freckled lad with violet eyes. He ran up to the homicide table and said, "Sergeant! You work homicide, don't you?"

"Yeah," said the detective trying to remember the young cop's name. "What can I do . . ."

"Sergeant. You aren't gonna believe this!"

"Could you maybe kick back a little and . . ."

"Sergeant!" The young cop wiped his sweaty face on the blue sleeve of his uniform. "They found this bag in Lafayette Park! Two-A-Forty-three found it and . . ."

"That's not my area," said Mario Villalobos. "See Detective Sanford and . . ."

"Sarge! They thought it was crappy diapers in the bag. Or old Kotex or something. At first. It looked like a rotten melon! All purple and black!"

"What?" Mario Villalobos sighed.

"The head!" the young cop cried. "There was a *head* in the diaper bag. I thought it was a rotten melon! It's a man's head! I think! They're watching it there. We called for the dicks but nobody came. We waited five minutes and . . ."

"Wait a minute, son," Mario Villalobos said. "First of all, that isn't my area. Detective Sanford will be glad to roll on that call. But you should try to settle a bit before you . . ."

"You should *see* it, Sergeant!" the young cop cried. "It looked like a rotten melon. I thought it was just diapers in the bag at first and . . ."

"Mellow *out*," said Mario Villalobos, grabbing the

freckled young cop by the shoulder. "Listen to me. Did it still have the eyes in it?"

"Eyes? Eyes? Yeah, I think so. Yeah! It still had eyes!" the young cop cried.

"Well then you can't *bowl* with it, can you? So what *good* is it? Just go get yourself a can of soda pop, and after you settle, go see Detective Sanford? Okay?"

So while Sergeant Mario Villalobos was wrapping up his morning's paper work and the freckled cop with violet eyes was trying to mellow out by thinking, what the hell, you can't *bowl* with it, The Bad Czech was about to get mad enough to commit murder. It all began when he decided to hang the wino.

The wino was one of those real pain-in-the-ass winos. One of those play ragpickers who push a shopping cart around Pico and up Alvarado clear to the freeway, pretending to pick up trash and bottles, stealing whatever isn't chained, locked, screwed or nailed. One of those winos who, in addition to being a thief, also had a fetish and foraged through MacArthur Park stealing the underwear from old women who couldn't put up a fight. One day he pulled the stockings right off the old shocks of a snoozing grandma in a wheelchair and was chased by The Bad Czech clear to the water's edge, where the wino waded and swam to Duckie Island and had to be arrested by helicopter. The Bad Czech's uniform was covered with duck shit and had to be dry-cleaned twice. The Bad Czech didn't like that wino one little bit.

His name was Elmo McVey. He was a cadaver with a crewcut who smelled like the Vernon slaughterhouse. It was particularly frustrating because he was ruined by alcohol yet somehow could still outrun The Bad Czech.

The two cops spotted him while they were making their first pass through MacArthur Park, hoping they wouldn't observe any assholes pulling a pigeon drop on pensioners, or mugging checker players, or purse-picking commuters on the way to the bus stop. The last thing The

Bad Czech wanted to see when he was *this* cranky was Elmo McVey. But there he was.

The skinny wino was sneaking up on a young Guatemalan couple who were necking on the grass. They had a prize in a carrying bag next to the wooden bench some distance away. The prize was a big silver stereo, which wasn't switched on but was protruding tantalizingly from the bag. Elmo McVey was creeping toward that bag like a mangy cat stalking a grasshopper.

The Bad Czech said, "I'd like to hang that wino."

"So would I," said Cecil Higgins, not knowing that The Bad Czech was feeling mean enough to do just what he said.

As they were watching Elmo McVey wriggling along the grass fifty yards away, a toothless woman with chin whiskers came wheezing along the path through the park and said, "Officers, are you watching that dirty wino?"

"Yeah, lady," Cecil Higgins answered. "What'd he do, steal your purse?"

"He stole my bra!" the whiskered woman answered. "From the clothesline outside my window!"

Cecil Higgins took off his police hat and rubbed his loose rubbery bald scalp, which was starting to lose its chocolate sheen what with all the futile experiments with hair-growing preparations. All the cops said it was beginning to look like a moldy coffee bean. He also used Lady Clairol on his moustache, which if left untouched would be dead white. "Lady, even for Elmo McVey that's a new low," said Cecil Higgins. "Wonder what he'd do with a size fifty, E cup? Pretty hard to peddle it, I imagine."

"I want you to put him in jail!" the whiskered woman demanded. "The worse kind a scum."

"He's the kind a pain-in-the-ass wino that really gives me a headache," said The Bad Czech absently. "I'd like to hang that wino."

"Too good for him, you ask me," the whiskered woman said. Then she spun around huffily and went wheezing back down the path.

He never heard them coming. Elmo McVey was suddenly lifted two feet off the ground by the back of his army field jacket, looking into the demented gray eyes of the biggest, strongest and unarguably the *meanest* cop in Rampart Division. The Bad Czech let him dangle for a moment and he did indeed resemble a mangy cat, wiggling and hissing.

"I ain't did nothin," Elmo McVey spat. "I jist wanted to hear the score a the ball game!"

"There *ain't* no ball game, Elmo," Cecil Higgins said, while The Bad Czech continued to suspend the wino by the scruff of the neck and glare at him.

"Well, I *thought* there was a ball game, is what I thought," Elmo McVey said. "Once a Met fan always a Met fan. I thought the Dodgers was playin in New York today. I was jist gonna tune in that radio to catch the score, is what I was gonna do."

"Why don't you go *back* to New York, Elmo," Cecil Higgins said as The Bad Czech lowered the wino to the ground, but continued to hold him by the nape of the neck.

"Too cold in New York. L.A.'s my kind a place," Elmo McVey said, getting quite uncomfortable what with The Bad Czech's hand, the size of a catcher's mitt, clamped around his neck.

The Bad Czech finally spoke: "I musta asked you a thousand times to take your act downtown to Main Street, Elmo. Did I ask you a thousand times or not?"

"Don't like Main Street. Too many winos down there," Elmo McVey said, looking fearfully up into The Bad Czech's deranged gray eyes.

"Well I ain't gonna ask ya no more," The Bad Czech said.

"Whatcha gonna do?" Elmo McVey asked.

"I'm gonna hang you," The Bad Czech answered.

And while The Bad Czech walked Elmo McVey south through MacArthur Park, Cecil Higgins followed along reluctantly, wondering what this latest bullshit trick was all about. He felt vaguely uncomfortable because The Bad Czech's loony eyes looked a little loonier than usual today. Just the hangover, Cecil Higgins finally decided.

Until they got into the secluded alley east of Alvarado and north of Eighth Street.

"I noticed this when we walked through yesterday," The Bad Czech said to Cecil Higgins when they arrived in the alley.

"Noticed what?" Cecil Higgins looked around. The alley was away from traffic, and quiet. There were some wooden boxes separating a pink stucco apartment building full of Latin American aliens and an auto parts warehouse, which had more alarms, barbed wire and steel bars around it than Folsom Prison. Aside from the wooden boxes and the derelict remains of a bicycle, there was nothing else in the alley.

"I saw *this*," the monster cop said.

Tucked behind a peeling metal downspout was a twenty-foot length of rope which someone had tied over the bottom step of a fire escape that was held in place at the second floor by a rusty cable. All business, The Bad Czech began fashioning a noose with the oily length of rope.

Cecil Higgins and Elmo McVey looked quizzically at each other, and Elmo McVey giggled uncomfortably and said, "I thought capital punishment was abolished in this state."

"They brought it back," Cecil Higgins said. "But they ain't used it in a long long time." Then to his partner: "Hey, Czech, what the fuck're you *do*-in?"

"I told him a thousand times to take his act on the road. Down to Main Street," The Bad Czech said, cinching up the noose, checking the snugness of the knot as it slid down to the size of a thirteen-inch neck. Then he opened the noose wide and left it dangling there from the fire escape while he crossed the alley in three giant steps and picked up a wooden box.

"This ain't much of a scaffold," The Bad Czech said, "but it's all we got." He placed the wooden box under the noose and said, "I asked you a thousand times to . . ."

"Ain't this gone far enough?" Elmo McVey whined nervously. He wisely decided to talk to the black cop, who, though an evil looking old nigger, was nevertheless more agreeable to Elmo McVey than the gigantic madman with the eyebrows all over his face.

"Hey, Czech, let's go git some soul food," Cecil Higgins offered, also sounding a bit nervous. "Little gumbo cleans up a hangover in no . . ."

But suddenly The Bad Czech lifted the mangy wino up on the box until he stood eye to badge with the beat cop's silver hatpiece. Then The Bad Czech grabbed the squirming wino under the throat, quickly slipped the noose over his head and cinched it tight. The monster cop stepped back and reckoned that the wino's feet would never come closer than twelve inches to the ground.

"Boys, this is some kind a fun," Elmo McVey giggled, grabbing at the rope. "I mean, I been rousted by cops from Manhattan to Malibu. I learned to appreciate the weird sense a humor a you guys. Now kin we jist wrap this up and take me to the slam or . . . or . . ." Then for the first time he looked *deep* into the demented gray eyes of The Bad Czech. "Or . . . or beat the crap outa me! OR DO SOMETHIN REASONABLE!"

"Let's go git some gumbo, Czech," Cecil Higgins said. "Now!"

"Fuck it. How do ya know Elmo's real, anyways?" The Bad Czech said.

And he kicked the box clear across the alley.

When Elmo McVey dropped, so did the fire escape. The rusty cable holding it up snapped with the wino's weight and both the fire escape and Elmo McVey crashed down in the alley. The fire escape nearly creamed Cecil Higgins, who yelped and jumped into a doorway. It missed The Bad Czech by less than a foot but he didn't seem to notice.

"Aw shit!" The Bad Czech said. "Let's tie it to the railing and try it again."

But by now Cecil Higgins was prying the rope from Elmo McVey, who was gasping and squeaking and about the color of the cops' uniform.

"He . . . he . . ." Elmo McVey croaked and coughed and babbled and touched the rope burn and took several gulps of air and finally said, "HE LYNCHED ME!"

"Take it easy, Elmo," Cecil Higgins said, dusting off the wino's army-surplus jacket. "Don't make a big deal outa it."

"HE TRIED TO HANG ME!" Elmo McVey screamed hoarsely as The Bad Czech worked silently to redo the noose and find a better gallows.

"Elmo, I was you," said Cecil Higgins, "I'd forgit all about this here . . . *fantasy* about some cop tryin to hang ya. I mean, I was you I'd take one more hard look at my partner and take your act on the road, right down to Main Street."

"I want a lawyer!" Elmo McVey screamed.

"Elmo," Cecil Higgins said shakily, "if ya was to make some kind a crazy complaint about bein lynched and all, would anybody believe ya? And even if they did, whaddaya think The Czech would do when he hunted ya down in a alley sometime? I bet he wouldn't hang ya by the *neck* next time, is what I bet."

Then Cecil Higgins reached in his pocket and took out two dollars. "Go git yourself a bottle a Sneaky Pete and forgit this fantasy. And git your shit together and take your act on the road."

Elmo McVey's eyes were still the size of poker chips but his face was only slightly lavender when he left that alley holding his neck. "Well," he said, "Main Street's got its good points. There's a mission down there where the food ain't bad and nobody's gotta hear *too* much Jesus crap. And down there stealin bras and panties ain't a *hangin* offense."

Actually, after the rope burn healed, Elmo McVey could not be sure that the hanging wasn't some terrible alcoholic dream. Even he wasn't sure that it was real.

Five minutes later, after having disposed of the gallows and rope while The Bad Czech ate a beef-and-bean burrito from a taco truck, the old beat cop cadged a free cup of coffee from the Mexican vendor and decided it was time for some heavy conversation.

"Shouldn't oughtta eat from these roach wagons,"

Cecil Higgins advised The Bad Czech, who was drinking grape soda pop and devouring a burrito like any whiskey-ravaged hangover victim.

"Nother one," The Bad Czech said with his cheeks full of tortilla. The Mexican, having served burritos to freeloading cops from Tijuana to L.A., just chalked the freebies up to public relations.

After The Bad Czech was belching hot sauce and feeling less cranky, the old beat cop took his giant partner by the arm and walked him over to a bench by the water in MacArthur Park. When The Bad Czech finished his soda pop, Cecil Higgins said, "Know somethin, kid? I been noticin that ya ain't so happy lately."

"I ain't?" The Bad Czech said, belching up a green chile seed which stuck to his wiry black moustache.

"No, you ain't. Is it maybe your divorce?"

"I'm used to them. After three I oughtta be. I ain't got no money for the lawyers to take no more."

"Maybe it's the booze," Cecil Higgins offered. "Maybe nobody oughtta go to Leery's ever single night."

"I think I'd *really* get grouchy if I didn't go to Leery's ever single night," The Bad Czech said.

Cecil Higgins, still boozy from last night, was being hypnotized by the green pepper seed on The Bad Czech's moustache. He pulled himself together, plucked off the fiery seed and threw it in the water, where a white duck bit into it and got totally pissed off, quacking furiously.

"I know what it is!" Cecil Higgins suddenly cried. "It's the fuckin newspaper. You're gettin goofy from readin the *L.A. Times*!"

"Ya think so?" said The Bad Czech. "Ya think I'm gettin goofy?"

"Kid, the *Times* ain't good for your head," the old cop said. "Ya take it too serious."

"Maybe you're right." The Bad Czech nodded. "But, Cecil, am I *really* gettin goofy?"

"Czech, I think you're aware that hangin went out in this state, oh, maybe eighty years ago. Like, they ain't even gassed nobody in years. I mean, the chief, the mayor, the public defender, the A.C.L.U., even Alcoholics Anonymous, almost *everybody* I can think of would not like it one fuckin bit, they was to catch ya hangin winos."

Then The Bad Czech turned his demented gray eyes toward Cecil Higgins and said, "But Cecil, how do ya know for *sure* that wino was *real*?"

"Gud-damnit!" Cecil Higgins yelled, getting up and throwing his police hat down on the bench.

Then he pulled out his nightstick and whacked a palm tree which brought a little palm frond down on his bald scaly bean and he said, "There ya go again with this *real* BULL-shit!"

"Cecil, don't get cranky!" The Bad Czech pleaded. "Look, the chief justice a the state supreme court says that smugglers shouldn't have to get rid a their Gucci luggage and buy sniff-proof containers for their dope. Don't ya get it? Even a dog can get his balls slapped for search and seizure. Don't ya *get* it?"

"Get what?"

"It ain't *real*. I mean it ain't *really* real in . . . in . . . a . . . a *philosophical* way."

"Philo-fuckin-sophical!" Cecil Higgins groaned. Then the old black cop paced back and forth snorting disgustedly. "I shoulda knowed. Ever since ya took that night-school class at L.A. City College. Up until then the biggest word ya ever said was enchilada. Philosophical. Shit. Night school's fucked up your head worse than the *L.A. Times*."

"But ya said yourself, Cecil, that even *you* ain't always sure what's . . . *really* real and what ain't."

Then Cecil Higgins sat down on the bench. A burly man in his own right and, when standing erect, at least six feet tall, he had to look straight up at The Bad Czech, who had most of his great height in his torso. Like John Wayne, he always bragged.

"Okay, Czech, I'm gonna tell ya what's *real*," Cecil Higgins said. "What's *real* is that nobody, I mean no *civilian* outside a the fat broad with the whiskers is gonna care about what's *really* real when it comes to hangin winos. And if ya insist on hangin winos, or anybody else

for that matter, what's gonna happen is they're gonna
send some headhunters out to throw ya in the slam and
then they're gonna send ya to San Quentin. And up in Q
there's these gangs a bad-news niggers like the Muslims
and so on. And one day in the prison yard old Elijah X
or some other headshaved motherfucker is gonna give the
signal and all these spades is gonna jump on your bones
and pull your pants off and about eighty a them's gonna
lay more tube than the motherfuckin Alaska pipeline and
your asshole's gonna end up lookin like the Second Street
Tunnel and you're gonna be able to carry your bowlin
ball and six armadillos no hands for the rest a your fuckin
life which is gonna be real short anyways. AND THAT'S
WHAT'S REAL! KIN YOU DIG IT?"

It was the longest speech Cecil Higgins had ever
made. The Bad Czech seemed impressed. "Okay, I won't
hang no more winos," The Bad Czech said, "If ya
promise not to ask to work with somebody else. You're
the only person left I kin talk to."

For once, The Bad Czech's demented gray eyes
didn't seem to smolder. The old beat cop brushed a palm
nut off his scaly noggin and looked at those eyes and—
well, he had to admit it: the big wacko had started to
grow on him. Truth to tell, Cecil Higgins didn't have anybody to talk to either, outside of the other losers at
Leery's Saloon.

"Okay, kid," Cecil Higgins said. "I promise to work
with ya right up to my thirty-year pension. Which I don't
expect to live to see anyways. I jist hope I don't end up in
San Quentin with a asshole big enough for a motor
scooter to turn around in."

THREE

The Stubborn Chopstick

Melody Waters and Chip Muirfield were feeling all warm and rosy from the brunch of steak tartare. They did *not* have Chardonnay as Mario Villalobos expected; they both drank Perrier. Full of steak tartare and designer water, the young detectives now did what they loved to do best: they headed for the coroner's to gawk at all the maimed and butchered carcasses of former human beings.

First they had entertained each other out in the hall playing with a stiff on a gurney. A Mexican had been shot three times in the chest for walking on the wrong street during a gang war in which he was not involved, nevertheless satisfying the gang's blood code by his demise. Chip Muirfield had stood behind the body and grabbed the top of the body bag and lifted the head a bit and made the cadaver, who stared with sad and sleepy eyes, respond to all of Melody Waters' questions.

"How's the accommodations down here?" Melody giggled.

"Is okay," Chip said in a gravel voice, shaking the body bag so that the stiff nodded.

"You wouldn't want to spend a lot of time here, would you?" Melody asked the corpse.

"Is not *that* okay," Chip said in the gravel voice, moving the bag so that the stiff shook his head.

They only knocked it off when Mario Villalobos caught them and said, "If you two could tear yourselves away from the grossout gags, could you please pay a *little* attention to business?"

Mario Villalobos, while awaiting the arrival of the shoulder holster kids, had given his crime report another perfunctory looksee. It was better than standing around the autopsy room watching them scoop out Missy Moonbeam like the honeydew melon filled with Häagen-Dazs ice cream that Chip Muirfield and Melody Waters had had for dessert. It was better than watching them replace her insides not with little balls of Häagen-Dazs ice cream, but with the scrambled heaps of guts shoveled back in by the morgue tech, who wiped the inside of her now brainless skull with soggy paper towels, which he stuffed inside the empty skull along with his sandwich wrapper when he was through.

As it turned out, Thelma Bernbaum a.k.a. Missy Moonbeam was one of those unhappy wretches whose "funerals" would consist of a few words muttered by a grumpy undertaker who thought the county was screwing him by expecting him to plant this stiff in something remotely resembling a casket for the paltry amount the county was willing to pay to dispose of the little hooker.

Thelma Bernbaum's next of kin in Omaha were struggling to make it, what with the recession and unemployment, and weren't about to spend a bundle of hardearned bucks to bring what was left of Thelma back to a place she always said was about as stimulating as the Gulag Archipelago. (Thelma had read a book or two. What else was there for her in Omaha?)

But upon arriving in Hollywood she had stopped reading anything except *Daily Variety* and *The Hollywood Reporter*. She stopped reading altogether when the money was gone, along with the hopes and dreams. And when they lose their hopes and dreams in Hollywood, it's like sliding bare-assed down a splintered two-by-four, they say. It hurts *all* the way to the basement.

She'd started out as a $500-a-night call girl. Even a police mug shot could not obscure the fact that she had been a pretty girl at first. Then the inevitable: hash, dust, uppers, downers, speed, coke. She never got to heroin, but she might as well have. On one of her arrests she admitted to a coke habit big enough to keep her on her back and knees eighteen hours a day without a shred of real rest or untroubled sleep.

The last mug shot of Missy Moonbeam looked like something that needed an exorcist. Mario Villalobos sighed his peculiar sad sigh and lit yet another cigarette and looked at his watch. It had been a marathon brunch. He wished he hadn't let the lieutenant talk him into taking on Chip Muirfield for his "seasoning" session, with help from Melody Waters. Mario Villalobos' regular partner, Maxie Steiner, was recovering from a heart attack, thanks to Leery's Saloon, lousy diet, lack of exercise, two packs of cigarettes a day, middle-of-the-night meetings with murdered people, a rotten marriage and a divorce. In short, everything Mario Villalobos had experienced, except that Maxie Steiner was ten years older and Mario Villalobos had had *two* rotten marriages and divorces.

Such troubling thoughts caused Mario Villalobos to look into the room, at the slab of lung a technician had placed on a steel table. It looked like a chunk of coal. That poor bastard had probably smoked as much as Maxie Steiner, which meant he smoked *almost* as much as Mario Villalobos. The thought of finally going end-of-watch as the result of something as relentless as lung cancer scared the crap out of Mario Villalobos. Better to look his .38 in the eye and smoke it. As he stared at that lung on the gut pan, gleaming like a chunk of anthracite, he got so tense his hands started to shake. To settle them he lit a cigarette, the thirteenth of the day.

Well, if he didn't die from lung cancer, and if midlife crisis wasn't terminal, and if he survived this feeling of dread and despair which more or less clouded every waking moment, he might soon start looking on the bright side. His youngest son, Alec, was nearly eighteen, which meant the child-support payment would end. His oldest son, Frank (he would never permit his boys to be cursed with a handle as Hispanic as Mario when followed by a Villalobos), was safely warehoused in San Diego State majoring in surf bunnies, and bleeding his old man for about $200 a month. The detective didn't mind the $200 donation as much as the child-support payment for Alec which the court *ordered* him to pay. In any case the court-ordered payment would soon be stopped and he could send money to Alec directly, of his own free will. He'd still be as bankrupt as International Harvester but at least it would be by *choice*, and that made all the difference. A man like Mario Villalobos needed at least to *pretend* to order his own destiny, but he'd been a cop long enough to know that a vagary of fortune probably had as much to do with destiny as any exercise of free will, in the world he inhabited. That is, in the emotionally perilous world of the policeman, where *nothing* is as it seems.

If he could only stop his hands from trembling. This was something new in his life. He'd noticed for several years that Maxie Steiner's hands shook for most of the morning. He felt like taking his own pulse but he was afraid to know, and he didn't want to resemble Rumpled Ronald with the look of doom on his face.

When Chip and Melody had finally arrived, Mario Villalobos thought he could see it in their shining eyes: incipient romance. Or was it just their common love of gore? It was so touching he wanted a double vodka.

"Glad you two could make it," Mario Villalobos had said to the brunchers.

"Sorry, Mario," Chip Muirfield apologized. "We couldn't get served as fast as . . ."

"Okay, okay," the detective said, feeling every one of his forty-two years whenever he looked at the surfer's body and seamless face of Chip Muirfield.

Mario Villalobos was once a good police department handball player, but he was now soft in the belly. He had to let out his pants to a size 35. He weighed more than 190 pounds now, and whereas he used to be nearly six feet tall, he was now less than five eleven. Middle age. He was shrinking in height, expanding in girth. He didn't have a frame large enough to carry 200 pounds. What would he look like in five more years? Could it be worse than this, smack in the vortex of a world-class mid-life crisis?

While the shoulder holster kids dived into their work, he looked around at the stacks of stiffs waiting to be sawed, chopped, sliced and emptied. There were racks of cadavers in the "reefer" rooms, bodies of unidentified John and Jane Does which could be kept refrigerated for months. There were bunches of bodies in the "decomp" room, decomposed bodies, lying putrid under ceiling fans which could never dispose of the unforgettable smell. There were gurneys loaded with corpses, in one case two on a gurney: a shriveled pair of pensioners, married fifty years, who died as a result of an unvented heater and lay sandwiched in death as they had lain sandwiched in life during damp and drafty nights in their pensioners' hotel. He wondered how many of *them* had survived a world-class mid-life crisis. Or if anyone *ever* did. Or was what he was experiencing more than a mid-life crisis?

Then he saw his face in the reflection of the window glass. In the opaque reflection he had eyes like The Gooned-out Vice Cop. Eyes like bullet holes. He was starting to feel inexplicably scared when Chip Muirfield, with a grin as wide as a surfboard, said, "Don't you want to watch her being posted?"

"No, you go ahead and enjoy yourself," Mario Villalobos said, "but don't get too close."

The L.A. county coroner had recently been the object of disciplinary action and was criticized for a backlog of bodies. As a result, the pathologists were doing maximum autopsies these days. The last postmortem that Mario Villalobos attended had been on a victim who was head shot. Formerly, a cop could hang around the length of time it took to smoke a few cigarettes, waiting until the pathologist popped the slug from the corpse's skull. Now the cops had to stand around for two hours. The pathologists, not wanting any more criticism and complaints, were going at it swashbuckler style. They were flashing more steel than the Three Musketeers, everyone said. Even for a head shot they'd open up that stiff from head to toe.

Every corpse became a kayak these days, which didn't displease the shoulder holster kids.

This was only the third autopsy that Chip Muirfield had ever witnessed. He enjoyed each one more than the last. Mario Villalobos thought that if Chip started liking them any better, the kid might start moonlighting at Forest Lawn. The pathologist and technician were trying like hell to get this one zipped in time to watch *Days of Our Lives*.

The former Western Avenue prostitute, who had delighted Chip Muirfield by dying not in Hollywood Division where she worked but in Rampart Division where she lived, was not broken up too badly by the fall from the roof, at least not her face. Mario Villalobos thought of the early mug shot of this face now peeled inside-out like a grapefruit. A natural blonde, fair and slight; he wondered if she drove them wild when she got that tattoo of the man-in-the-moon. It was on the inside of her left thigh, high enough to have been a very painful job. In death she looked thirty-five years old. Her identification showed her to be twenty-two.

Mario Villalobos was one of those homicide dicks who somehow revert to uncoplike sentimentality during mid-life crisis. That is, Mario Villalobos, like his old partner Maxie Steiner, gradually came to resent needless mutilation of corpses by cutlass kids who, quite naturally, are extremely unsentimental about carcasses in which detectives have a proprietary interest.

What Mario Villalobos didn't see while he was roaming the autopsy room, thinking of how dangerous it is to go to The House of Misery every single night, was Chip Muirfield's interest in the man-in-the-moon tattoo high up on Missy Moonbeam's torn and fractured femur, close to the inn-of-happiness which the bored pathologist figured was *really* what was interesting the morbid young cop.

It was a professional tattoo. The man-in-the-moon had winked one eye at Chip Muirfield and with the other glanced up at the blond pubis of Missy Moonbeam. It was a very cute idea, Chip Muirfield thought, but the leg was so destroyed by the fall that the upper thigh was ripped open and hanging loose.

"I wonder if the photographer thought to shoot a picture of that tattoo?" he mused aloud to the pathologist, who shrugged and said, "What for?"

"Identification," Chip Muirfield said without conviction.

"I thought you already knew who she was," the pathologist said.

"We're not certain," Chip Muirfield lied. "I wish it weren't so damaged around that tattoo. It's all ragged and bloody and it's hard to see. Snip it off there and I'll have the photographer come and shoot a close-up of it that we can use."

The pathologist shrugged again and sliced away the flap of tattooed flesh and placed it on the steel table. Chip Muirfield could hardly contain himself. He saw that Mario Villalobos was off down the hall. This might top all the macabre gags that old homicide detectives pulled on each other, if Chip Muirfield could think of something really funny to do with the slice of tattooed flesh which he slipped into a small evidence envelope.

While Melody Waters roamed the autopsy room enjoying the show on the other tables, Mario Villalobos returned and noticed that Chip Muirfield was so intensely interested he looked ready to crawl inside Missy Moonbeam.

"If I were you, Chip, I'd stand back a bit," Mario Villalobos said, lighting a cigarette, promising himself to cut down before he ended up under the swashbuckler's knife.

Chip Muirfield was so enchanted by the ragged bloody shell that used to be a girl from Omaha that he ignored the older detective's admonition.

Mario Villalobos looked at the butter-brickle three-piece suit worn by Chip Muirfield, hesitated a moment, and then said, "Even Boris Karloff wasn't so eager, Chip. If I were you I'd step back just a bit."

But Chip Muirfield didn't seem to hear him, so Mario Villalobos went for coffee. The pathologist pulled off his gloves and called it a wrap. The technician looked up at the clock and . . . Jesus Christ! *Days of Our Lives* was going to start in three minutes!

That did it. He reached for the faucet over the gut pan to get this baby zipped. He wasn't paying any attention to a young surfer-cop in a butter-brickle suit. He was eying that clock like a death-row convict and he cranked the faucet full blast. The water hit the gut pan with a crash. And Chip Muirfield was *wearing* Missy Moonbeam.

His butter-brickle three-piece suit was decorated by a geyser of blood. A piece of Missy Moonbeam was plastered to his necktie. Another little slice of her hit him on the lapel. A swatch of Missy Moonbeam's purple gut plopped on his shoulder and oozed like a snail. But worst of all for Chip, who was yelling and cursing the technician—who couldn't care less—Chip Muirfield had a wormy string of Missy Moonbeam's intestine dangling from his sunburned surfer's nose.

Chip Muirfield and Melody Waters couldn't come along on the trip that Mario Villalobos made to the Wonderland Hotel that afternoon. Chip and Melody had to drive straight to Chip's apartment in Venice so that Chip could change his blood-spattered clothes. Then they hastily dropped off the butter-brickle suit at a local dry cleaner's.

When the pants presser who was working the counter saw all the bloodstains, he said, "My gosh, what happened?"

To which a very cross and cranky Chip Muirfield replied, "I cut myself shaving. Just write the frigging thing up. I'm in a hurry."

Chip Muirfield's smart mouth ruined the remainder of the pants presser's miserable day. The pants presser was getting sick and tired of chemicals and starch and burning his fingers on the hot iron and he didn't need some prick poor-mouthing him just because he asked about some bloodstains. Suddenly the pants presser found a little envelope in the pocket of the suit. It had something soft in it. Maybe a few bucks folded up? Serve the prick right if the pants presser nicked him for it, which is what he decided to do. He looked around slyly and tore open the envelope and . . .

"GET OVER HERE RIGHT AWAY!" the pants presser screamed into the phone to the desk cop at Venice Police Station. "Get the homicide detectives! Call the press room! Get the six o'clock news team alerted!" Jesus Christ, he better shave and change his shirt before the television crew got here!

The Venice detectives arranged a stakeout for that evening at the address given by one Chip Muirfield, who was a new tenant and unknown to his neighbors. When the young man finally showed up with a tipsy Melody Waters, who had told her accountant husband that she had to work all night on a murder case, they were jerked out of Chip's car by four detectives with shotguns and spreadeagled across the hood of the car by a big cop who got fairly frantic when he discovered that their man was carrying a gun.

The upshot was that Chip and Melody eventually got to identify themselves and explain the piece of Missy Moonbeam that Chip carried in his pocket. They made peace with most of the cranky detectives who had thought they had an L.A. version of the Yorkshire Ripper, but they didn't make peace with the big detective.

When Chip got yanked out of the car by the big detective, he resented being spread over the hood of his car, and yelled, "Knock it off, asshole! Do you know who I am?" And he made the big, *big* mistake of trying to shove the detective at the same moment that the detective saw that his man was carrying a gun.

Chip found himself on the wrong end of the controversial police choke hold which the L.A. police chief had promised would be curtailed when he made his famous statement about the veins and carotid arteries of some blacks failing to open like those of *normal* people.

The choking of Chip Muirfield was good for lots of carotid artery jokes around The House of Misery for several weeks. They would say things like, "It proves that the veins and arteries of surfers open just like those of normal people."

For several days Chip Muirfield had a little surfer imprinted on his neck from the charm he wore on his gold chain. Otherwise he looked like normal people. And it was a very unhappy Chip Muirfield who said goodnight to Melody Waters that night and sent her home to her accountant husband because Chip was too sore and shaken to put a move on her. It was a sad young cop who painfully swallowed, and gave Melody Waters a wistful little kiss as they stood for a moment heart to heart, shoulder holster to shoulder holster.

The pants presser reluctantly agreed to give Chip Muirfield a freebie on the dry cleaning after the outraged young detective threatened to sue for physical and mental anguish. It was an unhappy affair for all concerned. The pants presser didn't get on the six o'clock news, and Chip Muirfield, still a very young cop, for the first time began to wonder if anything is *ever* as it seems.

One of the tiny vagaries of fortune, which veteran policemen like Mario Villalobos strongly suspect decide great events, was about to occur while The Bad Czech stuffed his face in the dining room of the Pusan Gardens, a Korean restaurant near Olympic Boulevard.

The Bad Czech was, to the chagrin of the chief, downing his second order of volcanic *kimchi* cabbage pickle, and dusting off a load of *yukkwe* raw beef which had been meant to feed six people at an intimate party that night. The Korean chef was so mad that he dumped enough hot sauce on that minced beef to blister porcelain, but all it did was make The Bad Czech sweat like a whore in a hot tub and order *more* Japanese beer, which stimulated his appetite.

The chef conceded that it was hopeless. The restaurant owner insisted that the beat cops, who so sympathized with his "police problem," were worth a few free snacks—which turned into these gastronomical orgies, causing the chef again to run out to the market in Korea Town before he could get the menu ready for the evening.

Between huge bites of red snapper and bean cakes and bottles of Japanese beer, The Bad Czech sang for his supper, as it were, commiserating with every waiter and busboy within earshot who couldn't have cared less if the cops threw their boss in jail for life.

"I think it's a damn shame the vice cops waste their time hasslin the good people who run clean establishments like this one," The Bad Czech announced theatrically.

"Uh huh," Cecil Higgins mumbled, trying to quench the flames with water, since the Japanese beer didn't seem to be doing it for him.

The Korean dilemma, the dilemma of many bar owners from the Orient, was that they could not convince the police department that their customs were not a threat to public safety. And that what is at most unsavory in America is commonplace in Seoul and in most of the rest of the Orient and southeast Asia.

"It's a damn shame that in this day and age the vice squad still wastes time and money and manpower to infiltrate fine places like this and pose as customers just to write a few lousy tickets to B-girls," The Bad Czech said for the benefit of a nighttime cocktail lounge B-girl who doubled during the afternoon as a food waitress.

She knew that the opinions of a lowly public servant like the monster beat cop carried about as much clout with the chief of police as the message in a fortune cookie. Still, she went along with the charade with Korean forbearance.

"Yes yes," she said. "Too bad."

"I mean, look at it this way, Cecil," The Bad Czech said to his partner, who was wiping the dripping perspiration from his face with a napkin. "The vice squad spends maybe a hundred bucks buyin drinks in the bar here, pretendin to be customers, until they finally get one poor little hostess to ask them to buy her a drink. And then they go, 'Dum, de dum dum!' and pull out the shield and write her a ticket for solicitin drinks. Big deal. They protected the public morality? I ask you, is that police work in this day and age? What with the streets overrun with maniacs and insane people and murderers and rapists and all the other things we owe to the Democrats? I ask you."

"Uh uh," Cecil Higgins mumbled, wondering if a glass of milk would put out the fire.

"It's just the Oriental culture, for chrissake! They like to come into a place and meet pretty girls and they don't mind if the pretty girls ask them for a drink and tell them how manly they are. Hell, I used to love that when I was in Nam and Thailand and Cambodia and Japan. That's what it's all about."

"Uh huh." Cecil Higgins had his lines down pat.

"The city licenses taxi dancers. *Round*-eyed taxi dancers. I think they dump on these people cause they're foreigners."

The Bad Czech looked toward the waiter clearing the next table and the waiter nodded at the monster cop and said, "Light on," which The Bad Czech understood to be "Right on," but which were the only two words the Korean knew, and he didn't have the faintest idea what the monster cop was babbling about and wished he'd get the hell out.

It was tough getting The Bad Czech to stop singing for his supper. When the boss was here, his expressions of sympathy and understanding with the Asian plight might have gone on for half an hour. But he was tired and it was time to close the show, which always ended with The Bad Czech making a gesture to pay the bill. Of course it was always refused, with lots of bogus smiles and bowing by long-suffering people who wished the boss would dump these two big dummies and start concentrating on bribing politicians and other people who *counted*.

Unlike Cecil Higgins, who in a more traditional fashion would halfheartedly reach in the pocket with a mumbled, "Whadda we owe ya?" The Bad Czech had panache, and took the trouble to display his credit card, saying, "How much for the *lovely* chow?"

The employees would grin through tight flesh and say, "No, no. On house. Come back soon."

And The Bad Czech would look surprised and say, "Really? Why, that's awful nice. Thanks a lot. And if I can ever help ya in any way . . ."

But then a singular thing happened. Not singular in itself but, as he later would consider it, something that helped Mario Villalobos come to the inescapable and troubling conclusion that most Big Events are decided by the falling of *less* than a sparrow. Of a leaf, perhaps.

Or in this case, of a chopstick.

When The Bad Czech was doing his act with the credit card he stepped on a dropped chopstick. The chopstick lodged between the ripples of The Bad Czech's ripple-soled shoes. The chopstick clicked along the parqueted floor when The Bad Czech took a step. He looked down and tried to kick the chopstick out of his ripple sole. The stubborn chopstick became lodged more securely.

"I got a chopstick in my shoe," The Bad Czech complained to Cecil Higgins, who was belching lava.

"Ooooohhhh, I knowed we shoulda had gumbo," Cecil Higgins moaned. "This *Ko*-rean soul food gives me heartburn."

But The Bad Czech wasn't commiserating with Cecil Higgins. He was dancing around in the darkened cocktail lounge on one foot, bitching and groaning and trying to extract the stubborn chopstick.

"I can't get it out!" The Bad Czech cried.

Cecil Higgins belched fearfully loud, moaned, and said, "Gud-damn, Czech. I know it ain't your day but I can't help ya with this one. Ya gotta take chopsticks outa your own shoes. My stomach hurts too much to be takin chopsticks outa anybody's fuckin shoes."

The Bad Czech sat down crankily and took off his size 15 EEE shoe, and broke off the chopstick trying to dislodge it from the rippled rubber, and finally grabbed a soup spoon and dislodged the broken shaft of the stubborn chopstick.

And after he did, he got up grumpily and picked up an American Express card which he had apparently dropped on the floor while he was dancing around on one foot. He had an American Express card because Karl Malden played a cop in their commercials.

Except that he hadn't dropped *his* credit card. It was still on the table where he had put it when he started fretting about the chopstick. The Bad Czech's credit card was later thrown into the lost-and-found drawer by the busboy who eventually cleaned and reset the table.

Mario Villalobos would come to understand and explain to The Bad Czech how it really worked, the thing called *destiny*. How an insignificant event could connect with something so great, something that signified for some men the ultimate honor that one human being can bestow upon another. And for some men even *more* than that.

The Bad Czech, despite the fact that he wondered if it was really real, would become linked with a double murder and a Nobel Prize for science.

And it happened because he mistakenly picked up a credit card from the floor. It happened, in the final analysis, because he had a stubborn chopstick in his shoe.

FOUR

The Spike

Dilford and Dolly, The Personality Team, constantly sulked while on patrol, turning one persecuted face to the other persecuted face only when it was absolutely necessary.

It hadn't been easy for Dolly to adjust to an out-and-out chauvinist like Dilford. It was bad enough with the run-of-the-mill chauvinists who couldn't adapt to the idea of females on patrol even though women were now undergoing academy training identical to the men's.

Dilford was one of those who never tired of short-people jokes when he had a male audience.

"Hey, Rumford," Dilford might yell to one of his pals from the morning watch, "bet you thought I was working alone. I got a partner: Too-tall Dolly. Stick up your shotgun, Dolly, so Rumford can see you."

Then while all the other jackasses hee-hawed, Dilford might yell, "Hey, Dolly, put a bicycle flag on your Sam Browne. Let the sergeant know you're here."

Things had gotten off on the wrong foot the very first day that Dolly was assigned to work with Dilford, after completing her one-year probationary period as a police officer. First thing he did was say to her the same old things she'd heard since academy graduation: "I *have* to work with you. It's not my idea. So let's just pretend it's a *date,* shall we? Except I don't open the door for you and I don't light your cigarettes."

And so forth.

"Does that mean we don't do any police work, Dilford?" the sorrel-haired, hazel-eyed mini-cop said to her tall, lean, sarcastic partner, himself only a three-year policeman.

"That's what it means, Shorty," said Dilford. "We put our blinders on so I don't get tempted to do police work with nothing but a split-tailed munchkin to back me up if I get in trouble."

"I see." Dolly nodded sweetly. "And what time does this *car* get hungry?"

That was another thing the other chauvinist pricks had taught her. The *car* ate at a given time. Regardless of when *she* might be hungry, the *car* ate when the *man* got hungry.

"I'll let you know when the car gets hungry," Dilford said, and the war had begun.

There was no question who drove and who did the paper work. He drove. Unless he was too hungover to drive and then she drove *and* did the paper work.

On the third day of their partnership he had made her so furious while she was loading the shotgun that she jammed the third round into the magazine and broke the nail on the ring finger of her right hand. Dolly lost her composure and yelled, "SON OF A BITCH!" scaring the crap out of Dilford, who was checking behind the seat of the black-and-white Plymouth for dope, knives, guns or time bombs which might have been left by prisoners from the last watch.

And then she made the further mistake of crying out, "Fifty bucks for this acrylic job, and *look* at it!"

The fingernail was snapped off cleanly, and along with it went the hand-painted stripes and racing-car decal that had adorned that particular nail.

"Well, no shit." Dilford grinned, calling all his pals to commiserate. "Looky here. The mini-cop lost her fingernail. The one with the Porsche racing stripe. It's really true. A policeman's lot just *isn't* a happy one!"

And if that wasn't bad enough, she got in a foot pursuit with a car thief that very afternoon while Dilford the wheel man circled the block in the car and tried to cut off the thief in an alley north of Temple. But another radio unit had intercepted the suspect and the foot race was over. Almost. In that the police department dressed the female officers in the same uniform as men, there just wasn't a place to keep certain essentials. When Dolly came hot-footing it down Temple that day, the suspect was already hooked up with Dilford's handcuffs. And Dolly dropped one of the *essentials* from her sock.

She thought Dilford's eyes, which slid back three inches past his pale eyebrows, might *never* come out of his skull when he saw a little Puerto Rican kid running up to Dolly to present her with the dropped essential.

"This is your *new* police force!" Dilford yelled, loud enough to scare the pigeons in Echo Park. "Double pierced earrings. Striped fingernails. And *Tampax* in their socks. Oh mercy!"

It had all come to a head three weeks earlier when the Cuban drag queen did a rough impression of Pele and tried to kick Dilford's *bolas* through an imaginary soccer goal.

That was a very bad day for Dilford, who was still tender from his vasectomy. Dilford had decided to become the only bachelor cop in Rampart Division to get one. Two of his academy classmates had been slapped with paternity lawsuits by a couple of grossed-out groupies from the Chinatown bars. Dilford said that if he ever got married he'd have the plumbing reattached, or adopt some little rug rats, or maybe marry a rich broad who had her own rug rats.

Dilford and Dolly had both been extremely cross and grouchy that day. He from the vasectomy, she from starting her period and having two humungus pimples blooming on her chin. She always felt that what happened was poetic justice in that Dilford deliberately antagonized the drag queen, knowing as he did that male homosexuals generally did not like being questioned, detained, searched or in any way handled by female officers.

Female police officers could hand-search either sex, according to department regulations. Male officers could not hand-search females unless it was a dire emergency. The bull-dykes on the other hand *loved* to be searched by the female officers. In fact, a great but unheralded contribution by female officers was their ability to pacify fighting bull-dykes simply by sweet-talking them. Or when necessary, by talking dirty.

Dilford, who kept his taffy-colored hair meticulously styled and sprayed, never missed a chance to pounce on any cop-chasing groupie who happened by Rampart Station at change of watch, but had been morally indignant and evinced biblical wrath when earlier that day Dolly had talked a two-hundred-pound fighting-mad bull-dyke into jail after the dyke had broken the jaw, nose and rib of a U.S. Marine (male sergeant) who had been screwing around with the bull-dyke's girl friend. Dilford had been outraged when Dolly smiled at the dyke, batted her lashes seductively and gave a sexual promise to the bull-dyke which, though the dyke didn't believe it, so charmed and enchanted the scar-faced street fighter that she dropped her boxing pose and came along like a kitten.

After they got the bull-dyke booked, Dilford had sneered, "I suppose *all* you females dig that kind of thing. Probably got to have a tendency in that direction to even want a man's job."

"Look, Dilford," she answered, "if I wanted to get in fights I'd get married. Would you rather fight with people or do the job the easy way?"

"If you were a full-sized *man* like cops're *supposed* to be, we wouldn't have to *embarrass* ourselves by offering tits and ass to a frigging bull-dagger," Dilford sneered.

"I wonder if you're gonna be one of those . . . *assholes* who deliberately gets his female partner in a physical altercation to try to prove something, Dilford?" Dolly asked, her voice shaking. "I know my limitations, Dilford. I don't want to get in punch-outs with these people out here. I'm not trying to *prove* anything." And then she made the mistake of adding, "I'm secure in *my* sexual identity, Dilford."

"What's that supposed to mean?" Dilford asked, slamming on the brakes at the intersection.

It was then he spotted the drag queen sashaying down Eighth Street, trying to shag passing motorists and get twenty-five bucks for a head job, and leave the customer thinking he had been partying with a real woman. Which seldom happened in that the drag queen was six feet two inches tall and had shoulders like Mean Joe Green.

Dilford, as bitchy as he was, knew full well how bitchy drag queens got with female cops, especially if male cops made flashlight-and-nightstick jokes during a pat-down search by a female officer.

"Let's see what the Cuban drag queen's up to," Dilford said. "I think that's the one sometimes carries a loaded thirty-eight in his purse."

Dolly figured right off that the only .38 the Cuban had was the 38 D-cup filled with latex attached to his chest. And she suspected that Dilford was bitchy enough today to get her into a fight deliberately. Dolly was nervously fiddling with a lock of her sorrel hair which the lieutenant made her pin above her collar with a dumb barrette to comply with ancient department regulations, when her off-duty below-the-collar hairdo was infinitely more attractive. Then Dolly stopped fiddling with her hair and decided that even Dilford couldn't be enough of a prick to deliberately get her hurt. On the other hand . . .

"Sure is a *big* drag queen," Dolly said.

"You scared?" Dilford grinned nastily. "*Scared* of a mincing faggot?"

"I heard about a drag queen on Alvarado who tore the uniform and even the T-shirt right off Cecil Higgins one day. This wouldn't be the one, would it?"

"I don't know." Dilford shrugged. "What if it is?"

"Well I'm down to my last T-shirt," Dolly said, trying her best to make an overture in case Dilford had evil intentions. "I own fourteen T-shirts, fourteen pair of socks and fourteen underwear. So I only have to go to the laundromat every payday. I'm down to my *last* pair." She tried a conciliatory smile when she said it.

"Fourteen underwear," Dilford sneered acidly. "Do you wear jockey shorts like me?"

"Let's talk to the frigging drag queen," Dolly said, muttering, "Prick!" under her breath.

"Let's do it," Dilford said, parking the radio car and jerking open the door, muttering "Bitch!" under his breath.

The drag queen was wearing a red lamé dress and silver pumps with ankle straps, and was also feeling pretty bitchy that day in that not a single trick had been had. And it was smoggy and the drag queen's boyfriend Pablo had not slapped him around lately, no matter how bitchy the queen acted or regardless of how much he deserved it.

The drag queen had once been the happiest hod carrier in Havana, lunching on bricklayers, so to speak. Then Castro got it in for homosexuals and started throwing them into jails for crimes against the state, finally loading them on leaky boats and sending them to Miami. In short, this drag queen had been very unhappy the last few years and was in no mood for some stinking roust by a couple of cops. Which is exactly what the queen said when they stopped him.

"I was not doing notheeng," the drag queen said. "I am in no mood for some steenking roost!"

"Watch your mouth, *seester*!" Dilford said. "And open that purse so my *leetle* partner can take a look."

It took only a few minutes of Dilford's smart-mouthing and mock Spanish accent before the big drag queen got *really* bitchy and said, "Thees ees not Cuba. Eef I have done sometheeng wrong, take me to yale!"

"Listen, rat breath," Dilford sneered, standing nose to nose with the tall drag queen. "I'll take you to Yale. I'll take you to Harvard, or I'll take you to the fucking *dog* pound if I feel like it. So don't give me any of your . . ."

But that was almost all he said that day, other than when he was on the sidewalk, howling like a bloodhound.

Dolly had always been a football fan and she said that the drag queen didn't have to take any steps like place-kicker Jan Stenerud. But the drag queen did a Jan Stenerud on Dilford, all right. The queen kicked Dilford's balls so hard he had pubic hair in his throat for a week, Dolly said. And Dolly became a more popular girl around Rampart Station because she took out her stick and, using the toe of it, buried it in the crotch of the drag queen, right up his panty girdle. It caused the drag queen to join Dilford down on the sidewalk, howling like a coyote.

That was a very noisy afternoon on Alvarado. Especially when the paramedics were loading Dilford into the ambulance, while he held his wounded testicles. Dilford was foaming like a mad dog and cursing the former President of the United States for being outfoxed by Fidel Castro, and cursing the Catholic Church for helping to settle the Cubans here in central Los Angeles. Dilford's eyes were about as deranged as The Bad Czech's when he began to imagine that his sucked-up testicles would never fall into place. As the paramedic was closing the door, Dilford screamed: "Thanks a lot, Jimmy Carter, you dumb cracker! Ooooohhhh! Thanks a lot, Pope John Paul, you dumb polack! Ooooohhhh, my nuts!"

As Dilford was being driven away by ambulance, the last thing he saw was his partner Dolly chattering away with Jane Wayne and three other cops. Dolly was warning that the girls should always use a pencil eraser to unload their shotguns so they didn't break a fingernail.

"Goddamn acrylic nail job costs fifty bucks," Dolly complained to Jane Wayne, who looked at Dolly's fingernail and clucked sympathetically while Dilford nursed his nuts and moaned.

Those bad old days were in the past. Things weren't much better now but they were quieter. Dilford and Dolly weren't openly hostile anymore. They were resigned to finishing out this month as partners, so they turned one persecuted face to another persecuted face only when it was absolutely necessary.

It was to be their Boat People Day, as Dilford explained it that night at Leery's Saloon, when Dolly got so bombed that she bought drinks for the entire gaggle of losers in The House of Misery. The afternoon began, appropriately enough, in Fu's Fast Foods, a Chinese version of an American greasy spoon, where cops ate because it was free to them or half price. Since there were no spoons in Fu's, Dilford called Fu's a greasy stick joint, but he ate there anyway. And he provided wonderful lunchtime conversation for the ever-suffering Dolly, who was starting to roll her eyes a lot, just like her lanky partner. She'd even started to whine like Dilford when she was bitching back at him. Partners often took on each other's characteristics, usually the worst ones.

"You oughtta go in that kitchen sometime," Dilford said through a mouthful of mu shu pork as he clicked his sticks expertly and looked toward the take-out counter, where the boxes of chow mein were being bought by Mexican factory workers as fast as Fu could get them up.

"Why would I wanna go in the kitchen?" Dolly said, eating her shrimp fried rice gingerly, extremely doubtful as to the true nature of the "shrimp."

"Fu's so glad he can fry a cockroach without making it dance. All that old oil in those woks goes up on the ceiling and drops back on the floor. In fact, it *isn't* a floor. It's more like an oil slick. The cockroaches can't even walk on it without cleats."

"Jesus Christ!" Dolly yelled, leaping up and knocking her plate off the table. "My mushroom *moved*!"

The later events of their Boat People Day were what caused Dolly to get so drunk at Leery's that she bought drinks for the house. And *that* is about as drunk as anyone ever got.

It was an "unknown trouble" call, which is very unsettling to police officers who, finding police work unpredictable enough, would prefer to have a more precise idea of the nature of their radio calls. In this case, a neighbor recently arrived from Cambodia by way of Bangkok had trouble explaining the problem to the operator at communications, hence the unknown-trouble call.

Jane Wayne and her partner Rumpled Ronald—now only thirty-four hours and fifty minutes from his pension and thus fearing just about everything, especially unknown-trouble calls—had arrived at the apartment building near Ninth and Catalina streets before Dilford and Dolly arrived.

Jane Wayne's shag was purple-streaked in the sunlight from her recent cellophane job, and she looked brazenly handsome in her tailored blues, with her broad shoulders, crimson mouth and narrow hips.

"We'll back you up," Jane Wayne said, uncoiling her long body from the radio car while her partner reluctantly followed, feeling his forehead for the tenth time this morning.

"I think I'm getting a fever," he said. "Wouldn't that be something? Drop dead from an Asian virus the day before my pension?"

It was near Korea Town, and many of the buildings were occupied by boat people, like the Cambodian who placed the call. Those who had survived war and famine, pirates and cutthroats, and arrived in California alive.

The apartment house was one of the many stucco buildings with Spanish tile roofs built in the late 1920's for the burgeoning population in central Los Angeles. It was pressure-packed with refugees now, and like the Latinos on other streets in other pressure-packed apartment buildings, they had to park their battered cars blocks away, since each apartment unit contained three or four times the people it was built to house. Parking tickets often wiped out the meager salaries these boat people earned in a day, working as they did in the same kinds of places that hired the illegals from Latin America.

The stench of pork was overpowering. *Rotten* pork. And gamy chickens that restaurants in Chinatown or Korea Town or Thai Town had disposed of. The four cops looked at each other, and Dolly thought she might just vomit.

There was a community kitchen serving the entire building. It was at the end of the darkened hall, and when Dilford yelled, "Police Department. Who called?" and got no response, the cops walked into the kitchen, which was the size of Leery's dance floor.

It had one apartment-size gas range and oven. Two hot plates were on the sink and the kitchen housed a noisy old refrigerator. Jane Wayne nudged open a door and saw it was a darkened pantry. Suddenly a dark scum of water began to flow out on the floor into the kitchen from the pantry.

Except that it wasn't water.

It was a *wave* of roaches. Jane Wayne, despite her macho ways, let out a yelp and instinctively pulled up her pants legs. So did Rumpled Ronald, who instantly wondered if roaches carried plague. So did Dilford and Dolly, Dilford saying, "Back! Back!" to the wave of roaches, scrambling, crawling, *flowing* around their feet like sewer water. Dilford stomped on a few dozen, and shiny bodies crackled like bacon frying. Dolly said, "Let's get *out* of here!"

Which they did. And fast.

"Eeeee!" Rumpled Ronald cried as he shook some roaches off his pant leg.

"Dis*gust*ing!" Jane Wayne cried, shivering.

"Re*volt*ing!" Dolly cried, remembering the mushroom that moved.

Then they saw the paws in the petunias.

At first they didn't know they were paws. They looked just like two white petunias among the pink and mauve ones. They were tucked inside the petunias, and the entire bouquet was wrapped in foil and left outside one of the doors on the first floor of the apartment house as though it were a love offering.

Dolly thought for a moment it was the dusky light and shadows on the napless, greasy, urine-befouled carpet. Then she bent down and looked. She gingerly *touched* the paws in the petunias. She felt the little black nails and the rigored toes.

"What the hell is *this*?" Dolly said.

Rumpled Ronald said, "It's two paws, is what. Dog paws in the petunias. Jesus! It's gonna be disease and pestilence that gets me on the next-to-the-last day. Don't get that thing near me."

"Dog paws?" Jane Wayne said incredulously. "*Real* dog paws?"

"They're real all right," Rumpled Ronald said. "The Chinese gangs send them as warnings. They also send dog's heads. There's a lot a heads and paws around here but I ain't never seen a dog's body. Wonder what they do with the body?"

"You been to Fu's for lunch lately?" Dolly said, turning chartreuse around the mouth.

"Fu woks his dogs," Dilford said, but nobody laughed.

"Somebody probably didn't make their extortion payment," Rumpled Ronald said as they ascended the stairs. "Maybe somebody works in a shop in Chinatown or . . . OH, SHIT!"

They found the dog's head. It had been a dirty bone-colored mixed-breed. The dog's head was attached to a door on the second floor. A swatch of muddy-looking blood had coagulated on the door where the head was attached. It was a dire warning all right. The head was pinned to the door by an eight-penny nail driven through the animal's distended tongue. The ragged mutilated collar of fur was peeled back from the severed neck, and the dog, obviously killed nearby, had bled quite a lot onto the floor outside the door of the doomed man's apartment. A baby rat had been happily frolicking in the gluey ooze, and ran with a blood-glistened grin right past the faces of Dolly and Dilford, who were nose-high with the second-story landing.

Dilford drew his revolver and was trying to show he wasn't nervous by making a few more cracks about the menu at Fu's Fast Foods. The others were silent. Dolly was grimly trying not to vomit.

"Police!" Dilford shouted in the second-floor hallway, in the seemingly deserted apartment house.

There were signs everywhere of Southeast Asian boat people jammed into the filthy little rooms. Paying exorbitant rents to the slumlord who, as it turned out, was one of the fun-loving Westsiders who paid $10,000 for a gold-plated .38 revolver engraved with his name by Bijan, the Happy Iranian of Rodeo Drive, who had created them for the design-conscious clients at his Beverly Hills men's store.

Still there was no answer in the upstairs hallway. Most were out doing their unskilled labor in the many shops and businesses owned by Thais, Koreans, Laotians, Vietnamese, Cambodians and Chinese, or in the downtown sweatshops owned by round-eyes who considered themselves keepers of the American dream by sweating the Asian boat people as diligently as they'd sweated the Mexicans before them. The four cops—now with guns reholstered, since there seemed to be no more mutilated animals lying around to scare the crap out of them—decided to try the third floor in the hopes of finding out who the hell called the police in this spooky place.

The four cops climbed to the third floor, their Sam Brownes creaking, keys jingling, breath coming hard, not from the easy climb but from the anticipation of more Oriental warnings left on people's doorsteps by cutthroats the boat people had failed to elude as they had eluded others in their journeys across treacherous seas in terrifying boats, hoping to escape rape, robbery and murder, only to find it again and again during their journeys.

These were the lucky ones, those survivors who had been miraculously delivered to freedom here in central Los Angeles, where gangsters from their own and neighboring countries nailed dog's heads to their doors if they didn't cough up their hard-earned greenbacks.

"Screw it," Dilford said. "I don't know who the hell called and I don't care. This place makes The House of Misery look happy. Let's get outa here."

Then they heard a woman moan. It was the kind of moan that is almost a chant, the moan of people who have watched the skies too many years for fire and explosion, who have nothing more than cries of anguish with which to entice mercy from oppressors.

"Who the hell's that?" Jane Wayne said.

And the tall young woman crept toward the third door on their left, one from which the brass door number had long since been stolen, along with the copper plumbing now replaced by plastic. Jane Wayne, using her stick, tapped on the door and all four cops stood well clear of it. The moaning rose and fell in tinkling, chantlike undulations.

Then the door was opened by a little boy of nine. He was a frail child with lashless eyes. He bore a homemade haircut that left him with whitewalls clear to the top of his head.

"You speak English?" Dilford asked, and the child, wearing an "I love L.A." T-shirt and short pants and hand-me-down sandals tied to his feet with strings, only stared. Unblinking.

"Shit," Dilford said nervously. Then he stuck his head into the apartment, which had been divided in half with a plywood partition by the ever-resourceful slumlord in order to double the number of tenants in each apartment.

Dilford said, "Hey, anybody here speak English?"

The chantlike moans from the back room stopped momentarily and resumed. Then a man walked out of the moaning room. He was ageless, had spiny black hair, was gray-yellow and gaunt. He wore pants six sizes too large, tied by a cracked leather belt. He wore rubber shower sandals with a thong between the toes. He wore a dirty sweat-stained undershirt.

And he wore a thousand cuts.

"I don't *need* this shit," Rumpled Ronald blurted. "I only got another day and a half." But Rumpled Ronald left the company of the three young cops and came forward. He took the ageless man by the arm and nodded.

"Okay?" Rumpled Ronald said. "Okay? No hurt. Okay?" And he pulled up the dirty sleeveless undershirt, baring the bony torso of the ageless man, and he said, "A thousand cuts. I don't *need* this shit."

And the ageless man, who did not understand a word of English, looked at the rumpled cop as though to say, "Neither do I."

Although Dilford was senior to Jane Wayne and Dolly, and with his three years of police service fancied himself a salty veteran, he had not worked long in Asian neighborhoods, not among the boat people.

"These Chinese gangs do it," Rumpled Ronald said. "This guy doesn't look Chinese." Then to the ageless man he said, "Cambodia? You?"

The ageless man stared at the wall, accepting whatever fate might be his. The little boy with the lashless eyes stared at the police officers, unblinking.

"What *happened* to him?" Dolly said. Then she came forward and touched his right arm. Every inch of flesh between his throat and navel was crisscrossed by slivers of scab and healing tissue, as though his entire body had been written on in Arabic script.

"They use sharp knives," Rumpled Ronald said. "They don't cut arteries. They want the guy to be able to work and earn the money to give them their payoffs."

"Payoffs for what?" Jane Wayne cried.

"For the right to *exist,* for chrissake!" Rumpled Ronald looked at his watch and counted the minutes.

"I'm reporting this to the Asian Task Force," Dolly said, her voice trembling. "These people have *got* to learn to come to the police for protection and . . ."

"What *is* that?" Jane Wayne said suddenly.

Jane Wayne, who stood almost as tall as Dilford, was looking into the squalid little moaning room.

"What *is* that?" Dilford said, and both Dolly and the rumpled cop walked cautiously over to the doorway.

A woman was kneeling and moaning. She was perhaps thirty years old, not ageless like the man. But she had the same look about her. The look that said: *Whatever you do to me cannot be worse than what has already been done. And I expect no better.* In short, she had the look of the boat people.

"It's a baby doll," Dolly said, standing on tiptoe to see over the broad shoulder of Jane Wayne.

"It's a baby!" Dilford said. "I *think.*"

One couldn't be sure. It was lying naked on a straw sleeping mat. The windows were covered with musty velvet drapes left over from a time long past, not stolen by previous tenants, because they were so torn and stained by the Latino illegals who occupied these rooms before the boat people came. It was dark in the room and the baby did not stir. The woman knelt beside the naked baby and chanted her moan of anguish.

"Is that baby sick?" Dolly asked.

"Is that baby dead?" Dilford asked.

"That's a strange-looking baby," Jane Wayne said. "It's all . . . *deformed*."

And the tall young woman squinted through the gloom into the squalid corner of the room where the baby lay. Then she walked softly into the room, past the moaning woman, and stood over the deformed baby.

Except that it wasn't deformed.

Jane Wayne groaned when she saw the gleaming splinter of bone protruding through the shoulder. The left leg was jackknifed and nearly touched the hip of the baby where the broken shards of bone had not torn the flesh. But they had torn through near the elbow. The child's left arm was fractured into two pieces and the crimson slivers punctured the flesh. There was very little blood.

The mother of the baby had not tried to rearrange the body into the whole child it had been. She had merely knelt beside the broken naked infant and moaned.

Jane Wayne and Rumpled Ronald were very glad that Dilford and Dolly had gotten the call. They only stayed long enough to call the detectives and the police department's Asian Task Force, and await the arrival of a translator, Vietnamese as it turned out.

They stayed long enough to learn who killed the baby. It was the ageless man, the baby's father, who, the translator explained, had been in America less than two years. Who had seen his parents, two sons, and his former wife killed in the war. By the time he finally arrived in America he was sick and tired of rape and robbery and torture and murder, and he flatly refused to pay when three lieutenants of a former South Vietnamese colonel who owned a string of grocery stores in Los Angeles decided that all the expensive military training given them years ago by the United States government should not be wasted. These lieutenants decided they should receive compensation for the years of broken promises and the final defeat of their country, so they began their own guerrilla war, a reign of terror against the people in the Vietnamese communities. But occasionally a stubborn customer, like the ageless man, just got sick and tired of it and decided that they shouldn't have the Vietnamese version of a mink blanket from Bijan's, not if his family was sleeping without *any* blankets. And he decided not to cough up twenty percent of his weekly paycheck for the right to exist. Hence, the thousand cuts.

And after the thousand cuts, the moaning woman told the translator that her husband stopped working and became very despondent. And one afternoon the baby *wouldn't* stop crying. . . .

When the Beverly Hills investment counselor who put together income-property investment syndicates heard about one of his nameless tenants being arrested for murder, he concocted a gross-out gag for the gang at the Polo Lounge.

"One of our tenants been watching *Monday Night Football*," he told them. "And apparently he liked the way our red-hot running backs spike the football into the turf after scoring a touchdown. This morning he tried to spike his baby! Six points! Just goes to show, these boat people can learn a lot in America!"

"Tell that one like it is, Howard Cosell!" his date giggled.

While Dilford and Dolly were assisting the detectives, Jane Wayne and Rumpled Ronald resumed patrol. The rumpled cop felt absolutely certain he would be killed in a traffic accident and hoped it would be merciful and swift. He was now thirty-three hours from his pension.

As it turned out, the translator's statement by the ageless man caused problems for Jane Wayne, as did the act of baby spiking, as did the thousand cuts. Ditto for nailing dog heads to people's doors and tucking paws in the petunias. Jane Wayne decided she didn't like any of these things a bit. After sixteen months as a police officer, Jane Wayne wanted to go to Leery's Saloon tonight and talk to Dolly and ask if baby spiking and paws in the petunias weren't different from cops-and-robbers and car chases and fun things she had always *expected* from police work.

Except that the more she thought of it, she couldn't wait until tonight. Jane Wayne, who wore her makeup too severe (the female officers had to wear it more "natch-your-all," according to the captain), suddenly noticed that her mascara was starting to run. Jane Wayne, who drove the black-and-white while Rumpled Ronald rode shotgun and took his pulse, was starting to cry.

The tall young woman hadn't cried since she was twelve years old and her mother died of cancer. She couldn't believe it. Jane Wayne furtively wiped her eyes and smeared her mascara and glanced at Rumpled Ronald. He didn't notice, and these days wouldn't see an elephant on the sidewalk unless it directly threatened his life. Jane Wayne knew she had to talk to someone. Pronto.

There was only one person who would do. She had an overwhelming urge to find her favorite sex object, not because he was her favorite sex object, but because he was the only person she knew who was absolutely, positively, undoubtedly, certifiably *crazy*, and therefore might understand. She began cruising the Alvarado beat, searching for The Bad Czech.

After hanging the wino and fighting with the stubborn chopstick, The Bad Czech was pretty well under control for the rest of the day. That is, he was doing ordinary things like lipping Cubans.

The Bad Czech had never stopped reciting his list of grievances against the former President for being outfoxed by Fidel Castro.

"Patriots!" he moaned. "Freedom lovers. Sure. There was thirty-two freedom lovers on those fuckin boats from

Cuba, and one hundred and twenty-five thousand thieves, rapists, murderers, lunatics, insane persons and faggots! Why couldn't *Billy* Carter have been President? You could get him drunk and *talk* to Billy!"

Lipping Cubans meant that every time The Bad Czech encountered someone he considered to be a Cuban hoodlum, after a pat-down for weapons and preliminary questions as to what the thug was up to, The Bad Czech would suddenly grab the lower lip of the suspect and pull it down to see if there was a tattoo.

Fidel Castro, when he was outfoxing Jimmy Carter, went to the trouble of tattooing all the lunatics, insane persons, murderers, robbers and drag queens whom he loaded on the leaky boats and sent to Miami, the reason being that if any of them ever tried to sneak back into Cuba they would be readily identified by that tattoo. At first some tried to bite the tattoo and obliterate it. Until the Cuban authorities smashed their teeth with rifle butts.

The more he thought of it as he foraged about his beat, lipping Cubans, the more The Bad Czech decided to write in Fidel Castro's name the next time he voted for a United States President. Castro was his kind of guy.

The Bad Czech, ever a diligent cop, kept a little notebook full of the names, addresses and descriptions of all the tattooed people he lipped. Ditto for those Cuban boat people who wore an additional tattoo on the left hand, a practice of the Cuban prison gangs identifying their criminal specialty, be it mugging, burglary, rape or murder.

Cecil Higgins thought it was unsanitary to lip Cubans, and tried in vain to convince The Bad Czech that some day he was going to get rabies sticking his hands in people's mouths.

"Czech, ain't you lipped enough people for one day?" Cecil Higgins griped. "How 'bout you go wash your hands? I'm gettin queasy thinkin where your mitts've been."

The Bad Czech obediently went inside Leo's Love Palace, kicked two fruits and a dope peddler out of the rest room, and washed his hands and face, deciding to sit in the park and feed the ducks and call it a day.

Jane Wayne spotted Cecil Higgins and was out of her car when The Bad Czech emerged from the saloon. While Cecil Higgins walked over to the radio car to try to persuade Rumpled Ronald that the odds of surviving a day and a half were excellent, Jane Wayne approached The Bad Czech and walked him into the doorway of Leo's Love Palace, out of view.

"Hi, hon." The Bad Czech grinned. "How's *your* day been? I sure had a hangover and . . ."

"I had a pretty bad day, Czech," Jane Wayne said, and for the very first time he saw Jane Wayne's chiseled chin begin to tremble. And her eyeliner was wet. "I had a pretty bad day. I don't like it when babies get broken and they put paws in the petunias," she said.

And as The Bad Czech stood with Jane Wayne in the grimy doorway of Leo's Love Palace, she began spilling it in a cracking voice, while her mascara ran and The Bad Czech's eyes gradually looked less demented.

Jane Wayne told The Bad Czech that when the cops from the Asian Task Force got the Vietnamese translator to the detective squadroom, she and Rumpled Ronald stayed long enough to hear the translator tell the detectives that the ageless man had been sick and tired of war and napalm and pirates who had robbed him and raped his wife during their journey on the leaky boats. And he was sick and tired of displaced persons' camps, and after finally arriving in Los Angeles, he was sick and tired of seeing his boss get extorted by the Vietnamese lieutenants. And after he stood up to the former soldiers, they decided to teach him to mind his manners and gave him the thousand cuts in the presence of his wife. Then a strange thing happened. He just got sick of being sick, and tired of being tired, and this morning when the baby wouldn't stop crying he just . . . well, he wasn't sure *what* he did until he saw the baby all broken on the floor.

And then, through the translator, the ageless man made a request of the detectives. He asked the detectives if they would please observe a custom of his homeland. If he signed whatever document they might require, could they please take him out and shoot him at once. For this he respectfully thanked them in advance.

The Bad Czech was thinking about asking Jane Wayne to come home with him after they got off duty, and it occurred to him that for the first time in his police career he was thinking of having a woman come home without the slightest thought of jumping on her bones. He suddenly felt that lipping people was unbearably lonely work and he wanted to be with her. Except that before he could ask her, Jane Wayne started to *sob,* and she said that nobody told her police work was about people who wanted to be taken out and shot, and dog heads nailed to doors. And broken babies.

The Bad Czech took the tall young woman in his arms and he patted her back and said, "There, there. It might not be real anyways. I mean, not *really* real."

And then The Bad Czech decided to try to cheer up Jane Wayne and he said, "Hey, tell you what! Let's go for some barbecue after work, and then we'll go bowlin, and then we'll go to Leery's, and we'll play all the good old rock 'n roll numbers. We can frug and jerk and . . . there, there," he said, patting her back.

Just then a middle-aged hairdresser from Hollywood came mincing down Alvarado looking for a twenty-two-year-old gay-bar hustler named Cubby, who had "borrowed" three hundred bucks from the hairdresser saying that it was needed for his sick mother who lived on Alvarado Street at an address which turned out to be Leo's Love Palace. The Hollywood hairdresser was mightily bummed-out and was standing there hands on hips looking at the seedy bar and thinking of the damage he would like to inflict on that little bitch Cubby when he saw two figures in the shadows of the doorway. It was silly, but they looked like cops.

They *were* cops.

The Hollywood hairdresser thought he must be going mad. One big cop and one *monster* cop were hugging in the doorway of Leo's Love Palace. In full uniform.

The monster cop partially obscured the other one but there was no mistaking that he was also a big one. The Hollywood hairdresser could hear their black leather creaking and their nightsticks clashing together as they embraced!

It was possibly the most erotic sight the hairdresser had ever seen. This topped every fantasy he ever had. The hell with Hollywood! *This* is where it's at!

Before he sped home to say adieu to his landlady and look for an apartment around these parts, he clearly saw the monster cop *kiss* the other guy while he burped him, saying, "There, there. There, there."

FIVE

The Play Pimp

The cause of death, reduced to ordinary language, was that Missy Moonbeam a.k.a. Thelma Bernbaum suffered enough damage in the fall from the roof of the Wonderland Hotel to splinter her spine, explode her spleen, and purée her kidneys. Moreover, her skull had a hole in it big enough to accommodate a nest of hotel mice.

On the way back from the morgue Mario Villalobos drove to the Wonderland Hotel to talk to the clerk who had mentioned a white pimp from Western Avenue. The Wonderland Hotel was what Mario Villalobos had expected: a sagging old whore of a hotel held together by paint and putty, now a home for pensioners and welfare recipients. Also living there were three Western Avenue hookers, five dope peddlers and two members of the Screen Actors Guild.

The hotel clerk's name was Oliver Rigby. He was about sixty years old, had a bald narrow skull and dentures that threatened to fall out of his mouth when he talked. And he talked as often as he could find another human being to hold still for it. But he wasn't thrilled to see Mario Villalobos.

Oliver Rigby had been bookmaking, panhandling

and hotel clerking in these parts for nearly forty years. When he saw the middle-aged guy in the five-year-old blazer and one of those reject neckties with the little stitched flaws that made it look like it was strafed with bug shit, and which he knew came from a little Jew on Los Angeles Street for five bucks, he knew even without the cynical brown eyes that this was a cop.

"Name's Villalobos." The detective halfheartedly opened his coat and flashed the shield pinned to his belt.

Oliver Rigby squinted through the cigarette smoke, his and the detective's, which cast a pall over the counter in the seedy lobby. He read the rank on the badge.

"Yes, sir . . . Sergeant," he said. "What can I do for you? Is it about Missy Moonbeam? Sad thing, sad thing. Little girl in the first bloom. Sad thing."

"Yeah, well what was this about a white pimp?" The detective examined the report made by another investigator Saturday night when they couldn't find Mario Villalobos, who was shacked up with a Chinatown groupie.

"Yeah, I think I seen this guy over on Western. I go over there to get the racing form every day."

"What makes you think he's a pimp?"

"Big pinstripe suit. I think I seen him last week talkin to some a the street hustlers on Western, is what made me think. Maybe he's a *play* pimp?"

"See him with Missy Moonbeam on Saturday night?"

"No," Oliver Rigby said, almost losing his upper plate, pushing it back in place with both thumbs. "But I seen him comin down the elevator that night. He may a been a visitor a somebody's." Then he quickly added, "Course I don't rent to girls, I know their hustlin tricks. I don't keep no rooms with hot beds. I don't allow none a that. I don't . . ."

"Yeah, go on," Mario Villalobos said with his peculiar, sad sort of sigh, lighting another cigarette.

"Anyways, once in a while I find out some a the girls're hookers on the avenue. But long as they don't bring tricks here, I can live with it. They gotta act like ladies and don't bring no tricks. This white pimp, this tall guy with black hair, you don't think he was a pimp?"

"Anything's possible," Mario Villalobos said. "But finding a white pimp alive and well on Western Avenue would be about like finding a blue-footed booby nesting on your roof. Which reminds me, is the door to the roof unlocked?"

"Yeah."

"Isn't it dangerous, as Missy Moonbeam proved?"

"Some a the tenants like to sit up there and get the sun in the . . ." He snapped his fingers and finished it in tune: ". . . the sun in the mornin and the moon at night!" Oliver Rigby looked disappointed when the detective didn't smile.

"What makes you think the play pimp was involved?"

"Cause I heard her scream. Then the cars outside started screechin their brakes and there she was layin in the street. He came rushin through the lobby."

"Who was her best friend in this building?" Mario Villalobos asked.

"The kid never had no friends in this hotel, far as I know," Oliver Rigby said, lighting a new cigarette with the butt of the last while Mario Villalobos wondered what *his* lungs must look like. "She only been stayin here, oh, six months maybe."

"She live with her old man?"

"A *real* pimp? I don't allow niggers around here. I let these white girls stay, they behave. But I tell em, you do what you want on the streets but don't bring the streets home to the Wonderland Hotel. I don't want no trouble with no vice squad and I . . ."

"I'm sure this is a hotel fit for the Moral Majority." Mario Villalobos nodded wearily. "Ever see someone, a righteous pimp, let's say, hanging around outside?"

"No niggers in the Wonderland Hotel," Oliver Rigby said. "And no greasers neither." Then the hotel clerk looked at the dark eyes and coloring of Mario Villalobos, realized the name was Hispanic and quickly added, "Course I ain't got nothin against clean *decent* Mexicans, you understand."

"Yeah, yeah," Mario Villalobos said.

"I *love* Fernando Valenzuela and all the other greas . . . all the other Mexicans and foreigners on the Dodgers," the hotel clerk said.

"Me too." Mario Villalobos sighed. "We're from the same *pueblo* but I took a Berlitz course in English. Now can we get back to Missy Moonbeam? Did she *ever* bring a trick home with her? Trust me, Oliver. I don't work vice. I catch people who kill people. I don't care who turns tricks on my beat. I don't care who books horses or does dope and I don't even much care who steals hubcaps as long as they're not mine. I only care about catching people who kill people. And then only if they do it on my beat. See where I'm coming from? Don't lie to me, because your hotel happens to be on my beat and somebody pushed somebody off the roof. Don't tell me any lies or I'll get *really* mad at you, Oliver."

Oliver Rigby looked at the deep lines around the mouth of the detective and at his hair too gray for his age and at brown eyes that for sure had seen most of it. He knew who he could screw with and of course he knew from an unhappy life on the streets who *not* to screw with. He said, "She took a *few* tricks upstairs. On'y a few, you understand."

Mario Villalobos knew of course that Oliver Rigby would know *exactly* how many tricks Missy Moonbeam took to her room because the Oliver Rigbys of this world demand a piece of the action from the Missy Moonbeams of this world for letting them take tricks to their rooms, and keeping it quiet, and even warning them if someone who looked like a vice cop should get on that elevator and go up to the fifth floor where she lived.

"Did she take a trick up to her room on Saturday night, Oliver? Sometime between nine o'clock and when she did her header off the roof? Think carefully, Oliver. And don't make a mistake that causes me to do extra work."

"I swear to God she din't," Oliver Rigby said. "There was just this guy, this tall guy, came down a few minutes after I heard the scream and the cars slammin on their brakes out on the street. Look, I don't want no problems. I wish I din't even mention the guy in the pin-stripes to the cops that came out Saturday night. I bet Missy tossed her own self off the fuckin roof is what I think. We had two other girls toss theirselves off the roof over the years. It ain't no big thing."

And that, Mario Villalobos had to agree, was a fitting epitaph for all the Thelma Bernbaums who ended up on a steel table in the coroner's by way of the streets of Hollywood: it ain't no big thing.

But there was one problem with the suicide theory of Oliver Rigby. A big problem which kept them from closing the book on Missy Moonbeam and calling her a jumper, which of course Mario Villalobos would like to have done. The first police on the scene Saturday night found one of Missy Moonbeam's shoes in the hallway leading to the roof. They found a piece of her panty hose torn from her leg and hanging from the air-conditioner *on* the roof. They found two of Missy Moonbeam's false fingernails on the step by the door to the roof. Unfortunately for Mario Villalobos, Missy Moonbeam was probably *dragged* from her room on the fifth floor, out to the roof, ending up dead under the cutlasses of swashbucklers who wanted to watch *Days of Our Lives*.

The room of Missy Moonbeam had been gone over pretty well by the detectives who got the call Saturday night. There were no readable latent prints that showed promise. There were no signs of a fight inside the room. It was probable that the killer overpowered her while she was standing outside the door or in the doorway. The door was unlocked and the keys were still in her purse, so it was possible that the killer was known to Missy Moonbeam.

It would have been very natural in these unnatural situations to have assumed that the killer was someone she had picked up as a trick. But she was fully clothed when she hit the roof of the panel truck from five stories up. There was no money in her purse or tucked inside her panty hose or bra. The bed was neatly made, so the possibility of a deadly customer was not likely. There had been no seminal fluid in her vagina, anus or mouth. Mario Villalobos had checked with Hollywood, Wilshire and Central divisions. There hadn't been a street whore murdered for several months, and earlier victims were not killed like this one.

Mario Villalobos, using the passkey given to him by Oliver Rigby, broke the coroner's door seal, entered, and sat on the bed in the dismal little room of Missy Moonbeam thinking how much he'd love to have a double shot of vodka. He'd just about conceded that this had the earmarks of a case that faded away under a deluge of "investigation continued" follow-up reports, and finally was forgotten. When street whores were done in by unknown suspects, the possibilities were infinite. It usually became one of those "an arrest is imminent" gags when the lieutenant asked about it every month or two.

Even Missy Moonbeam's trick book was pathetic. It bore the names of every superstar in Hollywood along with phone numbers allegedly belonging to the superstars. He smoked and shook his head wearily, and imagined the frail little coke freak with the man-in-the-moon tattoo on her thigh, stroking the ego and the limp penis of some john who couldn't get it up until she showed him how lucky he was to be turning a trick with a girl who regularly balled the biggest superstars in Hollywood. And here were their names and phone numbers in her trick book to prove it. And as often as not, when the john started looking at those names and imagining himself treading the same ground that his favorite movie actors had trod, so to speak, it was the ultimate aphrodisiac. Burt and Clint and Warren, and . . . Jesus Christ! Look out, man-in-the-moon! I'm coming through!

It was *such* a corny old game that it made the detective pity all the Thelma Bernbaums he had known. Then when he picked up the trick book he saw another piece of writing on the back of the book. There were doodles around the name, squiggly lines and jagged, manic, red slashes. There was a red ballpoint pen lying beside the book. A name and phone number were scrawled within the jagged doodles. The entry was not written neatly, as were the other names and numbers, by an Omaha child raised with the Palmer penmanship method. It was written by the same hand all right, but it was scrawled, no *slashed* across the book. It was on the page not with the play phone numbers, nor the real ones, the numbers that turned out to be sisters in Omaha, an aunt in Kansas, a V.D. clinic in Hollywood, an answering service favored by street whores. All the numbers that counted. It was slashed across the back of the book, and it aroused his curiosity.

The name was Lester. The telephone number was not a metropolitan Los Angeles number. When he got back to the squadroom, Mario Villalobos ran the telephone number and it came back to the Division of Chemistry and Chemical Engineering, at the California Institute of Technology in Pasadena, one of the foremost institutions of scientific learning in all of America.

Mario Villalobos wondered if Lester was some student or professor who, tiring of science all day, occasionally enjoyed a little of Missy Moonbeam's "art" in the drab little room on the fifth floor. But that didn't seem likely. His was the only name among the important numbers. A relative? Family friend? He wondered how many Lesters there might be in the faculty, staff or student body of Caltech. Probably hopeless, or of no value in any case. He'd make one quick phone call to Caltech to satisfy the lieutenant and that would be that.

Before leaving he checked her clothes and saw that Missy Moonbeam had favored hot pants, which never go out of style, not with the street whores of Hollywood. And she had three pair of thigh-length plastic boots: one red, one green, one yellow. Mario Villalobos supposed that the boots must have just allowed the tattoo on her leg to peek out between the hot pants and boot. He replaced the coroner's door seal with another that he kept in his briefcase. He took a last look at her yellow plastic boots, sighed wearily for the sheer squalidness of it, and locked the dismal little room.

The squadroom was almost empty when he put his case envelopes in his drawer. He was going to drop by the restaurant on Sunset where cops often ate on payday. It wasn't payday but he needed a good meal tonight. The trouble with the restaurant was that it was too close to The House of Misery. He told himself he shouldn't go there two nights in a row, not having a death wish as yet.

Well, maybe he'd stop for *one* drink before going home.

There were big problems at Rampart Station late that afternoon before the uniformed cops could go end-of-watch. And no matter how mad The Bad Czech got because the entire day watch was being held over pending an investigation by Internal Affairs, they stayed. The captain and the lieutenant and the headhunters from Internal Affairs would not have agreed with The Bad Czech, who was stomping around the locker room saying that they were overreacting and that it wasn't anything to get excited about. However, it wasn't every day that one of the cops tried to murder a sergeant.

The uniformed cops were instructed to remain in the assembly room while a latent-prints specialist dusted a locker for fingerprints at the direction of the headhunters.

"Nobody tried to murder no sergeant!" The Bad Czech thundered. "Somebody just played a little trick, is all. I think it's the fault a Rose Bird and the supreme court. Nobody around here has a sense a humor no more."

As it turned out, Sergeant Milo Jones certainly lost his sense of humor. He lost it at the exact moment a pin was pulled from a hand grenade, and the spoon went flying in his face, and a grenade that never blew up blew Milo Jones right into the hospital.

Sergeant Milo Jones, all the cops knew, was a snitch, a direct conduit to the brass for everything the troops did. He rarely snitched on anyone above the rank of sergeant, since he feared higher authority.

Milo Jones was a man who, like Mario Villalobos, had shrunk an inch in middle age, but he was never very big to begin with. Unlike Mario Villalobos, he didn't spread out but somehow got skinnier after a duodenal ulcer and a frequently fluttering heart. It was quite obvious that police work was very dangerous for the Milo Joneses of this world. In addition to the stress on an already anxious man, the years of snitching on errant cops had so far resulted in the tires on his private car being filled with cement, in his police hat being super-glued to a toilet seat, and in an assault by a sleeping "wino" in an alley who coldcocked Sergeant Jones from the blind side and was seen to be wearing suspicious black ripple-soled shoes when he made his escape over a fence in his rag-picking garb.

Milo Jones was one of those supervisors they called by various names such as "S.I.S." Jones (snoot in the shit) or "A.I.T." Jones (anus in the teeth), referring of course to his relationship with the brass. The cops settled on a handle for Sergeant Jones when one day in the locker room The Bad Czech was bitching because most of the patrol cops, male and female, enjoyed relaxed standards these days so far as wearing the police hat was concerned. But the beat cops like himself and Cecil Higgins still had to keep the lid on while on foot patrol. He said the only reason the brass knew who was or wasn't wearing hats was because they always had their asses in the faces of certain sergeants who spoke to them through the chocolate tube.

"*Real* cops got balls that clang when they walk," The Bad Czech announced. "Our leaders got balls that chime like Baccarat."

When Sergeant Milo Jones heard this he got cross and grumpy, but not *too* cross and grumpy because his eyeline only touched the third button on The Bad Czech's uniform shirt. Sergeant Jones said, "You wouldn't say that to the captain's face!"

To which The Bad Czech replied, "Hell, I just *did*. Everybody knows you're a *pipeline*."

That did it. From then on, Sergeant Milo Jones was Pipeline Jones. They say that even his wife started calling him Pipeline when she was feeling bitchy, and that didn't help the duodenal ulcer.

Sometimes though, Pipeline Jones was handy to have around because the cops could feed him bum information which they knew would get back to the brass. For instance, two cops could speak *sotto voce* in the coffee room, knowing that Pipeline Jones was lurking around the corner. They could say things like, "I just saw The Bad Czech over at the hospital with The Den Mother!" when they knew full well that The Bad Czech was innocently eating a pastrami sandwich in MacArthur Park.

That bit of news might send Pipeline Jones flying to his car and off to a hospital on the border of Hollywood and Rampart divisions where a certain nymphomaniac nurse, called The Den Mother, worked in the emergency ward and did her civic duty for the boys in blue by going down on every injured cop they ever brought in on a stretcher. She was the kind that gave a little flower lapel pin to each one, her signature. The cops said they were going to have a flower child convention some time, but that it would have to be held at the L.A. Memorial Coliseum, which seated 90,000.

Things got out of hand with The Den Mother when cops from San Pedro to Foothill were asking to be taken to her hospital when they were injured on duty. One evening there were more cops with phony bandages in the waiting room than had attended the nightwatch roll call. Some of the uniformed cops weren't even on duty. That's when Pipeline Jones and the other supervisors were ordered to put a stop to it.

The Final Order came from on high, as it were. From Deputy Chief Delmore Downs, the chaplain of the police department and a fundamentalist Christian who wasn't born again because, the cops said, he came here by immaculate deception the first time. Deputy Chief Delmore Downs went so far as to offer a *prayer* at Rampart Division roll call when he was giving a hellfire warning about the Hollywood cops who had just been exposed in the media for having engaged in everything from grand theft and burglary to sex encounters in Griffith Park, with everyone from street prostitutes to girl scouts.

Deputy Chief Downs hadn't liked it one bit when someone pulled a dirty trick on him that day. An unknown lyricist had penned a disgusting religious song with bawdy biblical allusions. It was recorded on cassette and broadcast from the deputy chief's own car radio to all hands. The religious song was dedicated to Deputy Chief Delmore Downs and was sung by a male soprano.

The final straw was when some unknown cop penciled out a bogus crime report alleging multiple counts of child molestation around the playground in Echo Park and listing as the suspect someone who unquestionably fit the description of the gangly deputy chief, who was speaking to an Echo Park citizens group that day. The rumor that the deputy chief was a child molester spread like herpes. There were hundreds of cops only too willing to believe it. Finally, a cartoon appeared in the vilest underground newspaper in Los Angeles. It was penned by someone who identified himself as the Renoir of Rampart Station. It was a picture of a huge ugly chickenhawk carrying off a baby. The chickenhawk wore the hat and insignia of a deputy chief of the Los Angeles Police Department.

Deputy Chief Downs took Pipeline Jones aside on his last visit to Rampart Division. He told the little sergeant that he knew he could be trusted. He said that he would be eternally grateful for his help. He wanted the balls of the "artist" who drew the scurrilous cartoon.

Pipeline Jones was everywhere. Cops complained that they saw him in their rearview mirror wherever they went. That he watched them with binoculars from the roofs of buildings. That their lockers were disturbed each time they returned at end-of-watch, and the glove compartments of their private cars were ransacked. Of course, the majority of the complaints were symptoms of the paranoia that inflicts police everywhere. Pipeline Jones could not have done a fraction of the things he was accused of, but he did in fact poke through lockers when the cops were out on the streets. He sprung a few of their traps, which proved it: broken threads and tiny bits of paper which paranoid police officers attach to the doors of their lockers.

And after two frustrating weeks of not finding a single lead in the locker room of the troops, Pipeline Jones on his own authority checked the locker room of fellow supervisors, even those who outranked him, which was about the bravest act of his police career. The reason he considered such a daring maneuver was that he heard two cops in the rest room (they couldn't hope for privacy even sitting on the toilet) engaged in a conversation about a certain lieutenant being an "artiste." In that same conversation he heard one of the cops announce to the cop in the neighboring stall that the lieutenant said that Deputy Chief Downs likes to read the Old Testament while he makes your asshole tight.

What Pipeline Jones *didn't* know was that for three days every cop on the day watch was talking *sotto voce* about that certain lieutenant, *hoping* to be overheard by Pipeline Jones. It finally worked, in the toilets.

Pipeline Jones immediately crept into the supervisor's locker room and with fluttering heartbeat approached the locker of a very salty twenty-five-year morning-watch lieutenant whose balls *really* clanged when he walked.

With his own balls as cold and clammy as his hands and armpits, Pipeline Jones held his breath and, using the master key, *dared* to open the locker of the salty lieutenant, dreaming of the glory that would be his if he found some evidence. He didn't know that the morning-watch lieutenant had been on vacation for three weeks. But the day-watch troops knew it for sure.

When Pipeline Jones opened the locker, a loop of fishing line pulled the pin from a hand grenade. The spoon flew in the face of Pipeline Jones, giving him a shiner. He yelped, grabbed his eye, heard a hiss, smelled sulfur or cordite, and even before the "explosion," which was the equivalent of a cherry bomb but sounded much louder within the locker, Pipeline Jones was on the deck experiencing what they called a mild heart attack. He ended up in the emergency ward of the hospital where

The Den Mother gave him the E.K.G., leered, and offered him a little flower.

It was a U.S. Army practice grenade which proved to be untraceable. The vacationing lieutenant knew nothing about it but wasn't particularly sorry when told that someone used his locker for the dirty trick. Pipeline Jones went off, I.O.D. (injured on duty), and began to display every stress symptom known to medicine including asthma attacks.

The Bad Czech and the others were allowed to leave after the headhunters interrogated everyone for three hours. That meant that he and Jane Wayne ended up at The House of Misery at eight o'clock and settled for two bowls of disgusting gruel which Leery called clam chowder.

They were half blitzed, but both Dolly and Dilford were totally wrecked when Mario Villalobos came in at ten o'clock.

"Dis*gusting*! Rc*volting*!" Jane Wayne said of her chowder as Mario Villalobos took his accustomed seat at the end of the bar.

The detective thought that Jane Wayne was looking particularly androgynous tonight in her cowboy shirt, riding boots and skin-tight jeans. The Bad Czech was reading the *L.A. Times* while eating chowder at the bar and was wearing his brand new Jordache jeans.

Which caused Dolly to say, "I see The Bad Czech has on his Sergio Valente portlies. If someone told him to haul ass, it'd take two trips."

"Those big buns're so bound up I don't think he could fart," Dilford noted boozily.

"That's okay with me," Dolly said, weaving on the stool.

"I'll have a *very* dry vodka martini," Mario Villalobos said to Leery, who nodded and gave him three ounces of straight vodka, no twist, no rocks.

Leery winked at Rumpled Ronald as if to say, *very* dry martini. Sure. Give Leery straight-vodka drinkers every time.

Rumpled Ronald turned his rumpled face to Mario Villalobos and scratched his rumpled belly and said, "I only got twenty-five hours and fifty minutes to go. I think I'm gonna make it!"

"That's wonderful, Ronald," Mario Villalobos said.

"I ain't givin odds on makin it to thirty," Cecil Higgins observed, gargling his Johnnie Walker Red. "Bein partners with The Bad Czech I don't think I kin last that long without landin in San Quentin and gettin my asshole stretched big enough for ten midgets to dance a polka in."

Dilford sipped his Scotch and turned to Dolly saying, "Maybe it ain't gonna be so bad after all, working with the *crack* squad. Maybe there's a place for broads. Okay, so you're a five-foot mini-cop. We'd probably have Toulouse-Lautrec walking a beat if he was around today."

"I'm glad John Wayne isn't alive to see what police work's come to," Dolly said sarcastically.

Suddenly Jane Wayne yelled, "Goddamnit, Leery! There's something in my clam chowder with six legs and it's doing a backstroke medley!"

"So drop it on the floor and break its neck," The Bad Czech said. He hated yelling and screaming while he was reading the *L.A. Times,* which was nerve-racking enough.

Then The Bad Czech started yelling and screaming: "Goddamnit, listen to this! It says here, 'California's foreign born is the highest in the whole country, most from Latin America and Asia. Los Angeles is the port of entry for the world. Four times as many refugees as New York. Hollywood High has students from forty-three countries!"

"If I live to get my pension I gotta get outa here!" Rumpled Ronald suddenly cried boozily. "I went to the department shrink the other day and told him I should get a seventy-five percent stress pension. I got symptoms. I'm a burnout. He asks me if I got a pension what would I do? Can you imagine? What would I do? I'D MOVE BACK TO THE UNITED STATES OF AMERICA! What does he *think* I'd do? I'm sick a El Salvadorans and Nicaraguans and Cubans and Puerto Ricans. I'm sick a Cambodians and Laotians and Vietnamese and . . ."

"I just don't like people putting paws in petunias," Jane Wayne said very softly, and The Bad Czech patted her hand as if to say, there, there.

To change the subject and get Rumpled Ronald quieted down, since everyone knew he was totally bonzo from being so close to his pension, The Bad Czech said, "Here's one for ya. It says in the *Times* that the Russians caught some official sellin large amounts of caviar to a Western firm. Get this. He labeled it smoked herring and pocketed the difference. Whaddaya think ya get in Russia when they catch ya sellin dead fish to a capitalist? Anybody wanna guess? Siberia? Castration? Nope." The Bad Czech tossed down his seventh double of the night and said, "I'll tell ya. Ya get *exceptional means of punishment*. That means a bullet in the back a your fuckin *head*. Whaddaya get in L.A. for blowin away your neighbor cause he won't let ya steal his stereo? Ya get a hunnerd-dollar fine for shootin a gun in the city limits is what ya get."

"Maybe I oughtta *move* to Russia," Rumpled Ronald cried. "Maybe there *ain't* no U.S.A. no more!"

"Lighten up, Ronald," Dilford whined. "Somebody call the animal shelter and shoot a tranquilizer dart in his ass!"

"Wait'll you're twenty-five hours and fifty . . ." Then the rumpled cop looked at his watch and said, "No. *Forty* minutes from a pension. *Then* you'll see!"

Dolly turned to Jane Wayne, who was trying to persuade The Bad Czech to dance, and said, "Didn't you give Ronald his lithium today?"

"Did I have a pulse when I came in here?" Cecil Higgins said in deadly earnest to Mario Villalobos, who of course didn't know about the hanging wino and the paws in the petunias. All he knew was that it must've been an off day. *Everyone* was cranky.

Suddenly the ordinary yelling and griping was interrupted by a god-awful howling outside in the street. It sounded like Woooooooooo!

"Oh no!" Leery cried. "It's Ludwig!"

When the door came crashing open to admit Ludwig, Hans and two groupies from Chinatown, you couldn't be sure if man was leading dog or dog was leading man. One end of the leash was attached to Ludwig's off-duty choker chain and the other to Hans' hand-tooled western belt with the big silver buckle studded with red glass.

"I told you to keep that goddamn animal outa here!" Leery screamed, hopping around behind the bar and furiously banging an empty beer mug on the keg, breaking it off at the handle and showering everyone with glass, which *really* made them mad.

"Goddamn you, Leery!" Dilford screamed.

"You got glass in my clam chowder! I want *new* clam chowder!" The Bad Czech yelled.

"How'd you like to find out if the carotid artery of seventy-year-old misers opens like *normal* people!" Dolly cried, drunk and belligerent.

Dolly was beginning to impress the hell out of Dilford. "Hey, Dolly," he said. "Do you dickless Tracys beat the shit out of civilian guys when they don't satisfy you? Tell me dirty stories. I'm starting to like broads in uniform."

"I ain't serving you and I ain't serving that dog!" Leery yelled, acting as though he was going to pick up the telephone. "You better get him outa here, Hans!"

"Put that fuckin phone down or I'll shoot it off the wall!" The Bad Czech bellowed, scaring the crap out of everyone but Ludwig. "I don't like Hans and his fuckin mutt any more than *you* do, but there ain't nobody gonna call the cops in my drinkin spot!"

"But, Czech, I can't *serve* that dog," Leery whined, while Ludwig, who had already hit two saloons in Chinatown, began howling, rising up with his front feet on the bar, glaring at Leery and going Woooooooooo!

"I'll buy the beer for the fuckin dog!" The Bad Czech screamed dementedly, holding his hands over his ears. "JIST STOP THAT FUCKIN HOWLIN!"

"Settle, Czech. Settle, baby," Jane Wayne said soothingly, tugging The Bad Czech's furry eyebrows and stroking his temples. "Mellow, mellow. That's better." Then she said, "Leery, the noise in here'd make the Falklands war sound like baby farts. I suggest you give that creature a glass of beer."

After Hans and Ludwig were reluctantly served, the entire establishment quieted down. Ludwig was the only one to know when he'd had enough, and was getting sleepy and eyeing the pool table next to the three-coffin dance floor where Jane Wayne and The Bad Czech rubbed their Jordache jeans together and bit on each other's ears. Hans and the groupies were getting very tense by telling outlandish and fanciful accounts of orgies they'd allegedly attended. Dilford and Dolly were so bombed they were not only talking to each other but Dolly had her arm around Dilford's shoulder, saying, "I don't want to have nightmares about what we saw today. I don't want to wake up to ugliness."

Which caused the eavesdropping Cecil Higgins to say, "You should see my wife. I *always* wake up to ugliness."

"I killed another parakeet," Rumpled Ronald suddenly announced weepily.

"Nobody asked ya, Ronald," Dilford said. "I had enough dead things for one day."

Cecil Higgins said, "My wife's uglier than Yassir Arafat, Tom Hayden and Kareem Abdul-Jabbar."

Rumpled Ronald had spoken only in non-sequiturs for the past hour, and made announcements. "I killed four *other* parakeets," he said. "If she knew it was me killing the parakeets she'd dump me like she did her first husband. *She* owns the house and car. And then if I didn't get my pension I'd end up living at the Midnight Mission on skid row. And selling my blood."

Suddenly Rumpled Ronald's voice broke, causing Mario Villalobos to say, "That is freaking *it*! Crying jags. Time to go home."

In that Leery was the only coherent one in the saloon, he got curious and said, "Why do you kill parakeets, Ronald?"

"They're filthy. They shit everywhere," Rumpled Ronald said weepily. "My old lady lets them outa their cage and they fly all over the house. How would you like parakeet shit in your Cream of Wheat?"

"I never even cook Cream of Wheat, living alone like I do," Dilford said. Now *he* was getting weepy and feeling sorry for himself. "You should see my bacon, Dolly. It's all green with hair on it. I hate living alone. Nobody *cares* for me!"

"*How* do you kill the parakeets?" Leery wanted to know.

"It's for great truths like these that you stay in business and don't retire to Sun City," Mario Villalobos noted. "It's not the money."

"I spray them in the snoot with a little spray starch," Rumpled Ronald said. "It's a merciful death and undetectable. They just do a little header right off the perch."

"I think you're dis*gust*ing," Dolly said, pugnaciously. "Somebody oughtta squeeze your carotid artery."

"Somebody oughtta squeeze my prick till I *scream*!" Hans cried to the groupies, making Dolly call him a pervert.

"I *love* to see tiny girls get hostile," Dilford said. "Hey, Leery, I wanna buy Dolly a drink and break down her resistance."

"This could be the beginning of a beautiful friendship," Leery said happily, while he poured the booze, grabbed Dilford's dough and leered like a gargoyle.

"There's a place in Nevada this wholesome," Mario Villalobos said. "It's called The Mustang Ranch."

"I like that!" Hans suddenly shrieked in his irritating singsong voice while one of his groupies sucked on his neck. "She said you should never run over a Mexican on a bike cause it might be *yours*!" Then Hans remembered the counterfeit Mexican and said, "No offense, Mario."

Just then the door opened and a lithe slender figure with shoulder-length hair floated through the gloom and smoke and sat at the bar, silently signaling for whiskey. They all quieted down a bit. They were vaguely troubled

by him and didn't know why. It was The Gooned-out
Vice Cop.

The others resumed their conversation when The
Gooned-out Vice Cop swallowed the double shot of bar
whiskey. He stared at his mirror image in Leery's spider
web of a pub mirror. The Gooned-out Vice Cop smiled
ever so slightly at his bifurcated face, green from neon
light. The Gooned-out Vice Cop signaled for another,
drank it down, left his money on the bar and stood up.

In the time he had been coming to Leery's he had
never spoken to anyone, and Dilford impulsively decided
to make him speak. Dilford said, "Better be careful.
Leery's bar whiskey'll make you go blind."

The Gooned-out Vice Cop just smiled serenely with
eyes like bullet holes and said, "That's all right. I've seen
enough. Haven't you?"

And then he floated through the gloom and smoke
out onto smog-shrouded Sunset Boulevard.

It was a fairly ordinary night at The House of
Misery, all things considered. The only thing unusual happened when The Bad Czech tried to pay the evening's tab
with his credit card.

"You know I don't take credit cards no more,"
Leery said. "Too much hassle. Cash on the barrelhead."

"Long as I been comin here, you ain't gonna honor
my card?" The Bad Czech glared, and with a melo-
dramatic flourish slammed his hand down on the bar,
nearly flattening the embossed name on the plastic card.

As old as he was, Leery still had the eyes of a vul-
ture. He looked down at the card and said, "Well, I sure
as hell ain't gonna honor *that* card. Not unless your
name's Lester Beemer."

"What're you talkin about?" The Bad Czech said,
picking up the credit card and trying to read it. But he
was seeing two credit cards, two Leerys, two Jane
Waynes.

Then two Mario Villaloboses walked up to him and
said, "What's the name on that card?"

"Lester Beemer," Leery said. "Better call bunco-
forgery. The Czech's trying to hang bad paper."

"Goddamn! Where'd I *get* this card?" The Bad Czech demanded of Leery.

"How the hell do I know?" Leery grumbled. "I just want my money. You owe me thirty-three bucks."

"Hon, where'd I *get* this card?" The Bad Czech demanded of both Jane Waynes propping him up.

"I dunno, Czech," she answered, "but I gotta hire a wheelbarrow and get you home."

"Where'd I *get* this credit card, Cecil?" The Bad Czech demanded of his partner Cecil Higgins, who was snoring louder than Ludwig, with whom he shared the pool table.

"Can I have that credit card until tomorrow, Czech?" Mario Villalobos asked the monster cop. "When we're both sober enough to think?"

"This is a freakin mystery!" The Bad Czech cried, giving the card to the detective. "I *hate* mysteries!"

SIX

The Vampire

It was a day to remember, all right. First, because all of the losers who had been at The House of Misery the night before, thereby evincing at least an unconscious death wish, had the world-class hangover usually reserved for The Bad Czech. Secondly, because a marathon foot pursuit, destined to go down in police folklore, took place. And finally, because a good cop died.

Everyone was looking a bit demented that morning. The Bad Czech was completely bonkers because he couldn't for the life of him figure out where his credit card was and how he had one belonging to a Lester Beemer.

"I dunno, Mario!" he groaned to the detective, who questioned him immediately after roll call.

"When was the last time you saw your own credit card, Czech?" Mario Villalobos coaxed. "Try to think."

"Try to think? Try to think?" The Bad Czech moaned. "Do you know what my head feels like?"

"About like mine," Mario Villalobos said.

"Well how the hell can I think?" The Bad Czech was feeling extra sorry for himself and was extra cranky, so there was no point continuing.

"If it occurs to you later, gimme a call," Mario Villalobos said.

"What's so important about the credit card anyways?" Cecil Higgins asked.

"Probably nothing," Mario Villalobos said. "It's just that the name Lester came up in a homicide I'm handling."

"Ordinary name," Cecil Higgins said. "I got a cousin name a Lester. Gud-damn! What's Leery put in that rotgut he serves, Agent Orange? I feel like a fruit fly that got maced. I gotta go out and get some fresh smog in my lungs."

"Okay," Mario Villalobos said. "Call me if you remember, Czech."

Before being permitted to get some fresh smog in their lungs, The Bad Czech and Cecil Higgins were grabbed by the weary day-watch lieutenant, who, having lost Pipeline Jones on the hand grenade caper, was down to one sergeant. The lieutenant was not a snitch like Pipeline Jones, and The Bad Czech didn't dislike him as much as he generally disliked supervisors, but the lieutenant hadn't been known to do any work of any kind for at least fifteen years. Answering a telephone or signing a report fatigued him so, he'd have to recuperate with a two-hour lunch break. The troops referred to him as Too-Tired Loomis.

"Cecil, you and The Czech come in here, will you?" he said as the beat cops were limping toward the back door with thumping heads.

"What's up, Lieutenant," Cecil Higgins mumbled.

"I need someone to help out on the desk for a bit." Too-Tired Loomis sighed. "I gotta do *everything* around here. I'm short one sergeant. I've got the regular desk people doing my roster. I don't know what everyone expects of . . ."

"Okay, Lieutenant." Cecil Higgins sighed. "C'mon, Czech, let's work the desk for a while and let the lieutenant rest. He's exhausted from all the tension."

Five minutes later, while working the front desk at

Rampart Station, The Bad Czech got a call from the Laser Lady.

"Oh God!" The Bad Czech said, holding his hand over the mouthpiece. "Cecil, it's the Laser Lady. Why don't you talk to her?"

"I can't take it when she's feelin grumpy. Is she in her God-bless-you mood today? Or her fuck-your-mother mood?"

"I dunno." The Bad Czech sighed, resigning himself to whichever mood she was in. Then into the phone, "Okay, it's me again. Gimme the grid coordinates."

The Laser Lady said, "The grid coordinates are thirty-six latitude and forty-five longitude. You must hurry, Officer. They're shooting lasers right into my head!"

"Okay, okay," The Bad Czech said, holding his own head in his hand, elbow on the desk, furry eyebrows protruding through fingers as thick as shotgun barrels.

"Do you have the shield up to forty-five milligrams?" the Laser Lady asked frantically.

"Yeah, yeah," The Bad Czech muttered.

"Well then, raise it to sixty-five milligrams, you stupid fucking cocksucking donkey!" the Laser Lady screamed.

"Ow!" The Bad Czech whined. "Cecil, she's yellin in my ear! I'm gettin a migraine! *You* talk to her!"

"Gud-damnit, Czech, my head's hurtin too. Jist raise the fuckin shield where she wants it. I can't do everything."

"Okay, okay," The Bad Czech said to the Laser Lady. "We usually gotta call Jet Propulsion Laboratory to raise it to sixty-five milligrams, but I'm doin it now. There, you feel better?"

"Oh, that's wonderful, Officer!" the Laser Lady cried. "All the lasers are being deflected now. Thank you *very* much."

"Yeah, yeah," The Bad Czech said grumpily. "Kin I hang up now?"

"You've been *very* kind, Officer," the Laser Lady said. "God bless you."

After The Bad Czech hung up he said, "Her headache's all better and mine's worse. I feel like they're shootin lasers in *my* fuckin head."

Just then Too-Tired Loomis trudged exhaustedly to the desk bringing with him the smallest male officer in Rampart Division. Sunney Kee was half Chinese, half Thai. He was twenty-two years old, had been in America only four years, yet could speak, read and write English with such excellence that he was at the top of his police academy graduating class. And though he was hardly taller than Dolly, he had come close to setting a new police academy record for the dreaded obstacle course which the recruits had to conquer. Of course he had a pronounced accent and was quite hard to understand when speaking over the radio or on the telephone.

It was really bad when he was teamed up with Carlos Delgado, a young cop from Ecuador, who when trying to broadcast license number VVA 123, actually said, "Beek-tore, beek-tore, adam, wan, two, tres."

It drove the communications operators bonkers but in the era of Equal Employment Opportunities, they all had their little crosses to bear.

"Sunney can help you out," Too-Tired Loomis said. "His partner had to go to court."

"Help out?" The Bad Czech said. "Why can't he jist take over and let us get out to our beat?" He was dying to get to Leo's Love Palace and drink an Alka-Seltzer and some raw egg in tomato juice.

"Sunney has trouble making himself understood on the telephone," Too-Tired Loomis said. "I can't be translating for him all day. Do you know how much work I have to do because Sergeant Jones went and got himself scared half to death by a hand grenade?"

"Aw, Sunney kin talk okay, Lieutenant," Cecil Higgins moaned.

"I don't know," Too-Tired Loomis said, scratching his gray head, looking doubtfully at the ever-affable Sunney Kee, who hadn't stopped smiling since he got this job which paid a good middle-class wage and allowed him to support his parents and six sisters.

The Bad Czech said, "What if I show ya he can say somethin real hard?"

"I don't know," Too-Tired Loomis said. "How hard?"

"I got it," The Bad Czech said. "How about if I kin teach Sunney to say Magilla Gorilla?"

"Okay," Too-Tired Loomis said wearily. "Make him say an understandable Magilla Gorilla and I'll be satisfied he can work the desk."

"There ain't nothin to it, Sunney," The Bad Czech said. "Why, when my old man came to this country from Czechoslovakia, he probably talked funnier'n you."

Sunney Kee just nodded and smiled agreeably.

Thirty minutes later Sunney Kee was not smiling. The Bad Czech, sweating 80-proof bourbon, with his head banging like the shotguns on the police range, was staring dementedly at the little rookie, saying, "No, no, no! Goddamnit! I told you a hunnerd times now! Go-ril-la. Go-ril-la. It's easy. Say it."

Sunney Kee, who was also starting to sweat right through his blue uniform, looked fearfully up at the crazed gray eyes of the monster cop and said, "Go-lee-la. Go-lee-la!"

"No! No! No!" The Bad Czech screamed, causing Cecil Higgins to say, "Czech, take Sunney in the coffee room. Git some orange juice. You're jist makin your head worse and my head worse and you're scarin the eggrolls outa poor Sunney."

"Say gorilla," The Bad Czech said, his voice flat and deadly. "I got a world-class hangover. I got a carnival in my colon. I gotta get out to my beat. Say gorilla, Sunney. Or I'll *kill* ya!"

"Go-lee-la," Sunney Kee said, looking up in terror into the blood-crimson demented eyes of The Bad Czech.

Meanwhile, there was trouble on The Bad Czech's beat. A woman with wooden teeth was being whacked around like a tetherball.

Her true name was unknown, but all the people around MacArthur Park called her Wooden Teeth Wilma. She was a harmless ragwoman who wore Hedda Hopper hats and miniskirts and boots that showed off her bony, varicosed, sixty-five-year-old legs, which she thought were beautiful. She was not as unkempt and dirty as most ragwomen, so it was thought that she might have a little income and actually live somewhere. Some policeman years earlier had started a rumor that she had been married to a cop, and when he was shot and killed by a bandit she haunted the area he used to patrol. It was probably without substance, but even cops need a little soap opera in their lives, so they chose to believe it and she was given handouts from time to time by The Bad Czech and Cecil Higgins.

As to the wooden teeth, it was a total mystery. She would only smile slyly when asked why she had dentures made of wood, and where she got them. She didn't talk much, since even ragwomen in MacArthur Park thought it imprudent to tell all. The only answer she gave was that she had heard George Washington also had wooden teeth and look how people loved him.

But Earl Rimms didn't love George Washington or Wooden Teeth Wilma. Earl Rimms didn't love anybody. He had spent all of his forty-five years learning that love is expensive. Love can cost, and hate can pay.

Earl Rimms was not very discriminating when it came to victims, as long as they were defenseless. And he believed in quantity, not quality, so he'd steal the purse of just about anyone over the age of sixty who might break a hip or a shoulder when he knocked her to the ground.

The heat was on in his Watts neighborhood and old black women were starting to fight back. Earl Rimms wasn't getting any younger himself, so he'd decided to move to central Los Angeles last year. He had been arrested here twice by Cecil Higgins and The Bad Czech, who were well aware of his record of senseless brutality to robbery victims. The beat cops had come to hate him as much as he hated everyone.

When Wooden Teeth Wilma made the near-fatal mistake of strolling past Earl Rimms that Tuesday morning, he couldn't have known that the loony old lady carried only food for the ducks and dog food for herself in her oversized plastic purse. Earl Rimms was feeling particularly bummed because his girl friend threatened to call the cops when he took half of her welfare money and knocked her down the steps for resisting. He was thinking of what he was going to do to that ungrateful bitch when he finished with his day's work.

Wooden Teeth Wilma was wondering where The Bad Czech and Cecil Higgins were this morning. Maybe it was their day off, she thought, but there were no other beat cops around Alvarado. Traffic was medium light on this overcast, rather balmy Tuesday morning. The ducks always seemed more cheery when the weather was balmy.

She said, "Good morning!" to Earl Rimms.

He punched her so hard in the stomach that her wooden dentures shot from her mouth clattering across the pavement. He grabbed the red plastic purse at the same moment and jerked the frail woman, who whipped around him like a tetherball. She wanted to let go but was unable.

In order to keep someone from stealing her red plastic purse full of food for the ducks, she had wrapped the purse strap around her wrist. Earl Rimms was a powerful man and he whipped her in an arc until she slammed into a park bench cracking six ribs. On another pass she crashed into a palm tree, breaking her hip and the strap of the purse.

A Costa Rican newspaper vendor who was working on the corner saw the incident and started yelling. Earl Rimms ran like hell through the park and disappeared in the foot traffic on Alvarado with the duck food and Alpo hors d'oeuvres. Wooden Teeth Wilma ended up in the hospital and would unquestionably be on a walker for the rest of her life. When The Bad Czech heard about this later in the day from the Costa Rican newspaper vendor, he got mad enough to commit murder. And he did just that.

*   *   *

Mario Villalobos had no luck at all on the telephone to Caltech. No one at the division of chemistry knew a "Lester," nor why a deceased person named Missy Moonbeam a.k.a. Thelma Bernbaum might have the number in her purse.

The coincidence of the name Lester on The Bad Czech's mysterious credit card seemed to be just that, a coincidence. Mario Villalobos decided to send Chip Muirfield and Melody Waters over to Western Avenue in east Hollywood just to see if by chance they could spot a tall, black-haired guy in a dark pinstripe suit who might fit the hotel clerk's description of the man he saw leaving the hotel when Missy Moonbeam did her header.

"Take a pass or two down the avenue," Mario Villalobos told the shoulder holster kids. "The hotel clerk said he saw the guy talking to some street whores near the little newsstand north of Santa Monica. If you see a middle-aged guy in pinstripes, have a talk with him. If you feel hinky about him or if his name's *Lester*, bring him in."

"Okay if we stop for brunch first, Mario?" Chip Muirfield asked. "I'm feeling awful hungry and . . ."

"By all means stop for brunch," Mario Villalobos said, taking two more aspirin, which weren't helping the headache but were giving him a stomachache.

He started to feel a bit better just for getting rid of Chip and Melody. Suddenly The Bad Czech came charging in with the smallest Asian cop Mario Villalobos had ever seen. Both The Bad Czech and the little policeman had grins as wide as a nightstick.

"Hey, Mario, this here's Sunney Kee," The Bad Czech said. "He's a new rookie outa the last class. Sunney, this is Sergeant Villalobos."

After they shook hands, The Bad Czech grinned down at Sunney Kee like a proud dad and said, "Magilla?"

"Gorilla!" Sunney Kee answered, beaming.

"How ya like that, Mario?" The Bad Czech said.

"He's bright as a button!" Then to Sunney Kee he said, "Gorilla?"

"Magilla!" Sunney Kee answered, bright as a button.

"I'm sure there's some significance here that I'm missing," Mario Villalobos said.

"Lesterrr?" The Bad Czech said to Sunney Kee.

"Lesterrr!" Sunney Kee answered.

"See, Mario!" The Bad Czech said proudly. "Right as rain!"

"That's truly made my day," Mario Villalobos said, "but I'm a *little* bewildered."

"I remembered about the credit card," The Bad Czech said. "I mean, workin here with a goo . . . workin with Sunney here, I remembered the Korean restaurant yesterday. I got this stubborn chopstick in my shoe and when I couldn't get it out I ended up with the wrong credit card."

"Chopstick in your shoe," Mario Villalobos said. He'd heard for some time that The Bad Czech was totally around the bend.

"Magilla?" The Bad Czech yelled suddenly, scaring the crap out of Mario Villalobos.

"Gorilla!" Sunney Kee answered, right as rain.

Then Sunney Kee and The Bad Czech beamed at each other, with smiles *two* nightsticks wide.

Dilford and Dolly, cold sober and hungover, had gone back to their old ways. Dilford had some memory of their semi-cordial night in The House of Misery. Dolly had none. She didn't even remember driving home, but knew she had when she found her car in the garage and keys in her purse where they should have been.

She had to admit that she was feeling a little less persecuted as Dilford's unwanted partner, and she guessed that it was less the drunken night at The House of Misery than it was the experience with the boat people. Dolly was learning that shared horror diminished hostility.

With Dilford suffering a hangover, she was driving

today. He sat in the passenger seat with his head back, eyes closed, mouth open, dozing fitfully.

The radio calls had so far been routine, and most of them could be handled without disturbing Dilford. Dilford had enough police experience to be able to sleep through the noise of the radio calls, awakening only when he heard their unit number.

Dolly thought she'd missed a major hotshot call when she saw three black-and-whites parked alongside Echo Park. After she made a quick turn and cruised up to them, she saw that it was Jane Wayne and Rumpled Ronald talking with two K-9 cops, one of them being horny Hans. He was grinning and waving her over. Unable to get gracefully away, Dolly drove up to the other black-and-whites and parked. Jane Wayne said, "Wanna see something impressive, Dolly? Come watch them work these dogs."

"What's going on?" Dilford mumbled, opening one eye.

"Go back to sleep," Dolly said, getting out of the car and following Jane Wayne across the grass to where Hans, dressed in the dark-blue jumpsuit uniform of the K-9 cop, worked Ludwig with a protective sleeve over his arm.

Dolly sat on the grass and watched the huge black Rottweiler snarl and roar while he clamped onto that sleeve and eventually pulled the skinny cop flat on his belly.

The other K-9 cop and his partner, a feisty German shepherd, were raring to go. The dog's name was Goethe, and he was an old pal of Ludwig's back in the kennel in Hamburg. They were trained together, shipped to Los Angeles together, were both brought and donated to the police department by a Palos Verdes plastic surgeon, and underwent further police training side by side.

In that the American cops couldn't say "Goethe," the German shepherd became known as Gertie, which The Bad Czech said was a pretty faggy name for a male German shepherd. Hans and the other K-9 cop often met in various parks around central Los Angeles and worked their dogs to keep them sharp, issuing commands in German, which was all the dogs understood. They let the two animals romp on the grass as a reward for a good training session.

Ludwig was twenty-five pounds heavier than Gertie, but Gertie was faster, and they loved to play-fight and growl and bite each other affectionately and roll around like old pals from puppyhood. Perhaps in their canine memory they recalled the bad old days back home where the weather wasn't so good and they lived in kennels and didn't have their own humans as they did now.

The Los Angeles Police Department had been slow to acquire dogs, fearing the bad image of southern cops unleashing police dogs on black people in the old days of civil rights marches. Blacks were generally terrified of the animals, no doubt as a result of the archetypal myth of master, hound and slave, as well as of later use in crowd control. Whites were just about as fearful of snarling police dogs as blacks, but Mexicans were generally unafraid. Or at least their *machismo* demanded that they show no fear when faced with dogs. There had been several incidents of Mexicans challenging a police dog to a fight.

There were other more interesting things to learn. For example, police dogs tended to acquire the traits of the partners with whom they worked and lived. Gertie was like her partner, an energetic young cop, very action oriented and, according to his personnel reports, a bit too impulsive.

Ludwig, on the other hand, was more deliberate, like Hans. He enjoyed action, but wanted to know and understand his commands. Ludwig did building-searches in a more methodical way and handled suspect-encounters with less flair and energy.

Gertie had once leaped from one rooftop to another in hot pursuit of a burglar, very nearly suffering the fate of another dog who had lost his life. Ludwig would probably have stopped, looked at the yawning chasm of concrete and tried to figure out in his canine brain how the hell to continue without a death-defying leap.

There were of course other traits that Ludwig had picked up from Hans, such as beer drinking, which Hans would not want his supervisors to know about. And of late they shared a characteristic that Hans wanted *no one* to know about. This particular trait showed up earlier that very morning.

Hans had made a run to Rampart Station to see if a certain foxy little records clerk was on duty. While he was lurking around the watch commander's office, Too-Tired Loomis, who was wearily trying to get up the energy to lift his telephone from the cradle, spotted the huge Rottweiler staring at him with yellow menacing eyes.

"Officer!" Too-Tired Loomis said to the K-9 cop. "Is that animal safe to roam around this station?"

"Oh yes, sir," Hans said. "He's perfectly safe."

Then to demonstrate, he walked Ludwig, using his on-duty choker, toward the watch commander. Ludwig wore an L.A.P.D. identification card, complete with his photo, attached to his choker chain.

When Too-Tired Loomis looked at the enormous black face and the drooling tongue, it made him shudder.

"I like dogs," Too-Tired Loomis said, "but that dog has eyes like . . . let's see . . . his pupils are elongated. Those're the eyes of . . . a goat. That's a *decadent*-looking dog," the gray-haired lieutenant said.

"He's a wonderful dog, Lieutenant," Hans reassured him. "He's very lovable."

And then Ludwig crept forward a few steps and put his heavy head on Too-Tired Loomis' knee, and he looked up at the lieutenant with eyes as demented as . . .

"Now I've got it!" Too-Tired Loomis said. "He's got eyes like The Bad Czech. Officer, take this dog *out* of here."

But before Hans could take Ludwig away, a terrible thing happened. Ludwig stared up at the gray-haired lieutenant and wagged his tail. And got an erection.

"Oh shit!" Hans cried out, but it was too late.

Ludwig growled excitedly and stared at Too-Tired Loomis, and began ejaculating. Right on the lieutenant's shiny floor.

"It looks like he . . . uh . . . he *likes* you, Lieutenant!" Hans cried nervously.

"GET THIS FILTHY CREATURE OUT!" Too-Tired Loomis bellowed, scaring the crap out of The Bad Czech and Sunney Kee, who were giving each other one last Magilla Gorilla before the monster cop was released for foot patrol.

The Bad Czech came running into the watch commander's office, took a look and cried, "Ludwig jizzed all over the lieutenant's floor!"

"Don't you *ever* bring that animal in this station again!" Too-Tired Loomis warned the skinny K-9 cop.

"I think you oughtta start carryin a jizz rag, Hans," Cecil Higgins said.

But what the others didn't know, and what only a certain Chinatown groupie knew, was that a very strange phenomenon had recently occurred. Ludwig was not only adopting Hans' characteristics, as is usually the case with K-9 partners. The opposite had also occurred.

Being together so much was causing Hans to react like Ludwig! The last two times he had taken the groupie to a motel he had suffered the humiliation of premature ejaculation. He begged her to tell no one. It was only temporary, he promised her. There was some psychological explanation for the bizarre turn of events, he was sure. Ludwig and Hans were *both* premature ejaculators.

The last time that Hans fired too early in the motel room, the sneering groupie said, "You better start carrying *two* jizz rags."

Mario Villalobos had by now received the information he wanted regarding the credit card of one Lester Beemer. The card had recently been canceled upon notification by the secretary of Lester Beemer that he had passed away. The former client had been self-employed as a private investigator, with his residence and business addresses in Pasadena. The secretary of Lester Beemer had made no mention that the credit card was ever out of his possession and there had been as yet no unauthorized purchases made with the card.

Mario Villalobos took down the addresses and phone numbers and that was it. The only link was the mention of Pasadena. Caltech was in Pasadena.

There wasn't much of importance on his desk and there were no other leads in the apparent murder of Missy Moonbeam. It was more than likely nothing, but he had an uncharacteristic urge to take it just one step further. Pasadena was fifteen minutes from Rampart Station when traffic was light.

By the time The Bad Czech and Cecil Higgins finally got out on the foot beat with the sound of Magilla Gorilla ringing in their ears, they had already heard about Wooden Teeth Wilma being belted around like a tetherball.

They didn't know as yet the identity of the suspect, but they had a description supplied by the Costa Rican news vendor, and Earl Rimms was one of eight or ten people they suspected. The Costa Rican news vendor said that when the suspect started highballing it through the park, he almost fell on his ass. He wore what looked like brand-new brown and white patent wingtips.

"Brown and white," The Bad Czech said. "There ain't too many dudes around with brown and white shoes."

"We kin take a look around Leo's Love Palace," Cecil Higgins said. "Git us a Alka-Seltzer while we're at it."

"Wooden Teeth Wilma isn't a bad old broad," The Bad Czech said. "It makes me mad to think a somebody usin her like a tetherball. I'm feelin mad enough to murder any spade I catch wearin brown and white shoes."

"Let's jist hope Mayor Bradley don't go out on the streets today with brown and white shoes on," Cecil Higgins said.

And while The Bad Czech and Cecil Higgins started a search for Alka-Seltzer and spades in brown and white wingtips, the K-9 cops were getting tired of showing off their dogs to Jane Wayne and Dolly.

Gertie and Ludwig were having such a glorious time that they both had to be dragged toward their radio cars, heartbroken that their romp was over. The K-9 cops drove black-and-white Ford Fairmonts with the back seat removed. The animal stayed in the back and a metal mesh protected any potential prisoner in the front seat from the threat in the back. Gertie and Ludwig were both whimpering for each other when Hans and the other K-9 cop ordered them into their respective radio cars.

The other K-9 cop was nameless. All the K-9 cops were nameless to the people on uniform patrol. They knew the names of all the dogs, but the dog's partner, unquestionably the less important half of the team, was nameless. It was "Gertie and Gertie's partner."

The only reason they knew Hans by name was that he chose to do his drinking in The House of Misery among other haunts downtown. To the cops in Rampart Station who *didn't* drink at The House of Misery, the K-9 team would be "Ludwig and Ludwig's partner."

Rumpled Ronald would have stayed in Echo Park all day screwing off and watching the dogs work. The pension was officially his at 12:01 tonight. He was absolutely convinced that if he did any police work whatsoever on this day he was a dead man.

As they were getting into their cars, the call came crackling over the radio: "All units in the vicinity and Two-A-thirteen. Two-F-B-one is in foot pursuit of possible two-eleven suspect! In the alley north of Eighth Street and Alvarado!"

"That's The Bad Czech!" Jane Wayne said. "Let's hit it, Ronald!"

"Oh God!" Rumpled Ronald cried, reluctantly getting in the passenger side. "Oh God! This is it! I shouldn't be chasing robbery suspects today!" Then he yelled at the snoozing Dilford, who didn't even hear the hotshot call. "Dilford, clean out my locker if anything happens to me. Throw away the nude pictures of my girl friend before you call my wife. She'd piss on my grave if she saw those pictures! Oh God, this is it! A good cop's gonna die today!"

And as it turned out, Rumpled Ronald was right.

Cecil Higgins had spotted the suspect first. He didn't know it was Earl Rimms. He just saw the tall black man with the mean-looking body shove a drunk out of his way when he came in the back door of Leo's Love Palace. He could see that the man wore a stingy-brim straw hat and a sport coat, but that was all he could see until the door closed. Then the man was no longer backlit against the sunlight as he stood in the dark saloon trying to get his eyes in focus.

Cecil Higgins' eyes were already in focus. He could clearly see that the man was wearing two-tone wingtips. Then he could see the man's mean and threatening face. "Earl Rimms," he said to The Bad Czech, who was putting away his second Alka-Seltzer along with a glass of tomato juice with egg. "Look at his shoes."

The Bad Czech saw the shoes at about the same instant that Earl Rimms' eyes dilated and he saw the beat cops at the end of the bar. The foot race was on.

Back out the door went Earl Rimms, followed by the monster cop, who was yelling and moving fast for his size. Cecil Higgins put out the "officers need assistance" call on the rover radio unit he carried on his belt. There wasn't much point in his trying to keep up with The Bad Czech, who was thirteen years younger, so he tried to figure in which direction Earl Rimms would go once he realized that the alley off Eighth Street would lead him into a dead end.

Both K-9 units beat the others to the scene. Cecil Higgins had totally lost sight of Earl Rimms and The Bad Czech once they got to the alley. There was a ten-foot chain link fence at one end and though Cecil Higgins thought The Bad Czech was too hungover to scale that fence, he realized that's what must have happened.

Unit K-9-1 arrived before any other car. It was to be expected, in that Gertie's partner was super-hyped and burning for action. Gertie was fairly frothing by the time they arrived, even more hyper than his partner. The shepherd detected the radio urgency, the change in his partner's breathing and voice level. The dog smelled the new sweat.

Gertie was stoked. Gertie wanted to *go*. He was ready to attack. Gertie was as wild-eyed as his partner when Cecil Higgins, holding his hat in his hand, waved the careening K-9 car around the block, yelling, "Drive south two blocks! If you don't see them, head west toward Alvarado!"

Hans, being a more placid and plodding cop, was of course giving off enough vibrations to make Ludwig excited, but both members of Unit K-9-2 were in control when Cecil Higgins, standing on the corner directing traffic, waved them in a westerly direction in search of The Bad Czech and Earl Rimms.

Dilford and Dolly squealed around the corner at Park View and Seventh Street, and Jane Wayne along with a pale and clammy Rumpled Ronald (who thought he was looking straight into his own grave) began weaving through the traffic to the south.

"Why ain't I driving? Why am I in the death seat?" Rumpled Ronald wanted to know. "Why am I in this Burt Reynolds movie?"

"I hope the Czech's okay," Jane Wayne said, biting her lip nervously while her blue eyes, lined severely with black eyeliner, swept the streets.

"I probably shoulda been better to my wife," Rumpled Ronald said. "I know I shoulda been better to my girl friend."

It was Unit K-9-1 that first spotted The Bad Czech. He was lumbering north on Coronado toward Wilshire Boulevard. A black man in a stingy-brim hat and sport coat was fifty yards ahead of him.

Unit K-9-1 hit the siren, blasted past four panicked motorists, ran up over the curb to get past two cars at a red light, spun and swayed and straightened out, and skidded to a stop. The black and tan shepherd was given his command to attack.

"Fass!" the cop yelled. *"Fass,* Goethe! *Fass!"*

Earl Rimms turned in horror when he saw the roaring mass of black and tan disaster hurtling toward him. He instinctively ran straight up to the front porch of a triplex, kicked open the door, entered past a screaming hysterical child, slammed the door shut, kicked through the rear door and was in the yard and over the fence while Gertie frothed and growled and barked at the front door. Then Gertie heard Earl Rimms plowing through the rear yard and the dog leaped from the porch, vaulted one fence, scrambled gracefully over another, and spotted the terrified mugger sprinting across the residential street.

Gertie pursued wildly. In full throat. Ecstatic. With abandon.

Gertie never saw the car. It didn't have time to brake. Gertie was struck broadside by a Cadillac, lifted six feet head over tail and smashed against a metal light standard at the intersection.

Gertie immediately tried to stand on three broken legs. He pulled himself upright on the one good leg. Gertie dragged his bloody hulk down the sidewalk toward the fleeing Earl Rimms. After him still. Vomiting scarlet.

Jane Wayne had tried pushing her foot through the floor when the K-9-Unit broadcasted the sighting of The Bad Czech and the suspect. She was the first to careen onto Coronado and see the dog dragging his broken body down the sidewalk instinctively in pursuit of the man who had disappeared and was again scaling backyard fences.

She stopped the car beside the dog and said, "Oh, Gertie!"

The dog didn't seem to hear her. The pain and shock were by now overwhelming. He could only whimper and vomit blood. And vainly drag his ruined body after the vanished Earl Rimms.

"Somebody should shoot him now," Rumpled Ronald said.

Then they heard Unit K-9-1 screaming up behind them and Gertie's partner was out before the car skidded to a stop, slamming into the curb. He was quickly down on the sidewalk, wrapped around the bloody dog, babbling to him and crying like a child.

"Goethe, Goethe," Gertie's partner said, sitting down on the sidewalk, cradling the dying shepherd.

"He should shoot that animal," Rumpled Ronald said.

"Shut up, Ronald," Jane Wayne said.

It wasn't necessary to shoot Gertie. His head was hanging loose and he'd stopped whimpering even before his weeping partner picked him up in his arms and carried him to the black-and-white.

Hans and Ludwig had arrived and Ludwig jerked Hans down the sidewalk like a puppet, despite the pinch collar Ludwig was wearing. Ludwig was whimpering and barking and growling all at once, and trying to get into the back of Unit K-9-1 with Gertie. Ludwig obviously was confused and bewildered, and ignored Hans' commands. Ludwig almost pulled the chain clear out of Hans' grasp and had to be wrestled away by Hans and Jane Wayne and Rumpled Ronald before they could close the door on Gertie.

"Well, Ronald, you were right," Jane Wayne said as they got back in their car. "A good cop *did* die today."

Earl Rimms was by now as bonkers as The Bad Czech, and he was lots more scared. He'd gotten away from the dog, and every time he thought he'd eluded the monster cop he'd stop running and take a breather and wipe the sweat off his face and fan himself with his stingy-brim. And each time he thought it was cooling off, the giant beat cop would come scuttling around the corner and the chase would be on again.

They had run west on Wilshire Boulevard past the Sheraton-Town House Hotel, providing a great show for some tourists from Toledo. They were several blocks past the perimeter of search. They had run through apartment houses, in the front door, out the back door. They had crossed busy streets, climbed over walls, run through alleys. They had both been threatened by frightened dogs and had frightened humans when they scaled or crashed through fences.

The Bad Czech's face and hands were bleeding and he was convinced that he was about a hundred heartbeats from a coronary, but he simply couldn't stop himself. He was, like Gertie, a product of training and he pursued like a monster police dog.

Twice he almost had a shot at Earl Rimms, who leaped over a fence each time. Whenever they would get close enough almost to smell each other, the elusive mugger would manage to do something totally unexpected like dashing through the door of an interior design shop on Wilshire Boulevard and out the back while customers screamed. The Bad Czech yelled curses and threats at Earl Rimms and at a covey of shoppers who got in his way at Bullocks Wilshire.

It was a foot pursuit that would go down in Rampart Division legend. Particularly after its bizarre ending. It appeared that Earl Rimms had won. He left The Bad Czech at Seventh Street and Magnolia, with the beat cop staggering in exhausted bewildered circles. The sun and the smog and the traffic sounds combined to make the huge cop giddy and disoriented.

For a second The Bad Czech thought he'd been nuked. A noise in his head sounded like the incoming missiles back in Nam. He had to sit on the curb and put his huge head between his knees. The Bad Czech raised his sweat-bathed face after a few seconds. He was dying to kill. He wanted to *murder*.

So did Earl Rimms. After he'd won the pursuit, after his heart stopped banging in his throat and the fear subsided, he was murderous. He was mad at the whole world. At the old crazy who carried only dog food in her purse. At his own woman, who called the cops just because he knocked her down the stairs. At Los Angeles county, which didn't give his woman enough welfare money to support him properly, thereby *forcing* him to whack old crazies around like tetherballs. At lunatic monster cops who just kept coming like police dogs.

Then he spotted the spic in the pickup. Earl Rimms

would have preferred spotting an old woman in a
Mercedes, of course. Someone he could grab by the neck
and throw out onto the street. And have a purse left on
the seat to make this miserable day worthwhile, while he
drove a decent car out of this goddamn neighborhood
which must be overrun by cops looking for him. But he
didn't see a single person sitting in a parked car on the
old and seedy residential area around Magnolia and Lee-
ward, except the spic in the pickup.

The spic in the pickup was a Durango Mexican
named Chuey Valdez. He was a gardener and had the
back of the pickup truck loaded with lawn tools. He'd had
a bad day too. Two customers had stiffed him, promising
to pay him next week. Chuey Valdez had found that
money and mangoes were not growing on trees in Los
Angeles as he'd been promised by the *pollero* who hustled
him illegally across the Mexican border for two hundred
American dollars. He was working his ass off in Los Angeles and he was cranky. He was not about to let some
big sweaty *mayate* steal his battered pickup truck.

Chuey Valdez was eating his lunch of corn tortillas
and cold beans and the treat of the week—one whole
avocado—when Earl Rimms walked up to his truck.

"Okay, climb outa there, greaseball," Earl Rimms
said, his depthless black eyes snapping like a whip.

"Joo wan' sometheeng?" Chuey Valdez asked warily.

"I want your *neck*. I want your *balls*. I want your
fuckin *blood*! An I'm gonna *have* them if you don't get
the fuck outa that truck!"

So Chuey Valdez, as was his custom, shrugged in the
face of overwhelming odds as if to say, "Si, señor." He
picked up his sandwich bag and his avocado and his tortillas and got out of the truck. Then Chuey Valdez
reached into his sandwich bag and withdrew the kitchen
knife with which he had been peeling his avocado.

When Earl Rimms, feeling as deadly as a white-
lipped cobra, turned to give the little greaseball a shot of
knuckles in the mouth, Chuey Valdez plunged that
kitchen knife right into the sweating chest of Earl Rimms.
Right under the sternum. Right up to the handle. Then he

jerked the knife out and tossed it into the back of the truck and stepped away a few feet to survey the job.

Earl Rimms just stood there with his back to the truck, looking at Chuey Valdez. He clearly couldn't believe it. He held both hands cupped over the puncture wound and said in disbelief, "You little spic! You stuck me!"

To which Chuey Valdez shrugged noncommittally and said, "Joo made me mad."

"You fuckin little greaseball!" Earl Rimms said in wonder, and with each beat of his heart, with each word he spoke, a jet of blood would squirt out from his body and splash onto the asphalt.

Then Earl Rimms turned and began walking aimlessly toward Wilshire Boulevard while Chuey Valdez contemplated being a good American and calling the authorities, or being a smart wetback and getting the hell out of here.

As it turned out, he didn't have to decide. Jane Wayne, who was by now crazy with fear for The Bad Czech, came squealing around the corner of Magnolia in her black-and-white Plymouth with her nearly comatose partner, Rumpled Ronald. Earl Rimms stopped, pointed to his chest and at Chuey Valdez as if to say, "That little greaseball stabbed me!" and staggered across the lawn of a stucco duplex, collapsing by the driveway.

Within five minutes there were a dozen police cars blocking the street, their red and blue lights gumballing in all directions. Earl Rimms had dragged himself toward the backyard of the duplex and was lying there, getting very cold, waiting for the ambulance.

The other cops kept back the crowd of rubberneckers, directed the traffic past the police cars and waited to wave in the paramedics, while The Bad Czech, battered and exhausted, stood with his partner surveying the inert body of Earl Rimms.

"He ain't gonna make it, is he, Cecil?" The Bad Czech asked in the flattest tone of voice Cecil Higgins had ever heard from him.

"I don't think so. He musta bled two quarts already.

Course these miserable motherfuckers like Earl Rimms, somehow they live when anybody else'd cash it in. He *might* make it."

Then The Bad Czech said, "Cecil, go ask Jane Wayne if she radioed the paramedics that he's gonna need plasma right away."

"It ain't like you to be so concerned," Cecil Higgins said suspiciously. But he turned to see whether Jane Wayne had informed the ambulance as to the nature of the puncture wound.

The Bad Czech looked dementedly down at the inert figure of Earl Rimms and said, "I think you ain't breathin, Earl. You need CPR."

The Bad Czech rolled up his shirt sleeves and knelt at the head of the mugger, and began *giving* him cardiopulmonary resuscitation. The Bad Czech pushed down on the bloody chest of Earl Rimms and the blood shot two feet in the air. The Bad Czech put the stingy-brim hat of Earl Rimms over the puncture and pushed down on his chest and the jet of blood clattered against the crown of the straw stingy-brim. The Bad Czech began rhythmically pushing on the chest of Earl Rimms and the blood pounded and clattered against the inside of the straw hat.

An elderly black woman, who lived in the duplex where Earl Rimms had fallen, finally got enough courage after peeking through the lace curtains. She walked out on her back porch. The Bad Czech sweated as he worked on Earl Rimms.

The old black woman was overcome with emotion. "Oh, that's so wonderful, Officer," she said to the monster cop, who looked up, startled. "You're saving that poor man's life!"

The Bad Czech turned his crazed eyes on the old woman and said, "That's right, ma'am. He ain't breathin and this is his only chance. If I can resuscitate him."

"I'm going right inside and call the mayor's office," she said. "You deserve a medal."

As the geysers of blood thudded against the crown of the stingy-brim, while The Bad Czech pushed on Earl

Rimms' chest, Cecil Higgins returned. He said, "Czech! What the fuck're you *do-*in?"

The Bad Czech had his bloody hands pressed around the rim of the stingy-brim. When he straightened up and removed it, a *hatful* of blood washed over the body of Earl Rimms and onto the concrete driveway. The Bad Czech had to jump back to keep from getting splashed.

"You pumped him *dry!*" Cecil Higgins whispered.

"Quiet, Cecil," The Bad Czech said. "Don't make a big thing outa it."

"Czech! Czech!" Cecil Higgins said, grabbing the monster cop by the shirtfront, looking for a shred of sanity in those demented gray eyes. "That's murder! Did anybody see this?"

"I think he was dead anyways, Cecil," The Bad Czech said.

They heard the ambulance cut its siren and slide to the curb. A few minutes later The Bad Czech, Cecil Higgins, Jane Wayne, Rumpled Ronald, Dolly and Dilford, two detectives and a patrol sergeant were all in the street discussing the incident. The Bad Czech reassured Chuey Valdez that he wouldn't even be charged with littering, and the only way he could've done better was if he'd taken Earl Rimms' scalp like a fuckin Apache.

The paramedic walked out to the clutch of cops while his partner covered the body. "He's long gone," the paramedic said. "I never saw so much blood, even from a puncture like that. The coroner'll have to go to his spleen for a blood sample. He looks like something from Transylvania got to him."

Which caused Cecil Higgins to glance involuntarily at The Bad Czech, who said, "This ain't been my day. I want a burrito."

As they were preparing to leave, the old black woman who lived in the duplex hobbled out to the patrol sergeant and said, "I just want you to know that you should be proud of your men. That big officer there tried to save that poor man even if he *was* a criminal. That's Christian charity. I want his name so's I can write a letter to the mayor about it."

"Thank you, ma'am," The Bad Czech said shyly. "It don't hurt to remember that we're all God's children."

The Bad Czech insisted on getting a burrito from the roach wagon before they headed back to the station for all the reports. His uniform was a mess, but the paramedics had cleaned up the cuts on his face and hands. He'd drunk seven free Pepsis, much to the chagrin of the Mexican on the roach wagon, but all things considered, he looked remarkably fit after his ordeal.

Cecil Higgins was a *wreck*.

"Even when ya hung the wino, I thought ya wouldn't really do it," Cecil Higgins said, looking up at his belching partner, who had both cheeks full of burrito. "I mean *really*."

"It ain't easy to say about somethin *really*," The Bad Czech said, pondering it. "I mean what's real and what's really . . ."

"Don't be *talkin* that crazy shit again!" Cecil Higgins yelled.

"Look, Cecil," The Bad Czech said as he stared at the lake in MacArthur Park, groping for the words. "Consider the Laser Lady. Now she says the lasers are real. What's more real than when ya feel somethin painful? Who kin say they ain't real? It's her fuckin bean the lasers are shootin at. That might be *really* real, know what I mean?"

"What's that got to do with hangin winos and doin a Dracula on Earl?"

"Well, it's hard to explain but . . . it's like it ain't *really* real. Stuff like that."

"I ain't ready for San Quentin," Cecil Higgins said. "I ain't ready to have a asshole big enough for Evel Knievel to pop wheelies in."

"You ain't gonna ask to stop workin with me, are ya, Cecil?" The Bad Czech looked alarmed for the first time.

Just then the sergeant drove up and parked at the curb. "Hurry up and get into the station, Czech!" he yelled. "The captain got a call from the old lady who saw you trying to resuscitate the suspect. He thinks it might make a good public relations story, so a television crew's coming down!"

"Okay, Sarge, we're on our way!" The Bad Czech said.

And when the sergeant waved and sped away, Cecil Higgins could only look dumbfounded.

On their drive to the station Cecil Higgins said, "I been thinkin, Czech. There's a certain risk to workin with you. I got to face that. What could ya offer me if I'm willin to run the risk a spendin my old age in San Quentin with a asshole big enough for a bobsled race and the Lawrence Welk orchestra?"

"You're the on'y one I kin talk to, Cecil," The Bad Czech said eagerly. "I'll buy ya a drink *every* night at Leery's!"

"Ya do that anyways. Make it two drinks."

"Okay, two drinks!"

"Maybe you're on to somethin," Cecil Higgins said deliberately. "You're gonna be kissin babies and have your picture in the papers."

"Cecil, this really ain't worth so much stewin about."

"But that old woman *saw* you suckin him dry. I mean you looked like a big ol blue vampire bat, but she *saw* a compassionate Christian *hero*."

"Good thing I got a clean uniform for television," The Bad Czech said, warming up to the thought of it.

"I think maybe you ain't crazy," Cecil Higgins said. "I think maybe *I'm* crazy."

"I wish you could be a hero too," The Bad Czech said sincerely. "Damn, I sure hope they send that foxy little blonde from Channel Two!"

"When ya buy me my two drinks tonight, I want ya to explain it all to me," Cecil Higgins said. "I wanna know what's real and what's *really* real. I think I'm ready to listen."

SEVEN

The Russians
Are Coming!

The "offices" of Lester Beemer were not exactly what Mario Villalobos expected. The deceased private investigator didn't cater to the carriage trade of Pasadena. His office was on Colorado Boulevard, near the black ghetto, the pawnshops and secondhand stores, an eyesore neighborhood trying to save itself through urban renewal.

Urban renewal had passed Lester Beemer by. He was a former policeman from Fresno who had settled in Pasadena when he was still a young man. Lester Beemer was sixty-six years old at the time of his death on Saturday, May 1. He had been a licensed private investigator for thirty-three of those years and, from the look of things, hadn't been a total success.

The janitor admitted Mario Villalobos reluctantly. The office had been cleaned out. There were empty metal file cabinets. There were two 1950's vintage desks of ugly limed oak. There was a tinny old sunburst clock, same era. There was a hat rack, a manual typewriter, a few green metal office chairs, and that was all.

Mario Villalobos next went to the apartment house where Lester Beemer had lived for the last nineteen years of his life. His bachelor apartment was already rented to another tenant, but Lester Beemer's landlady, a surly hag with a whiskey voice, provided his epitaph: "He was a dirty old man but he always paid his rent."

"Whadda you mean, dirty old man?" Mario Villalobos asked, glad to be standing on the steps outside the apartment house which reeked of wine and seemed to be occupied by young blacks and white pensioners.

"He liked young girls," the landlady said. "Got a cigarette?"

She sucked half the cigarette inside her toothless mouth when Mario Villalobos held the match. She took two puffs and said, "He never had much money even when he was doing good. Reason is he drank too much and he screwed young girls. He always had some whore in this room. Whores he picked up in nigger bars in L.A. Sometimes he had white girls with whore written all over them. He liked niggers too."

"Ever see this girl before?" Mario Villalobos asked, showing the landlady a mug shot of Missy Moonbeam, an earlier one when she wasn't so ravaged.

"Yeah, could be," she said. "Course they all look alike, those whores. But this one? Could be. I pretty much figured he'd go like he did, screwing himself to death in some whorehouse."

Mario Villalobos asked a few more questions which didn't provide helpful answers, and then he gave his business card to the landlady. "If you think of anything else, either about the blond girl or Lester Beemer, just give me a call."

"He was a dirty old man," the landlady said, taking the card.

"But he always paid his rent," Mario Villalobos nodded.

The next stop was the residence of the part-time secretary of Lester Beemer, whose name appeared on the door sign at Lester Beemer's former office: PERSON TO NOTIFY IF EMERGENCY CASE.

She looked like an emergency case. Her name was Mabel Murphy. She had a red Hibernian face and drank a fifth of booze on an off-day. She was half bagged at four o'clock in the afternoon.

"Aw shit!" she said when Mario Villalobos showed her his badge. "I thought maybe you were an insurance man. I've been hoping old Lester left me a few bucks. Silly of me. The old geezer was always three days ahead of the light, gas and telephone companies."

"How long did you work for him, Miss Murphy?" Mario Villalobos asked, looking around her sixty-year-old wood frame house, built at a time when most of the Pasadena blacks were servants to the rich, and lived in. Mabel Murphy's house was now in the middle of a working-class black neighborhood.

"Off and on, fifteen years," she said. "Lester wasn't a bad guy. Drank too much"—and her eyes said *Don't we all?* "About time for my first of the day." She got up, waddled to the refrigerator, brought out half a quart of milk and poured it into a water glass which she topped off with Scotch.

"Ulcer?" Mario Villalobos asked.

"Iron stomach," she said. "I just like milk-balls. Learned it from the colored people in the neighborhood."

"Lester Beemer's landlady said he had a taste for prostitutes." Mario Villalobos lit a cigarette after Mabel Murphy got seated.

"Taste for them? You bet," she grinned. "All flavors. He wasn't picky. Just so they were young."

"Did you ever see this one?" Mario Villalobos asked, showing the mug shot of Missy Moonbeam.

She held it under a badly done Tiffany copy and said, "Pretty girl. No, I never saw but one or two of them. He didn't bring them to the office very often. But I heard enough phone conversations to know that he spent plenty of money lining up working girls for himself and for clients."

"For clients? What clients?"

"I don't know," she said. "Most of the work I did was telephone answering, correspondence, checking account, bill paying. Stuff like that. His files were slipshod and that's the way he wanted it. I don't think he paid ten thousand dollars in income tax the whole time I worked for him. He was a secret old bugger. Not the soul of honesty, you understand. Always paid my salary on time though. I used to work Wednesdays, Thursdays and Fridays. The rest of the time he used an answering machine."

"What did he die of?"

"Heart," she said. "Had open-heart surgery twice. The last time they installed a pacemaker. That didn't stop him from enjoying his booze and cigars and it sure didn't stop him from whoring around. I think he almost liked having a bad heart. He loved to tell everybody he was going to die before Christmas. Every Christmas for ten years. Got lots of sympathy that way. But I don't think he got much sympathy from his whores. He was always having me get him cash to pay for services. In advance."

"How often would he want money that you figured was for prostitutes?"

"Thursday and Friday, usually. And from the withdrawal slips, I knew he'd do it at least one other night."

"Apparently his heart wasn't *that* bad," Mario Villalobos said.

"As long as the machine kept going," she said. "He always said the little machine in his chest was a child of the god of science. One night the child of the science god took a holiday and that was it."

"Funny way to put it," Mario Villalobos said. "Child of the science god. Did he have an interest in science?"

"Did he have an interest? He was a groupie. He wanted to belong to the Caltech Associates. A lousy little private eye with his dirty necktie and Timex watch, wanting to rub elbows with all those people who give endowments and grants and such. He must've subscribed to half a dozen scientific journals in America and a couple from other countries. It was one of his hobbies. Science, golf and whores."

"Would he've taken a phone call at Caltech's division of chemistry sometime? I found a phone number in the book of a Hollywood prostitute, along with the name Lester."

"He might," she said. "He went over there once in a while. He had a few golfing pals who were members of the faculty. Professors, I guess. Could've been chemists."

"Know any names?"

"No, they never called him. Sometimes he'd just sit around Friday afternoons when he was bored and tell me about his golfing pals from Caltech who were hot candidates for big casino."

"What's big casino?"

"What else? The Nobel Prize. That's what he called it."

"Well, that does it," Mario Villalobos said, with his sad and weary sigh. "My murder victim probably knew Lester Beemer as a customer. She wrote his name on her book. She called him at least once at Caltech's chemistry division when he was visiting someone. Mystery solved."

"Murder victim? Who killed her?"

"Pimp. Customer. Who knows? There's one more thing. His credit card was found in a Korean restaurant near the neighborhood where the prostitute died. Did he ever mention someone stealing his credit card?"

"No, not as far's I know."

"Who collected his personal effects after his death?"

"His sister in Seattle, Louise Beemer. She was all he had left and she's got one foot in the grave. There wasn't much. The police were called because of the motel."

"Which police? Which motel?"

"Pasadena. He was found in one of those no-tell motels on Colorado. His wallet was where he always kept it, in his sock. Old Lester wore *garters*. And he kept his moth-eaten wallet in his *sock*. Can you imagine?"

"Was his credit card in his wallet when he was found?"

"I have no idea."

"How about the office files?"

"I destroyed everything. All files. All tapes. You have to do that in a confidential business like Lester's. And like I said, Lester wasn't the soul of honesty and discretion."

Mario Villalobos stood and wiped his runny nose on a handkerchief and sneezed a few times as one of her cats ran across her slippered feet.

"Allergic to cats?"

"Uh huh," he nodded. "Well, that about does it."

But it didn't quite do it. Mario Villalobos was no longer a slave to a completeness compulsion, as he had been in former times, when he couldn't put a case away and do the "arrest is imminent" follow-up gags if there was a strand still dangling. In the old days he was not one who could gladly turn a back-shot victim into a suicide with a bizarre theory (which actually happened in another division) thereby closing a sticky case.

He was a different man these days. He was tired as dust. All the time. He would have been more than happy to call Missy Moonbeam's death a suicide if he thought he could persuade his lieutenant that she simply lost a few fingernails and a patch of panty hose while strolling toward her swan dive. In fact, he had no idea why he was fretting over this one. Could it simply be megaboredom? Was he *so* bored and weary, unaccountably *scared* these days that he felt compelled to *do* something? Something nostalgic? Like police work?

The credit card bothered him. He knew a little about the Pusan Gardens, where The Bad Czech found the card. The vice sergeant told him that the restaurant proprietor regularly engaged Asian and round-eyed B-girls to solicit drinks from customers. He knew that the Missy Moonbeams of this world were usually able to earn more money from Asian customers than they could get from white men or black. Maybe Missy Moonbeam simply knew Lester Beemer from the streets of Hollywood. It wasn't inconceivable that she drove or cabbed it to Pasadena from time to time to service the old boy. And that she and Lester had their last fling in the no-tell motel where his body was found.

But why a motel? Why not in Lester's apartment—to save money if nothing else? Lester Beemer was hardly worried about what the neighbors might think. The biggest *why* was the scribbling of the name on her trick book, the name of a dead man, along with manic doo-dling, decorated with scrolls and lines like daggers. And the number of the division of chemistry at the California Institute of Technology? If she wasn't calling the dead man, who was she calling *about* the dead man?

"Goddamnit!" Mario Villalobos said aloud, turning off the freeway, to get back on again and drive north to Pasadena. He wouldn't let it go just yet.

Fifteen minutes later he was standing inside Llewelyn Brothers Mortuary on Lake Avenue in Altadena, talking with the man who had collected the body.

"Of course it *wasn't* a coroner's case, Sergeant," the mortician said.

He didn't look like Hollywood's version of an under-taker. He looked like a bodybuilder, which he was. Since the family business was located in what was now a black neighborhood, the scion of the mortuary thought it prudent that the Llewelyn boys keep themselves in shape. Twice in the past year thugs had tried to rob the mor-tuary, just as bandits traditionally robbed liquor stores. The genteel old days of Altadena were long gone.

"I take it that a doctor signed a death certificate," Mario Villalobos said.

"Absolutely," the mortician said. "Wouldn't have touched him otherwise, in a motel like that. As soon as the police found the pacemaker identification bracelet with the name of his physician, they called him. And he later told me he wasn't the least bit surprised that Mr. Beemer died the way he had, in a sleazy motel."

"Was it obviously his heart?"

"Obviously. Probably during foreplay because he was fully clothed. He was just lying there in bed. Naturally the girl had run off, whoever she was."

"Is the physician local?"

"Dr. Trusk? Been around here for years. Elderly man. Very competent. Knew Mr. Beemer well."

"The police had no doubts whatever?"

"I don't even get near a coroner's case, I assure you. I learned that at my father's knee."

"Was there a wallet on the body?"

"At first the police thought there wasn't. Then I found it in his sock." The burly mortician smiled. "He wore *garters*. I haven't seen garters like that in years."

"Was there money in the wallet?"

"No, but the identification was intact. He had a few dollars in his pocket and some change."

"Were there credit cards in the wallet?"

"Credit cards? No, no credit cards. I sent his personal effects to his sister. An elderly woman from . . . Portland."

"Could it be Seattle?"

"Yes, that was it, Seattle. She requested cremation. She was without funds and his insurance was minimal—veteran's insurance, actually."

This time Mario Villalobos decided that nothing was going to stop him from staying on the Pasadena Freeway and heading for the station. If his partner Maxie Steiner were with him none of this would be happening. Maxie wouldn't have put up with this kind of dumb chasing around. It wasn't as though he didn't have enough to do, what with babysitting Chip Muirfield and Melody Waters.

On the other hand, he was giving them the routine investigations and bothersome follow-ups, which freed him to indulge a whim concerning Missy Moonbeam and a Caltech connection. Now he was going to let it go. There wasn't anything else to do with it. He'd just book the credit card as found property, release it to Lester Beemer's sister or American Express, and that would be that. Almost.

Just *one* more little step to relieve megaboredom. Chalk it up to mid-life crisis. Half a step, really. He wanted to see if The Bad Czech knew anyone at the Pusan Gardens who might answer a *few* questions about the found credit card and Missy Moonbeam.

When he located The Bad Czech, the monster cop was standing in front of Rampart Station doing his impression of John Wayne. There was a blond television reporter, sweating in the sunshine, who was very sick and tired of this big ham ruining every take with speeches about how he was in the business of protecting and serving, and even saving the life of "assholes" like Earl Rimms.

On take two, The Bad Czech changed "asshole" to "scumbag" when someone told him what he'd said. On take three he softened it to "slimeball" on request. On take four he got it down to "puke," but by then he was so nervous he blew the first part of his statement about protecting and serving.

Between takes six and seven she tried to help the big dummy relax by offering to let him go into the station and get a drink of water so his cotton mouth would stop popping into the hand mike. When he said he'd rather have a *real* drink, she smiled, and he took it as an encouraging sign and asked her if she'd meet him after work in some place called Leery's Saloon.

She declined and they did takes nine and ten. The cameraman was on his last roll when The Bad Czech managed something resembling a quotable statement about saving the life of the "rotten mugger."

The Bad Czech begged for one more take, saying that his mouth was as dry as Rose Bird's giz, but she refused, and called it a wrap.

"If you change your mind about Leery's, gimme a call!" The Bad Czech was yelling to the retreating blonde when Mario Villalobos pulled into the station parking lot.

A few minutes later The Bad Czech, ebullient from his television debut, was sitting in the detective car, heading for the Pusan Gardens on Olympic, telling Mario Villalobos about the marathon foot pursuit and the death of Gertie.

The Korean chef was overseeing the evening's food service when the beat cop entered with the detective. He looked about as happy to see the cops as he was to see the Chinese Army thirty-odd years ago when they swarmed across the border and overran the Americans. At which time he scooted out of Seoul with one thing in mind: Hollywood. And a restaurant he dreamed of, called "Seoul Food."

The Bad Czech spotted the part-time waitress, full-time B-girl, who was still doing waitress duty this early in the day. They walked her into the cocktail lounge where it was dark and private.

"Hey, Blossoms," The Bad Czech said. "This here's a detective and he's got a few questions for ya. Don't worry, he ain't with the vice squad. He's workin on a murder."

"Do you know this girl?" Mario Villalobos asked the chunky B-girl.

Blossoms was thick through the shoulders and thighs. Her face was flat and unrefined, the face of a peasant. They could see from her nervous glance that she knew Missy Moonbeam.

"She got in jail?" Blossoms asked.

"She's the dead one," Mario Villalobos said. "Did she work here sometimes?"

"Some time," Blossoms nodded, nervously fidgeting with her pencil and order pad.

"A . . . hostess?" Mario Villalobos asked.

"Like me." The girl nodded.

"Did she work here Saturday night?" Mario Villalobos asked.

The girl thought for a moment, a decided effort. She wrinkled her brow and shuffled her feet nervously. "Before one day. Flyday," she said. "She here all night."

"Did she pick up some men?" Mario Villalobos asked.

"I good girl, no men," Blossoms said, glancing toward the kitchen where the chef was peeking through the open door.

"I told ya he don't work vice," The Bad Czech said impatiently. "Jist tell him the truth, for chrissake, Blossoms."

"Maybe *few* men," Blossoms said.

"Korean men?" Mario Villalobos asked.

"Yes," she nodded.

"Are you sure you didn't see her Saturday night? That was the night she died. It's real important."

"She not here after Flyday," Blossoms said.

"Did you ever see this?" Mario Villalobos asked, producing the credit card of Lester Beemer.

She held the card upside down and said, "Maybe."

"Can you read?" Mario Villalobos asked.

"No."

"Why do you say 'maybe'?"

"She have card like this one Flyday."

"It looked just like this?"

"Look just like," she said. "She say card no good sometimes. Sometimes good. We talk about . . . *ways* make money. I good girl. She not so good."

"She talked about credit card scams?" The Bad Czech asked.

"What?"

"Did she say she used cards like this one?" Mario Villalobos asked. "To buy things? Cards belonging to other people?"

"Yes," Blossoms said. "I tell her no. I good girl."

"And this card?"

"Funny card, sho say. Missy throw card on table and say no good."

"I don't understand," Mario Villalobos said, looking at the credit card. "It hasn't expired. It looks okay."

"I hate mysteries," The Bad Czech said. "They give me headaches. I like to know how things work and what's real and what ain't real and . . ."

"Did Missy leave the no-good card on the table Friday night?"

"I sink so," she said. "Card no good, Missy say. Not anysing on card."

"Not anything on the card?" Mario Villalobos said.

When they got back to the station Mario Villalobos left The Bad Czech, who was beside himself with excitement about being on the five o'clock and eleven o'clock news. The detective had an urgent telephone call waiting for him. The number looked familiar, but the caller had refused to give a name. While he was dialing it, he realized the number was the Wonderland Hotel.

Oliver Rigby answered: "Hello, Wonderland."

"It's Sergeant Villalobos," the detective said. "Did you call?"

"Yeah," Oliver Rigby whispered.

The detective could imagine him peering around the lobby and cupping his hand over the mouthpiece. "Why didn't you leave your name?"

"It's too urgent!" Oliver Rigby whispered. "Some guy came in here. He was askin about Missy! He looked like he was gonna have a heart attack and die in the lobby. He asked did she jump. He kept askin, did she jump? Or did somebody *help* her jump?"

"You get his name?"

"He wouldn't give it," Oliver Rigby said. "Then I told him you was workin on the case and he should call you. I wrote down your name and telephone number. Did he call?"

"No, yours is the only call I've got on my desk," Mario Villalobos said.

"Did she jump? Did somebody help her jump? That's what he kept sayin! I thought about grabbin him and callin the cops."

"What'd he look like, Oliver?"

"Look like? Like a screamin fruit is what he looked like," Oliver Rigby said. "He looked like a peroxided limpwrist from Santa Monica Boulevard is what he looked like. Do I get a reward if he's the killer?"

After getting a more detailed description of Oliver Rigby's visitor, Mario Villalobos sat smoking at the homicide table long after most of the others had gone home. The Bad Czech didn't hate mysteries any more than Mario Villalobos did.

He was almost out the door when the call came. The lieutenant said, "For you, Mario."

The male voice was falsetto, so he figured who it was. The voice said, "Sergeant, I've been told that you're investigating the death of Missy Moonbeam."

"That's right," Mario Villalobos said. "What can I do for you?"

"I *gotta* know something first. Did she jump? Or was she, like . . . murdered?"

"First, let me have your name and . . ."

"I have some important information for you, Sergeant," the voice lisped, rising an octave. "*Extra* important!"

"Yeah, but I'd like to know who I'm talking to and . . ."

"Listen to me!" the telephone voice cried. "It's more than Missy. It's . . . first, ya gotta tell me, was she *murdered*?"

In that the caller was getting hysterical, the detective said, "I believe she *was* thrown from the roof."

The caller was silent for a moment and Mario Villalobos could hear him beginning to hyperventilate. Then the voice disappeared from the phone.

"Are you there?" Mario Villalobos asked. "Are you there?"

"I . . . can't . . . I . . . can't get my *breath*!" the voice said.

"Get a paper bag," Mario Villalobos said. "Breathe into it. Try to relax. You're okay."

The telephone was put down for a few more minutes. Mario Villalobos smoked and looked at his watch. Then the voice came back and said, "I'm all right now."

"Tell me your name."

"I'm *real* scared," the caller said. "I think I'm the *next* to die!"

"I can come and see you," Mario Villalobos said. "Tell me where."

"I'm . . . I'm too confused!" the caller said. "I'll call ya at ten o'clock tomorrow morning. Will ya be there?"

"I'll be here waiting for your call," Mario Villalobos said. "But can't you tell me . . ."

"I can tell ya one thing, Sergeant," the caller said. "This is probably the most important case ya ever worked on. I don't know who killed Missy Moonbeam, but I know *what* he was!"

And then Mario Villalobos figured that his caller was as goofy as a waltzing mouse. As loopy as a laughing loon. As crazy as The Bad Czech. In a breathy voice full of melodrama, but also full of *fear*, the caller said, "Her killer was a Russian spy!" And then he hung up.

A few hours later, Mario Villalobos was watching the Angels getting themselves beaten by the New York Yankees. Mario Villalobos could sometimes get a complimentary ticket at Dodger Stadium because he moonlighted doing stadium security. But tonight the Dodgers were on the road, so he drove to Angel Stadium and paid.

He ate hot dogs and ice cream and drank beer and didn't give much of a thought to Missy Moonbeam or Lester Beemer, because with that call it had gotten out of control. Even before having grown as tired as dust, Mario Villalobos had been a logical, methodical, if sometimes compulsive investigator. And Russian spies spelled fruitcake, and fruitcake investigations produced nothing but more fruitcake.

Maybe he should turn this one over to the shoulder holster kids. He thought about announcing it tomorrow: "Chip, Melody, I've got a case for you to work in your spare time. It involves a murder by a spy. The Russians are coming!"

He would have laughed except that Goose Gossage was just brought in to fire tracers at the Angel hitters, and *that* wasn't funny.

As usual, the ventilating was started by The Bad Czech who sat at the bar very nervously. The television news team had promised him that his interview segment would be on the five o'clock news. It wasn't.

Leery switched off the TV when The Bad Czech called the station and was told that extra coverage of the Middle East had preempted him.

"Sure," The Bad Czech complained to the losers at Leery's. "Mideast war. Arabs and Jews been killin each other since Christine Jorgensen had nuts. But how many times you seen an interview of a policeman that tried to save the life of a scum-suckin piece of slime like Earl Rimms? There ain't that many cops around with kindness in their hearts. Goddamnit, I better be on the eleven o'clock news or I'll firebomb that fuckin TV station!"

"Settle, Czech, settle," Jane Wayne said, standing behind the monster cop, tugging on his eyebrows.

"Well, whaddaya expect?" The Bad Czech said, picking up his newspaper. "Nobody cares about real news anyways. Listen to this. It says here that the no-nuke demonstration attracted the usual locals. There was the National Association a Social Workers. There was the Lesbian and Gay Democratic Club. I wonder why they have to stick 'Democratic' in there? It goes without sayin. There was the Revolutionary Communist Party. The ACLU. The Catholic Workers. The Radical Fairies to Heal the Earth. There was women dressed in nuns' clothes with skeleton faces. There was paper helicopters piloted by Ronald Reagan dolls. And get this: about thirteen pages later there's a tiny article about a family a six gettin slaughtered out near Riverside. Kin ya dig it? Mass murder is about as important as the classified ads. Nobody kin tell the Hillside Strangler from the Freeway Killer without a program. A no-nuke march gets the press. So who cares about a cop doin a humane act, for chrissake!"

"Settle, Czech, settle," Jane Wayne said to the street monster, who was starting to froth like Ludwig. He was making everyone extremely nervous. The Bad Czech's face was scratched and bruised from the foot pursuit and his demented eyes were pinwheeling tonight.

"The Bad Czech looks like he's been chasing parked cars," Dolly whispered.

"The Bad Czech looks like he's been blocking punts," Dilford whispered.

"How da ya like my new political poster, Czech?" Leery asked, trying to change the subject and console the rabid beat cop. Up on the wall was a homemade sign which said JERRY BROWN USES VASELINE. GORE VIDAL USES POLYGRIP. THE ONLY DIFFERENCE IS AGE. VOTE STRAIGHT REPUBLICAN.

"I *better* be on the eleven o'clock news, that's all I gotta say." The Bad Czech was too cranky to be diverted by politics.

"At eleven o'clock I'll only be sixty-one minutes from my pension!" Rumpled Ronald announced. "It looks like I might make it! Except that my heart's starting to skip beats. Wouldn't *that* be one for the book? Heart attack at five minutes to twelve? Wouldn't *that* be something?"

"The Czech's about as cranky as the bus driver we busted today," Dilford said to Cecil Higgins. "He beat the crap outa this sixty-three-year-old blind man who started bitching at the driver for missing his bus stop. Driver didn't have an excuse except he was tired of unsatisfied customers."

"L.A. wasn't always like this," Cecil Higgins felt obliged to tell the younger cops.

"The *world* wasn't always like this," Rumpled Ronald said, taking his pulse. "I just wanna get outa this world alive!"

Things suddenly became subdued at The House of Misery. A group of ten civilians came roaring in and took over the dance floor. There were six young men and four young women, members of an insurance adjustors' softball league. They had some weeks earlier found Leery's Saloon after a game at Dodger Stadium and now came in from time to time after softball games.

They had been drinking beer and eating Cracker Jacks and were all wearing their team shirts and baseball hats. They put ten quarters in the jukebox and started some play-punk dancing to the Circle Jerks. They were genuinely having such good clean fun that the cops, who usually evinced only about as much paranoia and xenophobia as the Kremlin, were plunged into utter depression and started drinking with a vengeance.

Rumpled Ronald even forgot to count the minutes, so despondent was he after watching the young people. "Can you remember when you could have fun like that?" he asked Cecil Higgins, who just stared into the bottom of his glass.

"I can't remember back that far," Cecil Higgins said.

"It's really something to see . . . *regular* people having fun," Dilford said wistfully, as one pretty young woman jumped up on a chair and started dancing soft rock while the others whistled and cheered.

Even The Bad Czech was captured by the sight of the young people dancing and singing and offering to buy beer for the clutch of jaded strangers who had moved to one end of the barroom and were watching them with eyes full of suspicion.

Jane Wayne said, "It seems like a lifetime ago that I could feel like that. They don't know how . . . it really is."

"How what is?" Dolly asked.

"All of it," Jane Wayne said. "They don't know about . . . paws in petunias and other things."

"I used to be like that girl," Dolly said to Dilford, never taking her eyes from the carefree blonde dancing on the chair in her team shirt with her baseball hat turned around backward. "I sometimes think I'd like to *try* to be like that again. I date civilians but it just never works out when they learn about me. They get intimidated by a girl that carries a gun. Emasculated, I guess. They know we see things. That we're . . . different."

"I stopped being a girl more than a year ago," Jane Wayne said, still watching the pretty girl dancing.

"Me too," Dolly said. "I'm a cop now. And that's all."

They turned away from the pretty girl and went back to their drinks, nostalgia dissolved. They hardly noticed when the young softball players finished their beers and waved cheerful goodbyes to Leery and breezed out the door singing, "We are the champions."

"They just don't *know*," Jane Wayne said. "Another Scotch, Leery. A double."

"They're children," Dolly said. "Another bourbon, Leery. A double."

They didn't envy the young people. The moment had passed. Jane Wayne turned a cynical smile to Dolly's cynical smile and they gave each other a nod of understanding. And drank. They were both twenty-three years old.

With the civilians gone, the cops spread out to their usual places at the long bar and resumed what they did best at this time of night: bitching.

"I hear some detective from West L.A. smoked it," Cecil Higgins announced, and *that* quieted even The Bad Czech.

"Another victim of U.C.A.," Dilford said, which is how he referred to the Ultimate Cop Affliction.

"Right in the mouth as usual." Cecil Higgins sighed.

"Change the subject," Dolly said. "It's one thing to have to wear that thirty-eight-caliber crucifix, without worrying about eating it."

"Whatcha gonna do with that pension, Ronald?" Leery asked, halfheartedly wiping a beer mug which he'd halfheartedly washed.

"*Do* with it? I ain't doing nothing with it. You think I can afford to retire and live on forty percent a my salary?"

"Well why all the worry about living till midnight?" Leery wanted to know.

"Jesus Christ, Leery!" Rumpled Ronald said. "Because I *got* it then. No matter what. If I ended up in prison some day, it don't matter. It's mine. They'd have to send my monthly pension checks to San Quentin."

"Any cop goes to San Quentin, it don't matter he's gettin a pension or not," Cecil Higgins said, looking at The Bad Czech. "You'd be the richest con in the joint but your asshole'd still be big enough to accommodate four monkeys on mopeds and the Soap Box Derby."

"I don't care," Rumpled Ronald said, scratching his rumpled belly, rubbing his rumpled face, which was starting to get numb from the booze. "I just wanna *own* myself. If my old lady kicks me out, I won't have to get an old wino dog and some newspapers for blankets and settle down on skid row. At least I won't have to do that."

"My ex-wife threw me right out in the street," Dilford cried out suddenly, and the others noticed that he was pretty bombed and feeling extra sorry for himself.

"And after you did the manly thing," Dolly said sarcastically. "Got *her* replumbed instead of facing the knife yourself."

"*I* got a vasectomy. You know I did!" Dilford said boozily.

"Sure, after you were *single* again," Dolly said, more sarcastically. "So you wouldn't knock up some *groupie*."

"Go ahead, stick up for a woman you don't even know," Dilford said. "Never mind sticking up for your partner. She threw me right in the street, my ex-wife did. Right in the street!"

"Was that the time you was gone on a three-day binge with that typist from the police commission?" Cecil Higgins wanted to know. "They say you banged that little homewrecker right on Leery's pool table, Dilford."

"I'd *still* like to know what happened to my cue ball," Leery said, considering the possibility.

"And after you got that pansy nurse at the hospital to bandage your head and give you a room and pose as a doctor, and tell your wife you'd been in a traffic accident and had amnesia. You went to lots a trouble for your wife, Dilford," Rumpled Ronald said sympathetically, starting to get numb in the fingers.

"I even had to wreck in the side a my pickup truck to make it look good," Dilford whined. "That truck's had three face-lifts! And *still* she kicked me out! The heartless bitch. They're *all* heartless bitches!"

"My first wife was *always* kickin me out," Cecil Higgins said. "She had a habit a throwin my clothes out in the driveway. I wore out more clothes by runnin over them than I ever did wearin them. Least she wasn't ugly like the one I'm married to now. And this one's into pain. *Mine*."

It was ten-thirty when Hans and Ludwig came in, without a single groupie from Chinatown. Hans was morosely drunk. Ludwig was apparently sober, but did not get up on the bar.

"Ludwig understands that Gertie's dead," Hans said, in his lachrymose singsong voice.

"Bullshit," The Bad Czech said, as they watched Ludwig lumber over to the three-coffin dance floor and lie down.

"See that?" Hans said. "He didn't even get up on the pool table. When he saw Gertie laying dead he understood perfectly. I can't cheer him up."

"That's crazy," The Bad Czech said. "Dogs ain't got brains like that."

"He wouldn't have a single beer tonight," Hans said. "I tell you he *knows*. He saw Gertie all busted up and covered with blood and he knows his pal's gone for good."

"I don't doubt nothin no more," Cecil Higgins said. "You tell me Ludwig knows, I believe it. You tell me Ludwig wants a stress pension, I believe it. I don't know what's real and what ain't real no more."

"It makes me sad to see Ludwig sleeping on the floor," Jane Wayne said. "Make him get on the pool table, Hans."

"Might as well," Leery shrugged. "Many jizz stains as there are now, a few more ain't gonna hurt nothing. Maybe I oughtta just pour a bowl full a beer for Ludwig," Leery mused. He thought it over and said, "Naw, if he *is* able to think about Gertie, it wouldn't be good for his head."

"What a relief!" Cecil Higgins cried. "For a second I thought you was gonna give away a free drink, Leery! I thought for a second I really *had* lost my mind!"

The eleven o'clock news came and went. The Bad Czech couldn't believe it. They had *not* used his interview segment.

When Mario Villalobos showed up at 11:30 for a nightcap, a terrified drunk who had roamed into the bar three minutes earlier was running out onto Sunset Boulevard, hysterical.

"Don't go in that place, mister!" he warned Mario Villalobos. "There's a giant madman throwing beer glasses at the television set! And a woman in a black fur coat looks like she's dead on the pool table!"

138   THE DELTA STAR

"Don't worry," The Bad Czech said. "Does that one

EIGHT

Mother
Of The Year

Mario Villalobos thought it advisable not to tell his colleagues in the squadroom that the Russians were coming. At least not until he'd heard from his breathless caller at ten o'clock. That is, if he *did* call, and if the fruitcake caller had some information about Missy Moonbeam, and if he was able to keep his head clear enough of Russian spies to talk coherently. Fruitcake and caviar. It was a first for Mario Villalobos, since foreign agents usually didn't find Hollywood street whores of strategic interest. Nevertheless he was awaiting the call, proving that even homicide detectives are not immune to soap opera.

Meanwhile, Rumpled Ronald had been awarded a gold watch at roll call for having successfully completed twenty years' police service. The watch was made of chocolate candy, wrapped in foil. Rumpled Ronald told Jane Wayne that she could stop painting the no-bite medicine on his fingernails because he didn't think he'd be biting them anymore. Rumpled Ronald stood and took a bow and ate the gold watch and made a little speech which indicated that his pension made him more or less immortal, and that nothing could hurt him now.

Three hours later he was flat on his back at the hospital where The Den Mother worked as a nurse, and he was in too much pain even to *think* about letting her give him a blow job. It happened when they got a call from The Mother of the Year.

She lived on Westlake, south of Seventh Street. She was seventy-two years old and had been in a wheel chair for ten years. Her legs were arthritic and her fingers were as gnarled as oak and nearly as black from the number of cigarettes she smoked. Like most of the other elderly people in her apartment house, she lived on social security and bemoaned the influx of Asians, all of whom she called Chinamen, and of Latin Americans, all of whom she called niggers.

Her name was Aggie Grubb, but from this day forth, whenever she was discussed by the cops at Rampart Station she would be known as The Mother of the Year. She put in a call to the station because her little boy wouldn't get out of the house and stop sponging off her.

"I just can't make my boy get out," she said sadly to the cop who took the call. "He just sits around all day eating up what little food I have, and he won't get a job, and he won't do nothing I tell him to do. Can you send a policeman by here to talk to Albert and make him behave and get a job?"

"How old is Albert, ma'am?" the desk officer asked.

"He's thirty-nine years old," she said. "And I'm a poor crippled lady in a wheel chair and he won't do nothing I tell him. What's a poor old mother to do, Officer?"

The desk cop also had a poor old mother who wasn't in such hot shape, and he said, "You stop fretting, ma'am. We'll send a car by and have a talk with Albert. Is he living with you?"

"Yes, but he promised it was only temporary," she said, "and he's been here three months and I just don't have no food left, hardly."

"Now, now, don't you cry," the desk cop said, picturing his dear old mother. "We'll just try to talk sense to Albert and see if we can make your life easier for you."

"Thank you, son," Aggie Grubb said.

The call was given to Sunney Kee and his partner Wilbur Richfield. They were an odd couple, Sunney and Wilbur. Because the black cop had the last name of a famous oil company, he was called Thirty-weight Richfield. And naturally, when he was teamed with someone as small as Sunney, the little Asian refugee became "Twenty-weight Kee."

Actually, it wouldn't have mattered how much weight they had that day. It wouldn't have done any good at all. When they knocked on the door, they heard her screeching wheel chair rolling across the cracked linoleum floor. Then the door creaked open.

"Good morning, Officers," Aggie Grubb said.

The veins throbbed blue in her twisted hands. Her dress did not cover her white skeleton knees. When she smiled her single tooth glinted. Then she looked closer through her bifocals at the little Chinaman and big nigger. She couldn't conceal her disappointment. If she was some rich old lady from the West Side, they'd send her real cops, Aggie Grubb thought.

"We got a call that you're having a family dispute," Wilbur Richfield said.

"Might as well come on in," Aggie Grubb said. "Maybe you can talk some to my boy, Albert. Make him go live somewheres else. I can't be supporting him no more. Me on social security, with arthritis? That boy don't respect his mother."

"Where is he?" Wilbur Richfield asked.

"Where he always is," Aggie Grubb said. "In bed till noon. Then he gets up and makes himself a dozen eggs and goes back to sleep till night. I just can't be feeding that boy no more."

"Okay," Wilbur Richfield said. "Where's the bedroom at?"

"Through there," she said, motioning down the hall with twisted stick-fingers. "First door on the left."

"Dozen eggs," Wilbur Richfield said to Sunney Kee when they walked down the musty hallway. "Even The Bad Czech don't eat a dozen eggs."

Albert Grubb ate a dozen eggs. And he ate a pound of bacon with them. And he ate ten pieces of toast. And he drank a gallon of milk when his mother had it. And then he was still hungry.

"Is that *one* man under there?" Wilbur Richfield said to Sunney Kee when they opened the bedroom door and looked at the human shape snoring under the mountain of blanket.

"Is that *one* man under there?" Wilbur Richfield said to The Mother of the Year, who was snuffling and cackling from her wheel chair in the kitchen.

"Big boy, ain't he?" she said. "You shouldda saw his old man."

Wilbur Richfield, a fifteen-year cop, looked at his little Southeast Asian partner, and looked at The Mother of the Year, and looked around the room.

Albert Grubb had pinups on the wall. All the pinups wore skimpy bathing suits and were covered with oil and had unbelievable bodies. All of the pinups were men. Body builders. The largest man on those pinups did not have a chest like Albert Grubb.

There was a set of dumbbells on the floor beside the bed. Wilbur Richfield said to Sunney Kee, "I never thought ya could get that much weight on a dumbbell."

Sunney Kee was also getting a very bad feeling. He looked up and smiled at his partner, but not with conviction.

"Wake the lazy boy up!" Aggie Grubb croaked from her wheel chair in the kitchen.

And Wilbur Richfield bit the bullet and said, "Albert, wake up!"

The sleeping giant stirred and changed gears a bit, but the snoring continued. Like a chain saw. His head was twice as big as Ludwig's.

"Wake up!" Wilbur Richfield said, and this time he tapped Albert Grubb on his size 16 foot with his stick. Like Ludwig, Albert Grubb didn't like to be touched by foreign objects while he slept.

He raised his head. It was a bald head, clean-shaven, formed like something that goes into a gun—a 105 howitzer. He had a face like a huge oatmeal doughnut. His shapeless nose was blackhead-studded. He said, "Who the fuck's that?"

Sometimes, living up to what they imagine their image should be, cops do foolish things because of *machismo*. The foolish thing that Wilbur Richfield did, ignoring the instincts setting off whistles and sirens in his head, was not to use his rover radio unit to call for a backup unit right *now*. And *two* backup units would have been better.

Sunney Kee, who was half the size of Wilbur Richfield, and a rookie, and therefore not saddled with dangerous macho yokes, smiled affably at Albert Grubb and said to his partner, "One second." He stepped into the kitchen, took out his rover and requested the backup. Code-two, which meant hurry up.

Then he quickly returned to the bedroom, where Wilbur Richfield was surveying the colossus on the bed. Albert Grubb was as tall as The Bad Czech. But even bigger. He was lying on his back looking up at Wilbur Richfield and Sunney Kee, and he was feeling very, very cranky.

There were lots of things the cops didn't know about Albert Grubb but which they were going to learn. One thing was that Albert Grubb didn't get his muscle mass at Jane Fonda's exercise salon. He got his muscles from a place far away. In a prison in northern California where he had spent the last eleven years of his life. Where he had nothing to do all day except pump iron and be given ice cream and candy and cigarettes by other members of the Aryan Brotherhood for whom he served as hit man. Albert Grubb had *hated* niggers and slopeheads long before he went to prison and joined the Aryan Brotherhood. Albert Grubb hated niggers and slopeheads even if they *didn't* wear blue uniforms and wake him up in the morning. And of course he hated everyone *in* blue uniforms even if they weren't niggers and slopeheads.

There was something else that Wilbur Richfield and Sunney Kee didn't know about Albert Grubb: he was an institutional man.

Albert Grubb had been out of prison only three months, but he had left a trail like Hansel and Gretel in the forest. And still they hadn't rescinded his parole. Upon being released from prison, he had failed to report to his parole officer. Next, he had "forgotten" to show up for a job interview. Next, he had been "unable" to get a driver's license because he couldn't pass the exam. Then another missed opportunity for a job interview. Then, when he showed up at the parole office, he had liquor on his breath. Obviously. And his eyes were dilated from amphetamines. Obviously. And still they had not rescinded his parole.

Albert Grubb had only a 90 I.Q. but he was smart enough to know what was good for him and what was not. And he couldn't for the life of him figure out why his parole officer didn't know. Albert Grubb had had his sabbatical. He was sick and tired of life out on the street. He couldn't bear the thought of getting up and going to another job interview for some boring job he didn't want in the first place. Everyone expected him to do things which gave him a headache and made him grumpy. The fact is, Albert Grubb had an everloving, gut-twisting need to go *home*. Back to his eight-by-eight-foot cell. To his ice cream and weight lifting, and good-time rapes of every whiskerless kid in the yard, and bashing the faces of niggers and spics in the other prison gangs. To all the things that gave him *pleasure*.

The first of three backup units pulled up out front at about the instant that Albert Grubb raised up out of bed in his yellow-stained jockey shorts. The team of Jane Wayne and Rumpled Ronald was climbing the stairs to the apartment house at about the same instant that Albert Grubb picked up the dumbbell, hefted it, but decided he'd better not use weapons or they might shoot him.

Two other teams of cops were getting out of their radio cars at about the same moment that Wilbur Richfield decided that Albert Grubb could turn railroad tracks into monkey bars. At about the same moment that Albert Grubb let out a manic hyena laugh and said: "I'm *glad* they sent a slopehead and a nigger."

Wilbur Richfield partially ducked the first punch that Albert Grubb threw. It only caught Wilbur Richfield in the shoulder. It only dislocated that shoulder.

Sunney Kee drew his stick and tried all the tricks he had seen growing up as a child in Bangkok and later in Taiwan, in all the Bruce Lee movies. But he found out, as had a thousand cops before him, that they work only for Bruce Lee. In real hand-to-hand combat, people like Albert Grubb just refused to cooperate with the various martial-arts moves as all of Bruce Lee's enemies had done. Sunney Kee, who was small and quick and agile, was only making Albert Grubb madder by darting around the bedroom and slapping him with that nightstick, while Wilbur Richfield tried to reach his right-handed holster with his left hand, crying out in pain from the torn deltoid.

There was now absolutely no doubt in Wilbur Richfield's mind that he should shoot down Albert Grubb like a rogue elephant. But Wilbur Richfield couldn't get the holster unsnapped with his good hand, not when Sunney Kee came crashing into him after being thrown across the bedroom by Albert Grubb, who was just getting warmed up.

"Shoot him!" Wilbur Richfield screamed to the brave little rookie who still believed in the movies of Bruce Lee.

Sunney Kee didn't obey his training officer. Instead, he stood up, assumed a martial-arts pose with his stick, and struck Albert Grubb right across the wrist, shoulder and knee before the behemoth had a chance to react. But alas, police academy instructors—who, like Bruce Lee, always have the cooperation of *their* subjects when demonstrating self-defense—did not always tell it like it is.

"You'll break his wrist with that move," Sunney Kee had been promised by his police academy instructor.

"You'll paralyze his knee with that one," another had promised.

"You'll put him through the wall!" a dozen martial-arts films had promised Sunney Kee during his days as a devotee.

But all it did was make the Albert Grubbs of this world *mad*. In truth, given his size and power and love of pain, Albert Grubb might not have been stopped by Reggie Jackson with a Louisville Slugger.

"Shoot the motherfucker!" Wilbur Richfield screamed, thrashing with his ruined right arm, unable to get to the holster which had been twisted clear to the back of his Sam Browne when the body of Sunney Kee knocked him into the hallway.

And just when Sunney Kee, who had an I.Q. of 140, learned something that Albert Grubb with an I.Q. of 90 had known instinctively—that makers of martial-arts movies were full of shit—Albert Grubb landed a punch on top of the head of Sunney Kee, the portion of the body that the physical training instructor promised would break the fist of an attacker.

It nearly broke the skull of Sunney Kee. Actually, it knocked him loopy. Sunney Kee was trying to stand on boneless legs and was seeing all sorts of Taiwanese fireworks and couldn't get the measure of the words that Wilbur Richfield was screaming at him: "SHOOT THE MOTHERFUCKER!"

Albert Grubb then broke Sunney Kee's jaw and splintered his cheekbone and smeared his nose over to where his right eye could almost look inside.

Sunney Kee never saw Rumpled Ronald slamming Albert Grubb across his howitzer head with a stick, nor did he hear the four other cops who responded to the call, nor did he see Jane Wayne riding Albert Grubb like a jockey as the giant roared into the kitchen knocking over tables and chairs, spinning his dear old mother right out of her wheel chair onto the linoleum floor.

Rumpled Ronald in the heat of battle showed why Mace is so risky a proposition in violent combat. He drew his can of gas, pointed it at the thrashing mastodon and triggered it. But the upside-down nozzle was pointed at himself. He Maced his own armpit. Right up the short-sleeved uniform shirt. His armpit was on fire!

The most extraordinary part of the brawl was the

behavior of Aggie Grubb. With Sunney Kee bleeding from nose, mouth and ears, and Wilbur Richfield still trying to get at his gun, and Rumpled Ronald lying on the floor with two cracked ribs, and Jane Wayne and the other four cops trying to squeeze off Albert Grubb's carotid artery no matter what the police commission and the city council and the press thought about the outlawed choke hold, and while screams of pain and curses terrified the entire apartment house, Aggie Grubb managed to right her wheel chair and get back in it.

Two things happened that would go down in police folklore. First, Albert Grubb extricated himself from under the pile of bodies, staggered back into the corner of the kitchen smashing through a maple hutch and adding a few more cuts to his face and arms, and showed the cops what so far they had accomplished. There was one handcuff dangling from his enormous wrist. The thing he did next was what cops would talk about. He took the loose cuff and snapped it shut on his wrist. On the *same* wrist. Unencumbered now, wearing two cuffs on one wrist, he thought of San Quentin and gave them the grin of a happy boy going home.

He said, "Okay, *now* we fight."

And while five young cops, including Jane Wayne, faced the horrifying prospect, two wounded older cops who knew better came staggering from the hallway into the kitchen. One was Rumpled Ronald and the other was Wilbur Richfield, who was finally holding his service revolver in his left hand.

"No, we ain't fightin no more," Wilbur Richfield said hoarsely. "This little war's over."

Albert Grubb said, "You can't shoot me. I ain't got no weapon. You'll get in trouble."

Wilbur Richfield said, "You'll get *dead*, motherfucker. It's worth it."

Albert Grubb studied the black cop. He listened to the quivering voice, saw the hand trembling against the trigger pull, and knew that this nigger would shoot his face clear off if he twitched.

"Okay, boys," Albert Grubb said. "I'm all yours. Gentle as a lamb."

What happened next was what usually happens after a fearful fight or chase, when cops are raging and terrified. It horrifies bystanders and editorial writers and lawyers and judges when later the cops are charged with using excessive force. In such situations it has always happened and always will, despite all the training in the world. Five terrified raging vengeful people, those who were able physically to function after the maiming battle, leaped on their gentle lamb, and with punches, nightstick blows, kicks, choke holds and handcuffs, managed to play a little catch-up.

The other moment that would go down in police folklore occurred when Albert Grubb was down on the floor, covering his head, taking his not unexpected lumps, thinking how he'd get his turn when he got back home again and got to bash some spics and niggers in the prison yard.

What happened was that Aggie Grubb wheeled her gnarled skeleton body over to the pile of cursing, screaming, vengeful cops who were trying to inflict everything short of death on Albert Grubb. And she became a *cheerleader*.

"Kick him! Punch him! Use that stick!" she screamed.

And one of the cops thumping Albert Grubb looked up, stunned.

Aggie Grubb was really into it. Her brittle eyes were gleaming like handcuffs. She strained forward in her wheel chair to see a cop cracking the noggin of Albert Grubb with his stick.

"KICK HIM!" Aggie Grubb screamed, saliva drooling down her chin. "USE YOUR FEET! PUNCH HIS EYES OUT!"

It was probably the cheerleading of Aggie Grubb that stopped the game of catch-up, more than it was the exhaustion of the players. All the cops, Jane Wayne included, looked at the mother of Albert Grubb in wonder.

"WELL, YA AIN'T GONNA STOP NOW, ARE YA, YA CHICKENSHITS?" she screamed, baring her single tooth. *Drooling.*

Henceforth, whenever the cops of Rampart Division met to drink and ventilate and recall the bad old times, Aggie Grubb would be referred to as The Mother of the Year.

If there was any justice or irony to the situation, it occurred after Sunney Kee was taken away by ambulance—eventually to be given a medical pension for neurological injuries, and after Rumpled Ronald was driven code three to the hospital with two cracked ribs, in too much pain to accept a blow job from The Den Mother, who was the duty nurse that afternoon—when Albert Grubb, bleeding from a dozen head wounds, was being led down the stairway, his hands cuffed behind him. He was indeed as docile as a lamb, hoping they wouldn't keep him in county jail too long before sending him back home to San Quentin. Albert Grubb suddenly remembered that he might need his allergy medicine, in that the pollens had been blowing wild all week, what with the Santa Ana winds.

"How about tellin my ma to give ya my medicine?" Albert Grubb yelled to the cops.

"I'd like to give you some double-aught shotgun pellets," Jane Wayne said, wondering how badly Rumpled Ronald was hurt.

"Come on, sweet stuff." Albert Grubb grinned through bloody teeth. "I got asthma."

Jane Wayne had been thinking of how she failed to get the choke hold properly clamped to the twenty-two-inch neck of Albert Grubb. She was thinking of how the carotid choke hold was the only weapon of value against animals like Albert Grubb in the sudden hand-to-hand fighting that police officers have to do. She was thinking how impossible it would be to use taser guns in such situations without shooting each other. She was thinking how Rumpled Ronald Maced himself and could as easily have Maced one of them. She was coming to the inescapable conclusion that for one human being, even of superior strength, to overcome the resistance of another who really didn't want to cooperate, the choke hold was the *only* weapon, outside of deadly force.

She was thinking how the city council and the ACLU and the police commission and the press didn't like the idea of choking the necks of the Albert Grubbs of this world, fearing they might lose a few Albert Grubbs from time to time. She was thinking all this, and of how one city councilman stood up and said that the use of Mace was as rough as the cops should ever have to get.

"You need your asthma medicine, Albert?" she asked, with eyes as crazed and deranged as The Bad Czech's.

"Yeah, baby," Albert Grubb grinned. "I knew you wouldn't let a sick man suffer."

"Well, Albert, since we can't legally choke you animals anymore, here's a little *medicine,* compliments of your city councilman."

Jane Wayne drew the Mace can from her Sam Browne, and before Albert Grubb saw it coming, he had a snootful of gas and was writhing on the ground, yelling. After which she sprayed it in his *mouth.* Lots of it.

Because of incipient emphysema he ended up in the prison ward of the county hospital with respiratory complications, and nearly died. Three cops later swore to Internal Affairs investigators that Albert Grubb was gassed *during* the fight, and Jane Wayne was ultimately cleared of the charge of excessive force leveled by Albert Grubb, who they decided was a poor loser.

Aggie Grubb defended Jane Wayne by saying that of course he was Maced during the fight and she'd have given her eyetooth if they'd stuck the Mace can up his ass. She was just disappointed that the cops didn't do a *real* number on the bastard, who should have been douched to death when she had the chance.

The Mother of the Year became a Rampart heroine when she said that boys like hers not only proved that Father Flanagan of Boys Town was full of shit, but that kids like Albert could turn Mother Teresa of Calcutta into an abortionist.

*   *   *

Ten o'clock came and went and Mario Villalobos did not receive any intelligence reports on Russian spies. He was a little disappointed. It was a dreary day and there were a lot of routine follow-up reports to catch up on. A fruitcake call would have helped relieve the monotony.

And while Rumpled Ronald was being treated for his cracked ribs and was realizing that his twenty-year pension did not make him immortal, he was approached by a black woman who had seen him brought in by ambulance.

She was wearing green silk shorts, knee boots, a green jersey see-through top, with a sequined lime jacket thrown over her shoulders. She wore heavy orange lipstick and orange blush on her mocha-colored flesh. Her hair was not her own but was obviously a wig, done in orange spikes. In all, she wasn't the height of *haute couture*, but she sure as hell attracted attention walking down the street. And that was her business.

She stood watching Rumpled Ronald lying inside a cubicle in the emergency ward, and had seen them hang up his uniform shirt. She was nursing an ugly salve-covered burn on her left shoulder and she started toward Rumpled Ronald three times.

When the doctor left to check X rays, she approached. "Officer?" she said tentatively.

"Yeah?" He looked up at the hooker. "I can't be dealing with police problems, lady."

"My old man burned my shoulder," she said. "I been thinkin about makin a report."

"Call the station," Rumpled Ronald said. "I'm in no shape to be taking reports."

"But he's a pimp. I thought you all'd be interested."

"Call vice," Rumpled Ronald said. "They'll be glad to take a report. They don't like pimps."

"I got somethin else I wanna talk to the *po*-lice about," she said.

"Oh!" Rumpled Ronald said, moving around painfully on the stretcher, turning his rumpled face away from the hooker. "Gimme a break! I just survived a five-Pamper day!"

"It's about that white girl Missy," the hooker said. "I hear on the streets she got *pushed* off that roof."

"What white girl? What roof?" Rumpled Ronald moaned.

"The Wonderland Hotel," she said. "A girl got throwed off the roof. I thought I should tell you all I know if somebody's killin workin girls."

Ten minutes later Mario Villalobos got a telephone call from a voice he hardly recognized. The voice was full of anguish and misery and self-pity, and finally he realized who it was.

"Ronald?" he said. "What happened?"

"There's a hooker here with some information about a case you're handling," Rumpled Ronald said. "I got some busted ribs and my armpit got Maced and they had to shave off the hair, and I'm so sore I can't even accept a blow job from The Den Mother, and I only wish I could take my brand-new pension and get the fuck *outa* here and go back to America except that the animal that busted my ribs was an American and I'm getting involved in a homicide investigation and I don't want no *part* of it!"

Mario Villalobos drove to the hospital and had a brief conversation with the hooker who called herself Bo Derek Smith. They sat in the detective's car in the hospital parking lot. As was to be expected, she had changed her mind about making a pandering report or any kind of report against the pimp who had burned her with the cigarette. Usually he was nice to her, she said, and if she made the report he'd just get out on bail and set fire to her or pull her nipples off with a pair of pliers. So she thought it best to tolerate the shoulder burn and to go ahead and let him use her for an ashtray when she was bad. And to try to be a better girl in the future and make lots of money for him.

She did however decide to talk about Missy Moonbeam, because even pimps didn't like sicko-psychos who totally destroyed good merchandise.

"Two times I run into this guy last week on Western Avenue," she told Mario Villalobos. "This white guy. Sorta big with black hair. He ast about Missy Moonbeam, you know, like where she hustled and where she lived. Said he used to be her ol man and had some money for her."

"What kind of car did he drive?"

"He came walkin up. Once I was with three girls. Once I was with another girl. I wear different wigs so I don't think he knew he talked to me twice."

"Did he always ask the same thing?"

"Not the last time. Then he said it was real important because her mother was dyin and he was her brother."

"Ever see him before last week?"

"Never did," she said. "He wasn't no on-time guy. No kinda street guy. Had a dark stripe suit on and a necktie."

"See him on Saturday?"

"Last time was Friday afternoon."

"Did you tell him where Missy lived?"

"I never told him nothin. I never be knowin where she lived, matter a fact."

"Did any of the girls on Western know where she lived?"

"Prob'ly not. They mighta told him which corner she worked. If they believed him about having money for her. I never did believe him. I thought about callin you when I heard she went off that roof. He coulda followed her home or somethin. I didn't like his looks. Wearin dark shades you couldn't see through. Him and his phony moustache."

"How did you know it was phony?"

"Not many guys have a moustache *that* thick. I done a little work as a screen extra."

"Hooray for Hollywood," Mario Villalobos said. "Did his hair look real?"

"Couldn't tell. He wore a cap like you wear in a sports car. Not a pimp hat. That's why he looked so off-time. Probably a sick-psycho that tricked with her a few times. Maybe wanted to go home and stick needles through her eyelids but didn't know where she lived. I picked up a guy like that once."

"Do you know anyone who was a good friend of Missy?"

"No . . . well, yeah, but none a the *real* girls. There was this sissy, name a . . . name a . . . le's see . . . Dagwood, I think it was. Yeah, name a Dagwood. I seen Missy once or twice when she was workin over around Sunset and La Brea with this sissy name a Dagwood. Little teeny sissy with gold hair. Looks enough like a girl to be a queen, but wears guy's clothes, least when I saw him."

"Know where I can find the sissy?" Mario Villalobos asked.

"They got a few sissy bars not too far from there," the hooker shrugged. "I think I better be goin now. I ain't made no money all day."

"Okay, here's my card," Mario Villalobos said.

"I hope you catch him," she said. "Don't like them freaks that throw girls off roofs. Hard enough in this world tryin to make a honest dollar without some freak throwin you off roofs."

"If you change your mind about making a report against the pimp, give us a call on that," Mario Villalobos said. "You shouldn't have to put up with some dude using you for an ashtray."

"Well, he on'y be's mean to me when I'm bad," she said. "When I'm good, the man's full a love!"

Mario Villalobos nodded and opened the car door for the woman. He understood that even hookers need a little soap opera in their lives.

There was something nagging at Mario Villalobos. It was one of those relentless little aches that wouldn't take shape and wouldn't go away. There was something that was said to him yesterday, either by Lester Beemer's landlady or his secretary or the mortician who burned Lester Beemer and shoveled him into an urn. Something that didn't check.

When he looked at his watch to see if it was time to be hungry, it hit him. It was time to be hungry, but first he had to make a call or two.

"I just wanted to make sure I read your inventory correctly," Mario Villalobos said to the mortician on the other end of the phone. "You released keys and wallet and a little money to his sister, and that was it?"

"Yes," the mortician said.

"Was he wearing a wristwatch? His secretary said that he wore an old Timex."

"No, no wristwatch."

Next, Mario Villalobos made his first contact with the Pasadena policeman who responded to the call that night in the no-tell motel. He reached the cop at home.

"When I saw that pacemaker identification bracelet I called the doctor, who called the undertaker," the cop told him.

"Was Lester Beemer wearing a wristwatch?" Mario Villalobos asked.

"No, no wristwatch that I recall," the cop said. "You might ask the undertaker."

After Mario Villalobos hung up he lit his seventeenth cigarette of the day, reminded himself that he *had* to cut down, and thought it over. Then he called Mabel Murphy.

"When you helped Lester's sister retrieve the personal effects from the office and his apartment, did you find his Timex?"

"How did you know he wore a Timex?" she asked.

"You mentioned it yesterday in passing," Mario Villalobos said.

"Wasn't he wearing it when he died?" she asked.

"No, he wasn't."

"He *always* wore it," she said. "Bought a new Timex every couple years. He was a clock watcher. Very punctual."

"Did you find any claim checks in his personal effects? Maybe he had the watch at a jeweler's for cleaning or repair?"

"No," she said. "And anyway, he never bothered. That's why he didn't buy expensive watches. When the Timex stopped ticking, he'd run down and buy a new one. He was the same way about neckties. When they got too stained and sloppy, he threw them in the trash can and bought a new one."

When Mario Villalobos hung up he lit a new cigarette, forgetting he already had one cooking. Not only was Lester Beemer missing a credit card at the time of his death, but a worthless wristwatch as well. He wished they hadn't cremated the body.

He knew what would happen if he called Pasadena detectives at this juncture to suggest that maybe they had a whodunit homicide on their hands. They'd say thanks and politely kiss him off. He'd do the same in their shoes. A wristwatch that may have been lost or put in a jeweler's somewhere? A credit card that could have been left anywhere at any time by the old private eye when he was out romancing whores in downtown L.A.? The Pasadena detectives would suggest that if Lester Beemer had some connection with Missy Moonbeam, and was linked to *her* death, that was Mario Villalobos' problem. The little child of the science god in Lester Beemer's chest had just kicked off because he had his three hundredth whore of the year in a motel room and got all excited. Any other problem was not *their* problem.

After a futile check of the monicker file for a little swish named Dagwood, he decided to try to find him.

"Hey, Charlie," he said to the black detective lieutenant who was reading the sports page and eating an egg salad sandwich, "I'm going out barhopping tonight."

"And here I thought you never took a drink," the lieutenant said without looking up.

"Just thought I'd tell you in case the Hollywood vice squad recognizes me. I'll be looking in some Hollywood gay bars for some swish named Dagwood. Thought I'd better tell you in case you hear about it and worry that I'm turning gay."

"I don't care anything about your sex life," the lieutenant said, absorbed in the sports page. "Long as you don't wear dresses to work."

NINE

Fruitcake and Caviar

Mario Villalobos didn't bother to alter his appearance. This wasn't an undercover operation, and in any case he was the last person anyone would choose for an undercover assignment. He stood before the mirror and realized that in just eight days he'd be forty-two years old. Middle age wasn't that bad. No worse than herpes or tuberculosis. His mind occasionally tried to persuade him that he was thirty-two. His body, already sagging and out of shape, felt every one of the forty-two years. The face he saw in the mirror frightened him a bit. The hair was almost totally gray and he was losing plenty of it. The eyes were beginning to pouch, the mouth had deep lines on either side, and he could feel a pinch of loose insensitive flesh between his chin and Adam's apple. He looked down at the sink. He counted seventeen hairs lying there dead.

What he was experiencing, of course, made him want to cry for the many failures in his life. Especially for the two marriages and the two sons who were strangers. One son only ignored him, but the other actually despised him. His son Alec was the kind of boy who despised many things, mostly himself. He was a rather unattractive kid, puny and anemic, who in adolescence became addicted to drugs and had to be committed to a hospital at the insistence of Mario Villalobos over the objections of his wife. It was the final and most destructive blow to their bad marriage.

The detective learned one thing during the two months his son was in that hospital. First of all, he learned that a cop didn't earn enough money to pay for the hospitalization of an emotionally disturbed child. Secondly, he learned that his son despised and hated himself so much that he needed to despise and hate someone else in order to function.

Mario Villalobos, the symbol of authority for young Alec, the one who committed him to the hospital over the objections of the boy's mother, was the natural object of the boy's hatred. And Mario Villalobos also learned that being the natural object of his son's hatred was the most unnatural experience of his own lifetime.

He took upon himself a terrible responsibility after the divorce. Insofar as possible he continued to make the decisions, all of which his son hated. Insofar as possible he monitored the boy for surreptitious drug use which his son hated even more. Insofar as possible he insisted that his ex-wife continue the boy in psychotherapy, and this the boy hated most of all.

Mario Villalobos believed that by being hated he was committing the greatest act of love possible.

The detective breathed a weary sigh and decided that the man in the mirror looked ten years older than his chronological age. He didn't bother to change his suit or take off the necktie. The man in the mirror would be recognized as a cop no matter how he dressed, and in any case he wasn't trying to fool anyone. There was one great advantage to working homicide: people involved in minor vices or even major vices, people who functioned in a subculture, were generally unafraid of homicide investigators, since premeditated murder was usually not in their repertoire.

An ironic thing happened that night. He looked so much like a cop that the people in the gay bars did not think he could be a cop. A young hustler sat next to him within his first five minutes in Hercules' Heaven and asked him if he was looking for a date.

"I'm looking for someone named Dagwood," the detective said.

"Won't Blondie do?" The young man winked. "Or how about Daisy?"

"Not tonight," Mario Villalobos said. "Do you know Dagwood?"

"I know Elwood," the hustler said. "We can do a double if you like. You and me and Elwood?"

By ten-thirty he had drunk at least one drink in each of five gay bars. This one was called The Peanut. At least it had entertainment. A pretty good trio banged out some cool jazz and a male vocalist sang "I Only Have Eyes for You," which the detective enjoyed. By his estimate he had seen eighteen slender blond men, about five feet three inches in height, between the ages of thirty and thirty-five, who were potential "Dagwoods."

He had tried it every way possible. From "Hi, Dagwood," to "I'm scouting this location for a movie and could use some extras. Can I have your name?"

Just as he was about to leave The Peanut, the drummer played a roll and a spotlight illuminated the tiny dance floor where two gay couples were slow dancing. The couples cleared the floor and the piano player announced Miss Connie Creampuffs.

Connie Creampuffs wore ballet slippers and a pink tutu. Connie Creampuffs also wore a pink punk wig, a Wonder Woman headband, a padded pink bra, and a pink ribbon that dangled from under the tutu. Connie Creampuffs was a man, which was to be expected. But what was unexpected was that Connie Creampuffs, who stood only five feet five inches tall, weighed at least four hundred pounds.

"You want another?" the butch bartender said to Mario Villalobos, who watched Connie Creampuffs doing a burlesque bump while the crowd hooted and whistled.

"I can't leave *now*," the detective said, paying for another double shot of vodka. *This* was a show.

Connie Creampuffs had a Kewpie red mouth and eyelashes that extended past his nose. His belly, legs and back were particularly hairy. He moved with surprising grace and Mario Villalobos had to revise his guess. He believed that Connie Creampuffs weighed at least 425 pounds.

It was when Mario Villalobos was starting to decide that the "entertainment" at The House of Misery was pretty tame that Connie Creampuffs showed the howling crowd where the pink ribbon went. He dropped the tutu and everyone went mad. There were flaps and folds and rolls of flesh, but there was one particular mass of white hairy belly flesh that hung like a loincloth over the pubis of Connie Creampuffs. Each time the drummer would clash the cymbals, sweating Connie Creampuffs would grab that particular fold of flesh with two hands and show them the pink ribbon obviously tied to his genitals. Genitals that might never be seen by Connie Creampuffs without a mirror and could not be seen by anyone else, so deep within the tucks of flesh were they hidden.

In order to flash the crowd, this stripper didn't lift a dress, a skirt, or a spangle. This stripper had to lift his belly. With two hands, the way one would raise a lead-lined loincloth.

Things were pretty dull at The House of Misery that night what with the absence of Rumpled Ronald, who was home nursing his cracked ribs. And especially without the presence of the town crier in blue.

"Where the hell's The Bad Czech?" Cecil Higgins was getting worried.

"Maybe he *did* decide to firebomb the TV station," Dilford said, putting down his third double. "You think he's getting even loonier than usual these days, Cecil?"

"Well, he *does* sort a make me wanna bring bail money every time we hit the bricks in the morning," Cecil Higgins admitted.

"Why do you wanna work with the maniac?" Leery

asked Cecil Higgins, leering at the pile of dollar bills that Dilford had in front of him.

"I might regret it someday," Cecil Higgins said. "When I'm sittin in a prison cell needin all the astro turf in Houston to wipe my ass with. But ya know what? He never does bore me. Ain't nothin worse than bein bored."

"There's worse things," Dolly said.

"Everybody looks as cheerful as Bjorn Borg, for chrissake," Dilford said. "What's *wrong* with everybody?"

"The Czech isn't here," Jane Wayne said. "Mario isn't here. Ronald's hurt. And Sunney Kee, well, they say *some* neurological damage, maybe."

"I could get more belly laughs from the Ayatollah Khomeini," Dilford said miserably.

There were two Rampart cops sitting at the end of the bar in the place usually occupied by Hans and Ludwig during later hours.

"Hey, Leech," Dilford said to the younger one. "Is it true you're the one that sent out the APB teletype about the Japanese tourist group that got robbed?"

"Yeah," the young cop said. "And Too-Tired Loomis threatened me with two days' suspension just cause it said, 'Victims unable to describe suspect, but got three hundred pictures of him.' Something about cultural stereotypes, Loomis said."

"Two days. That ain't bad for a lightweight joke," Cecil Higgins said. "That's a low bail schedule."

"Where the hell *is* the Czech?" Jane Wayne wanted to know. "If he doesn't come soon, you can put my drink in a boozer bag, Leery, and I'll take it with me."

Meanwhile, Mario Villalobos could think of only two gay bars he hadn't tried. Tomorrow he was going to call the Hollywood watch commander to ask if any of the night watch knew of a pansy named Dagwood. He tossed down the vodka and decided he'd had enough to drink.

"Hi, Dagmar," the bartender said to the little man with a bleached blond perm who was perched on the first stool at the bar. "Didn't see you come in. What'll you have?"

Dagmar Duffy's heart began to beat faster when he saw the masculine gray-haired guy in the suit shooting him a smile of recognition as wide as Connie Creampuff's tutu.

Dagmar Duffy returned the smile and could hardly believe his good fortune. This guy *liked* him. This guy couldn't take his *eyes* off him. This guy came over to him as soon as Dagmar said to the bartender, "I'll have a scorpion, Waldo. And mix me up lots of ice cubes in your jolly blender!"

The man in the suit sat beside Dagmar Duffy, who batted his lashes and wondered if he should play hard to get.

"I've been looking for you all night, Dagmar," Mario Villalobos said. "Actually, I thought I was looking for Dagwood."

"Pardon me?" Dagmar Duffy said, wondering if the guy in the suit had a nice ass.

"I'd know your voice anywhere, Dagmar," the man in the suit said.

"I don't understand," Dagmar Duffy cried happily, shaking his golden perm. "But I don't *care* if I don't understand!" This was his night. Dagmar Duffy was so happy he could have laughed.

Five minutes later, Dagmar Duffy was so miserable he could have cried. He was walking down the sidewalk with Mario Villalobos and shaking like the ice cubes in Waldo's jolly blender.

"You got the wrong person!" Dagmar Duffy cried.

"I'd know your voice anywhere," Mario Villalobos said.

"Oh Lord! Are you arresting me? I haven't done nothing!"

"We're just gonna talk, Dagmar," Mario Villalobos said.

"Oh Lord!" Dagmar Duffy cried. He wrapped his arms around his bare shoulders and goosebumps formed on his bare thighs.

Mario Villalobos looked at the olive drab tank top and khaki shorts and said, "You oughtta dress warmer when you go out at night."

"I'm not cold!" Dagmar Duffy cried. "I'm scared! Where we going?"

"Anywhere we can talk," Mario Villalobos said. "Would you feel okay talking in my office?"

"Oh Lord!" Dagmar Duffy ran his hands nervously through his perm, and plucked anxiously at the single amethyst stud he wore in his left ear. "Don't take me to a police station!"

"If you don't calm down you're gonna start hyper-ventilating again," Mario Villalobos said. "Now let's hear what you know about Missy Moonbeam."

"Can we get some ice cream?" Dagmar Duffy asked. "My stomach's a mess."

"I'll be glad to buy you an ice cream, Dagmar," the detective said. "But I hope that doesn't mean we're going steady."

Things were getting tense at The House of Misery. Hans and Ludwig showed up drunk. Dilford was half blitzed and Dolly was bagged. Hans was making a move on Dolly, who was too drunk to be sickened by his sing-song little double entendres which usually made her want to puke. Two groupies from Chinatown were getting jeal-ous because Hans was making the move on Dolly. Hans and Dolly had already danced twice and were giggling all over the dance floor. And on top of everything else, Dil-ford was getting insanely jealous of Dolly and Hans.

"Look at my partner dancing with that K-9 weasel!" Dilford said to Cecil Higgins, who was staring into the bottom of his glass as usual. "Doing the twist. Huh! She's twenty-three years old. What does she know about the twist?" Suddenly he yelled, "Dolly, you never even *heard* of Chubby Checker!"

But Hans just giggled and waved bye-bye at Dilford, and leered down at Dolly while they did the twist.

"I don't really care if there's a brawl," Cecil Higgins

said. "Long as they take off their guns. Any shootin starts and somebody's gonna end up in San Quentin with a asshole roomy enough for two Christmas trees, a phone booth, and Shelley Winters."

"That pervert!" Dilford said, and made a quick move as though to stalk over to the three-coffin-sized dance floor and cut in.

The move was *too* quick. Ludwig was standing at the bar with his big clumsy front feet wrapped around a beer bottle to the delight of the two drunken groupies. Ludwig was trained to be wary of *any* fast moves toward his partner. Ludwig growled at Dilford. Ludwig sounded like a *lion*. Dilford got very pale and went back to his barstool.

"Just like the whiny noodle-neck pervert," a *very* jealous Dilford said of Hans. "Gotta have his big brother with him."

"Dilford, I wouldn't advise ya to push this," Cecil Higgins said. "I jist bet if you so much as spit on Hans, Ludwig would *eat* you. There'd be nothin left but a shinbone, I bet."

"Has to bring his big brother along when he steals someone's girl, the skinny little pervert," Dilford said.

That woke up Jane Wayne. "Have you lost your mind, Dilford?" she asked. "Dolly's your *partner,* not your girl! Do you think you *own* her?"

"I heard that!" the mini-cop said, breaking off from the twisting K-9 cop while old Chubby Checker's voice blared from the jukebox, encouraging everyone to do the twist. "How *dare* you tell me what to do when we're off duty? How *dare* you tell me what to do when we're *on* duty? I'm not on probation anymore, Dilford."

"I don't know why you even wanna *dance* with Hans," Dilford said, and now *he* was sounding whiny. "He's a pervert. He looks like he's seen too many steam rooms. Don't you agree, Cecil?"

"Leave me outa this," Cecil Higgins muttered. "I don't wanna get ate by Ludwig."

"He's so perverted he *reeks* of Mazola oil," Dilford said.

But the skinny K-9 cop wouldn't be provoked. He

giggled drunkenly and kissed his groupies and said to Dilford, "Just do unto others as you would do unto yourself. If you were double-jointed."

"He'd sleep with an Egyptian mummy," Dilford said. Then, deciding to make the insults political, he added, "I bet he's a Democrat!"

"At least I can say *government*," Hans said. "That's more than your Republican President can do. Guv-ment. He can't even *say* the word."

"You know, I'm sick of people like you thinking you *own* the female officers," Dolly said to Dilford as she staggered backward.

"Better sit down, Dolly," Cecil Higgins said to the mini-cop. "I don't wanna see a little cop flop."

"You know what it's like being the first full-fledged female officers on patrol in this police department?" Dolly asked boozily.

"You tell em, Dolly," Leery said. A good argument always made them *drink* more.

"You males are the worst gossips in the world," she continued. "You're *expected* to score with your female partners. I know *you*, Dilford. You don't say yes you did, but you don't say no you didn't. You just smile when they ask you about me, and let them draw their own conclusions."

"Want another double, Dolly?" Leery asked. He was leering for all he was worth.

Jane Wayne had had enough to drink to throw in with Dolly. "Yeah, Dilford, how would *you* like to be out on some assignment in full uniform and you can't take a leak? It's fine for you men. You just run in an alley for a few seconds. We need five minutes to take off our Sam Brownes and uniform pants. We just have to stand around tap dancing till we get a *chance*!"

It was obvious that Dilford, as drunk as he was, couldn't handle the two-pronged attack of Dolly and Jane Wayne. "Well, you women aren't always nice to us either," he whined. "You know that other bionic bitch that works Hollywood? I heard she went to a Japanese restaurant with her partner and when the sushi chef asked if they wanted giant clam, her partner said, 'No thanks, I got one.' And she popped him across the chops! In full uniform! In front a people!"

"And our makeup," Jane Wayne griped. " 'Don't look like a hooker,' they say."

"Pin up our hair with a dumb barrette like my mother did in grade school!" Dolly said.

"Goddamnit, cops shouldn't wear makeup, and have hair below the collars unless they're sex perverts like Hans!" Dilford sneered. His face was getting red and he couldn't take much more.

"Mahatma Gandhi liked daily enemas from his granddaughter," Hans informed them, sharing a beer with Ludwig. "Nobody called *him* a pervert."

"We can't wear shorts or tank tops when we're off duty and come in to pick up our checks," Jane Wayne said. "But the male officers can wear anything they damn well please. We can't be comfy like you."

"No shorts up the wa-zoo," Dolly said. "Do you know how many times I've heard that? Look at Jane. Cleavage for days and days. What's she supposed to do, hide them in a bra *all* the time?"

"I saw Dolly putting on lip gloss and combing her hair when we had a man-with-a-gun radio call!" Dilford said to Leery. "Does that sound professional to you?"

"You know what the department psychiatrist said to me when I was trying to get on the police department?" Dolly asked Hans, who was all ears, cheek-to-cheek with one groupie and Ludwig. "He asked questions like, 'Have you ever had sex before?' I asked him 'Before *what*?' Do you think the men got asked questions like that?"

"He asked me if I ever wanted to have sex with my sister," Dilford said to Leery, who replied, "Why don't you buy a few drinks and let's talk about it, Dilford."

"You know what *else* he asked me?" Dolly said. " 'During sexual encounters do you like to throw oranges?' "

"DO YOU, DOLLY?" Hans screamed suddenly, scaring the crap out of both the groupie and Ludwig. "DO YOU?"

"Do you smoke after sex? I don't know, I never looked," Leery said, but no one laughed.

" 'Have you ever had sex with an animal?' he asked me," Jane Wayne said.

"Did you know The Bad Czech then?" Cecil Higgins wanted to know.

"I'll bet he never asked *you* such things, Dilford," Dolly said. "You don't know what we women have had to endure to *become* cops. I really got mad when he said to me 'Do you climax big or little?' "

All of a sudden it got very tense and quiet down at Hans' end of the bar. One groupie was dressed like a bazaar in Istanbul. She wore so many metal bracelets she couldn't lift her drink with one hand. And now that she was blasted she began to side with the female cops. She shot a hostile look at Hans, whose eyes got big and round and scared. He feared the worst. And he got it.

"I happen to know somethin about climaxes," the groupie announced. She turned her fat dumpling face to Hans and said, "I happen to know that some a the male cops act like their *dogs*."

"Ludwig!" Hans cried out. "It's time to go! Leery, I wanna pay my tab!"

Just getting revved up, the groupie said, "I happen to *know* that some male cops can't keep it hard long enough to do a girl any good. They have a little P.E. trouble, if ya know what I mean."

"What's P.E. trouble?" Leery asked. It had been a long, long time for Leery.

Then she said it publicly: "Some guys gotta carry *two* jizz rags, one for their dog and one for . . ."

"YOU BIG-MOUTHED CUNT!" Hans screamed.

"Whaddaya think, we're married?" the groupie said huffily. "If we was, you'd have to sign a pre-ejaculation agreement. And don't call me a cunt or I'll let a rat crawl in my wa-zoo before you ever see it again!"

So they all knew. Jane Wayne looked sorry for Hans. Leery just leered as usual. Cecil Higgins thought, what the hell, jizzing too soon was better than not jizzing at all. But Dilford's grin was two nightsticks wide.

"Well, no shit!" Dilford said. "Go ahead, Hans, steal somebody else's girl. See how happy you can make her *with your P.E. problem.*"

"I'm your *partner,* scuzzbag!" Dolly yelled at Dilford. "I'm *not* your girl friend!"

And while the groupie was letting the cat out of the bag to the mortification of the doggie cop, Mario Villalobos was smoking his third cigarette in an all-night ice-cream parlor near Farmer's Market. He was watching Dagmar Duffy putting away a banana split and trying to pull himself together to talk about Russian spies.

"I just love hot chocolate syrup," Dagmar Duffy said, sweating from the tension.

"Uh huh," Mario Villalobos said. "How about wiping it off the end of your nose and let's talk about Missy Moonbeam now."

"Oh Lord!" Dagmar Duffy said, wiping off the syrup. "I was gonna call ya this morning, but I lost my nerve."

"Why?"

Dagmar Duffy shivered so palpably that his blond curls jumped. "I was scared to call ya and scared *not* to call ya."

"You know who killed Missy. Is that it?"

"I know *what*!" Dagmar Duffy said.

"Yeah, Russian spies." Mario Villalobos sighed. "Wanna cigarette?"

"I don't smoke. It's terrible for the complexion. It ages ya." Dagmar Duffy reflexively fluffed his perm when he said it.

"What's your connection to Missy?"

"Okay," Dagmar Duffy said. He pushed away the empty dish and licked the syrup off his lips, which had just a hint of clear gloss on them. "I knew her because she scored coke from Howard. He's my old boyfriend."

"Go on."

"Well . . . I don't wanna get Howard in no trouble. He only started selling because he was tooting about a thousand lines a day. I told him he was gonna be a rail-head, but he wouldn't listen. I *never* use drugs myself. I'm thirty-nine years old but you'd never know it, would ya? I'm not from the drug generation."

"Enough with your mid-life crisis," Mario Villalobos said. "I got my own to deal with. Get to the point."

"Then we became friends, Missy and me," Dagmar Duffy said. "I started shining on old Howard because of his flake habit and all. Missy wasn't a dumb girl. She used to read books and listen to good rock 'n roll. I really liked her. Sometimes we'd get together at my place when she wasn't hustling."

"Did she have an old man?"

"A pimp? I don't think. Like, she had to pay money to black guys sometimes just to make them leave her alone and all. She was a lonely kid. Reminded me a my little sister, Missy did."

"Tell me about the Russian spies," Mario Villalobos said.

"Oh Lord!" Dagmar Duffy shushed Mario Villalobos while the waitress removed the ice cream dish and brought fresh coffee. When she'd gone he said, "I don't turn tricks for money. I'm not that kind a person."

"Yeah," Mario Villalobos sighed.

"But this *one* time, Missy told me she had a special date. *Real* special. She said the date was all-time impor-tant and she could let me have a hundred bucks out a what she was gonna get."

"Yeah, and what did it involve, this special date?"

"He liked to party with two people, man and woman. That's all she'd tell me. It wasn't like her, cause she usually told me everything, we was such good friends. At first I told her no and she goes, 'I'll give ya more money.' Then I asked why it was so important and she said it just was, and she begged me. Finally I did it for the hundred bucks."

"You and Missy did a double?"

"Uh huh," Dagmar Duffy said.

"Where? When?"

"About the middle a April. It was a Saturday night.

We were in a hotel in downtown L.A. The tall glass one that looks like a pinball machine inside. Or maybe a jukebox."

"I know the one." Mario Villalobos nodded.

"There was lots of foreigners there. All over the lobby. He was a foreigner."

"Who made the contact with this foreigner?"

"I don't know. Missy had some friend who set him up. She never knew the foreigner before we saw him in the lobby. He was sitting near the glass elevators. Missy said he'd be fifty years old and be tall and blondish and be wearing a blue suit and a brown hat with a feather.

"She smiled at him and he smiled back, and I smiled at him and he smiled back. He offered to buy us a drink in the bar and we played a little hard to get for a minute. He was easy. We settled on twenty bucks apiece. He was so square he actually thought he picked us both up for forty bucks. Of course, somebody *else* had set it up and paid the *real* freight."

"What did he call himself?"

"Edwin. We had one drink and went to his room and turned the trick."

"Did he speak English?"

"Oh yeah, but with an accent."

"What country was he from?"

"Dutch is what I thought. He had blue eyes and milky skin. He was nice but I didn't dig it, turning tricks for money like that. I'm not a whore. When I can get a job, I'm a *great* housekeeper. You know anybody needs a macho maid, gimme a call."

"I'm sort of fond of my clutter and dust," the detective said. "How about any special instructions Missy gave you before the date?"

"Well, the sex was normal. I mean normal for us, you understand, but there was a scary part. It makes me scared when I think about it. We weren't really alone with him."

"Whadda you mean?"

"I'm not dumb. I mean I'm not smart, but I'm not dumb. I could see what Missy was doing. The way she turned in bed. The way she made *him* turn when we were on the bed. The way she said things and made him talk."

"What was she doing?"

"We were making a movie! Or at least we were posing for still shots. Maybe a tape recording. Like that. There was somebody there. Maybe in the closet, I don't know. Maybe in the other room, shooting pictures through a wall. I don't know how they do those things. But I know somebody was getting us down."

"Did the john guess?"

"He was totally square," Dagmar Duffy said, shaking his head. "He was drunk and into what he was doing. We made him crazy, Missy and me." Dagmar Duffy looked as though he wanted to take a bow. "When it was over, he thanked us and gave us each a ten-dollar tip. He was a real gentleman, drunk or not."

"That was a month ago. Did you see Missy after that?"

"A few times."

"Did she ever talk about that date?"

"Sort of. I mean, she said how much she appreciated me helping her. And that pretty soon she'd make it up to me and pretty soon she'd be off the streets. Poor Missy, she was doing coke like crazy at a hundred and fifty a gram. I knew she wouldn't be off the streets. Ever. Anyways, I knew what she meant."

"Extortion?"

"Whadda *you* think? I feel bad about it. He seemed like *such* a nice man."

"Now let's get on to the Russian spies," Mario Villalobos said.

"Oh Lord!" Dagmar Duffy said. "Well, the week before she went off the roof I seen her a couple times. Once was in her apartment. She was real excited, looking at magazines. One was *Time* or *Newsweek*, but it was from last year. It was open to a picture of the Russian sub that got caught by Sweden. Then I saw this other magazine that didn't look familiar. It had pictures of scientists in white coats doing experiments and things. I go, 'Whatcha reading?' She surprises the shit outa me by going, 'Dagmar, can you believe I'm gonna make a lotta money and get off the streets?' I go, 'Sure and I'm gonna be straight and start dating waitresses.' She goes, 'No lie. The *Russians*'re doing it for me.' Then she goes, 'My boyfriend's a Russian agent.' Then she blows a rail or two of coke and starts laughing like a maniac and she wouldn't say no more."

"That's it?"

"Don't ya see? We turned a trick with this guy. At first I thought he was Dutch, but I bet he was a *Russian!* Maybe he was a famous Russian scientist and the KGB was involved!"

"KGB."

"Yeah! And the KGB took pictures of us and they're now telling him he can't deflect."

"Defect."

"Yeah! And the KGB decides to get rid a Missy!"

"Why?"

"Cause Missy contacted the Russians and said she's gonna tell!"

"This isn't making much sense, Dagmar."

"Well I haven't worked it all out," Dagmar Duffy said. "Anyways, I'm next! I was in that room too!"

It was hard for Mario Villalobos not to sigh and roll his eyes. But it was easy to ask himself what the hell he was doing here. Russians? Fruitcake and caviar?

"Tell me, Dagmar, did Missy ever mention a friend of hers in Pasadena? An older guy named Lester? A private investigator?"

"Come to think, she knew an old geezer in Pasadena. I don't know his name, but he called the same day she was looking at the Russian's picture. She never said who he was, but after she hung up she goes, 'That's a friend a mine from Pasadena.' I go, 'Keepin the good stuff for yourself?' She goes, 'He only likes girls. And besides, he's too *old* to interest you.' Old guy in Pasadena! Is he connected with this?"

"No, he's dead," Mario Villalobos said.

"Dead? They got him too? Oh Lord!"

"Heart attack," Mario Villalobos said. "Try to calm

down, Dagmar, and tell me, do you know anything about Missy having a stolen or borrowed credit card belonging to a man named Lester?"

"No," he said. "No credit card. Well . . ."

"Puh-leese, Dagmar!" Mario Villalobos said, and this time he *did* show the whites of his eyes.

Dagmar Duffy said, "I mean, okay, like she was a coke freak, she was a hooker. Sometimes she lifted guys' wallets when she tricked with them. She talked about it, about how risky it was, but how it gave her a rush to do it. Like coke, she said. Trick with a guy and lift his wallet and run outa the motel. Crazy girl."

"And about the credit card?"

"Sometimes she'd take me out to dinner. We'd get dressed up real nice and she'd . . . I can't get in trouble, can I? I never did it."

"I'm only interested in murder."

"Sometimes she'd use a hot credit card and pay for the meal. She looked like a lady when she dressed up. She talked very nice. Her husband's card, she'd say. We did it a few times, no problem."

Mario Villalobos took Lester Beemer's credit card from his pocket. "Did you ever see this card?"

"American Express? All look alike, don't they? Don't leave home without it. I never looked at the names on them. Once we almost got caught with one a those American Express cards. It didn't work."

"Whadda you mean, didn't work?"

"It was a few days before she died. We went to a very nice restaurant on La Cienega. Ate about a hundred bucks' worth a food and she gave the waiter an American Express card and pretty soon he came back and he goes, 'There's something wrong with this card. Please talk to the manager.'"

"What happened then?"

"She got real huffy and snatched the card outa his hand and pulled a hundred and ten bucks outa her purse and threw it at him and said we were never coming back. He was apologizing to *us* all the way to the door. She was beautiful!"

"And maybe it was *this* card?"

"Maybe." He shrugged. "Same kind. She said she only kept them a few days after she stole them. Said tricks usually thought it over a few days before they figured out a good lie for their wives about the missing wallets. She was a smart kid. *Too* smart, maybe. Did she have that card when she died?"

"No, not when she died," Mario Villalobos said. "I'm gonna want your address and phone number. I've gotta think about this for a while and do a little more checking."

"Can I get police protection? You know, the Russians? Are you sure the old guy in Pasadena wasn't murdered? They can make it look like an accident!"

"Heart attack."

"Did he die the same day as Missy?"

"No, he died on the first of May."

"FIRST OF MAY!" Dagmar Duffy screamed, scaring the crap out of Mario Villalobos and the waitress, who spilled some coffee, and the only other customer in the ice cream parlor, an old woman who said, "Keep it down, you little screamer!"

"What're you *yelling* about?" the detective demanded.

"May the first! That's May Day in Moscow! A perfect time for Russians to kill their enemies!"

This time Mario Villalobos could *not* prevent his eyeballs from sliding back in his skull. Fruitcake and caviar.

The last of the regular losers to leave The House of Misery was Jane Wayne. There were a few other cops still there when she left. Three civilians had wandered in and were talking baseball to Leery. Jane Wayne wondered why the Bad Czech had not showed up. All in all, the evening had offered all the fun of an Ingmar Bergman movie.

While Dagmar Duffy was scaring himself with Russian spies, and Jane Wayne was longing for her favorite sex object, a feverish Laotian woman saw a giant with winged eyebrows in the corridor of a local hospital. She had been recuperating from a bone graft and was now allowed to hobble around pretty much when she felt like it. She had seen several Asian people in the ward that evening, but they did not speak her language. Two of them were middle-aged adults and the rest were pretty girls who were crying.

The Laotian woman was about one-third the size of the giant who stood awkwardly in the corridor. After all the Asians had gone, the giant tiptoed softly, on the largest pair of jogging shoes the woman had ever seen, to the room where the people had been. The patient in that room looked like a battered child. The white sheets and big bed made him look very small. And he was *very* battered. There were tubes everywhere, including one plastered inside a mound of bandages on his broken face.

The giant stood clumsily by the bed and watched the patient. The patient breathed fearfully shallow and hadn't moved or stirred or opened his eyes since the Laotian woman had first noticed him.

The giant whispered to the battered patient.

"Magilla?" he said.

The Laotian woman was extremely curious about the giant. He stood by the unconscious patient for nearly an hour. He was still there when the woman got very tired and had to shuffle back to her room. Every five minutes or so she could hear him.

"Magilla?" the giant said.

TEN

Madonna Of The Wogs

Mario Villalobos was awakened at 6:00 A.M. by the telephone. It was something that detectives got used to if they wanted to work homicide. It was what made most detectives choose to work burglary or robbery or auto theft, which were rarely considered important enough to get a detective out of bed. But homicide investigation was the only thing left in the world that occasionally stimulated his few still-living neurons. It was one of the few things left in life that gave him a little pleasure. Aside from an occasional baseball game, or pop music from the forties and fifties which lately made him miserable by reminding him of his hopeful youth.

He always felt exactly the same these days whether he slept a lot or a little: exhausted. He had seen the symptoms in other cops. He knew he was in trouble.

The detective let the telephone ring seven times as he always did when he was awakened bone-weary out of a sound or fitful sleep with news of another shooting, stabbing, strangling or mutilation. Seven rings gave him just about enough time to become partially alert.

A familiar voice exploded in his ear, "SERGEANT VILLALOBOS!"

"Jesus Christ, Dagmar!" Mario Villalobos yelped, jerking the phone away from his face.

"Sergeant!" Dagmar Duffy cried. "I just got home and discovered that you ain't been the only one looking for me! There was a guy with glasses and black hair and a moustache asking about me at the Adonis Club last night."

Now Mario Villalobos snapped his eyes open. "Yeah, what happened?"

"The stupid fucking bartender, some bitch I used to go with named Samson, told him where I lived!"

"Where're you now?"

"I'm home. I couldn't sleep with Howard so I came home. And somebody broke in my apartment!"

"I'll be right there," Mario Villalobos said. "Gimme thirty minutes."

"I got my door locked! If anybody tries to get in, they'll hear me screaming in Malibu. The guy had a *thick* moustache, I heard. Just like Joseph Stalin!"

Dagmar Duffy lived near Santa Monica and Normandie, not far from the Wonderland Hotel. He had a lovely view of a muffler shop and a Charlie Chicken take-out. Mario Villalobos practically had to give a recital to get in.

"Dagmar, it's Mario Villalobos," he said for the third time. "Open the goddamn door!"

Finally the door was cracked open and Dagmar Duffy said, "I'm getting crazy. I started to think that maybe the Russians knew about you and were impersonating your voice."

The sun was just rising on yet another overcast day. Mario Villalobos was unshaven, had his necktie in the pocket of his suit coat, and looked almost as haggard as Dagmar Duffy. The detective entered the apartment and peeked out the window at the three-story drop. He looked at the dead-bolt lock and the untouched doorjamb. He couldn't see any sign of forced entry.

"I leave my door unlocked," Dagmar Duffy said

sheepishly. "I know it's dumb, but I have this old boy-friend Arnold. Sometimes he likes to surprise me and I find him in bed when I get home."

"So then how do you know the Russians were here?"

"Things were moved!"

"Puh-leese, Dagmar," Mario Villalobos sighed wea-rily, eyeballs sliding up at the ceiling. "You interrupted my wet dream for *this*? How do you know Arnold or Howard, or Manny, Moe and Jack didn't come? Christ, you have more boyfriends than Linda Lovelace."

"I know none a my boyfriends did it. When they come in they leave everything all messed up. They're a bunch a pigs except for Howard and he was with me. Look, somebody opened every drawer and moved my things!"

Mario Villalobos stepped over to the veneer ma-hogany chest in the neat little one-bedroom apartment. There were ten pair of bikini briefs meticulously folded in the drawer. "Everything looks okay to me."

"No, no!" Dagmar Duffy cried. "I keep the persim-mon ones on the left. I keep the plum on the right. They've been reversed. Someone picked them up to look under them!"

"Puh-leese, Dagmar," Mario Villalobos said. "I don't *get* many wet dreams at my age."

"I'll show you something else," Dagmar Duffy said. "Look!" And he opened his closet revealing two rows of clothes poles bearing several pair of size 28 shorts and jeans, T-shirts, and two Members Only jackets, rose and powder-blue.

"It all looks okay to me." Mario Villalobos sighed.

"The *pockets* on two pair of jeans are inside out. I would *never* hang my jeans like that!"

"How do you know that Arnold didn't . . ."

"Here's how I know!" Dagmar Duffy pulled one of the jackets off the hanger. It was the powder-blue, which exactly matched his eyes. There was a roll of bills in the pocket. "My money's all here. Every boyfriend knows where I keep it. I tell them it's there so they don't have to tear up my apartment if they need money. I think that someone was looking for something else: film, tape, papers. This place was searched real careful. The way the Russians do it!"

Mario Villalobos conceded there was a remote possibility that Dagmar Duffy was right about the intruder. But it may have been an ordinary money burglar who missed the blue jacket. And it could have been a coincidence about a black-haired man with a moustache. Maybe.

"Okay, okay," Mario Villalobos said. "I'll have a fingerprint man come over this morning and dust for prints. Don't touch anything else."

"I'm not staying here alone!"

"Look, I have to admit there *might* be something to this, but I think you're safe."

"I want police protection. I'm a taxpayer. I mean, I *used* to be a taxpayer."

"Dagmar, I don't think I could explain you to my landlady."

"I'm *not* staying here. I'm moving in with Howard."

"Okay, just stay long enough for the fingerprint . . ."

"I'm *not* staying here one minute alone. Why can't I come with you? I can come back when the fingerprint guy gets here, and then I'll move my clothes out."

"Okay," the detective sighed. "Come with me to the station. We'll call prints and then we'll come back here and I'll stand by while you move your stuff. But with your dance card as full as it is, I don't expect we'll find any suspect's prints that we can work with."

The detective lieutenant at Rampart Station, who was drinking coffee and wondering if the Dodgers could ever pull out of their slump, gave more than a passing glance when Mario Villalobos came into the squad room leading a man with a golden perm and plucked eyebrows, in boy's size jeans and a Hollywood YMCA T-shirt.

"I see you weren't jiving about barhopping in Hollywood," he said to Mario Villalobos. "When's the wedding?"

"This is a witness," Mario Villalobos said, collapsing in a chair. "The Missy Moonbeam murder case is getting outa hand. I just gotta work on it for a few days. How about Chip and Melody taking over everything else for me?"

"Might as well," the lieutenant said. "Keep them from groping each other all day. I swear, a cold shower'd do them both good. Wouldn't be surprised if Melody's old man doesn't get *accidentally* shot some night when she *mistakes* him for a burglar."

"Have a seat over at that table, Dagmar," Mario Villalobos said. "I'll call latent prints."

There was a burly man with long sideburns and a macho moustache sitting at one of the long tables. He had on a burnt-orange sportcoat with a brown and red check pattern, and a fat blue print necktie, and brown doubleknit pants held up by a big belt with a cowboy buckle. In short, he looked pretty much like what he was, a burglary detective. The burglary detective did a double take when he looked up at the Hollywood YMCA T-shirt.

Dagmar Duffy batted his lashes shyly, offered his hand palm down and said, "Hi. Mind if I join ya? I'm working on a murder case!"

The Bad Czech and Cecil Higgins were in the police parking lot when they spotted the K-9 cop lurking around behind the radio cars. Cecil Higgins had already spread the news to The Bad Czech about poor Hans' P.E. problem. The K-9 cop looked as though he hadn't slept a wink. He was a nervous wreck.

"You wanna give up being a doggie cop, you can jist transfer over here to Rampart," Cecil Higgins said, startling Hans when he walked up behind him.

"I'm just waiting for Dolly," Hans said miserably.

"Got somethin on your mind?" Cecil Higgins asked, knowing perfectly well what Hans had on his mind.

"I just need to straighten something out," Hans said. "I hope you didn't believe what that lying bitch said about me last night?"

"Ain't my business," Cecil Higgins said.

"I never had a sex problem in my life. *You* didn't

believe her, did you?" Hans asked, getting white around the mouth.

"Ain't my business," Cecil Higgins said.

"I know Dolly wouldn't believe such a dumb thing," Hans said.

"You coming to Leery's tonight? You can catch Dolly there for sure."

The skinny K-9 cop shrugged, and felt his jaunty grin cracking like an egg and thought that he was never going to that miserable fucking saloon as long as he lived, and hoped that a police helicopter would fall on Rampart Station and incinerate everyone who was there last night when that vicious bitch he intended to *kill* told them about the P.E. trait he had picked up from Ludwig. And which he intended to discuss with the department psychologist this very afternoon. If ever there was a justification for a stress pension, this was it, Hans thought ruefully. He sure contracted his problem while doing police work.

But as it turned out, Hans was going to be unable to escape the company of The House of Misery losers. The K-9 cop was about to find himself in the middle of a homicide investigation. It happened because of another tiny vagary of fortune. Something nearly as insignificant as a chopstick in a shoe.

"Just what I need," Mario Villalobos said. "A flat tire."

He was standing with Dagmar Duffy beside his detective car intending to meet the latent-prints specialist who was to be at Dagmar Duffy's apartment house in ten minutes. Then he spotted a few of his House of Misery fellow sufferers.

The Bad Czech was getting in his car, preparing to drive down to the foot beat, when Mario Villalobos yelled, "Hey Czech, do me a favor? Drive this guy over to Santa Monica and Normandie, will you? There's a latent-prints guy on the way there and I gotta get my tire changed."

The Bad Czech looked doubtfully at Dagmar Duffy, who was flushed and beaming from all the attention and the undeniable thrill of being a potential homicide victim.

"What am I, a taxi?" The Bad Czech grumbled.

"I'll be there in ten minutes. Am I asking a lot?"

"Aw right," The Bad Czech muttered. "Come on, Cecil, we gotta give this little . . . *person* a ride home."

While the beat cops were delivering their little person, Mario Villalobos went looking for a garage attendant to change his tire, but the garage attendant was delivering a car to Parker Center. Another was off sick. A third, who had three police cars waiting for gas, suggested that the detective could *consider* changing it himself if he needed it right away.

It was when he was stalking back to his car, exhausted and grouchy, that Mario Villalobos saw Hans and Ludwig driving out of the parking lot. "Hans!" Mario Villalobos yelled. "Give me a lift to Santa Monica and Normandie, will you?"

Meanwhile, The Bad Czech couldn't get rid of the little person in the back seat of the police car.

"Whaddaya mean ya ain't gettin out!" The Bad Czech bellowed, turning around in the driver's seat and showing his demented gray eyes to Dagmar Duffy.

"I can't be alone!" Dagmar Duffy cried. Then he added, "I'm a possible murder victim."

"You're for *sure* a fuckin murder victim, you don't get outa this car!" The Bad Czech said, while Cecil Higgins rested his bald head against the doorpost and tried to shut out all the sound and fury.

"Czech, you wasn't at Leery's last night," Cecil Higgins said. "Have a little consideration for my poor head and stop yellin."

"Can't you wait till Sergeant Villalobos gets here?" Dagmar Duffy cried.

"He didn't say I hadda babysit," The Bad Czech said. "Where the hell *is* he, anyways?"

"He'll be here in a few minutes," Dagmar Duffy said. "I can't go in that building alone. There might be a *man* waiting for me!"

The Bad Czech took a gander at the blond perm and the plucked eyebrows and the Hollywood YMCA T-shirt, and said, "Yeah, a Roto-Rooter man, no doubt. And not for your *sink*. Now get outa my car, junior!"

Just then Dagmar Duffy was saved by the appearance of Unit K-9-2, delivering the frustrated detective to the apartment house.

"Did the prints man get here?" Mario Villalobos asked The Bad Czech when he got out of the K-9 car.

"Hey, Mario, this guy wants to marry me or somethin'," The Bad Czech said. "I can't get *rid* a him!"

Hans, who was still considering drinking hemlock, leaped out of the K-9 car while Ludwig snoozed as peacefully as Cecil Higgins, and with a forced smile said, "Czech, I guess you heard about the *lie* that bitch told about me last night at Leery's? Pretty funny, huh?"

"You guys can split," Mario Villalobos said. "I'll get a ride back to the station with the prints man when he shows up."

And while Mario Villalobos and Dagmar Duffy entered the apartment house and took the elevator up to the third floor to await the latent-prints specialist, a man in a pinstripe suit, with black hair and a thick black moustache and horn-rimmed glasses, came down the stairway. He paused in the lobby for a moment, looked at his watch, and walked out the front door. He almost ran right into two cops—one in a blue jumpsuit covered with dog hair, the other a monster cop in a regular blue uniform—who were standing on the sidewalk talking about miserable bitches who love to tell lies about real men.

The man looked as though he might start running. He stopped for an instant, reassured himself that this had nothing to do with him, and continued down the sidewalk. He was forced to pass between the two cops, since one of them was so huge he took up most of the sidewalk.

Both cops hardly glanced at him when he said, "Pardon me, please."

When Mario Villalobos and Dagmar Duffy were unlocking the door, Dagmar Duffy's neighbor across the hall popped her head out. She worked in the typing pool at

Paramount Studios and lived close enough to come home for lunch on days that she worked. Today she had blue rollers in her hair. She said, "Oh, Dagmar, there was a man looking for you."

"Damn," the detective said. "The prints man got here faster than I thought."

But there was no police business card in the door.

"What did the man look like?" Mario Villalobos asked.

"This is a detective," Dagmar Duffy explained. "Someone broke in my place last night."

"Really?" the girl said. "Well this man didn't look like a burglar. He wore a business suit like you," she said to the detective. "With pinstripes."

"Did you see his face?" Mario Villalobos asked.

"No," she said. "Just the back of him. He was sorta big and had black hair."

"Dagmar," Mario Villalobos said, "after we dust this apartment for prints, maybe you oughtta stay with Howard until I tell you to go home."

There were no readable prints that were not Dagmar Duffy's, but one hour later The Bad Czech, Hans and Ludwig were sitting in the Rampart coffee room, bitching loud enough to blister paint.

The detective lieutenant had made calls to Hans' commanding officer and talked personally with The Bad Czech's watch commander.

"Look, there's nothing to get excited about," Mario Villalobos assured them. "I only want you both available *if* I need you. Is that so tough to do?"

"But, Mario, *available* to a homicide dick means twenty-four hours a day," Hans griped. "I got a *date* tonight in Chinatown. I can't be on call!"

"Yeah, I got somethin to do tonight too," The Bad Czech griped. "What if I have to stop what I'm doin and come runnin to be your witness?"

"You, I know where to find *every* night," Mario Villalobos said to The Bad Czech. "Look, you two saw what the guy looked like. The only others that've seen him are a hotel clerk and a hooker. They're not nearly as reliable as two policemen. In fact, being as they're shorties, they say he's a tall guy. You two say he's not particularly tall."

"I also said I *might* recognize him," The Bad Czech said.

"Me too," Hans said. "He's maybe fifty or fifty-five. And now you say the black hair and moustache might be phony. I don't know if I'd recognize him or not."

"Look," Mario Villalobos said. "First I have to *find* somebody for you to recognize. I might not be able to do it, so you got nothing to worry about right now."

"I just hope my big night in Chinatown don't get interrupted," Hans whined. "I gotta find a *new* girl friend."

Mario Villalobos drove straight to the motel where Lester Beemer died. It was a no-tell motel all right. It offered closed-circuit television with X-rated shows. It promised a water bed in each room, but didn't deliver. The promises were on a marquee over the motel roof, which looked like it would leak buckets in a rain. The manager was no more happy than could be expected.

"I can't remember every guy that comes in," he said to Mario Villalobos. "Especially a month ago."

"It *was* a bit unusual to have one of your tenants die, wasn't it?"

He was a transient type who didn't own the place and stole only a modest amount from the cash he took in, thus was slightly more honest than the last five managers the owner had employed.

"The cop that came by when I found the body already asked me everything."

"And you gave him the same answers?"

"Yeah. I only remember an old guy renting the room in the afternoon. I was busy and he filled out the card. Gave the name a Lester Beemer and wanted the room for one night and that was it."

"You didn't see *another* person with him? Not a man nor a woman?"

"I didn't notice. I called the cops soon as I found the guy dead in the morning. I thought he checked out without turning in the key. He checked *out* all right."

"Lemme see the other register cards for that day," the detective said.

"Gimme a break. I'm busy."

Mario Villalobos glared at the manager who always kept his head down and crawled through life. Finally the manager said, "Aw right. Here, *you* go through them. I gotta clean up two rooms before three o'clock."

He left Mario Villalobos in the motel office and the detective sat and smoked and went through the stack of register cards. He supposed that one room could be rented four times on a good day with three of those day-rates going into the manager's pocket. Most of the customers gave obviously phony names and addresses and wrote fictitious license numbers.

There were eleven rooms rented on the day that Lester Beemer checked in using his true name, address and car license number. There no doubt were more than that, but he didn't expect the manager to tell him about the cards that got thrown away when he was stealing from the boss.

Three looked fairly legitimate. Two were out-of-state guests and the area codes on the phone numbers at least checked with the state given on the license. One was local and he decided to use the pay phone outside the motel and give it a try.

The male voice that answered the phone couldn't have surprised Mario Villalobos more if he had confessed to murder. What he did was to cooperate fully with a man who spent his life talking to people who lied when the truth would save them.

"Sure, I was at the motel that night," the man said. "Took my girl friend for a naughty birthday treat. Kind of a tacky motel, though. Wasn't what we expected."

"Tell me," Mario Villalobos said, "were you there when the police showed up the next morning?"

"No way," the man said. "A few hours in that tacky

place was enough for us. We left about midnight, maybe earlier."

"Did you see an older man who rented the room next to you?"

"No, I saw the girl though."

"*What* girl?"

"When I went out to the car to get our second bottle of champagne, I saw a skinny blonde running out of the room."

"Running?"

"Almost," he said. "She was in a hurry. Rushed out onto Colorado Boulevard and disappeared."

"Would you recognize a picture? Did you see her face?"

"Not really. Just a skinny blonde with long straight hair. Tacky-looking girl."

"Tacky how?"

"Cheap-looking and flashy. Like a hooker. She wore yellow boots that went nearly up to her shorts. Don't see that around Pasadena too often."

Mario Villalobos was able to secure quite a bit of information at Caltech without having to reveal that he was a cop. The last thing he wanted at this stage of a fruitcake investigation, which was spreading like spilled mercury, was to tell anyone at the university that he was investigating a murder or two.

Caltech was not a large university, some eighty acres, including playing fields. There were about seventy buildings, mixed rather capriciously as to architectural style. Some were old Californian, with tile roofs and Moorish arches. Others were contemporary, of concrete and glass. The male students outnumbered the females eight to one. There were only 1,700 students in all. The impressive off-campus facilities included the Jet Propulsion Laboratory.

He read the catalogue and learned that the professorial faculty numbered 266 with nearly an equal number of research faculty. There might be over a hundred visiting professors during any semester, he was told. And of course he knew that it was upon the faculty that he must concentrate his attention, particularly the chemists.

Mario Villalobos had known about as much as the average citizen knows about the handful of first-rate scientific institutes in America. That is, he had known next to nothing. He could see by the literature in the college office that virtually everyone had a Ph.D. after his name, which was to be expected. He learned that an extraordinary number of Nobel Prizes had been awarded to Caltech alumni and faculty, and that this small faculty had a higher percentage of members elected to the National Academy of Sciences and National Academy of Engineering than any educational institution in America. There were always Nobel laureates among the active faculty and in such a place it was to be expected that there were many more who had hopes and dreams of becoming one.

After reading the literature available to anyone who asked for it, Mario Villalobos walked outside and sat in the little amphitheater near a newly constructed chemistry laboratory. He watched the students come and go. He smoked, and enjoyed the little bit of sunshine the day offered. And he thought things over.

So far, he had one murdered hooker. He had one second-rate private eye who died in a motel he had shared with the now-murdered hooker. Why a motel, he had no idea. Maybe they liked dirty movies.

He had one "foreigner" who tricked with his murdered hooker, and a crazy pansy who believed that the murdered hooker and her private eye may have set up the "foreigner" for blackmail.

He knew that his hooker had the telephone number of Caltech's division of chemistry and he knew that the private eye was a science groupie, and may simply have come to Caltech one day and asked Missy Moonbeam to call him there. Maybe Lester Beemer had only been attending a lecture in the auditorium. They were open to anyone.

But there was the cryptic promise from his murdered

hooker to the crazy pansy that a Russian scientist was somehow going to enable her to get off the street. Hence, it *did* seem possible that the foreigner was a Russian being extorted.

Furthermore, his murdered hooker had done a little corpse-robbing and had stolen her former friend's credit card, which was understandable, given her tastes. But would she also steal his cheap wristwatch? That was *not* understandable, given her tastes. Or did someone *else* steal his wristwatch. And why? Did it reveal the time of death?

And finally, he had a tallish black-haired man in a pinstripe suit, who had been stalking one now-dead hooker and one live pansy, probably with a very bad idea in mind for the live pansy.

And all this added up to fruitcake and caviar, since it was absolutely wacky to suppose that there was a mad Russian prowling the streets of Los Angeles and Pasadena for a whore, a pansy and a sleazy old private eye who set him up in a badger game. In any case, it was hardly a motive for multiple murder: a threatened revelation to his wife or boss or commissar that he indulged in kinky sex while visiting Los Angeles, the home of kinky sex.

Some men might murder to hide such a secret. If it meant utter ruin. But homicide investigations usually entailed what was probable, and in this day and age, men might pay quite a bit and *do* quite a bit to keep an evening with Dagmar Duffy and Missy Moonbeam secret. Yet it was highly improbable that the exposure of bizarre sexual taste was worth throwing people off buildings.

And how in the hell was the private eye killed, if he *was* killed? Drugs maybe, which made it look like a coronary? He wished there hadn't been a family doctor so willing to sign the death certificate. He wished they hadn't cremated the body.

He had to find out if there *were* any Russian scientists presently at Caltech. He wanted The Bad Czech and Hans to see every face of every professor in the division of chemistry and chemical engineering, foreigner or not. He had no idea how to arrange it. There was one thing for sure if he was even going to *hope* to unscramble the mess of fruitcake and caviar before he died of exhaustion: he couldn't tell anyone how little he had. Because he had nothing, not a wisp of hard evidence. He didn't dare tell anyone at this institution what he was *really* doing here or they might call the L.A. chief of police, and he might get a stress pension sooner than he expected.

Therefore, there was only one thing for a sensible cop to do if he was going to pursue his nutty Russian clue at the California Institute of Technology: Mario Villalobos was going to lie like hell. But he needed a good one. A lie that would fly.

The detective offered a sample from his bag of lies to three people in the administration building. Each person referred him to another person, and finally the rather confusing police matter was referred from the office of the president to the office of the vice-president for institute relations, to the office of the vice-president and provost. He was getting sleepy and cranky. But then he suddenly perked up.

He wished he'd shaved a little closer when he suffered three gotcha cuts at the station after his early date with Dagmar Duffy. He also wished he'd combed his wind-blown hair to hide the bald spot. And while he was at it, he wished he'd worn his new suit and didn't have on a shirt with a frayed collar and that his necktie didn't have a coffee stain on it. And for a moment he didn't even care that her boss was at the Pasadena conference center for the day, because there was a secretary smiling at him with the largest eyes he'd seen lately, outside of Ludwig's. And her hair was even blacker than Ludwig's and much shinier. And then he was sure that his fruitcake investigation had made him bonkers because he realized he was comparing this Latino woman to a panting Rottweiler, and she was *anything* but a dog.

"My name's Lupe Luna," she said, smiling.

"Mario Villalobos," he said. "Los Angeles Police Department."

"Mucho gusto," she said, still smiling.

"I don't speak Spanish," he said. "Well, a little street Spanish."

"With a name like Mario Villalobos?"

Then it slipped out, the thing he had said a thousand times in his life: "I'm not Mexican."

She laughed and said, "I didn't *accuse* you. But I am. East L.A. Mexican."

"I didn't mean . . . What I meant was, my name's Spanish, but I'm not."

"Were you adopted?"

"No, but . . . oh well, I'm a counterfeit Mexican. I'll explain it some time if you give me a chance."

"What can we do for you?"

"I'm investigating a very large jewel theft," he said.

She was one of those steady gazers, the kind of mature, good-looking woman who always rattled Mario Villalobos. He knew he wasn't terrific to look at and she was. And she appeared to be smart. And the more he thought of his bag of lies, the dumber they sounded.

"This jewel theft makes my position delicate, as I'll explain." He drew thoughtfully on a cigarette, hoping he looked *sincere* and thought, Jesus, she has a slight overbite. He was a sucker for women with an overbite. No wedding ring and an overbite! "Uh, you see, this theft took place in a very chic Los Angeles restaurant. My victim is an elderly lady and she was dining there with a young man, a gigolo you might say. And a couple at the next table admired her necklace and they did some talking and became acquainted. The man at the next table was a Caltech professor and he was with a young lady. They didn't give their names."

The detective paused to smoke and he was almost starting to enjoy himself. First of all, because he had her attention, and secondly, he discovered that his story was turning into pretty good soap opera.

"Well, this is sad, all in all," he continued. "The young lounge lizard stole the old lady's necklace and disappeared from her life. We know who he is, but he denies ever knowing our victim and he has an alibi witness as to his whereabouts that night. Are you with me?"

"Yes," Lupe Luna said. "Where does our Caltech professor fit in?"

"Ah," Mario Villalobos said. "You see, your professor and his lady could corroborate my victim and destroy the suspect's alibi. *But*, and here's the delicate part: we suspect that your Caltech professor was not with his wife that night. The waiter and busboy who served his table said they were sure it was an illicit rendezvous. Thank God for busybody waiters and busboys." Mario Villalobos was starting to wonder if he wrote this as a script, could he *sell* it?

"Now we've got a problem, Miss Luna . . . is it Mrs. Luna?"

"It's *Ms*. Luna," she said, dashing his hopes, "but you can call me Lupe."

That restored them a bit. "I can't expect your college president to make an announcement asking who was at the restaurant that night. A married man with a young woman? I have to locate him in a discreet manner and assure him that it'll remain confidential."

"But you don't even know the professor's name."

"No. My victim knows what he looks like, but that's another problem. She's a distraught old lady. What I'd like to do is bring the waiter and busboy here and have them look at pictures of your faculty. And if we can narrow it down to people who look like the witness, maybe the waiter and busboy could see the professors in the flesh. In their classroom or laboratories or something? *Very* discreetly. We can't embarrass your professor if we want to make our case. We need his *full* cooperation, and if he's a married man having a night out, well . . ."

"I don't know how current all our pictures are. He may have been a visiting member of the research faculty. We have nearly two hundred research fellows."

"My victim thinks he was connected with the division of chemistry and chemical engineering."

"I can think of something that *might* help," she said. "Tomorrow night's one of our many open-house nights. Lots of chemists will be milling around along with outside people who donate money to Caltech."

"Do you have any visiting scientists from, say, the Iron Curtain countries?"

"What's that got to do with the professor you're looking for?"

"He, uh, he . . . mentioned a visiting scientist from . . . I think it was Russia."

"Might be biology." She held up slender fingers and ticked off the science divisions. "And we have chemistry and chemical engineering, engineering and applied science, geological and planetary science, physics, math and astronomy. Take your pick."

"How about chemistry?" Mario Villalobos asked. "Any Russians here now?"

"I haven't heard of any. When Russians come it's different than visitors from anywhere else, even Red China. Each Russian scientist travels with a party member and a security man. They stay, oh, six weeks to two months. And *no* women."

"They leave mama back home so they don't defect?"

"Exactly."

"Wonder if they ever feel like doing a little barhopping?" Mario Villalobos said it casually. "In some decadent capitalist place. Like Los Angeles, for instance?"

"I've heard they're pretty well under control," she said. "No barhopping without Comrade Vladimir tagging along."

"But they must get a little romance-starved, with Olga back on the Volga?"

"I'm sure it'll be okay if you want to come tomorrow night," she said. "I hear there's going to be wine and cheese set up in the Athenaeum patio for all the visitors. You like wine and cheese?"

"I like margaritas and *carne asada*," Mario Villalobos said. "Being a counterfeit Mexican and all."

"What's that about?" she asked, smiling again. "Your Hispanic name?"

"I'd love to tell you about it," he said. "Tomorrow afternoon I'll bring my waiter and busboy to look at all available faculty photos. If that doesn't help, we'll come to the open house for wine and cheese. You gonna be there?"

"Not much for wine and cheese and open houses," she said. "I've worked here for fifteen years. Been to too many of them."

"In that case, there's only one thing to do. Come with me *tonight* for margaritas and *carne asada* and I'll tell you all about how I became a counterfeit Mexican with the L.A.P.D."

"A counterfeit Mexican," she said, with some interest.

"You're not married, are you?"

"Divorced."

"Me too. Twice."

"I suppose twice is about average for a cop."

"You ever go out with cops?"

"Before I got married one of my boyfriends was a cop."

"Oh oh," he said. "You know cops. Does that mean I don't have a chance?"

She grinned and said, "You're not going to believe it, but I *was* thinking about a Mexican restaurant for a quick bite."

"I believe it," he cried. "Pick you up at seven?"

"Afraid not."

"Six? Five? Ten? Eleven?"

"Have to get home early tonight," she said. "My fourteen-year-old daughter's cramming for a history test and I'm supposed to quiz her."

"How about a *very* early supper when you get off work? A quick bite and a few margaritas? You can be home by six o'clock."

"A *few* margaritas?"

"Sure. Why not?"

"It's okay if you're an alcoholic."

"That's me," he said cheerily. "*Borderline* alcoholic, I like to think."

"You're sort of honest—I'll have to say that."

"Lupe," he said, "I'm middle-aged, not much to look at, got nothing in the bank. And the only thing I'm halfway good at is catching bad guys. I figure I *gotta* be honest."

"Honesty deserves to win once in a while," she said, not knowing that except for the personal data, every single thing he had told her was a lie.

"What time should I pick you up?"

"I'll meet you. Where do you want to eat?"

"You know where York and Figueroa is?"

"York *y Feeg*," she said with an affected Spanish accent. "Of course I know. I told you I'm an East L.A. Mexican."

"There's a restaurant about a block from the police station. The Villa Sombrero. I'll meet you there."

"Is it a cop hangout?"

"Lady, you are *not* a person I'd take to a cop hangout. The last woman I dated from a cop hangout looked like Golda Meir. Or maybe Menachem Begin, I can't quite remember. This is the best Mexican restaurant I know. I wouldn't kid you about anything."

"*That* remains to be seen," she said. "See you there at five-thirty."

And while Mario Villalobos was telling a lie that would fly, Dolly and Dilford were about to meet yet another person who would affect Dilford's testicles.

She would be described on television that night as a Bel-Air housewife. She was seen by one witness strolling along Bonnie Brae Street directly over the southbound Hollywood Freeway. The wind gusted that smoggy overcast afternoon. The wind blew her chestnut hair across her face and whipped it in strings around her sparkling green eyes. She wore a wine-red cloak with a hood which she had bought in London on one of several trips abroad.

She was forty-one years old, had three children, and had been married to the same man for twenty years. He sold commercial real estate and had it made. He dealt with Iranian and Arab investors who couldn't care less about Reaganomics and high interest rates, and who could buy mink horse blankets from Bijan in Beverly Hills and use them as bath mats.

The Bel-Air housewife owned a Mercedes 450SL and lots of diamonds, round brilliant cuts, of course, and coveted nothing on earth except a Ferrari which her husband refused to buy her. It caused a problem or two in their marriage, resulting in an occasional five-Valium day, but nothing to prepare her friends or family for what happened on Bonnie Brae Street.

In fact, no one on Rodeo Drive where she shopped could *understand* why the Echo Park area. Even tacky people who lived in the 500 block well south of Sunset wouldn't go bananas in such a low-rent neighborhood. This was a woman, everyone knew, who could get into Spago's for Wolfgang Puck's show biz pizza with only *one* day's notice!

It was as though anyone could understand someone doing what she did but they couldn't *begin* to comprehend someone doing it in a district that advertised cheapie trips to Manila. It was a low-rent neighborhood *full* of Filipinos, Mexicans, Cubans and other wogs.

The first witness driving southbound on Bonnie Brae saw her climbing the guardrail and drove straight to a pay phone to call the cops. The second witness was a Good Samaritan and he leaped out of his car and ran toward her, but froze and retreated when she let go of the guardrail with one hand, pointed a bejeweled finger directly at his face and unleashed a spine-arching scream.

By then, unit Two-A-Ninety-nine was exploding onto the scene like a cruise missile, and two hot dogs, Stanley and Leech, were running toward the Bel-Air housewife, who was looking at the speeding cars on the freeway below.

The second police unit contained Dilford and Dolly, who had the presence of mind to radio communications and request that the Highway Patrol stop all traffic on the southbound Hollywood Freeway approaching the Queen of Angels Hospital.

With sparkling green eyes, the woman watched the hot dogs running toward her, running hellbent for heroics

and maybe a medal of valor. They stopped when Dilford
cut them off and screamed, "STOP, YOU ASSHOLES!" right
in their faces.

For an instant the two hyped-up hot dogs took a
look at their jumper and saw quite clearly that she was
watching them. Her chestnut hair was whipping in the
wind, and her wine-red cloak was flapping around her
slender shoulders, and her hands were cupped in front of
her. Which meant that she was holding on to the stan-
chions with her *knees*.

The Bel-Air housewife then looked directly at Dilford, who had one hand on each hyper hot dog. And, still
holding her hands cupped in front for whatever gift she
thought she was about to receive, she looked at the tall
young cop with the bulging blue eyes and the taffy-
colored hair blowing straight back from an already
clammy forehead.

She said to Dilford, "Come here."

By now six cops and several civilians and one roach
wagon were all gathered on Bonnie Brae and all traffic
was stopped both ways except that the traffic southbound
on the Hollywood Freeway continued to roar beneath
them. Nonstop from the north. From the blind side.

The Mexican on the roach wagon, who had lost
many pesos lately due to The Bad Czech's voracious appetite for free burritos, tried to make a buck or two from
selling soda pop to the gathering crowd, who only stopped
yelling, "Jump, lady!" when Dolly said she'd shove her
stick down the throat of the next son-of-a-bitch to open
his mouth.

"Don't do this," Dilford pleaded with the woman in
the wine-red cloak. "Let's talk about it. I know it can be
worked out."

Her voice was calm. She said to Leech and Stanley,
"You two. Go away."

And then she suddenly unleashed another eerie
shriek, as piercing as a sparking knife blade on a grinding
stone. And she began to sway in the wind. At which time
Stanley and Leech thought they might be getting in over
their wired-up heads, and what the hell, maybe they

ought to just boogie on out of here and get their medals some other time.

"Come closer to me," the Bel-Air housewife said to Dilford, whose taffy hairstyle was going electric. He was looking for a sergeant. He was *alone*.

"Don't do this to me, lady," Dilford pleaded. Which was something many cops before him had said in such a moment. Don't do this to *me*.

"Closer," she said calmly, her eyes bright as a bird's. She even smiled for an instant. A beatific smile. The smile of a martyr marching to glory.

Dilford was advancing ever so slowly and the wind began to moan on the overpass, or so he thought. Her wind-blown hair hid her face like a mask. Except for the sparkling green eyes.

"Maybe if we talk about it?" Dilford said. He looked like he was going to cry. "Let me go get a sergeant. Please. I'm just a . . ."

"Closer, closer," she coaxed with her beatific smile.

She began breathing hard then, facing the Queen of Angels Hospital up on the hill in the distance. And perhaps that's how she perceived herself. The Queen of Angels. The Virgin of Bonnie Brae. The Madonna of the Wogs.

"Don't, lady. *Please* don't," Dilford said, with his hand outstretched. He inched closer until he was only two feet away.

And that's when she gave herself to eternity. With outstretched arms, she imitated every painted plaster saint and martyr she had ever seen.

"DON'T, LADY!" Dilford shrieked, leaping forward and grabbing a fold of the cloak for an instant.

She looked at him with the sparkling eyes and sanctified smile of every fanatic who ever quested for crucifixion or drank soda pop in Jonestown. Her body remained still and rigid as though indeed it were painted plaster. With arms outstretched in forgiveness for the world, she did her back dive, head first, and gave up her spirit. To the Hollywood Freeway.

As often happens, the frustrated, smog-burned,

crazed drivers on the Hollywood Freeway didn't even know they had mutilated The Madonna of the Wogs. The first three who ran over the wine-red bundle didn't know what the hell it was. One thought he'd hit an Irish setter. Another thought it was a plastic trash bag. A third heard something bump into the bottom of his car and thought he'd dropped his transmission.

Dilford had a delayed reaction to his meeting with The Madonna of the Wogs. He and Dolly did a creditable job on the reports at the station. Except that Dilford kept wondering over and over why The Madonna of the Wogs had chosen him and not the hyper hot dogs. And whether he had done enough, or too much, or said enough, or not enough, or chosen the wrong words.

"Was it something I *said*?" he asked Dolly while they sat penciling out their report.

"What?"

"I thought she was going to take my hand. She looked like she was going to take my hand. Why did she reject me?"

"You did just right. Even the sergeant said so. Forget it, Dilford."

"I often wonder if my personality alienates people," Dilford mused, staring with sweat-rimmed, bulging blue eyes. "Was it something I *said*?"

Dilford's delayed reaction hit him later, almost the moment he walked inside The House of Misery after work. Dolly was following him in her car and she noticed nothing unusual about his driving. But once inside The House of Misery, in the presence of Leery, The Bad Czech and Cecil Higgins, an odd thing happened.

Dilford said, "I feel like I got a jock full a popsicles. And my hands. They're like ice. Turn down the air conditioner, Leery."

"It ain't on," Leery said. "I ain't even got the smoke eaters going."

"It's freezing!" Dilford said. And suddenly he felt his jaw twitching. His teeth started clattering together.

Dolly put her cold hand on Dilford's cold hand.

"I'm *freezing*!" Dilford said. "I must be getting the flu!"

"Give him a double," The Bad Czech said.

"A jock full a popsicles," Dilford laughed, but his teeth were chattering. "It's c-c-cold!"

"It probably wasn't even real, kid," The Bad Czech said to Dilford. "Give him another one, Leery."

"He ain't paid for that one yet," Leery said.

"Bring the fuckin drink or I'll squeeze your turkey neck till ya gobble!" Then The Bad Czech said to Dilford, "Just shut your eyes and swallow it down."

Dilford had three double shots of Leery's bar whiskey, guaranteed to make you go blind, before his teeth stopped chattering and his balls thawed out.

The second strange thing that happened to Dilford was that Dolly matched him drink for drink and neither of them got particularly drunk. She even talked civil to him and continued to hold his freezing hand. In the evening they ate a bowl of Leery's disgusting clam chowder together and talked about movies.

Mario Villalobos had already drunk three vodkas by the time Lupe Luna arrived at the Mexican restaurant.

"Hi, Sarge," she said, sitting with him at a table in the barroom.

It was a surprising little restaurant to find on the barrio fringe. The waiters wore jackets and black ties and each table had a linen tablecloth, cut glass and a long-stemmed rose. The women's rest room was full of flowers, another surprising touch Lupe Luna noted. Of course there was the inevitable painting of an Aztec chief weeping over his dead maiden, proving that even Aztecs needed a little soap opera in their lives. Mexican music played on a tape deck and the *salsa* was fresh and hot, as were the tortilla chips with which Mario Villalobos ladled the *salsa*.

"Does a waiter help me lift this margarita?" she asked.

It was a fishbowl-sized snifter. He licked the salt off

the rim of his glass and said, "Have *two* of them. I'm capable of any dirty trick with a woman like you. I'd even take you out to my car and play the police radio if I thought it would help."

"Yeah?" She smiled, showing him the overbite that was driving him crackers. "Does cops 'n robbers *usually* help?"

"Lady, *nothing* helps at my time of life," he said. "All my neurons're almost petrified. About the only pleasure I get these days is from solving murders."

"Murders? I thought it was a jewel theft?"

"Yeah, well . . . I *prefer* solving murders is what I meant. Right now it's a jewel theft."

"I don't know how sexy I might find a police radio," she grinned, lifting the enormous glass with two hands. "But I confess to liking cop shows. And I read mysteries."

"I hate any kind of mystery," he said. "Mysteries drive me bonkers. In fact, I might go bonkers if I don't solve the one I'm working on. It's making me work. I'm too tired to work. I haven't worked so hard in years."

"Nothing very mysterious about it, is there? You just have to find out which professor was chasing around with a young girl in the restaurant that night. Pretty straightforward."

"Pretty straightforward," Mario Villalobos said. "How do you like the *salsa*?"

She scooped up a portion on a tortilla chip and said, "Just like mother used to make. Even better."

The music and conversation was interrupted occasionally by the whirring blender mixing margaritas, a not unpleasant sound to a borderline alcoholic like Mario Villalobos. He was starting to glow.

"Are you being nice to me so I'll help you with your investigation?" she asked.

"Cops're like basketball players," he said. "We peak early and then we drop like a sandbag. I'm being nice because I don't have much time left. And I *love* white teeth and an overbite."

She chuckled and said, "Do you have kids?"

"Two," he said. "I know a cop named Ludwig with eyes as big as yours. But his're yellow and yours're chocolate."

"Yellow? He must look like an animal."

"He does," Mario Villalobos said, and he was getting more than a glow. "Alfonso!" he called to the waiter. "One more margarita. The *big* one!"

"Do your kids live with you?"

"They live with my ex," he said. "My first ex. My second ex wasn't around that long, lucky for her."

"What's it like having sons?"

"I don't know," he said. "One of them ignores me. The other hates me."

"Hates you?"

"Yeah, I give him a target. That way he doesn't hate himself. How about another margarita?"

"You're a curious person."

"Whadda you expect from a counterfeit Mexican?" the detective said, and he was getting bagged in a hurry. "How do you like the huge American flag at York and Figueroa? Patriots, us Mexicans. No wonder we win so many Medals of Honor."

"Okay," she said. "*Tell* me about your Hispanic name and how you came to be a counterfeit Mexican."

"First, there's absolutely no chance of my making a move on you, is there?"

"Not tonight," she grinned. "I'm going *straight* home to my daughter."

"In that case I may as well get wrecked and tell you how I became a counterfeit Mexican. It's a boring story but it's all I got. I can tell you one thing: everybody dumps on the poor beaners. Even on counterfeit beaners . . ."

Jane Wayne came to Leery's from a beauty parlor appointment after work. She looked startlingly new-wave when she stalked into the bar in leather pants, boots, cleavage for days, and a steel-banged hairdo that shocked the crap out of everybody but The Bad Czech. He said she looked sweet and cute and adorable, even if she *did* sort of resemble Adolf Hitler.

She played some heavy-metal rock on the jukebox and the two of them got up on the dance floor and started doing some play-punk which involved make-believe slams. It ended in an erotic slow dance that got everyone except Leery and Ludwig aroused, and excepting Dilford, who was just happy that his teeth stopped chattering and his body temperature got back up to 98.6 degrees Fahrenheit.

The only thing that almost ruined the evening was that The Gooned-out Vice Cop showed up. He wasn't wearing a headband or thong this time. His long sandy hair was parted in the middle and hung softly around his rather delicate face. He wore an old army shirt and faded jeans and hiking boots, and he went straight to his favorite barstool.

Before he took his first drink of Leery's bar whiskey, he looked strangely at Dilford, and Dilford thought he *knew*. But he couldn't have known. Dilford had by now stopped shivering and Dolly was no longer warming his hands with hers.

Dilford got nervous when The Gooned-out Vice Cop looked at him. Dilford suddenly made an unsolicited statement. He said, "The suicide rate is terrifying these days."

Dolly followed with a non sequitur of her own. She said, "Homicide is one of the leading causes of death of *children* in America."

Jane Wayne, who had returned to the bar with The Bad Czech, said, "When parents start killing their children, it's the most unnatural thing imaginable."

"Kiddy porn, child murder, suicide," Cecil Higgins said, looking up from the bottom of his glass. "Maybe it's the end a the world."

The odd thing was that they were not so much looking at each other when they made these uncharacteristic, unsolicited remarks. They were looking at The Gooned-out Vice Cop, who was looking at nothing but his own bifurcated image in the broken shards of pub mirror. His face was green from the neon, and his mirror image resembled a Cubist portrait. His eyes were like bullet holes.

The Gooned-out Vice Cop had two shots of bar whiskey, never grimaced when he downed them, paid Leery, and left without comment.

As usual, he walked on cat feet, like a vice cop. And he seemed to float through the smoke and gloom out onto Sunset Boulevard.

When he was gone, The Bad Czech said, "I think that vice cop is gooned-out on PCP. A duster is what I think."

"Really?" Dolly said. "I was thinking he's more the free-base type."

"Uppers, is what I think," Jane Wayne said.

"It's coke," Dilford said. "Internal Affairs is gonna nail him one a these days."

"Naw, he's a hardballer," Cecil Higgins said. "That's what speed and Mexican brown does to ya. A hardballer."

Never one to discourage any paying customer, Leery said, "Long as he pays his tab, he don't bother me."

"I don't like cops havin zoned-out eyes," Cecil Higgins said.

"He looks like the freaks on our beat," The Bad Czech said. "Maybe he ain't real. Next time he comes in let's make Ludwig bite him. See if he's *real*."

Jane Wayne, with her new steel bangs and evening makeup, didn't look quite real herself when she said ambiguously, "It's the most *unnatural* thing imaginable." Then she said, "Well, if it's the end of the world, let's have another dance, Czech."

After a few more drinks no one thought about the end of the world or The Gooned-out Vice Cop, and everyone got back to normal.

ELEVEN

Brave New World

Because of Mario Villalobos, The Bad Czech and Hans were in the detective squadroom the next morning, dressed not in their uniforms but in civilian clothes. Hans wore a blue leisure suit and a pink nylon shirt with a pastel necktie. The Bad Czech wore a sportcoat that looked like something that should go over an animal at Santa Anita, and was about the right size for it. His necktie ended halfway to his belt, so lengthy was his massive torso. They were all dressed up and on loan to Mario Villalobos. It made them *really* cranky.

"I'm no freaking detective, for chrissake," The Bad Czech griped to the black detective lieutenant who was trying to figure what would happen if the Dodgers beat San Diego and Atlanta got knocked off by Chicago.

"Whaddaya think, I asked for this?" Hans said in his whiny singsong voice which was driving The Bad Czech goofy this early in the day.

"It's enough I gotta listen to ya at Leery's when I got a drink and can *cope*," The Bad Czech said to the skinny K-9 cop.

"I got Ludwig all locked up in the yard at home. He misses me. You think I *like* this?"

"Just try to make the best of it," the detective lieutenant said, deciding that if Fernando could stop them one more time and Garvey could start to hit, the Dodgers might get their shit together yet.

Mario Villalobos, who was off getting the work of Chip Muirfield and Melody Waters sorted out for the next few days, strolled into the squadroom drinking a cup of coffee. After his early date with Lupe Luna he had, unbelievably enough, gone straight home and listened to Cole Porter's "Just One of Those Things," which he had actually taken to be a happy song when he first heard it as a youth. He was not hungover and was not as weary as usual. But he could see that The House of Misery victims were not feeling good about things.

"Look," he said, anticipating the gripes. "We'll go up there to Caltech and just look at some photos of the faculty. And then . . ."

"Mario, I didn't get a good look at the guy!" The Bad Czech complained. "He jist walked by on the sidewalk, is all."

"I hardly noticed him," Hans whined. "You think I look at every guy walks by? Gimme a break, Mario."

"Here's my problem," Mario Villalobos said, lighting his eighth cigarette of the morning. "The guy at the Wonderland Hotel described him as a tall guy in a pinstripe suit with black hair and a black moustache."

"So?" The Bad Czech said.

"So the whore said she thought the moustache was phony, and maybe the hair was too. Except he wore a hat."

"So?" Hans said.

"Both the whore and hotel clerk see this tall dude, probably with a phony moustache. Maybe with a wig. You're better witnesses."

"How do ya know that?" The Bad Czech demanded. "He had the same moustache when I saw him."

"And horn-rim glasses," Hans added.

"And black hair," The Bad Czech said. "I don't know if it was a wig or what. Whaddaya mean, better witnesses?"

"You both said he wasn't as tall as the whore and the clerk thought he was," Mario Villalobos said. "You both thought he was in his fifties. They thought he was much younger."

"Maybe it's a different guy," Hans said.

"I know it's the *same* guy," Mario Villalobos said. "I can sense it."

"Sense it!" Hans whined. "Who do you think you are, Ludwig? And that reminds me, I was supposed to give Ludwig a bath today. How would you like it if nobody ever gave you a bath?"

"Listen to this shit!" The Bad Czech groaned. "On top of everything else, I gotta put up with this noodleneck doggie cop all day. Gimme a break, Mario!"

Finally the lieutenant put down his sports page, unable to solve the problems of the National League with all this bitching going on. "Fellas," he said, "the bottom line is that two policemen should be a sight more reliable than a street whore we can't even find and a hotel clerk who drinks a fifth a day."

The Bad Czech almost asked the lieutenant how the hell much he thought *Hans* drinks, but he could see it was no use.

He looked at Hans and thought, he had to trade Cecil Higgins for this?

Hans looked at The Bad Czech and thought, he had to trade Ludwig for this?

Mario Villalobos pulled out the American Express card and said, "If it weren't for you finding this, we wouldn't have a single clue in our clues closet, Czech. If anything comes outa this, I'm gonna ask the lieutenant here to write a nice 'attaboy' for your personnel package."

"I can't *wait*," The Bad Czech grumbled. Then he said, "That reminds me, on the way to Caltech let's stop by the Pusan Gardens. They got *my* American Express card in their lost-and-found drawer."

"Hope nobody used it to buy won ton," Mario Villalobos said as he got his reports together. Then he looked at the dead private eye's credit card for a moment and said, "I wonder why this card didn't work for Missy and

Dagmar? The American Express people didn't know Lester Beemer was dead, and he kept his bill paid."

"Mine always works." The Bad Czech shrugged.

"This couldn't be a forged card, could it?" Mario Villalobos wondered. "When we pick up your card, I wanna compare the two of them closely."

"What's the credit card got to do with murder, for chrissake?" The Bad Czech asked.

"I don't know what anything's got to do with anything," Mario Villalobos said. "I've told you guys everything I know."

"This is just a goddamn fishing expedition," Hans whined. "Ludwig should be getting groomed today. I hope Ludwig don't get ringworm or something."

"I *hate* mysteries," The Bad Czech complained. "This case is gettin as complicated as this doggie cop's fetishes."

Mario Villalobos and Hans waited in the detective car while The Bad Czech went into the Pusan Gardens to collect his American Express card. When he returned to the car, Mario Villalobos had Lester Beemer's card in his hand. He examined them side by side.

"That's a legit card," The Bad Czech said. "Looks jist like mine."

"The same," Hans agreed, leaning over the front seat of the car.

"Damn," The Bad Czech groaned. "You smell like Ludwig. Sit back, will ya?"

"The Korean B-girl said Missy complained about the card not working, remember, Czech?" Mario Villalobos noted.

"Yeah, so what?"

"It didn't work when Dagmar and Missy used it on Restaurant Row either."

"Mario, we gonna screw around all day?" Hans whined. "Let's get this over with."

"Okay," Mario Villalobos said. "Lemme just make one stop. I wanna take this to a bank and have them run it through in a normal transaction and see if it's an ordinary legit card."

And while both Hans and The Bad Czech moaned about Mario Villalobos, and detectives in general, they stopped at a downtown bank on their way to the Pasadena Freeway.

The bank officer returned with the credit card and said to Mario Villalobos, "Sergeant, there's no information on this card. That's the problem."

"Whadda you mean, no information? Is it a forged card?"

"No, it's a proper card," the man said. "But the magnetic stripe doesn't contain any information."

"Why's that?"

"It's been erased. I don't know how. I've heard that a magnet can do it."

"A magnet can wipe out the information on the magnetic stripe? Like the magnetometer at an airport terminal?"

"No, I've carried mine lots of times in airports. A strong magnet can do it, that's all I know. Why don't you use our phone and talk to someone who knows more about it?"

The Bad Czech and Hans both turned their persecuted faces to Mario Villalobos when he returned after thirty minutes.

"If we had Ludwig, we'da sent him looking," Hans said.

"A strong magnetic field can erase the information on these cards," Mario Villalobos said. "That's why it didn't work for Missy and Dagmar!"

"So, what's that mean?" The Bad Czech asked.

"Mean? Nothing, yet."

"It's amazing the irrelevant things that make detectives so happy," Hans said.

The K-9 cop looked unhappily out the car window at the downtown pedestrians dodging and careening into one another. An army of blinded worker-ants sweating in the smog.

*   *   *

Mario Villalobos wisely decided to buy Hans and The Bad Czech something to eat before going to Caltech, so they wouldn't be quite so difficult. The Bad Czech insisted on Chicken McNuggets, so they stopped at McDonald's and he ate four orders of them, and had two chocolate shakes and three bags of fries. So that he could cope with the afternoon.

They went straight to Lupe Luna's office and found her working away on a typewriter, looking even better than Mario Villalobos remembered her from last night. He thought that if he were a *real* Mexican, he might have beautiful hair and teeth and skin like Lupe Luna.

"Hi," she said brightly when the detective walked in with The Bad Czech and Hans. "Thanks for dinner last night. It was great."

The Bad Czech and Hans gave each other a look that said, Is *this* why we're here? To give old Mario a crack at a foxy secretary?

And then Mario Villalobos almost panicked when he suddenly remembered that he had forgotten to include one detail when he briefed the cops as to the nature of their "work" as restaurant employees. He'd never told them what *kind* of employees they supposedly were.

He never got the chance. When he introduced them to Lupe Luna as "Czech" and "Hans," Lupe Luna said, "Which is the waiter and which is the busboy?"

In that Hans thought quicker, he said, "I'm the waiter."

And when The Bad Czech caught on, his demented gray eyes started to bulge and pulsate. Mario Villalobos prayed that he wouldn't scream something like, "I GOTTA PLAY LIKE I'M A FUCKIN BUSBOY?"

But Lupe Luna said, "Let's get started. It'll take you a while to look at all the pictures."

Mario Villalobos offered a placating glance at the monster cop, who was glaring murderously at Hans because the K-9 cop started giggling. He was the waiter and The Bad Czech was the busboy!

* * *

They reminded Mario Villalobos of typical witnesses looking through police department mug books. At the start, witnesses have some interest and diligence. Very quickly diligence wanes and confusion reigns. Then they give the photos a perfunctory glance and realize that they *must* see the person in the flesh if they're even to have a chance.

At four o'clock that afternoon, Mario Villalobos said, "Enough. There's no point looking at them again."

"I just have six *maybes*," Hans sighed.

"I jist have four *maybes*," The Bad Czech sighed.

"Lemme go talk to Lupe for a minute," Mario Villalobos said. The Bad Czech rubbed his eyes and leaned back in his chair, stretching the fabric on his doubleknit pants with a pair of thighs the size of Hans' waist.

When the detective returned he was grinning. "Lupe's taking us to their bar. We're gonna get some *drinks*, compliments of her boss."

"Aw right!" The Bad Czech said.

"A couple drinks helps me recognize people," Hans said.

"Let's not take advantage," Mario Villalobos warned. "Her boss is gonna get our bill."

As it turned out, the afternoon's bar tab wasn't as high as it once was when Lupe Luna's boss hosted a cocktail party for thirty in the Caltech dining room. But it was close.

The Caltech Athenaeum was one of the older buildings. It was built in 1929, just before the crash, during the golden age of California architecture. An age of tile roofs, Moorish arches, Corinthian columns and vaulted gold-leaf ceilings. Lupe Luna took them on a tour of the building, past an elegant dining room into an enormous sitting room.

The Bad Czech said, "Primo! You could play basketball in here!"

Hans walked on the Oriental carpet and said, "That rug's big enough for a hundred ayatollahs to roll around on!"

"What a fireplace!" The Bad Czech said. "It's big enough to roast Ludwig in."

"Look at the patina on that walnut paneling," the detective said. "They don't make things like this anymore."

"I never saw a busboy so big," Lupe Luna said suspiciously to Mario Villalobos.

The detective hushed her and whispered, "He's sensitive about it. He used to be a waiter and got demoted for dropping dishes."

She looked as though she didn't believe that either. They passed back through the lobby to the Hayman Lounge. It was a restful cocktail lounge with upholstered chairs and a bartender in black tie.

"This is where donors and trustees drink," Lupe Luna explained. "The students and faculty prefer it downstairs."

"Let's go downstairs," Mario Villalobos said.

The downstairs Athenaeum bar was in a basement lined with sturdy, unpretentious wooden tables and chairs. The floor was thinly carpeted and the basement walls were painted concrete. But the bar, even without the upstairs luxury, had a pub quality which Hans and The Bad Czech were comfortable with.

Mario Villalobos liked it here because it was obviously the kind of "neighborhood" saloon in which people talked. And as all detectives knew, *talk* was finally what solved crimes, "scientific" detection serving only as public relations sop. He just hoped he could pay attention to business, what with Lupe Luna distracting him.

The students had decorated the walls of the bar with allusions to current events. A chalkboard posed a question: "Should 40,000 Falkland penguins be guaranteed political asylum?"

Another offered an answer: "Only if they wear 'Save the Whale' stickers epoxied to their flippers."

The dress of scientists, be they student or professor, seemed to range from careless to grungy. There was a slim, attractive woman tending bar and she was just opening for the evening. The Bad Czech took one look at her and made himself right at home on the first stool by the door.

"Bourbon on the rocks. Double," The Bad Czech said, wondering how long was considered polite in high-powered science institutes before you made a move on lady bartenders.

"Scotch on the rocks. Double." Hans leered, not caring what was considered polite.

And Mario Villalobos thought, so much for worrying about other people's bar tabs.

Lupe Luna gave him a shrug and said, "We believe in supporting our local police, as they say."

"Okay," Mario Villalobos said. "A very dry vodka martini on the rocks. Double." And when he added, "Hold the vermouth. Hold the olive," the woman behind the bar displayed a knowing bartender's smile and gave him a *very* healthy shot of vodka over ice.

The Bad Czech said to Hans, "This might turn out to be pretty good duty after all." And then he saw the dish full of Goldfish bar tidbits, and a huge plastic bag full of popcorn on a table.

"You give away free Goldfish and popcorn?" The Bad Czech asked the bartender.

"All you want," she said.

"This here ain't like Leery's, eh, Mario?" The Bad Czech said. "You get somethin free!"

Lupe Luna, who was sitting at one of the wooden tables with the detective, said, "Where's Leery's?"

"That's the, uh, owner of the restaurant where they work."

"He calls you by your first name? Are you so intimate with all your witnesses?"

"I believe in being an approachable cop."

"Uh huh."

"Speaking of intimate, when're we going out again?"

"Have you told me the *whole* truth about this . . . jewel theft you're working on?"

"Would I lie?" Mario Villalobos asked, swallowing the double vodka.

"*That,*" she said, pointing to The Bad Czech, "is a busboy?"

"Do you think I could have just one more drink on your boss's tab? We'd buy our own if this wasn't a private club."

"I'll get it," she said, and he knew that the lie might not fly.

"Tell her a vodka martini . . ."

"Very, *very dry.*" Lupe Luna nodded.

"She knows I'm full of crap, and still she buys us drinks. I think I'm in love!" Mario Villalobos mouthed the words to The Bad Czech, who just shrugged.

When Lupe Luna returned she brought him a double vodka and a whiskey sour for herself.

"I'm gonna get you drunk and take advantage of you," she warned him playfully.

"You are?" Mario Villalobos cried. "Along with *free* drinks?"

"Yeah. Then I'm gonna find out what you're really investigating. I'm getting *excited.* I love a mystery." She looked at him over the rim of her whiskey sour with mischief in her eyes.

"I hate a mystery," Mario Villalobos said. "It drives me bonkers. But I'm getting excited too. I *love* overbites."

Meanwhile, The Bad Czech and Hans were no longer cranky at all about their detective assignment, and the bar started to get crowded. They were both working on their second double and The Bad Czech was threatening to break the pub record for eating Goldfish, previously held by the chairman of the division of chemistry.

In fact, The Bad Czech began giving a lecture to two "postdocs," young women who were postdoctoral research fellows, one doing work in physics, the other in chemistry, after having received their doctoral degrees. The Bad Czech's lecture to the two young women was on how to eat Goldfish.

"Some people eat a Goldfish by chewin off the tail first," The Bad Czech said. He took the little fish-shaped cracker and held it in fingers as big as 50-milliliter test tubes. "It's real interestin sittin at a bar and seein how people eat Goldfish," The Bad Czech said. "There's these tail biters. Some bite the tail edgewise and some do it flat. Then there's these types that put the little fish between their teeth and kind a split it down the middle. Then a course, there's people that jist gobble them up and all the crumbs jist flop outa their mouths. I ain't much interested in meetin people like that. I see you two're tail biters. I *like* tail biters. I wish I could buy ya a drink, but we're jist guests here."

"That was a *very* enlightening talk on Goldfish," Hans said, and his whiny voice and smart-aleck tone made The Bad Czech mad.

Then the skinny K-9 cop whispered to his postdoc, "Your girl friend's looking at the big dummy like he's a booger on her finger. The girl's got taste."

Both postdocs wore Levi jeans. One wore a red T-shirt and moccasins. The Bad Czech liked her big chest, and he also eyed the other one, who wore a baggy work shirt and deck shoes. In general, they dressed not unlike off-duty male cops.

"Who're you guests of?" the postdoc in the T-shirt asked.

"That woman over there with the guy in the suit," The Bad Czech said. "Luna's her name."

"What do you do?" the other postdoc asked Hans, who was slinking closer along the bar as was his custom.

"I'm a waiter," Hans said. "He's a . . ."

"We're *both* waiters!" The Bad Czech said, glaring at Hans. "We work in a real nice joint over on Restaurant Row. Ever eat over there?"

"Can't afford it," the postdoc in the T-shirt said. "Starving young scientists trying to make our place in the world. Next year we'll get real grown-up jobs doing science and maybe we can eat in a restaurant."

Just then a clutch of noisy graduate students came banging down the stairs and into the bar. They wore cutoffs and jeans and grubbies of all kinds. They didn't look any smarter than college kids the cops had occasionally jailed when they drove drunk through Rampart Division on their way to USC or UCLA. The difference was that all these *were* smart or they couldn't be here. One kid with a beard full of lint said to another, "Physics is like fucking. Mathematics is like masturbation."

The Bad Czech didn't get it, but at least it had to do with sex. The two unglamorous postdocs were starting to look better. "Another double," he said to the bartender, who was now having to move fast to keep up with the noisy crowd of drinkers.

The postdoc with the baggy shirt, who was getting more appealing to Hans, said to the other, "Have you heard the one about the theoretical physicist who drowned in a lake he theorized had an average depth of six inches?"

Both young women laughed like hell, and The Bad Czech, who didn't get that one either, said, "Maybe if ya bite the Goldfish vertical it means you're Caucasian, and sideways you're Oriental."

"Whadda you do?" Hans asked the postdoc in the baggy shirt. He was leaning on his elbow now and sidling ever closer, as The Bad Czech had seen him do many times before. He was the sneaky type that bellied along a bar, much as a police dog bellies close to the ground before attacking.

"Right now, colloidal interface chemistry," she said.

"Wow! That sounds *erotic* to me!" Hans cried.

"I wish that little pervert'd get back to his side a the bar," The Bad Czech whispered to *his* postdoc. "Tell ya the truth, he ain't even a waiter. He's my *busboy*."

Just then a man entered the barroom. He was older than the graduate students and postdocs. He was obviously a member of the faculty. The Bad Czech signaled to Hans to turn around on his stool and take a look. The man was neither fiftyish nor tall enough to be the one they saw outside of Dagmar Duffy's apartment house. He was a visiting research fellow, it turned out, and had just spiced up his lecture in bio-inorganic chemistry with a theory as to how vampires came to be.

One of the students who was drinking beer and twirling a Frisbee on his finger said to the professor, "Could you tell my friends here your theory on vampires?"

Which caused The Bad Czech to stop ogling the postdoc and come up off the bar and turn around and pay attention. They were talking about vampires! And he *was* one!

"It's quite credible, really," the professor said with a British public school accent. "It deals with the disease of porphyria, which is a genetic disease, so it could be regional, say around Transylvania, and . . ."

The professor was interrupted by one of the most enormous men he'd seen lately, with eyebrows like fingers of fur, who was sitting at the bar looking tense. "How do ya spell that disease?" the huge man asked.

"Uh, that's p-o-r-p-h-y-r-i-a," the professor said. "And to continue, my theory is that it's the making of too much porphyrin, which with iron in it makes blood red, that gave them their problem. Drinking blood slows porphyrin production, so they would attack cows and drink their blood."

The Bad Czech suddenly relaxed. "Drinkin cows' blood ain't got nothin to do with *me*!" he said to the postdoc, who looked puzzled.

"Now it happens that garlic can block an enzyme that gets rid of porphyrin," the professor continued, "so that plays right into the legend of garlic warding off vampires."

"Thou shall not covet thy neighbor's cow," Hans giggled to his postdoc, who was ignoring him completely.

"As it happens, quinine also blocks the enzyme," the professor continued, "so . . ."

"That means ya can't give a vampire a gin and *tonic*!" The Bad Czech said, and for the first time his postdoc paid attention to him. He was right!

"Next time I accept a blind date I'll give him a gin and tonic test," she said, examining The Bad Czech, who with his black hair, furry eyebrows and Slavic features *did* look something like an archetypal Dracula—a very large one, to be sure.

"I could tell a *real* vampire story," The Bad Czech whispered, "if I get to know ya better. I can see ya *like* vampires."

Two male students who were going bonzo over the approaching deadline for submitting a doctoral thesis were arguing about whether or not one of their colleagues had jumped or fallen out of a window while loaded on nitrous oxide. Apparently science prodigies also had their stress problems.

The Bad Czech, who was working on his fourth double and charging into all the conversations, said, "He *jumped,* ya ask me. Everybody's jumpin these days or slashin their own throats or smokin their thirty-eights. Or killin their kids or . . ."

"The restaurant business can't be *that* bad," one postdoc said to him.

"So what's that these guys're talking about, this reaction dynamics?" Hans demanded boozily from *his* postdoc, who couldn't get away from the K-9 cop and had already noticed that he smelled like an animal.

"How molecules bump into each other," she said.

"*Everything* ya say sounds erotic to me!" Hans cried. "Write down your phone number, will ya?"

"I don't think so," the postdoc said, rolling her eyes at her colleague.

"Well, write down your area code," Hans begged, getting hotter by the minute.

"Not tonight," she replied, whispering, "Nerd alert!" to her girl friend.

"Well, then write me down a formula," Hans cried. "I'm crazy for smart girls!"

"Ya know what I like about gettin ripped in this place?" The Bad Czech said to the lady bartender, who was pouring his fifth double. "Everybody here's smarter than me. Where I usually drink, I'm smarter than everybody else and it makes me feel guilty cause I should know better than get drunk with all the dummies."

"Smarter, huh!" Hans whispered to his postdoc. "He's as smart as a box a rocks. He ain't even a waiter. *Busboy* is what he is. Been one for twenty years. Oldest freaking busboy on Restaurant Row." He waved at the bartender and said, "Can I have a refill, lovely lady?"

Just then another professor entered the barroom. He was rather tall and had dark hair and was at least fifty years old. He didn't wear glasses and didn't have a moustache, but The Bad Czech got excited for a minute. He nodded to Hans, who craned his noodle neck and shrugged.

When the man came to the bar to order a gin martini, The Bad Czech was already getting numb around the nose and chin. He also was having some trouble keeping his elbow on the bar.

He wanted to hear the man's voice. He said, "I like to drink down here better than the fancy lounge upstairs. How 'bout you?"

The man looked at the boozy giant and smiled congenially, and didn't respond.

"They tell me the lounge up there, whadda they call it, the hymen lounge . . ."

"The Hayman Lounge," the bartender corrected him.

"Yeah, the Hayman Lounge, is where most a the people drink who donate big bucks."

The man stood at the bar sipping his martini and looked at his watch.

"It's a pretty bar up there," The Bad Czech said, "but I like the people down here, don't you?"

"Uh huh," the man said.

"Do you bite the tails off Goldfish or eat them all at once?" The Bad Czech wanted to know.

"Are you connected with Caltech?" the man asked.

"Naw, I own a restaurant," The Bad Czech said. "In fact, I own about six a them. Might give a few bucks to the college if I like it around here."

When the man smiled and walked away, The Bad Czech shook his head in the negative and Hans went back to making a move on one of the postdocs.

There wasn't much to deaden the sound in the concrete basement and the din was nerve-racking to Mario Villalobos, who was learning all about Lupe Luna's own failed marriage, and her life with a teenaged daughter, and her work at Caltech. He did everything he could to keep her talking so she wouldn't ask him too many questions. He was afraid if she knew the true nature of his investigation she might feel honor bound to report it, which he was positive would be the end.

Distilled right down to the bottom of the test tube, as it were, was nothing but a detective's hunch and instinct that someone in this place was running amok, and had killed a private eye and a hooker and was trying to kill the macho maid, Dagmar Duffy. Each time Lupe Luna tried to pump him for more specific information, he'd change the subject. After his third vodka he tried to get the conversation back to where it belonged: sex.

"And is your dance card pretty well filled up around here?" Mario Villalobos asked. "I imagine there's a few prospects among the faculty?"

"Not that many," she said. "These scientific types seem to have a biannual rutting season. They sublimate their sex urges for study and research and then suddenly go into a rutting frenzy like moose. That's when I start getting phone calls. How about cops?"

"They're not so consumed by their work," he said, taking a look at the two at the bar. "But they tend to get very tired in later life."

By now the two postdocs had scooted off and were replaced at the bar by two faculty members who did not remotely fit the description of the man in the pinstripe suit. The Bad Czech and Hans were both moving on the lady bartender.

"It's really true," Lupe Luna told Mario Villalobos, "that pure science can be very erotic to these people. I've dated scientists who described their work the way you'd describe an orgy."

"I couldn't describe an orgy," Mario Villalobos said, "but if you have any orgy stories, let's have them!"

"What time do you want to mingle at the open house?" she said, looking with antelope eyes over the rim of the glass.

"About eight o'clock," he said. "This is a long shot, but it's a way to see lots of chemistry professors at one time. In the flesh."

"Then we don't have time to get into orgies," she said, clearly not used to three whiskey sours.

"I'm starting to feel the neurons bubbling," the detective said, reaching across the table and rubbing his finger along hers. "I was starting to think that catching crooks was *all* I had left."

"I'm feeling strangely sexy myself," she said, and the words were getting slurred. "I think this mystery is a turn-on."

"Agatha Christie never made you feel like this?"

"Uh uh," she said, and he felt her slender ankle touch his under the table.

Meanwhile, The Bad Czech had found a graduate student who was chestier than the postdoc. Except that she wore very grubby cutoffs and a man's BVD T-shirt without a bra. She was by no means the most unglamorous woman in the place.

"I'm a rookie gynecologist and I'm giving free Pap smears," Hans whispered to the grad student, who tried to ignore him.

"Let's wet that T-shirt down and get a weather report," Hans said slyly, as he nearly fell off the barstool slinking closer to her.

"Get lost," she said, glaring at the skinny guy in the leisure suit who obviously didn't belong here.

"If it was wet, I'd either know how cold it is or if maybe you *like* me!" Hans cried, skulking along the bar in her direction.

"Nerd alert!" she yelled to the other women and Hans decided she was probably as nasty as that cunt who told everyone about his P.E. problem. Which gave him an idea: he wondered if he could find a hotshot chemistry professor who might help him out.

Meanwhile, The Bad Czech gave up eyeballing the grad student in the T-shirt when one of her male classmates said, "Some of the women around here are slightly *more* than feminist. *That* one gives lectures on how to live a lifetime without men."

"She looks too old anyways," The Bad Czech said to the gangly student, having to shout to be heard over the noise in the basement bar.

"I know one guy who was in graduate school ten years. He was gray when he got out," the kid said.

With just enough booze in him to make him play detective, The Bad Czech said, "There must be a lot a stress around here. You ever know a professor to go wacko and maybe do somethin . . . violent?"

"A professor?" The student ran his fingers through his snarled hair. "I heard of a student who bludgeoned his adviser at Stanford. Typical science student. He put a bag over the adviser's head to keep from bloodying his papers. Then he told the judge that after ten years of graduate school, Folsom Prison would be a piece of cake."

"Can't think of any violent ones?"

"Hard to say. Lots of them are nuts."

They were interrupted just then when the grad student in the T-shirt yelled at Hans, "No, I don't want to learn how to do a choke hold! I can take care of myself!"

"But it's the carotid artery hold!" Hans leered. "You know, the one they talk about in the news where the cops choke peoples' necks and they croak sometimes?"

"I do *not* want you choking my neck, man!" the grad student yelled.

"How about you choking *my* neck?" Hans cried. He was unstoppable when he was horny like this.

"No, I don't want to choke your goddamn neck!" she shouted.

"Then how about *spanking* me?" Hans screamed.

The graduate student grabbed her beer and stalked off to one of the tables while The Bad Czech said, "Ya can't behave nowheres, can ya? Ya gotta always be disgustin!"

The K-9 cop waved hornily at the bartender and said, "One more double, my dear! For the freeway!"

Returning to business, The Bad Czech asked the student, "Which professors are the most . . . *emotional*. Like which ones get really overexcited if things don't go right in their experiments or whatever. Is there a certain field a study that attracts, say, *aggressive* ones?"

"I think you oughtta ask her," the kid said, pointing to the lady bartender, who was listening.

"Most of the people you see here right now are into chemistry," she said to The Bad Czech. "They're the jovial ones and they drink like fishes."

"I don't think they sleep around much at their conferences," another student piped in. She was in chemical engineering and looked very disappointed that chemists didn't sleep around much at their conferences.

"Maybe they drink to many chemicals with their booze and they *can't* sleep around too much." The Bad Czech shrugged, and that again reminded Hans that he *had* to talk to a likely chemist about his recent "problem."

"Biologists are clean-cut and healthy," the bartender said. "So they *do* sleep around at their conferences and have lots of fun."

"Physicists have great integrity," one of the postdocs piped up.

"That's true," the bartender said. "They always pay their bar tab. But they're the least concerned about clothes and shaving and combing their hair."

"I think geologists are womanizers," another postdoc offered. "They get horny looking for rocks out there in the desert."

"Engineers are the cheapest," another student said. "They let someone else buy. They actually try to sneak their own cheap wine in here sometimes."

"Well, in terms of quantitative science, chemistry is a lot *harder* than biology," one student argued. "So you tend to drink more."

"Physics is more rigorous," another told The Bad Czech.

"Geology is in the basement," another told him.

"Physicists keep their word," the bartender said. "They also eat better food when they're not forgetting to eat."

And so forth.

The Bad Czech realized he wasn't getting anywhere trying to find a criminal "type" and was about to try another tack when one of the students told a riddle.

"Here's an ellipsoid swimming pool riddle," the student said. "If you dive in at one focus, will water splash at the other focus? Not allowing for water viscosity, of course?"

"Not *another* theoretical physicist," one student groaned.

"Water waves aren't like light waves," a student noted.

"A swimming pool isn't the Whispering Dome," another joined in. "Water waves aren't *like* sound waves."

"Because of the uneven depth of the water, the waves won't hit the focus at the same time," still another offered.

"I said, not *allowing* for relative depth and viscosity," the riddler reminded.

"The answer is yes," three of them said at once.

And The Bad Czech was getting dizzy. He walked over to Hans and said, "They might as well be talkin Cambodian!"

"Might as well be talking in tongues," the K-9 cop complained. "I thought I was getting somewhere with the one in the T-shirt."

And then, feeling confused by all the jokes he didn't understand, and wishing he was in The House of Misery where at least he was the smartest one at the bar, The Bad Czech prompted another of those tiny vagaries that trigger more significant events and seem to indicate that all men are linked in a great and mysterious chain.

Either that, or as cops tend to believe, it's all a freaking accident. It came to pass because The Bad Czech took a pee on a tree.

It never occurred to him that there was no downstairs rest room, and he walked through a basement door and found himself roaming down a long corridor into another, and finally found a door which led him outside at dusk. The need had come on him fifteen minutes earlier, but with all the confusing talk he had waited. Now he was bursting.

Once outside, he roamed near the tennis courts and didn't see anything like a rest room. He had to go and he was cranky. He started back and was startled to learn that he had already drunk himself into double vision. He was getting mad at the world. He looked around and saw an olive tree waiting in the dusk.

When he got to the tree, he unzipped his fly and began urinating. Suddenly a bellowing Spanish-accented voice in the shadows said: "Ees magnificent to find a human being in thees Meeckey Mouse place who has the *huevos* to pee on a tree!"

The Bad Czech quickly finished, zipped up the fly on his doubleknits and saw a man step forward. The man was of medium height, middle-aged, and resembled Benito Mussolini. His feathery hair looked like the topknot on a cockatoo.

"Ya scared me!" The Bad Czech said.

"I was just trying to get away from the Meeckey Mouse *estupidos* at the open house," the man said. He reeked of wine from having consumed nearly half a gallon at the cheese and wine table which was a bustling center of activity in the garden.

The man wore a suit about as shapeless and cheap as Mario Villalobos', and he wore a yellow bow tie with flowers on it. His frayed shirt was stained by red wine and he was nearly as bombed as The Bad Czech. When he got close, The Bad Czech could see that the cockatoo hair was the color of red pepper.

"Peeing on the tree to show contempt!" the man said. "I admire that!"

"Naw, I jist hadda take a leak," The Bad Czech said. "I got lost. I gotta find my way back to the downstairs bar."

"I refuse to go een that Meeckey Mouse bar!" the man announced, and his topknot bounced and danced.

"I thought it was a nice joint," The Bad Czech said. "Course I drink at a better place."

"I am Ignacio Mendoza," the man announced. "Call me Nacho. What do they call you?"

"Everyone calls me Czech cause my folks came from Czechoslovakia."

"I came from Peru, but nobody calls me Perry," Ignacio Mendoza said. "What are you doing at thees Meeckey Mouse place?"

"I was jist takin a leak," The Bad Czech explained. "I was . . ."

"No, no, no!" Ignacio Mendoza bellowed. "I mean thees Meeckey Mouse social setting. I am a professor. I have no choice. There are bourgeois requirements in my life."

"Well, see, I'm jist at this here open house to look around. To get my feet wet. To see if I wanna become a . . . *donor*. See, I own a string a restaurants in L.A. and I been thinkin about donatin some money."

"I see!" Ignacio Mendoza said. Then he put his arm around the oxlike shoulder of The Bad Czech and said, "There ees some great research to be done here and I shall be your guide. You have just found a friend!"

"Thanks, Nacho," The Bad Czech said. "First, can you take me back to the bar, cause I'm lost. And second, can you buy me a drink or two cause I ain't a member here and I can't buy my own, even though I'm a rich guy and own about six or seven restaurants."

"Eet shall be my pleasure, Czech!" Ignacio Mendoza said.

Mario Villalobos thought he was *really* blitzed when he saw the pair coming through the downstairs door. The Bad Czech in his yellow sportcoat and Ignacio Mendoza with his red-pepper cockatoo topknot made Mario Villalobos put his drink down.

"Een the old days a man did not have to pee on a tree," Ignacio Mendoza explained to his new friend. "The Hayman Lounge, before it was a bar, used to be the world's greatest men's room. There were more than a dozen peeing places. A plethora of pissoirs. Very tall pissoirs."

"I like tall ones," The Bad Czech said, happy because his new friend bought him a drink.

"Eet was wonderful," Ignacio Mendoza said. "Can you imagine resting on the john and considering that Albert Einstein himself took a dump een the same place een nineteen thirty-two! Come, let us go to a table and perhaps I can persuade you that money would be well spent here."

Mario Villalobos was by now looking at his watch, realizing that open house was in full swing and that he had to get his cops upstairs. Except that Lupe Luna had her hand in his and they were leaning across the table looking into each other's eyes.

"I see your busboy got teamed up with Ignacio Mendoza," she said.

"Who's that?" Mario Villalobos asked.

"Chemistry professor," she said. "Wild man even when sober, and now he looks drunk. He was eighty-sixed from this bar for jerking out the plug when a hundred people were trying to watch the Sugar Ray Leonard–Thomas Hearns fight on pay TV."

"Couldn't they plug it back in?"

"He jerked it out of the TV, not the socket. He said that prizefighting was bourgeois and primitive and had no place in an academy of science. He's also been kicked out of most of the bars in Pasadena."

Mario Villalobos saw that he was perhaps the right age and he wondered if The Bad Czech was onto something. "Does he always wear that silly bird wig?" the detective asked.

"That's his hair," Lupe Luna answered.

As The Bad Czech and the Peruvian professor passed the horny K-9 cop, Hans was trying to engage the bartender in conversation while she was trying to stay at the other end of the bar, having picked up the scent of dog on Hans' leisure suit.

The Bad Czech whispered to Ignacio Mendoza, "That's one a my waiters, Nacho. I brung him here for a big night out. Got to take care a your employees."

"That ees wise." Ignacio Mendoza nodded. Then to the bartender, "Give my friend a double and one for his waiter."

"His *waiter*?" Hans said. "Did you hear that? I'd like to break his eyebrows is what I'd like to do, the big phony! I'd like to make him a *canceled* Czech!"

"I'd like to have him on our team," a big baby-faced kid said. "We need somebody that size at defensive end."

"What kind a football schedule would a place like this have?" Hans asked, knowing he'd better soon get something to eat. He loosened his pastel necktie and took deep breaths to make his head less fuzzy.

"Well, we tried to play Tijuana Tech but their team didn't show up. I think Lopez-Portillo was on a tour and needed the rental bus. But we played Tehachapi."

"The prison?"

"Yeah, the refs were all inmates so of course they were crooks. One of them got beat up when he called a penalty against the other crooks. So he called all the rest of the penalties against us."

"Rampart used to have a good football team," Hans said. "The Czech played for them. Morale's low everywhere now. Everybody's dumpin on us co . . ." Hans stopped running his mouth when he saw the big kid looking at him in puzzlement. "Uh . . . Rampart's the name of our *restaurant*. Ever eat there? Right next to Lawry's? Rampart House of Ribs?"

"Waiters have a football squad?"

"Yeah, and busboys," Hans said. "I gotta get some coffee. I'm too drunk to touch my nose."

"I'm not too drunk to touch his nose," the braless graduate student said to the bartender, clenching her fist.

"Haven't seen you around lately, Nacho," one of the new arrivals at the bar said to Ignacio Mendoza. He was about six feet tall and fiftyish. He had a receding hairline and blond-gray hair. The voice was close to being right.

"I don't frequent thees Meeckey Mouse place very often," he said to the man. "The last time was nearly a year ago on Bastille Day. Somebody actually started complaining because I sang the Marseillaise." And then Ignacio Mendoza relived the moment by humming a few bars: "Da da da Dum da Dum da Dum da da . . ."

He was interrupted by the graduate student with the Frisbee who was getting smashed. "*Casablanca*!" the kid said. "Paul Henreid!"

"No, *estupido*!" Ignacio Mendoza thundered. "*Casablanca* was . . ." And breaking into lyrics he sang: "You must remember thees. A kees is steell a kees, a sigh ees just a sigh!"

"Same movie, but Paul Henreid sang the other one," the kid with the Frisbee insisted.

"Come, Czech!" Ignacio Mendoza roared. "We are getting out of thees Meeckey Mouse place! Call your waiter!"

Mario Villalobos caught up with them as they were climbing the steps, very unsteadily. The Bad Czech and Ignacio Mendoza were arm in arm. Hans struggled along behind them. His pastel necktie hung like a noose from his skinny neck.

"Where're you going?" Mario Villalobos shouted from the bottom of the landing.

"We're goin to the open house," The Bad Czech said, winking about as subtly as a left jab to the mouth. "We're gonna meet the *faculty* with my friend Nacho here."

"Take a *good* look around, understand?"

"Yeah, yeah, yeah," Hans mumbled.

"Meet me at the wine and cheese table in an hour," Mario Villalobos ordered.

"Who ees that person?" Ignacio Mendoza asked The Bad Czech.

"He's one a my headwaiters," The Bad Czech said. "They're all alike. Bossy types. I humor him cause ya can't find good help these days, Nacho."

When they got outside the Athenaeum, Hans began throwing his arms up in the air and taking deep breaths. They started across the campus past the student dorms where so many famous Caltech pranks were perpetrated by very creative young minds, toward the amphitheater where Mario Villalobos had conjured up his lie that would fly. When they arrived at Mead Laboratory, Hans was tired and cranky.

There were hundreds of people there for open house, in small and large groups, roaming through four buildings that housed chemistry laboratories.

First, Ignacio Mendoza took them to one of the teaching laboratories, a glass-walled instrument room full of visitors. The tourists stood in several groups listening to various students and faculty members demonstrating chromatographs, melting-point apparatus and other equipment. The shapes and structure of tubing connected with some of the devices delighted The Bad Czech.

"All them tubes goin up and down and around! Like the old Rube Goldberg cartoons. I like stuff like that. It's pretty."

"I can see you are a man of sensitivity," Ignacio Mendoza said.

"I'm feeling better," Hans said, "but I'm getting hungry. I'm going back where the wine and cheese is. I'll catch ya later."

"There ees nothing but Meeckey Mouse women there," Ignacio Mendoza warned.

"So what's wrong with big ears and a few whiskers?" The K-9 cop leered. "Ya stay till midnight, they all look good."

"Go on, but keep your *eyes* open," The Bad Czech said.

"Eyes open for what?" Ignacio Mendoza asked, when Hans was gone.

"He falls asleep all the time," The Bad Czech said. "Can't take him anywheres."

Next, the Peruvian chemist took The Bad Czech to Noyes Laboratory, where they joined a queue of people watching laser spectroscopy in a small room.

"Thees shall be an attempt to understand the nature of the interaction between light and matter," Ignacio Mendoza said to The Bad Czech, who got really excited watching the ultra-short pulse-lasers used to excite molecules in different phases.

"These things could make great weapons for cops and people like that!" The Bad Czech said. "Burn the freaking eyes outa some a these pukes. You know, we had . . . I mean, I *read* about a couple a Cuban boat people down in Los Angeles shot at some cops last month while they was robbin a market. When they get to trial they claim they're just poor hungry refugees tryin to steal food for their families. Sure. The food is kept in the *safe*? That's where the cops found them. Lasers like this, you could shoot right through a wall and burn the bastards up. Outa sight!"

The Bad Czech was next led by Ignacio Mendoza toward the solar photochemistry demonstration. Ignacio Mendoza said, "I myself am exploring the chemical processes occurring on a variety of catalytic surfaces."

"Can you do pretty experiments like they did with the lasers?"

"Maybe you will like the next demonstration," Ignacio Mendoza said. "Eet's very pretty."

"No lasers?"

"No, but they are trying to effect a practical and efficient production of hydrogen and other fuel from water. You understand, eef eet could be done by producing a high yield, the Pacific Ocean would be a gas station!"

"Primo!" The Bad Czech said.

"The Middle East could return to being a place to raise goats and date palms. Not worth fighting for. I hope you agree that we have had enough bourgeois wars?"

"I had enough, Nacho. I was in Nam. My partner Cecil Higgins was in Korea. He had enough too."

"You are not the sole owner of your restaurants?"

"Well, my partner owns about three of em. What's goin on in this room?" he asked, to change the subject as they joined a throng of people.

"Thees shall be Dr. Harry Gray's group," Ignacio Mendoza said. "The research group deals weeth the synthesis of compounds containing rhodium and platinum and tungsten and so forth, which have the ability to capture sunlight and use the energy to produce fuels."

"Oh, that's pretty!" The Bad Czech cried, as he watched the chemist instructing one of the tourists on how to jiggle a test tube in a demonstration of chemiluminescence.

Two molecules were reacting to generate a new molecule which was so excited that it dumped off light. It had a beautiful luminescence which reminded The Bad Czech of a heightened version of the neon glow on the face of The Gooned-out Vice Cop.

Then The Bad Czech noticed that Professor Harry Gray was tall and had very dark hair and dark-rimmed glasses. He looked younger than the man outside Dagmar Duffy's apartment house, but then, the light was not good in this room. If he was wearing a false moustache . . .

"Is that guy a regular around here?" he whispered to Ignacio Mendoza.

"He ees the chairman of chemistry," Ignacio Mendoza said.

"A high-powered guy?"

"Yes."

"He ever been known to do anything . . . violent?"

Ignacio Mendoza looked quizzically at The Bad Czech and said, "You have a great eenterest een violence, my friend."

"Can I meet him later and hear him talk? I mean, talk to him?"

"At the wine and cheese reception. I weel be pleased to make you acquainted. Shall we go on to the next exhibit?"

And while Ignacio Mendoza and The Bad Czech moseyed across the campus in what turned out to be a balmy California night, Mario Villalobos decided wisely that he had had much more than enough to drink, and so had Lupe Luna. The two of them were in the lighted garden sampling cheese and strawberries when Mario Villalobos saw Hans staggering with a glass of white wine toward the reception area, where a quartet of students was playing chamber music. There were two violins, a viola and a cellist who looked like he was wearing a fright wig.

Hans sat down hardly noticing the music, very occupied in trying to suck a piece of strawberry out of his molar. Then he noticed a middle-aged man in a pinstripe suit holding a glass of champagne.

He stood perhaps twenty feet from the patio near a camellia bush, quietly humming the Bach melody while the students played. The man's hair was not black but gray. He was rather tall, well built, and was perhaps fifty-five years old. The pinstripe in his suit was subtle, but a man who liked pinstripe might also wear chalk stripes like the man in front of Dagmar Duffy's. Hans pulled himself together, stood up and strolled toward the camellias.

"Like the music?" the K-9 cop asked, sipping at his wine, trying to act sober.

The man nodded.

"I like classical music," the K-9 cop said, not knowing Dvořák from the Doobie Brothers. "Like, uh, Beethoven's my favorite."

"Some people might say that Beethoven wasn't a classicist," the man said, moving away and strolling toward the wine and cheese table.

The voice! Maybe, Hans thought. Maybe! Hans started to feel a little more sober. He pushed the knot on his necktie closer to his skinny neck and tried to tuck his shirt in. There might be some police work to do after all.

By the time The Bad Czech and Ignacio Mendoza reached the basement of Crellin Laboratory, the monster cop was running out of steam. He had pumped the Peruvian professor with about as much subtlety as he was capable of mustering, and had seen about six members of the faculty who were possibles but no one he was very certain about. He was also getting tired of visiting the various demonstrations, even if some of them were pretty. He was disappointed that he hadn't found anything else that offered promise that in the future, cops were going to have better weapons with which to preserve order and keep the peace—by blasting lots of puke bags into teeny bits.

"You might find the next one to your liking, Czech," Ignacio Mendoza said. "NMR spectroscopy ees one of the best ways to analyze chemical compounds."

"Yeah, sounds like fun," The Bad Czech said.

"Under a very high magnetic field all the protons een a molecule can be looked at. You understand that the nuclei een molecules have tiny magnetic moments? The spectrometer can be used to monitor structural changes een a molecule. Eet's like stepping out to the street and being able to see whether a stoplight ees red or green. Thees ees the most sensitive spectrometer een the world. There ees a very very powerful magnetic field, so leave your watch outside the room. Me, I don't wear one."

"Okay, Nacho," The Bad Czech said, taking off his watch and giving it to a student who was on duty.

They followed a group of seven visitors into the small room.

"Any chemist who needs to determine the structure of a molecule weel use the spectrometer," Ignacio Mendoza said. "The powerful magnetic field could damage your watch. There are stories of janitors trying to clean up around a spectrometer and their vacuum gets pulled right eento the magnet and topples eet."

It was a shiny metal cylinder about the size of The Bad Czech's apartment-size refrigerator. He was disappointed with the magnet because he thought it would look different. It weighed less than a ton, depending upon whether or not it was filled with helium, and squatted in the middle of a small basement laboratory. It was tied off at the top and affixed to the ceiling because of California earthquakes.

"I was hopin it was shaped like a big horseshoe magnet," The Bad Czech said. "I thought we could play with it. You know, like make a hairpin fly across the room?"

"Chemists like to use gases contained in heavy cylinders," Ignacio Mendoza explained. "And they say once a cylinder on a cart was drawn right eento the magnet."

"Can we go get somethin to eat, Nacho?" The Bad Czech asked. "I'm gettin hungry."

By this time Mario Villalobos had said good night to a very tipsy Lupe Luna, who had to be driven home by another secretary.

The detective had trouble finding Hans, who had followed the pinstripe suit through two of the laboratory exhibits and back to the reception area.

"Mario!" the K-9 cop said when the detective located him. "That guy's a *maybe*! I already found out he's a member of the chemistry division. And his voice is *close*. I dunno. I'd like the Czech to hear him."

"Where's the Czech?"

"I left him with that goofy professor. Where's the skirt?"

"I let her go home." He sighed. "Business is business."

"Here comes the campus couple now," Hans said to Mario Villalobos, who turned and saw The Bad Czech and Ignacio Mendoza, still arm in arm, strolling across the lighted walkway toward the wine and cheese table.

"Hey, Mario!" The Bad Czech called. "You should go over to them laboratories. Just like *Star Trek* and Disneyland. They got some *pretty* stuff over there."

"Could I have a word with you in private?" Mario Villalobos asked.

"Grab us a couple glasses a wine, Nacho," The Bad Czech said, "and get me a big dish full a cheese and strawberries and grapes and apples and lots and lots a crackers and Goldfish and anything else ya can find. I'll join ya in a few minutes. I want ya to introduce me to a few professors."

"Have any luck?" Mario Villalobos asked after he got the monster cop and Hans away from the milling throngs of people.

"The head a this chemical division is a suspect, far as I'm concerned," The Bad Czech whispered. "Name a Harry Gray. And I seen some others that . . . Hey, *there's* the guy!"

Mario Villalobos saw a tall man with nearly black wavy hair and dark-framed glasses standing with a group of people who were listening to the chamber music.

"He's about six-foot-two," Mario Villalobos said. "I thought you guys decided the guy wasn't over six feet?"

"He ain't that tall, is he?" The Bad Czech asked.

"Nobody seems tall to someone that looks like he was built by a mad scientist, for chrissake!" Hans said. "*Course* he's tall. I don't think it's him. But it *might* be him, Mario."

"Go listen to his voice, Hans," Mario Villalobos said. "We gotta get something outa this night besides a hangover. This fruitcake investigation's making me tired."

"Okay, but see the *other* guy, Mario? The guy over there by that nut case friend of the Czech's? The guy in the pinstripe suit? That's the one that I want the Czech to hear his voice. He's the most likely, I think. He could a been wearing a black wig the day we saw him."

"Okay. I'll talk to mine. You talk to yours," The Bad Czech said.

The monster cop lumbered over toward the man in the pinstripe suit. The man had an aquiline, refined face and seemed a bit standoffish. Nothing like the jovial chairman of the division, whom The Bad Czech could now see talking to Ignacio Mendoza while the K-9 cop lurked around behind them, about as subtle as Ludwig would have been in the same assignment.

The man in the pinstripe suit didn't seem anxious to chat, and he nodded politely from time to time to several of the people milling around. He seemed most interested in being alone and listening to music.

The Bad Czech said to him, "Kin you tell me where I kin find the john?"

"Right through that door," the man said. "First door on your left."

"Thanks," The Bad Czech said and, instead of going in the direction of the rest room, wheeled and ran back to Mario Villalobos, who shook his head and looked heavenward.

"Czech, make it less *obvious*!" Mario Villalobos said. "Was it him?"

"It might be!" The Bad Czech said. "The voice was *real* close, Mario!"

"Go listen to him some more," Mario Villalobos said. "I wanna talk to your friend Mendoza about the guy. Who did you tell Mendoza I was, another busboy?"

"Headwaiter," The Bad Czech said.

"Okay, go listen to that guy some more, and . . . Goddamnit! look at that freaking Hans!"

The K-9 cop was skulking backwards on one side of a tall azalea bush while Professors Ignacio Mendoza and Harry Gray stood on the other side making small talk.

"This looks like a Pink Panther movie!" Mario Villalobos moaned.

"I told ya we wasn't detectives, Mario," The Bad Czech said. "Whaddaya expect? I never had to pretend I wasn't a cop before!"

"Okay, okay, just go take another *close* look and try to listen to him talk. I'll find out from Mendoza who he is."

When Hans came running back into the shadows to report to Mario Villalobos, he said, "I found out two things. That guy Harry Gray likes country music. One of his favorites is Conway Twitty singing 'Tight Fittin Jeans.' "

"And what *else* did you find out?" Mario Villalobos sighed wearily.

"That it ain't him. The voice is different."

"Are you sure?"

"I'm sure. And he's too young. The other guy was at least fifty."

"Okay, we'll concentrate on pinstripes."

The K-9 cop ran back to the reception area, but found The Bad Czech already in conversation with Professors Harry Gray and Ignacio Mendoza. Hans was feeling a tiny bit sober, what with all the running around, so he did the expected thing: he had another glass of wine.

The Bad Czech was saying to Harry Gray, "You're pretty tall, ain't ya, Professor?"

"Not as tall as you," the chemist said, looking puzzled.

"Your hair's pretty dark," The Bad Czech said.

"Not as dark as yours," the chemist said, shooting a *very* puzzled look at Ignacio Mendoza, who by now was used to his new friend's eccentric questions.

The K-9 cop walked among them just then and said, under his breath, "Czech, Mario wants to talk to you and your pal about Mister Pinstripes. And I don't mean Joe DiMaggio."

The Bad Czech nodded and said, "C'mon, Nacho, I want ya to meet my headwaiter, Mario." Then to the tall chemist he said, "Dr. Gray, this here's Hans. We work together. Dr. Gray here's the head a the whole damned chemistry shebang."

Suddenly Hans got *very* excited. This guy might not be a suspect, but he was just the man the K-9 cop was looking for. He said, "Hey, Dr. Gray, you probably can mix just about any kind a formula there is, can't ya?"

"I don't know about *any* kind," the chairman of the chemistry division said, studying the skinny drunk in the leisure suit.

"Listen, Doc, let's suppose a person had a . . . *problem*. Like he was a real macho guy but all of a sudden a strange thing starts happening to him. This is hard to explain. Let's go over and get ourselves a few glasses a wine and maybe we can talk better."

Meanwhile, The Bad Czech and Mario Villalobos were being forced to come semi-clean with Professor Ignacio Mendoza.

"You are a police officer?" Ignacio Mendoza exclaimed, after examining the identity card of the detective.

"Yeah and *he* carries one too," Mario Villalobos said. "We're working on this very large jewel theft, you see. It involves a Caltech professor who was out with a young lady not his wife and . . ."

"You *don't* own all the restaurants, Czech?" the chemist asked, scratching his red cockatoo topknot.

"You ain't mad at me, are ya, Nacho?" The Bad Czech said boozily. "If I *did* have any money I'd give it to ya for research. But my three ex-wives can outspend Saudi Arabia."

"Let's go for a walk, Professor," Mario Villalobos said, "and I'll explain the jewel theft and what we need here."

And while Mario Villalobos was trying the lie that would fly on Professor Ignacio Mendoza, The Bad Czech got himself a couple of glasses of red wine. He didn't like it very much. He tried a glass of white wine and gulped it down. He switched to champagne. He wished he could find one of the postdocs he met in the basement bar. He wished he was *back* in the basement bar. They served lousy drinks up here. To pass the time he ate another apple and half a pound of cheddar cheese. He could see Hans gesturing wildly at Professor Harry Gray.

"C'mon, Doc!" Hans was *pleading* with the tall chemist. "You *must* have a chemical warehouse with everything in it!"

"Hans, I'm not a medical doctor," Harry Gray said. "I think it might be a problem for a . . . psychiatrist?"

"No no no!" the drunken K-9 cop cried in utter frustration. "It's just a little temporary thing that I know could be fixed up with some *special* chemicals. Keerist! Are you people some a the best in the world, or ain't ya?"

Mario Villalobos and Ignacio Mendoza sat on a concrete bench beneath a California live oak and drank some champagne while Ignacio Mendoza listened to the jewel theft flimflam.

It was then that The Bad Czech came scuttling down the concrete walk in the moonlight yelling, "Hey, Nacho!"

"Over here," Mario Villalobos called, "by the big tree."

When The Bad Czech came puffing to a stop he said, "I left my watch down in the basement."

"Can you remember how to get there?" the chemist asked the monster cop.

"You kidding? All these big buildings look alike."

"Okay," the chemist said. "Back we go. I don't

know why people carry watches anyway. Time ees relative."

Mario Villalobos looked at his watch. It was 9:30. "Why'd you take your watch off?" he asked.

"Because a the big magnet," The Bad Czech said. "It can stop a watch."

The Bad Czech and Ignacio Mendoza were halfway down the walk in the darkness when they heard Mario Villalobos scream: "WHAT BIG MAGNET?"

Five minutes later Ignacio Mendoza, The Bad Czech and Mario Villalobos were locked in a little office in a basement, having a *very* private conversation in which Mario Villalobos was, for the first time at Caltech, telling the *whole* truth about his homicide investigation to a *very* interested chemist.

Every few seconds the detective would pause and consider a very big and very strong magnet. One that could break a wristwatch, and erase the magnetic stripe on a credit card. And most certainly could stop the wearer of a pacemaker dead in his tracks.

TWELVE

The Martian Mouse

The office of Ignacio Mendoza was in a sub-basement. It was there that he chose to think alone, behind locked doors, in impossible clutter. He refused to admit janitors, and his footprints showed _in_ the dust as he paced the floor. He walked three steps in one direction and three back, whirling quirkily at the completion of each three paces. His cockatoo topknot jerked and fluttered, throwing strange shadows on a green chalkboard affixed to the wall. The chalkboard was covered with written formulas. For once, Ignacio Mendoza was silent, and so were Mario Villalobos and The Bad Czech. The cops had confessed the _whole_ truth and were asking for help.

Finally the Peruvian chemist stopped pacing and said, "Why did you not tell the truth from the first? Why all the bull-cheet?"

"Dr. Mendoza, I didn't know _how_ to tell it. I didn't have any evidence. I still don't. I figured that the president of the university might throw me out if I told the truth."

"You suggest that a member of the faculty has murdered a private investigator by using our six-hundred-thousand-dollar spectrometer? And then murdered a

242

prostitute by throwing her off a roof? And ees stalking a fairy to murder heem also? You have no motive whatsoever, and the identity of the professor remains a mystery?"

"That's about it." Mario Villalobos nodded.

"Correct. He would throw you out of the office."

"Are *you* gonna throw us out, Nacho?" The Bad Czech asked.

"That ees what I am contemplating," Ignacio Mendoza said, beginning his pacing again. Three steps to and fro, cockatoo topknot fluttering crazily.

"Is there a bathroom down here, Nacho?" The Bad Czech asked.

"We are below the water table. The johns don't work. Use a beaker." He waved in the general direction of a pile of glass tubes and beakers on a table.

"Just hold it for a while," Mario Villalobos said.

"If I held it last time you wouldn't a met Nacho here!" The Bad Czech said grumpily, "and he's your only chance a gettin somewheres." Then to the chemist he said, "Nacho, sometimes a person shouldn't *know* the whole truth. The whole truth can make ya *sick*. And that's the *truth*."

"Een the final analysis, you are correct, Czech." Ignacio Mendoza pointed one finger heavenward while he addressed the seated cops. "There are two things which eenterest me here. First, that our meeting was no more part of a grand design than the collision of two small stars een the galaxy."

"Because I took a pee on the tree," The Bad Czech noted.

"Exactly. I know precisely that there ees no prime mover een the universe. No *mysterium tremendum*. And I am always looking for ways to prove eet. Secondly, I don't like Meeckey Mouse people, so my choice of friends ees limited een the bourgeois world where-een I function. Therefore. I find a worthy friend perhaps once every ten years." Ignacio Mendoza pulled something out of his pocket and put it in his mouth. He loosened his yellow flowered bow tie and took half a pint of Scotch from a drawer. He swallowed whatever he had put in his mouth, washing it down with booze. He didn't offer the cops any and put the bottle back in the drawer.

"Are you saying that you won't help me?" Mario Villalobos asked.

"Don't tell me what I am saying!" Ignacio Mendoza shouted, his pouting lip glistening in the lamplight. "Only Ignacio Mendoza knows what he ees saying!"

"Sorry, Professor." Mario Villalobos sighed, glancing wearily at The Bad Czech, who was only looking at the drawer that held the bottle of booze.

"Czech," Ignacio Mendoza said, "I believe that you possess a philosopher's heart. Ignacio Mendoza selects you as a friend!" With that the Peruvian chemist marched to the seated cop and placed a hand on one of The Bad Czech's monster shoulders. "You are a poet, Czech. I sense eet." Then he turned to Mario Villalobos and announced, "Sergeant, for the sake of my new friend, Ignacio Mendoza ees at your service!"

Mario Villalobos tried not to show visibly his relief at receiving help—and at having the speech concluded—while the Peruvian posed like Il Duce and smiled down at his big new friend, who only looked at the drawer containing the booze.

"Whadda you think we should do first, Professor?" Mario Villalobos asked.

The scientist resumed his three-step pacing and wheeling, and said, "During the Martian probe we were called to Jet Propulsion Laboratory as consultants when a very strange event occurred that could not be readily explained. You see, they eenjected food from the space vehicle onto the surface of Mars. Eet was converted eento products een a manner that suggested metabolism of the substance witheen a few seconds. Een other words, metabolic processes and oxidation and carbon dioxide release. What organisms must be present! Super life! Everybody was very excited. Eet reminds me of your position, Sergeant. You are looking for the same thing that these scientists were looking for. You are looking for the mouse who ate the cheese."

"So, *did* the Martian mouse eat the cheese?" Mario Villalobos asked.

"Of course not! The only rational chemical theory ees that Mars ees bombarded by ultraviolet radiation from the sun. Radiation we do not get on earth because of the ozone layer. The food was oxidized instantly by a combination of ultraviolet radiation and the special nature of the planet's surface which ees highly oxidizing because of the bombardment. Can I *prove* my theory? Of course not. Perhaps some physicists or astronomers or engineers or biologists are walking around today preferring to believe that the Martian mouse ate the cheese. But I ask you, ees eet rational?"

"So where does that leave me?"

"You have no rational theory on your side. Eet ees preposterous to think that one of our own people would seek to compromise a visiting Soviet scientist. For what? To get the scientist on the staff? The best chemistry een the world ees done een America, and een West Germany and Britain. As a matter of fact, we chemists at Caltech are even accused of being elitist by our colleagues een other divisions. Do you suppose we need the Soviets? There ees no mouse for you here, my friend."

"How do you know my mouse, my *theoretical* mouse, would have to be in the chemistry division, aside from the telephone number in the hooker's book?"

"The NMR spectrometer," he said. "Eet ees primarily a tool of chemists. Others usually know the structure of molecules they work with. When a structure ees already determined, they wouldn't need it."

"Let's forget the motive," Mario Villalobos said. "Pretend that one night an old private eye with a pacemaker kept a date with someone down in that laboratory, and they sat and talked, and the magnetic field played a cha cha on his heart machine and he expired. The person then carried the body up the elevator, put it into a car and dumped it in a motel where maybe the meeting was originally to have taken place. Is any of this implausible? All you people have keys. You can get in at night. In fact, people work in these labs every night."

"But why would he *do* such a thing?"

"He's being blackmailed by the private eye and the hooker. They have pictures of him. The badger game."

"Someone commits *murders* for being caught een a ménage?"

Now it was Mario Villalobos up and pacing. Ignacio Mendoza finally noticed The Bad Czech staring sadly at the desk drawer, so he opened it and took out the bottle of Scotch and a small glass beaker. He handed it to the smiling giant, who poured four ounces into the beaker and was about to put it to his lips, but stopped abruptly.

"Ees okay, Czech, I don't pee in that one," Ignacio Mendoza promised, and The Bad Czech happily guzzled.

"The Russian part's a problem," Mario Villalobos said. "There *had* to be a Russian here last month when Missy and Dagmar had their date with the foreigner."

"When Russians come, we *know* eet," Ignacio Mendoza said, shaking his head.

"Well, what the hell was going on that could have attracted Soviet agents?"

"Nothing whatsoever."

"Jesus Christ!" Mario Villalobos said. "It's hopeless."

"Jesus Christ was just a gifted confidence man," Ignacio Mendoza said to The Bad Czech, who was amusing himself by playing with tubes and beakers, pouring Scotch back and forth into them.

"Okay, Professor, what happened of *any* consequence in the chemistry division that brought in one or more *foreigners* who might have stayed at a downtown hotel rather than a Pasadena hotel?"

"The Pasadena hotels are not much. Lousy dining rooms. The Biltmore downtown has a very good dining room. But then, scientists are not necessarily gourmets."

"Last month," Mario Villalobos pleaded.

"Ees possible that the members of the Nobel Committee have gastronomical requirements which may persuade them to stay een downtown Los Angeles."

"What committee?"

"A very important member of the chemistry committee was here for an address on the chemistry of explosives. Eet didn't tell anything new, but of course, eet was a very popular lecture. Though hardly worth attracting Soviet spies."

"What's the Nobel Prize worth?"

"Worth?"

"In money."

"Two hundred thousand dollars, depending on the value of the Swedish krona."

"Now we're cooking," Mario Villalobos said.

"Lot a guys'd knock ya off for a lot less than that, Mario," The Bad Czech observed.

"How many get Nobel science prizes each year?" Mario Villalobos asked.

"Three to nine, depending on whether eet ees shared. A prize can be shared."

"Is it like winning . . . Wimbledon?" Mario Villalobos asked. "I mean, you don't get television commercials, but can it be turned into *more* money?"

That jiggled the cockatoo topknot. "Money! Just like a cop! Bourgeois mentality!"

"Money is the motive in badger games, Professor, at least in my experience. Can it be turned into more money? How about lectures? Could a winner command a big fee?"

Whatever Ignacio Mendoza had downed with his Scotch was taking effect. His pupils were clearly dilated and he was standing mannequin-stiff, rocking on heels and toes, his hands behind his back. He looked as if he might go straight up in the air like a hummingbird.

"All right!" he said with overwhelming disgust. "We shall be bourgeois for a moment, like cops." He pulled open *another* drawer, withdrew *another* half pint, cracked it open and handed the bottle to The Bad Czech, who was ecstatic. "A man gets the Nobel Prize and decides to make money. A man who has been doing fine work for a long time and getting lecture expenses when he was lucky. Now with the prize he can command three to five thousand dollars a lecture. He does four lectures a week, yet thees ees merely mad money. He ees a celebrity with total peer recognition. Now he can set up a multinational company. Venture capital people come to him. Raising money ees trivial for a Nobel laureate. There ees a man from Harvard, for example, who now heads a fifty-million-dollar company. Does that supply for you the bourgeois motive that you need?"

"That's definitely worth killing for!" Mario Villalobos said.

"That ees *not* worth killing for and not worth dying for!" Ignacio Mendoza bellowed, kneading his fingers, his eyes popping.

"The Russian connection," Mario Villalobos said. "Give me the names of a few professors of chemistry who're *hot* right now."

"Hot?"

"Hot candidates for big casino. For the Nobel Prize. Do you have one here at Caltech?"

"Only one. He ees working on actinide photochemistry and . . ."

"What's he look like?"

"Your friend was talking to him."

"The pinstripe suit?" The Bad Czech cried.

"That one." Ignacio Mendoza nodded. "Hees name ees Feldman. And he has done some famous work on the chemistry of electronically excited organoactinide molecules."

"And what's the practical application of that?" Mario Villalobos asked.

"Separating isotopes for nuclear chemistry and many other applications."

"*Nuclear* applications?" Mario Villalobos noted.

"You are back to the Russians!" Ignacio Mendoza shouted. "You are making Ignacio Mendoza angry!"

The Bad Czech, who was leaning his head back against the wall, opened one eye and said, "Have a drink, Nacho. Don't get mad."

"The scientific community *frowns* on exploiters!" Ignacio Mendoza cried, his dilated brown eyes sparking. "The Nobel laureate who would accept a chairmanship een the research division of a multinational company, when he could be doing split-brain research or curing epilepsy, would be *speet* on by his peers! Yes, there are a few who have done eet, but there are also those who gave away the prize for the resettlement of refugees! Perhaps the Meeckey Mouse young men of today might exploit eet, but the prize does not go to young men. Eet ees given ten or twenty years *after* your best work can be seen een perspective!"

"So, who *else* is a hot candidate for this year's prize?"

"No one else here at Caltech, I don't believe. There ees a man at Stanford perhaps. No one can say for sure. Eet ees a closely guarded secret. There are no leaks een the Nobel operation. A very elaborate procedure goes on all year. They screen hundreds of applicants from all over the world."

"Don't you try to promote your own people?"

"Of course!" Ignacio Mendoza said. "There ees politicking as to fields and subfields. But to badger our colleagues? To write letters to the Nobel Committee? Thees ees considered, how you say, bush league. Eet would be very important to know which field of chemistry was going to be chosen so that the proper candidate could be promoted by our people. But eet ees a complete secret."

"How many members on the Nobel Committee?"

"For chemistry? Five. They have been members for ten to fifteen years. They have great power."

"And you had one of the chemistry committee here giving a talk?"

"They say he ees the most influential committee member."

"Describe the Stanford competitor of your hot candidate, Feldman."

"What do you mean?"

"Could he be middle-aged, fair-haired, with milky white skin?"

"Hees name ees Van Zandt," Ignacio Mendoza said. "I have a photo of him."

The Peruvian professor rummaged through the clutter on one of the tables and produced a Caltech newspaper which had a front-page photo of ten men in suits, including himself, toasting each other at a banquet. The man who stood next to the chairman of the division was, Mario Villalobos hoped, a man that Dagmar Duffy would recognize.

"He *does* fit the description of the guy in the badger game!" the detective said.

"He *might* be considered for the prize over Feldman eef the prize were going to be given for organic photo-chemistry," the scientist said.

Mario Villalobos was smiling slightly. "Professor Feldman hired a private investigator who was a science buff and knew people at this university. He planned the extortion setup."

"Preposterous!" the chemist said.

"Okay, here's how it goes." The detective was cooking now. "Your Professor Feldman knows of some unusual sexual preferences of his Stanford rival, Van Zandt. You boys have attended conferences together for years and there've been a few rumors from time to time."

"I never heard the rumor."

"Feldman did. And he hired a local private eye to set up his rival Van Zandt in a little badger game with a little kinky sex and it was recorded by the private eye on film. The private eye is supposed to forward the picture to the Nobel Committee, who surely wouldn't give the prize to a man with such pictures of him floating around."

"Preposterous!" Ignacio Mendoza said.

"Don't you see? The private eye Lester Beemer got to thinking like a bourgeois cop. He got maybe two thousand bucks for setting up and photographing the action in the badger game. He got to computing the value of a Nobel Prize just like we did. How Professor Feldman could turn it into *real* bucks and how those bucks could be shared with him and Missy Moonbeam, his little conspirator and girl friend. So they turned the tables on your Professor Feldman, who hired them. They threatened to expose his game to the university and the Nobel Committee if he didn't get very generous when he won the prize."

"Eef he won the prize."

"Yes."

"And the Russians?"

"It was just some wacky private joke between Missy Moonbeam and the private eye. I don't know."

"So Doctor Feldman, knowing of the private detective's pacemaker, entices him to the room with the spectrometer?"

"Yes."

"And then he hunts down the prostitute and eliminates her?"

"Yes."

"Well, een that you have such a near-perfect theory, I can supply the last piece to your puzzle. Feldman was born een Odessa. He ees a Russian Jew who came to America as a small boy."

"That's it, then! It was a little joke between Missy and Lester Beemer. They called their employer their *Russian agent*!"

"And now Richard Feldman wants to murder the fairy, the last person he feels can expose the badger game conspiracy?"

"Yes, that's it!"

"I have only one thing to say: YOU ARE FULL OF BULL-CHEET!"

"Please, Dr. Mendoza, can I borrow your newspaper? To show the picture of the Stanford chemist to Dagmar Duffy? And I'd like to get Professor Feldman's address and phone number from you. Is it in your Rolodex?"

"At your service, Sergeant," Ignacio Mendoza said mockingly.

Mario Villalobos was exhausted but elated when he shook The Bad Czech awake in his chair.

"I'll return the newspaper," Mario Villalobos said, writing Professor Richard Feldman's number. "If I get a positive identification of Dr. Van Zandt as the badger game victim, I'll be a little closer to something concrete."

Suddenly the Peruvian chemist looked as though he was coming down to earth in a hurry. His eyelids were drooping. "I shall see you later, Sergeant. This ees bull-cheet, but eet's more fun than a Pac-man game."

When The Bad Czech and Mario Villalobos found Hans, the K-9 cop was sitting morosely on a bench, covered with wine stains. There were a dozen people still lingering at the reception table but the waiters and bartenders were cleaning up. The musicians had called it a night and lights were being turned off in the garden.

Professor Harry Gray, chairman of the chemistry division, almost got away, but Hans spotted him and scurried down the walk after him, grabbing a sleeve.

"I gotta go," the chemist said to the skinny K-9 cop, who was holding on for dear life. "Let go!"

"Not until you help me, Doc," Hans warned, and his eyes were as deranged as The Bad Czech's. "I only want you to get something from the lab to keep it stiff! That ain't asking too much!"

"Let me *outa* here!" the chemist cried.

"Not until you help me!"

"Okay, okay, let me go and I'll tell you what to do."

"Yeah?" Hans said hopefully, releasing the scientist's sleeve.

"Shellac it!" the chemist cried, and ran like hell through the darkness.

The telephone rang a dozen times before a sleepy male voice answered. "Hello," the voice said.

"Is your name Howard?" Mario Villalobos asked.

"Yeah, who's this?"

"Lemme speak to Dagmar. It's urgent."

"Is this Arnold?" the voice said testily. "Dagmar don't want nothing to do with you."

"Tell him it's Sergeant Villalobos, goddamnit!" the detective said.

A moment later Dagmar Duffy said, "Sergeant? Did you catch the guy that's after me?"

"No, but I'm getting closer. I want you to meet me at your apartment in twenty minutes."

"Meet ya? I'm not dressed!"

"Get dressed."

"I'm scared to go there."

"Have Howard go with you."

"He's zoned out. He can't go."

"Drive over there and you'll see my detective car in front. I'll be waiting for you. Now get on it."

"You *sure* you'll be there?"

"I'm standing by the Pasadena Freeway right now. I'll be there in fifteen minutes. Move!"

Ten minutes before 1:00 A.M. Dagmar Duffy was driving his boyfriend's beat-up VW bug down Santa Monica Boulevard, looking very unhappy. He was relieved to see Mario Villalobos' detective car parked in front of his apartment house.

Dagmar Duffy got out of the car and trotted. His hands, held in front like a rabbit, flapped at the wrist as he ran. "I hurried fast as I could!" he said. "Who's that sleeping in your car?"

"The two cops you met here the other day."

Dagmar Duffy peered through the darkness into the Plymouth. The Bad Czech was lying down, jammed into the back seat. Hans was snoring in front with his knees up on the dashboard.

"What's so important I had to get outa bed?"

"You got me outa bed yesterday. Come on."

"Where we going?"

"Up to your room."

"What for?"

"I want you to give me your key. I'm sending these two home in the car and I'm staying."

"With me?"

"No, you already have a boyfriend," Mario Villalobos said. "I'm sending you home too. I don't wanna take a chance that I might miss my man if he comes back looking for you. I'm gonna set up a proper stakeout tomorrow, but for tonight, I'm staying."

"Won't he be too scared after seeing the cops yesterday?"

"As far as he knows those two cops were just writing parking tickets. He'll be back because he wants to kill you. He thinks you were in on the scheme of Missy Moonbeam to extort him."

"Is he a Russian?"

"No. He's an American. So is the man with the phony accent that you and Missy tricked with. That's who I want you to identify. I have a newspaper picture of him. Let's go inside."

While the detective and Dagmar Duffy walked into the apartment house, a man in a dark suit with a tweed cap and a moustache stood outside the door of Dagmar Duffy's apartment on the third floor. He put his ear to the door and listened. Then he walked down the hall toward a window which overlooked the Normandie side of the building. He looked down, and then he walked back to the door and listened again. When he heard the elevator being activated in the lobby, he crept down the hall to the stairway, unscrewed the stairway light, and backed down the stairs crouching in the darkness. He quickly stretched upon his hands a pair of surgical gloves. Then he withdrew a small syringe from his pocket.

Mario Villalobos couldn't help feeling satisfied when he pulled out the folded newspaper and showed the picture of ten grinning scientists to Dagmar Duffy.

Dagmar Duffy looked at the picture, held it closer to the light sconce in the elevator, and worried Mario Villalobos with his silence. Finally he said, "Yeah, it's him. He was a real gentleman. I hope he don't get in trouble."

With his biggest grin of the week, Mario Villalobos said, "Gimme the key to your room."

He was only two seconds late following Dagmar Duffy out of the elevator when the doors opened. The man in the shadows saw the little man with the blond perm and moved a bit soon. Mario Villalobos caught the movement with his peripheral vision and yelled, "Hey!"

The man in the pinstripe suit bolted for the staircase but stumbled on the first step. The detective leaped onto the man's back, trying to draw his service revolver. The man was strong and agile and sober. He spun and threw a wild left-handed punch that hit the staircase wall, causing him to scream. But he hit the detective square in the face with his elbow and then with his good hand punched him on the side of the neck, knocking him down the stairs to the bottom of the landing.

While Mario Villalobos lay on his back looking loopily at Dagmar Duffy, who stood at the top of the landing screaming in terror, he got a subliminal flash. *Déjà vu.* He staggered to his feet and ran down the stairs after his attacker. He descended only five stairs. Then the back spasm hit. He was down on the floor yelling about as loud as Dagmar Duffy up above him.

By the time Dagmar Duffy got The Bad Czech and Hans awake, along with half the apartment house, the back spasm had subsided enough to allow Mario Villalobos to hobble up the stairs. It would of course have been the logical time to call the Pasadena police to intercept and arrest Professor Feldman before he got back to his home.

It would have been the logical thing to do except for something that occurred when The Bad Czech and Hans got Mario Villalobos into a chair inside Dagmar Duffy's apartment. Dagmar Duffy took another look at the newspaper photo which Mario Villalobos had thrown on the bed, while the detective lit a cigarette with shaking hands and examined the syringe his suspect had dropped.

"You were right about the Dutch accent," Mario Villalobos said to Dagmar Duffy. "His name's Van Zandt, so he probably used an accent he was familiar with. No doubt he's descended from Dutch parents."

"We shoulda had Ludwig here," Hans said.

"Why're the names wrong under the picture?" Dagmar Duffy asked.

"What?"

"His name's Jan Larsson, according to this picture."

"Lemme see that!" Mario Villalobos said, crying out in pain from the wrenched back as he tried to jump up.

"Want me to call Pasadena P.D. and have them

stake out Feldman's house?" The Bad Czech asked, while Mario Villalobos gaped at the picture.

"This guy here!" the detective said, pointing at the Stanford chemist Van Zandt.

"No, *that* ain't him," Dagmar Duffy said. "It's *this* guy. The guy right in the middle that they're all toasting. It says his name's Jan Larsson."

"The Nobel Committee member?"

"You want me to call the Pasadena P.D.?" The Bad Czech asked.

"I gotta get Feldman's house on the phone!" Mario Villalobos said. He furiously dialed the number he had gotten from Ignacio Mendoza. When a woman answered he said, "Mrs. Feldman?"

"Yes?" she answered.

"I'm sorry to disturb you, but this is the police department and we've found a wallet belonging to your husband. It may have been stolen by a burglar."

"My God!" she said. "Richard, it's the police! They've found a wallet of yours!"

A groggy male voice came on the phone saying, "Yes? What is it?"

"Talk to him!" Mario Villalobos whispered to The Bad Czech, holding his hand over the mouthpiece. "Is it the guy in the pinstripe suit?"

"Uh, Mister Feldman. I think we have your wallet," The Bad Czech said.

"My wallet? But that's impossible. My wallet's right here on the nightstand. I haven't lost a wallet!" the voice said.

"Is this Henry Feldman?" The Bad Czech asked.

"No, I'm Richard Feldman!" the voice said testily.

"Real sorry," The Bad Czech said. "Wrong Feldman. You can go back to sleep."

He clicked the receiver down and handed the phone to the detective. "That's the guy in the pinstripe suit, Mario. He's got an unusual voice. It's him."

"Then who the hell attacked me?" Mario Villalobos cried. Suddenly he scared the crap out of Dagmar Duffy by yelling, "Nacho Mendoza was right! I'M FULL OF BULL-CHEET!"

When they were helping the emotionally depleted detective into the car, and Dagmar was waving bye-bye, it occurred to Mario Villalobos who Dagmar Duffy had reminded him of in that moment of *déjà vu,* after he was knocked loopy. Standing on top of the landing, his blond perm bouncing, one hand pressed to his mouth and the other outstretched while he screamed, Dagmar Duffy looked *exactly* like Fay Wray in *King Kong.*

THIRTEEN

Mysterium Tremendum

Mario Villalobos couldn't sleep, not a wink. He lay in bed twitching, with a heating pad under his wrenched back. Both eyes were swollen and marbled and his nose felt fractured. He had drunk so much coffee that he could hardly close his eyes. He could only twitch, and wait for the dawn.

He was at his desk very early. He was shaved, showered, combed, and wore a fresh suit. He thought he looked acceptable.

"You look like *hell*!" the detective lieutenant said upon seeing him. "You look like the phantom of the opera."

The detective bureau was closed on weekends, but given the extraordinary events of the previous evening, the lieutenant was called from home to meet Mario Villalobos for a briefing. Ditto for a crime lab forensic chemist who bitched for half an hour about working on Saturday. He gave a preliminary report that the syringe contained sodium cyanide and that unfortunately it was an ordinary syringe, sold in any first-class pharmacy.

It was noon before his lieutenant was completely informed about the sad state of affairs. When Mario Villalobos was finished, the lieutenant said, "That's *it* for roaming around alone at night all over Pasadena and Hollywood."

"Whadda you mean, that's *it?*"

"That's *it*, Mario. You can stay on this with Chip and Melody helping you, but no more playing solitaire."

It was a relief, actually. His reach had too far exceeded his grasp. He was too tired to sleep. Too tired to think. He was wired to a short circuit from coffee, booze, cigarettes and exhaustion. He was *inadequate*.

"Maybe it *would* be good to give it a rest," Mario Villalobos said.

"Go home," the lieutenant nodded. "And rest your back and put some ice on your kisser and go to sleep for a couple days. See you Monday."

By 1:00 P.M. Mario Villalobos was in bed trying to sleep. He couldn't remember when he'd been so tired. He couldn't remember when he'd been so embarrassed, nor when he'd been such a failure. He couldn't remember when he'd felt so sorry for himself.

At 1:30 P.M. he switched on the radio, turning from the Dodger network to a local station that played music of the forties, day and night for lots of people like Mario Villalobos, obsessed with Time.

At 2:00 P.M. he was in his private car on the Pasadena Freeway heading for Caltech, dizzily thinking of all the poor sharks in the sea. Never able to rest. To stop moving was to die of anoxia.

Saturday and even Sunday were by no means days of rest at the university. There were always research groups at work. In fact, some scientists worked only at night due to the nature of their experiments or by personal preference.

He made inquiries of a group of postdocs and found Ignacio Mendoza in a lecture hall in Noyes Laboratory. The lecture hall contained some ninety theater seats in six graduated rows descending steeply to a lecture platform.

Ignacio Mendoza, dressed in a pink and green aloha shirt, gym shorts, sandals and black socks, was addressing his research group while they ate Kentucky Fried Chicken. The pink flamingos on the aloha shirt slithered on a field of slimy moss. The shirt was greasy from food, chemicals and perspiration.

Behind the scientist were three enormous green chalkboards rising twenty feet, nearly to the ceiling. The chalkboards were covered with exotic chemical formulas, and Ignacio Mendoza, who was holding a pointer as long as a deep-sea fishing pole, could not have reached the top ones with it. That problem was solved when the Peruvian chemist touched a switch and the chalkboards were raised or lowered on a mechanical slide.

Ignacio Mendoza did not see Mario Villalobos enter. The students came and went as they pleased during Ignacio Mendoza's informal presentation on solar energy conversion.

The Peruvian chemist was saying, "A particularly intriguing redox-active energetic species ees the delta to delta-star singlet excited state of octachlorodirhenate dianion, whose energy ees one-point-seven-five electron volts and whose excited state lifetime ees one hundred and forty nanoseconds een acetonitrile solution at twenty-five degrees centigrade. Various electron acceptors such as tetracyanoethylene, chloranil, and the phosphorus-twelve tungstate trianion, quench the delta to delta-star luminescence een solutions, thereby producing the octachlorodirhenate anion and the reduced acceptor."

Mario Villalobos liked the sound of it. It was mysterious and hopeful and soothing like the pop music of his youth, music which lately had begun to call forth nostalgic sentimental moments he was afraid to indulge, given the wreckage and waste of his life.

The informal lecture was over thirty minutes after the detective arrived. For the first time in thirty-two hours he had managed to doze a bit. He remained in his seat until all the students had gone. Ignacio Mendoza was gathering his papers when he noticed the detective sitting in the top row of the elevated lecture hall.

"You have returned, Sergeant Villalobos," the Peruvian said.

"Yes."

"You have been playing football since last night?"

"I had an accident, Professor. I ran into the killer I've been looking for."

"Yes! Go on!"

"He beat the crap outa me. It *wasn't* Professor Feldman."

"Of course not. Who was eet?"

"I don't know. He got away. He had a syringe full of sodium cyanide for the little pansy."

"My God!" the chemist said. "I thought eet was *all* bull-cheet!"

"It is."

"But you have *part* of it! A sodium cyanide solution ees the favorite method of suicide for scientists. You are getting somewhere!"

"I don't think so. I'm too beat-up and tired and inadequate. I'm ready to use the old 'police are baffled but an arrest is imminent' gag and let the whole thing slide."

"What do you mean, slide?"

"The guy that got sucked into the badger game wasn't the Stanford Nobel candidate. It was Jan Larsson, the Nobel Committee member."

"My God!" Ignacio Mendoza cried.

"For a guy that's so sure He doesn't exist, you sure call His name a lot," the detective said, lighting a cigarette.

"Ees just an expression," the chemist said. "But Sergeant, that ees fantastic!"

"Naturally I expect you to treat this confidentially."

"Of course! But Sergeant, I cannot believe this. What then? Someone ees trying to influence the committee?"

"You could say *that* for sure," the detective said, rubbing his neck and moving painfully in the seat.

"But Feldman ees the only logical chemistry candidate, Sergeant," the Peruvian exclaimed. "Thees ees madness! We have other men who have done notable work but not approaching Feldman's body of work. Madness!"

"I don't know," Mario Villalobos said, resting his head on the back of the seat. "I'm not thinking too well since he beat me up. Maybe Van Zandt's behind it. Maybe he'd resort to this to win."

"But he's up een Stanford. Not here with access to our NMR spectrometer."

"I know, I know," Mario Villalobos said. "Maybe if I go home and let it alone for a few days and get some sleep . . ."

"Let eet alone? GET SOME SLEEP?" the chemist screamed. "*Estúpido!* Gringo with Hispanic name! You are on the verge of discovery and you talk about sleep? How did you get your Hispanic name? No, don't tell me! I don't even *want* to know!"

Then Mario Villalobos gaped at the Peruvian chemist in his nutty aloha shirt, with his red cockatoo topknot fluttering electrically as he charged up the steps in slapping sandals to the top row of the lecture hall. The scientist took a white capsule out of his pocket and boldly shoved it into the mouth of the astonished detective.

"Here, *gringo!*" the Peruvian thundered. "To help you live up to your noble Hispanic name!"

"What is it?" Mario Villalobos said.

"Swallow eet!" the chemist thundered.

It took three tries before he could get it down. When he did, he said, "If I die before I wake . . ."

"Talk about death later, bourgeois cop!" the scientist shouted, descending back to the podium. "Die when your work ees completed and there ees *time* to die!"

"But I don't *know* what to do next, Professor!" the detective said.

"I don't know! I don't know! That ees what I *hate* about Meeckey Mouse people een this bourgeois world!" the scientist roared, pacing back and forth on the stage at the bottom of the lecture hall. "Ees why I don't own a gun or knife! Think! And you shall know!"

Three steps one way, three steps back. Whirling quirkily. Topknot jumping on his cockatoo's head. His fingers kneaded each other, as though he were weaving the warp and woof of the *mysterium tremendum*. Finally he said, "I am going to write for you a formula that even a Meeckey Mouse bourgeois cop can understand."

He wrote on the blackboard, in letters two feet high: NP = I.

"What's that?" Mario Villalobos asked.

"All the BULL-CHEET you throw at me! To blow my mind!" the chemist shouted up to the detective, his topknot dancing. "Bull-cheet about *money* motivating a scientist to compromise a Nobel Committee member! And after being blackmailed himself, to murder once, twice! Eet ees not rational, but I let myself be seduced by *estúpid*, irrational cop thinking. Money? MONEY SUCKS! But een your own way you were achieving some rational results with irrational reasoning. Would Ignacio Mendoza murder for money? Never! But Ignacio Mendoza *would* murder."

"For *what* then?" the detective asked, staring down at the crazy chemist, who was standing on tiptoe, his index finger pointing heavenward.

"One can work an entire life doing science. I have. One can do great and famous work een science. I have. One can receive fulfillment and satisfaction beyond the dreams of ordinary people. I have. But until some *estúpid* bourgeois Meeckey Mouse *cocksuckers* in Stockholm select my name, I cannot live *forever*! The money directly or indirectly gained ees meaningless. For the same reason that Khufu killed ten thousand slaves constructing his monument, I would kill. For nothing more nor less than immortality!"

He pointed to the NP = I and said: "Nobel Prize equals *Immortality*!"

Suddenly he started erasing the formulas on the lower chalkboard. He dropped the eraser, cursed in Spanish, picked it up and frantically wiped.

He drew three enormous symbols on the chalkboard:
δ δ *

"There ees the key to your solution."

Mario Villalobos was starting to feel an energy rush. The scientist's "medicine" capsule was working. "What's that mean?"

"Eet's delta to delta-star!" the scientist thundered, cracking his pointer against the chalkboard until it snapped in two. "Eet ees a new kind of excited state whose peculiarly long lifetime was discovered here at Caltech. Let's call eet a lingering *excited state*. Look at you. A cop burnout. Anyone can see eet. Still a young man and yet you project like you are seventy—no, eighty years old! Eef you could ever get eento a delta to delta-star excited state, just long enough to be creative for once een your bourgeoisie cop life, perhaps you could find what you are looking for!"

"Delta to delta-star?" the detective said.

"Did you see my research group?" the scientist said. His topknot red as sunset threw fluttering moth shadows. "They are all smart. One was a prodigy who entered university as a child. Are they necessarily creative? Not at all. I believe that pure creativity can only be achieved een an excited state. Like an electron gone mad! I am not asking you to be smart. I am asking for infinitely more than that. Show me a *dramatic* change een your creativity. Show me the excited state of delta to delta-star!"

At four o'clock that afternoon, Mario Villalobos lay on the campus grass beneath a California white oak that was perhaps 150 years old. At first he felt as old as the tree. He watched a sparrow veer on the wind and wondered if its fall would be of any more cosmic significance than that of a leaf or a Hollywood whore. The clouds were white as linen over the university and darting squirrels played on the limbs of the ancient oak.

The "medicine" that the scientist gave him was causing him to see things differently, like a drop of water glistening on the petal of a camellia, sun-splashed among mottled shadows. He saw a hawk hanging like doom directly overhead and he feared for the carefree squirrels. He dozed and awoke days or seconds later. He watched students come and go, and they all walked lightly on cat's feet or floated before his eyes like The Gooned-out Vice Cop.

Gradually things assumed more familiar essences and he was left with a residue of unaccustomed energy. He was a man, he thought, who had been a consummate failure up to this moment in his life. He was, he thought, without the love of a single human being on earth, and had had not a moment in forty-two years of which to be particularly proud. And his mortal machinery was now taking him frighteningly fast toward the last end-of-watch.

He decided that for once in his life, for whatever reason, he was going to seek the answer for the sake of knowing. And he'd have to be far better than himself in order to do it. He also realized that unless life imitated soap opera, no one was going to run up to him and confess to being the man he sought, and without an admission of guilt he had absolutely no chance of arrest and conviction.

Still, it seemed that for the first time in his life he felt an exquisitely urgent *need* to know. For the sake of knowing.

When he tried to stand, his back sent a shaft of pain straight down his right leg all the way to the knee. He walked apelike until the back permitted him to walk like a human being.

He thought it the greatest of ironies when, upon entering Millikan Library, he saw the man in the pinstripe suit. Even on a weekend Professor Richard Feldman wore a suit and tie. He was a refined, well-tailored man. Nothing like the scientists the detective had seen in the basement pub. Nothing like Ignacio Mendoza.

He couldn't help noticing that Professor Feldman's graceful fingers were unmarred. He would have given a great deal if another scientist had walked into the library with a bandaged left hand from punching plaster walls in the night.

The library on weekends was open only to faculty and students. A student was on duty to check identification and was impressed when the detective showed his badge. The boy eagerly helped the detective find what he wanted.

Mario Villalobos read all that he could absorb about the Nobel Prize. He read old Caltech newspapers with accounts of the ceremonies in the Stockholm concert hall. It appeared that the whole country closed down to entertain the Nobel laureates. The detective paid particular attention to whatever news items he could find on American chemists who had traveled to Sweden for the festivities, and there were many. He saw pictures of some from Caltech in the concert hall in Stockholm, dressed in white tie and tails for an event that was sold out ten years in advance.

He could see that most of the chemistry prizes were given to Americans, and he read of complaints that other nations had tried to exert national pressure on the committee to bridle the American race for prizes. And that some scientists believed Japan had been recently successful in exerting national pressure.

One of the articles showed a map of Sweden and told of the tour of a group from Caltech, Stanford, Harvard and M.I.T. The tour took place during the Nobel festivities of 1981, just a few weeks after a Soviet sub ran aground near the Karlskrona naval base and shocked the nation.

The detective looked at the map and considered the Swedish navy at Karlskrona facing the Soviet colossus directly across the Baltic in Kaliningrad. And of course he could not help but think of a coked-out street whore from Normandie and Santa Monica who months later was reading of an event which all but the Swedes had nearly forgotten.

He had not slept for thirty-five hours. He read until the print started to blur and it became impossible to continue. He politely thanked the student and went out to his car and drove toward the Pasadena Freeway and home. He tried not to think of how pathetic and dreary his life's work had been when seen in light of delta to delta-star.

FOURTEEN

The Gooned-Out
Vice Cop

Mario Villalobos was able to sleep for three hours. He awoke in pain. He had been grinding his teeth as he slept and had bitten the inside of his cheek. His hands were trembling and he was instantly alert. When he sat up, his head hurt. He walked to the window of his apartment and looked out at the smog-shrouded streets of the Los Feliz district. It was dusk and the sun was fiery copper against a mauve and redolent sky.

He looked at his swollen eyes in the mirror. The eyes looked dead and gutted. The marbled flesh was precisely the color of the Los Angeles smog-layered sky at dusk. He went into the kitchen in his undershorts and took one of his week's supply of TV dinners from the refrigerator. He smoked a cigarette and stared at the tinfoil tray for a moment and put it back. Instead, he poured himself a very large glass of orange juice and whipped three eggs into it.

He drank it, and smoked, and listened to "Stella by Starlight" on his favorite radio station, and experienced what he supposed was an unconscious pathetic try for a creative moment. He got dizzy, or rather, light-headed with occasional dizziness. He felt alternately as though he were going to have a coronary, faint or vomit. He was so weak that his knees actually buckled as he paced the kitchen. He knew that he was too tired to sleep without drugging himself with alcohol. He sensed that while asleep his brain had been working at capacity, thus allowing him little rest.

"I can't!" he actually cried aloud.

Mario Villalobos believed that if he kept this up he'd blow his usually desensitized neurons right through his marinated brain matter. Delta to delta-star might be very injurious to what was left of his health.

Mario Villalobos concluded that he could not be better than himself. He could not imitate the excited state of an electron gone mad. Not with his slaughtered senses. The future and past were one. He showered, shaved, dressed in casual clothes and went to The House of Misery to get drunk.

They were all there, in that it was Saturday night. Even Rumpled Ronald was back, getting lots of attention and sympathy for his broken ribs and, of course, loving it. The Bad Czech and Hans had already informed them of the Caltech experience, and Mario Villalobos was spared explanations of why he looked worse than Gerry Cooney after Larry Holmes beat him up for thirteen rounds.

Ludwig was sitting beside Hans at their end of the bar, looking cranky because he wanted to sleep, and the hyper hot dogs, Stanley and Leech, were playing a game of nine-ball on his bed.

A groupie with a face like tapioca pudding was draped around Hans, who wasn't looking too happy since he'd gotten nothing from the hotshot chemist at Caltech but advice to shellac it.

Jane Wayne was tugging on the eyebrows of The Bad Czech, who was reading the *Los Angeles Times* and howling from time to time, which would set off Ludwig into louder howling and make everyone get cranky and start yelling at each other to shut up.

Dilford and Dolly were sitting together and commenting on one of the town crier's editorials. Cecil Higgins was staring into the bottom of his glass, and Leery was setting them up for all he was worth, playing a sonata on the cash register while he sucked his teeth and leered happily.

Mario Villalobos just nodded when Leery said, "Whatcha having, Mario, a very dry vodka martini?"

The detective hadn't taken his first sip when the door opened and through the smoke and gloom floated a young man with shoulder-length hair and a delicate face. He took his place before the broken spider web of mirror and signaled for bar whiskey.

Before everyone got a chance to quiet down and get unaccountably edgy in the presence of The Gooned-out Vice Cop, the hyper hot dogs, Stanley and Leech, finished their nine-ball game and came swaggering into the bar for more beer.

"Look who's here!" Stanley said to Leech. "Hey, Bartholomew!"

The Gooned-out Vice Cop was moving his face from side to side, making the ghastly neon illuminate various shards of mirror in his cubist self-portrait. He didn't seem to hear.

"Hey, Bartholomew!" Leech yelled, and both hyper hot dogs charged down to the end of the bar and clapped The Gooned-out Vice Cop on the shoulder.

"Haven't seen you since the academy!" Stanley cried.

"How's it hanging?" Leech cried.

"Just kicking back lately," The Gooned-out Vice Cop said, turning and smiling placidly at the hyper hot dogs.

"Man, that was all-time what I read about you in the paper last January! All-time!" Leech said.

"You did the *right thing* on that one!" Stanley said, winking at The Gooned-out Vice Cop.

And of course all the cops in the barroom knew that

"the right thing" in police jargon means that one has blown some pukebag into eternity.

"Musta scared the shit outa ya, that scuzzball leaping out with a knife when you're creeping through a backyard on a little gambling raid."

"So what if he was sixteen? He tried to do a little East Hollywood surgery on ya, didn't he? Bet *he* was surprised when he was looking outa two more eyes on each side of his nose. How many rounds did ya fire? Any misses?"

The Gooned-out Vice Cop continued to smile serenely and did not reply, but there was seldom need to reply to hyper hot dogs like Stanley and Leech.

"You guys hear about his shooting?" Leech asked, giving no one a chance to answer. "Big deal on TV when the little puke's Cuban mama says how her little boy was out playing with his pigeons in the yard and gets killed by a trigger-happy vice cop. Sure. With a goddamn *knife* in her baby's hand and PCP in his pocket."

"Did they find any angel dust in the autopsy, Bartholomew?" Stanley asked.

"Bartholomew made a good Cuban outa him before he had a *chance* to get dusted out," Leech answered.

"Garbage. All garbage," Stanley said.

The Gooned-out Vice Cop continued to smile until the hyper hot dogs got tired asking and answering their questions. He shook his head when they tried to buy him a drink, and they returned to their nine-ball game.

Except that Ludwig had established his idea of eminent domain and was lying on the pool table with his head on the rail, slobbering all over the felt by the corner pocket.

"Hey! Get that fucking dog off the table!" Stanley said to Hans, who was moving on his groupie, worrying about doing it without shellac, and feeling generally grumpy from listening to the two hot dogs babble.

"*You* get him off," Hans said.

"Get the fuck *off* that table, asshole!" Leech said to Ludwig, and banged on the table with his cue stick.

This time Ludwig did not come up with a roar. He barely raised his head. But despite stories about animals avoiding eye contact, *this* animal looked directly into the eyes of the young hot dog. Ludwig's goatlike eyes were amber yellow and the whites were red-webbed from the smoke in the saloon and the beer he'd consumed. It did not become a roar, nor was it interrupted by breathing. It was a primordial growl, from the neighborhood of the La Brea tar pits where saber-toothed tigers lay interred. And except for Leery, Hans and The Gooned-out Vice Cop, every human being in that bar reached slowly toward a gun.

Leech never broke eye contact when he put his cue stick against the wall, very carefully. He didn't break eye contact when he ever so slowly backed out of the pool table area into the main barroom. He didn't even break eye contact when he paid Leery and said, "Come on, Stanley. If they're gonna permit animals in this place, we'll just drink somewhere else."

"Don't be hasty, boys!" Leery yelled anxiously as the hyper hot dogs scooted toward the door. "Come back! You can drink down at the other end of the bar!" Then he turned to the K-9 cop and said, "Goddamnit, Hans, Ludwig's gonna ruin my business yet! Get that freaking dog off the pool table!"

But Hans, who was half bagged, just giggled and drank his beer and whispered something lewd into his groupie's ear.

Then for the first time, The Gooned-out Vice Cop uttered an unsolicited comment. He said, "Here's a syllogism: people are nothing more than garbage. I'm a person. What am I, finally?"

The Gooned-out Vice Cop looked around the bar and no one could answer for a moment.

The Bad Czech spoke first. He said to The Gooned-out Vice Cop: "Them two bigmouthed hot dogs gimme a pain in the ass. Maybe you'd like to get acquainted with us here?"

The Gooned-out Vice Cop said, "What if once you

got *real* scared. You ever do a job every day and suddenly one day you get scared? For no reason?"

"I can understand that," Mario Villalobos said to The Gooned-out Vice Cop.

"Did you ever see a kid get shot in the face?" The Gooned-out Vice Cop asked.

Cecil Higgins said, "A sixteen-year-old jumps out in the dark with a knife? I mean nobody can blame . . ."

"What if he *didn't* have a knife?" The Gooned-out Vice Cop asked. "What if someone panicked? What if someone then planted some dust and a throwaway knife to cover it? Have you ever been absolutely *positive* your heart was going to bang a hole in itself and bleed all over the inside of your belly? Have you ever been *that* scared?"

But it was too late for anyone to formulate answers. The Gooned-out Vice Cop took one last look at his image in the broken glitter of glass. At his mirror image in black shadow and ghastly neon green. Then he was off the stool moving on a vice cop's cat feet toward the door.

He turned for an instant and smiled serenely at them, with eyes like bullet holes.

"Hey! He didn't pay for his drink!" Leery said. "Hey!"

"I'll pay for his freaking drink!" The Bad Czech said, and that made Leery quiet down and go back to leering happily at the amount he'd taken in so far.

Then the cops began talking about The Gooned-out Vice Cop.

"I was sorta scared of him before," Dilford confessed.

"I sorta thought he looked like *me* sometimes," Hans confessed.

"I had eyes like that when we found the paws in the petunias," Jane Wayne confessed.

"I thought he might not be *real*," The Bad Czech confessed.

"I thought he might be a devil," Rumpled Ronald confessed.

"If he was a devil, he wouldn't be *here*," Cecil Higgins said into the bottom of his glass. "This place ain't got enough *class* to be hell. Purgatory, maybe."

"Well, he's not so spooky anymore," Mario Villalobos said, feeling an overwhelming desire to *survive*. "Next time he comes in, somebody should buy him a drink and talk to him."

And with that, Mario Villalobos picked up his bar change and got off the stool. Everyone was utterly dumbfounded. Mario Villalobos hadn't even touched his drink!

"You ain't leaving, Mario?" Leery cried.

"Catch you later," Mario Villalobos said.

"It's the shank of the night!" Leery cried.

"Was it something I said?" Dilford wondered, remembering The Madonna of the Wogs. "I seem to alienate people."

"Have to see someone," Mario Villalobos explained.

As he was going out the door he could hear Leery screaming, "It's *your* fault, Hans! You and that goddamn dog! He scares off *all* my customers!"

Later that evening Lupe Luna opened the door and gasped in shock when she saw the detective's battered and swollen face.

"Don't make me explain it," he said. "Just a little police problem."

"Maybe you should go into some other line of work," Lupe Luna said, admitting the detective into a feminine and cozy three-bedroom house in South Pasadena.

"I can't. I don't know anything else and I don't know any better."

"When you called it was like you were reading my thoughts," she said. "When my daughter went to spend the weekend with her dad, I started thinking about calling *you*."

"Got a record player?" Mario Villalobos asked.

"Sure. Why?"

Mario Villalobos opened the paper bag he was carrying. In it was a bouquet of white carnations, a bottle of good California Zinfandel, and a record album he'd brought from home.

"Moldy oldies," he said, putting the record on the turntable.

Lupe Luna picked up the album and said, "Oh, Mario! 'Stardust'? Is *this* what you listen to?"

"I just came from a bunch of confessors," he said. "I may as well confess too. *That's* what I listen to. I'm from another time and I'm going to hell in a hurry. I love your new sporty haircut. You're a knockout, kid."

"You look like you've been knocked out enough lately," she said, as the Hoagy Carmichael classic melted out of the dual speakers.

"Wanna dance?" Mario Villalobos asked.

"Oh, Mario," she said, shaking her head incredulously.

But she moved into his arms and put her head on his chest and they danced in the living room of the little house. She said, "You're the most peculiar guy I've met in quite a while."

"If only I could find some stardust. Just once. Maybe I could go for it," he said.

"For what?" she asked.

"If only I could be like an electron gone mad. Just for a moment."

"What *are* you talking about?"

"I don't know," he said. "Maybe the excited state of delta to delta-star."

They were barely moving, only swaying when she kissed him, slant-eyed, heavy-lashed, smoldering, her glistening overbite white in the glow from the lamp.

"Come on," she said, taking his hand and leading him through a hallway to her bedroom.

"I didn't come here for this, believe it or not," he said, feeling a sudden drumming in his blood. "I only wanted to dance to 'Stardust.' "

"I don't care *why* you came here," she said, pulling his jacket off his shoulders. "Since meeting you I've been in my *own* excited state." Then she said, "Get in that bed, Mexican."

FIFTEEN

The Delta Star

The detective didn't get back to his apartment until 4:00 A.M. Lupe Luna couldn't persuade him to stay the night. He didn't know why he had to spend the rest of the dark hours alone, but he had to. A feeling was coming over him. It thrilled and frightened him. He was light-headed, unsure of whether he might faint, vomit or have a coronary.

Something was generating a kind of energy. His neurons were being bombarded with sensations. He lay in the dark, neither awake nor asleep. He watched sparkling images on his eyelids: Lupe Luna. Black matted lashes. Nipples like berries in buttercup. Then in whiter light like pale cherries in alabaster.

He opened his eyes to watch the black sky through his bedroom window. A dark star showed faintly through the smog. He closed his eyes for seconds or days. When he opened them the star had flared to life! It was spinning in the blackness like an electron gone mad. The star as huge as the sun powered upward in stellar fire. An instant of cosmic excitement!

Then, rising silence. Silver starlight and rain. Cumulus as white as lace. Moonset.

277

At 5:30 A.M. in a river of sweat he came up out of bed like Ludwig off the pool table. If he could have managed the Rottweiler's roar, he might have. At 5:35 A.M. Ignacio Mendoza was cursing into his telephone in Spanish.

Mario Villalobos, his eyes bulging and pulsating, said, "Please, Professor, try to understand that I wouldn't wake you if it wasn't urgent! Now let me repeat the question: Who's the Soviet chemist most likely to be a candidate for the Nobel Prize?"

"Estúpido!" Ignacio Mendoza thundered, causing the detective to hold the phone a foot from his ear. "I told you that the best work ees done een America! With some een West Germany and Britain! Not Russia! You wake me for a Meeckey Mouse cop question?"

"Please don't hang up, Professor!" Mario Villalobos pleaded. "I think I've been into the excited state of delta to delta-star."

Ignacio Mendoza quieted down and after a few seconds said, "Anatoly Rozlov. He works een Dubna, the Soviet version of Los Alamos. He would be the only possibility, but eet ees so remote that . . ."

"In what area has he done the most notable work?" Mario Villalobos asked.

"Organometallic diradical chemistry, to be sure," the Peruvian answered. "Specifically, een studying diradical species as catalytic intermediates. The importance ees een the development of cheap synthetic fuels."

"Okay, now give me the name of the Caltech scientist who has done the most notable work in *exactly* the same area of diradical chemistry. I'm referring to a man who's made similar discoveries, if not identical discoveries."

"Noah Fisher," Ignacio Mendoza said immediately.

"Is he a candidate for the prize?"

"You don't understand, Sergeant!" the chemist cried in exasperation. "Chemistry ees not the kind of science where a piece of work has instantly recognizable and far-reaching implications! We don't make fundamental discoveries as een physics or biology. Eet's the *body* of a man's work, a *package* of science. I believe that the work of Noah Fisher needs at *least* five more years to . . ."

"But his achievements pretty well mirror the best work of Anatoly Rozlov?"

"They have done a lot of separate but identical work."

"Thanks, Dr. Mendoza," Mario Villalobos said. "I'll stay in touch."

The detective's hands were shaking when he whipped the eggs into the orange juice. He almost gagged it back up when it splashed into his empty fluttering stomach, but he concentrated on holding it down.

He showered, shaved, and dressed just as he would for duty, except that he wore his best suit and a new necktie. He dropped the keys trying to unlock the door to his BMW and had to pause for a moment to get his nerves quieted. He drove straight to the Hollywood Freeway and fairly raced around the ramp to the Pasadena Freeway north.

It was 8:00 A.M. before the detective was able to locate the home of Noah Fisher in northwest Pasadena. It was a very nice house on a very nice street lined with flowering trees which shed white and purple blossoms from curb to curb. The woman who answered the door was about the detective's age.

Mario Villalobos decided not to identify himself. He said, "May I speak to Dr. Fisher?"

"He's not here. I'm Mrs. Fisher. Can I help you?"

"I'm a friend of Lester Beemer's," the detective said. "And I was told that he left some property of mine with Dr. Fisher."

"Lester Beemer? I don't think I know him," she said.

"He passed away," Mario Villalobos said. "*Lester?* Did your husband know a man named Lester?"

"Lester?" she said. "Is that the Lester he played golf with at Altadena Country Club?"

"Might've been," Mario Villalobos said. "A few months ago?"

"He called for golf dates. He *died*?"

"Yes, and as a matter of fact he left a pair of golf shoes in your husband's car. They belong to me."

"Oh. I'm sorry. It must be an oversight. I wonder if Noah knows the man died?"

"I think he knows," Mario Villalobos said. "Is he in his laboratory this morning?"

"He's at the track," she said. "He likes to lift weights and jog at the Caltech track."

Mario Villalobos sat anxiously in the second row of bleachers on the south side of the quarter-mile dirt track. The San Gabriels loomed to the north and were still snow-capped despite the heat in the valley. He would have taken his suit coat off were it not for the gun and handcuffs. He watched four sweating men making labored trips around the track. One appeared to be eighty years old and shuffled on legs veiny and bowed. But still he shuffled, and did not stop until he'd covered a mile.

There were three other men lifting free weights to the north of the track near the university swimming pool, but they were young men. Two women suddenly appeared from the direction of the basketball courts and started to jog slowly around the track. They turned to wave to a man some distance behind. They encouraged him to hurry. He feigned exhaustion and pretended to stagger with his tongue hanging out, and the women laughed and waited.

He was about six feet tall and in excellent condition. He wore a gray sweat shirt cut off at his bruising shoulders and was very bald with only a black fringe around the ears. His legs were hairless and well developed, with the large calves of a tennis player. He didn't notice Mario Villalobos in the bleachers on his first pass around the track.

The detective guessed him to be in his early fifties, and also guessed that he was very lucky that the scientist hadn't had a better chance to overpower an out-of-shape detective and stick that syringe full of sodium cyanide right where he lived. The detective could see that the man intended to continue jogging with the two women in warm-up suits. On his second pass by the bleachers, the detective clearly saw the abrasions on his left fist, and he yelled, "Hey, Dr. Fisher! I'm Lester Beemer's friend!"

The two women smiled up at Mario Villalobos and both looked to Noah Fisher for a response. He slowed his jogging pace and stared up at the detective in consummate disbelief.

The detective smiled grimly and sat back down.

On Noah Fisher's next pass around the track, his breathing was far more labored than it should have been. He waved the women on, and stopped. He held his hands on his hips and looked up at the man in the bleachers as though it were a dream. Then he began jogging again, his face dead-white when he passed those bleachers alone.

"I want to talk to you about my friend Missy Moonbeam!" Mario Villalobos said.

Noah Fisher could only gape at the man in the bleachers as though he were dumbstruck. Then he resumed jogging as before. He quickened his pace. He began *sprinting,* as if he could outrun this specter in the bleacher seats. He passed everyone on the track.

When he got to the opposite side of the track he stopped and held his hands on his knees until he got his breath. Then he stared across the track at the man in the bleachers. He turned and began walking to the gymnasium locker room. When he got near the door he turned again.

Mario Villalobos was standing. He'd moved down to the front row of bleacher seats. He cupped his hands to his mouth and shouted, "I'll call you at home!"

Noah Fisher turned and entered the locker room without ever uttering a word.

The detective called the residence of Professor Noah Fisher twice that Sunday afternoon. Each time, the chemist's worried wife informed Mario Villalobos that her husband had not returned from his workout and that she was concerned.

He made another visit to Millikan Library, found the same student on weekend duty, and spent hours reading journals, magazines and newspapers, for biographical data. He learned that Anatoly Rozlov was seventy-seven years old, suffering from a serious undisclosed illness. He learned from a newspaper story that Noah Fisher had three handsome sons, and a mentally gifted daughter at the University of California at Berkeley. And of course he read more on the Nobel Prize.

At dusk Mario Villalobos was wandering around the nearly deserted Caltech campus. He saw that there were some chemists coming and going from one of the laboratory buildings, where Ignacio Mendoza had his office. Mario Villalobos was considering another call to Noah Fisher, but instead walked impulsively into the building when he saw that they had left the door unlocked.

He strolled through the halls and heard voices from one of the chemistry labs where half a dozen young men and women were laughing and working alongside an older man who seemed to be in charge of the research group. He continued unhurriedly down the deserted corridor and found himself near the lecture hall where Ignacio Mendoza had first told him about delta to delta-star.

The detective entered the darkened lecture hall and lit a match until he found the light switches. He turned on the light over the lecture platform, and sat in the upper tier of seats looking down at the lighted stage below him. He sat like this for fifteen minutes. Then he got up and walked down to the lighted platform and found the switch under the chalkboard tray. The green chalkboards, which rose twenty feet up the wall, were set into motion and reversed their positions. The detective played with the switch for a moment and watched the giant chalkboards rise and descend on the metal slides.

Then he picked up some chalk and began writing formulas on the chalkboard. It was nearly nine o'clock when he stopped writing and started out of the building. He switched off the light and walked down the hall, passing an office where a janitor was cleaning. He stopped, smiled pleasantly at the Latino janitor as though he belonged there, and picked up the telephone.

Mrs. Fisher answered and said, "Yes, he came home." Then he heard her say, "Noah, it's that man who's been calling."

"Yes," Noah Fisher said, his voice as lifeless as The Gooned-out Vice Cop's.

"I'm in Noyes Laboratory," Mario Villalobos said, "in the lecture hall at the north end, first floor. I think you can find me."

Then he hung up and returned to the lecture hall and smoked, and revised his formulas, and waited.

It was nearly 9:30 when the detective heard the door to the lecture hall creak open. He stood on the lighted podium and didn't bother to peer up into the darkness at the top row of theater seats.

He could see the shadow figure move into the top row and sit down. Mario Villalobos was feeling calmer than he had in two days. He ground the cigarette on the floor and kicked it out of his way. Suddenly it occurred to him that he hadn't had an alcoholic drink in nearly forty-eight hours, a record to be sure.

He picked up the pointer, the size of a deep-sea fishing rod, and pointed toward the formula he had written on the chalkboard. The detective stood in the wash of light and faced the darkness.

He said, "I'm Sergeant Mario Villalobos of the Los Angeles Police Department."

The introduction made, the detective paced back and forth on the podium looking up at his formulas. He said, "All week I've been very upset because I couldn't formulate it." He pressed the switch and the top blackboard descended to his pointer.

"I bet you almost went bonkers when that Russian sub ran aground last year," Mario Villalobos said. "I bet they were crapping Swedish meatballs the size of BBs when that Russian captain drew his finger across his throat and the Swedes wondered if he was referring to himself or *them*. I bet you heard lots of talk about how *next* year the committee would have the screws tightened by their own politicians. To give the Russians something they'd like more than fifty golds in the Olympics. Right when they're trying to persuade Scandinavia to join in a nuclear free zone. I bet you figured if ever a Russian chemist like Anatoly Rozlov had a chance, it was *now*! But you probably got real nervous because Rozlov's very old and sick. And they don't give that prize to dead men. You probably concluded it better be *now,* in 1982.

"I bet you thought that if someone powerful on the chemistry committee in Stockholm was really pushing Rozlov, it'd give him at least a fifty-fifty shot this year. What you planned really wasn't much worse than what nations do. They try to exert pressure and badger the committee, don't they? That's all it started out to be: a simple, understandable, low-life *badger* game.

"You hired your pal Lester Beemer to set up the Swede, Jan Larsson." Then the detective pointed to his formula: BG + NP = WR

The detective said: "Badger Game, plus National Pressure equals Winning Russian. A pretty good formula. You weren't remotely considering murder. Just encouraging the most powerful man on the committee to push for the Russian chemist. An agreeable thing to do anyway at this time in Swedish history. I bet old Lester Beemer had a laugh when he contacted the Swede, with his filthy little tapes or photographs, and warned that Rozlov *better* be the winning horse next time. That must've been pretty funny. The sleazy little Pasadena private eye playing like a Russian agent promoting his Soviet countryman."

The detective pushed the button and the blackboard slid on the rails until he could reach the next one. "Then poor old Lester Beemer decides that *two* can play your game. He starts looking at the lousy thousand or two that he got paid by you and he starts computing what a Nobel Prize could be worth, not just the two hundred grand in front money, but in the *possibilities* for an ambitious Nobel laureate. After getting Jan Larsson all ready to cooperate, he tells you that *you* have a partner now. That the president of the university *and* the Nobel Committee were going to know about your extortion conspiracy *unless* he was your fifty-fifty partner from the day you walk into that concert hall in Stockholm and pick up big casino.

"*Now* where were you? From plain old low-rent badger game, you were facing the prospect of not just losing your chance now, but *forever*. Not to mention a criminal prosecution."

The detective pointed to a formula that read: $BC = I$

"Big Casino equals Immortality," he said. "But you were *never* going to be immortal if he informed on you. Now *this* is something to *kill* for, I've come to understand. Even I might kill for immortality, Professor."

The detective felt a rush of adrenaline when the shadow figure stood for a moment, but then sat back down. The detective kept his coat clear of his holster when he continued.

"The old Caltech science groupie had a *little* knowledge. And in this case, it was a very very dangerous thing. You probably made the date to meet him in the no-tell motel because it was a believable place to find a man like Lester Beemer with a dead pacemaker. Did you talk about getting one of his whores for you? Anyway, you changed the meeting place to here, late at night, in that little room with the NMR spectrometer. You didn't have to lift a finger to kill him, just to carry his body to the motel where they found him.

"But his girl friend showed up at the motel and found old Lester dead of an apparent heart attack. Missy Moonbeam was a smart girl. She decided *she* was going to be your partner. She phoned you and introduced herself. You were terrified to discover that Lester Beemer had let the whore in on the whole deal.

"It still could've worked out except for one little thing: simple, low-life greed. When she found his body she did a little low-life corpse robbing. You'd taken his wristwatch which the spectrometer had busted, but he kept his *wallet* in his sock! Can you imagine?

"She decided to have a little fling for a few days on his American Express card, but the magnetic stripe had been erased by the magnet. Isn't that something, Professor? Such a *little* thing."

The detective pointed to another formula that read: $I = 1DH + 1DP$

The detective said, "For you, Immortality *now* equaled One Dead Hooker, plus One Dead Pansy. But actually the pansy wasn't in on the scheme with Lester and Missy, so you would've stuck him full of sodium cyanide for nothing. But I suppose that one dead pansy more or less doesn't make much difference when the payoff is immortality."

And then it started closing in on Mario Villalobos: the bombardment of myriad sensations and the danger of the present moment. He remembered the syringe full of poison, and Missy Moonbeam, neé Thelma Bernbaum of Omaha, hanging in pieces from Chip Muirfield's ice-cream suit.

He could hardly keep his voice from trembling when he said, "I suppose that one dead hooker more or less doesn't make much difference either, when the payoff is immortality. After all . . ." The detective startled himself by shouting, "Khufu killed ten thousand slaves to become immortal!" Then he scared himself by screaming: "BUT I'LL TELL YOU SOMETHING, MISTER—HE DIDN'T DO IT ON MY BEAT!"

The detective felt himself go weak, and his knees started to buckle. His hands were shaking too much to let the man in the darkness see them, so he didn't light a cigarette though he needed one. He pushed the button which sent the last chalkboard down into range of his ten-foot pointer. He pointed to another formula.

"I could have figured it out earlier, *maybe*. No, I take that back," the detective said, holding on to the podium because his head was spinning. "I couldn't, because then I couldn't get into an excited state like a nutty electron. I came to learn that a *shared* prize is the same as an unshared prize. There's no asterisk here to show whether you hit sixty home runs in a short season or a long season. You're just as immortal as the guy who takes it alone."

He pointed to a formula that read: $\frac{1}{2}BC = I$

"In other words, One Half of Big Casino equals Immortality. If Rozlov was chosen by the committee, they *had to choose you with him,* because you'd done separate but identical work in the field of organometallic diradical chemistry. You'd get the prize right with him!"

Then the detective went to the chalkboard and feverishly drew three huge symbols: δ δ *

He turned and said, "I got into a state of delta to delta-star for a while, but I know there's no practical application of my theories. Yet in pure science the knowledge in itself is worth the quest. I've sought the answer for its own sake. You can believe me, if I *could* prove my theory in a court of law, I'D BE CLIMBING OVER THOSE FUCKING SEATS TO SLAP THE IRON ON YOUR WRISTS!"

He threw the pointer on the table and said, "That's it, Professor. Lecture's over. There's only one thing I can promise you: I'm calling Jan Larsson in Stockholm, and I'm explaining your badger game to him, and I'm telling him he has nothing to fear from a phony Russian agent who was just a blackmailing private eye hired by Dr. Noah Fisher. And if you wanna stop me, I suggest you get out your syringe and try it right now. You're *never* gonna get that prize! You're *never* gonna be immortal if I can help it!"

Mario Villalobos stepped down from the podium, not taking his eyes from the shadow figure seated in the darkness of the top row.

The detective walked cautiously toward the door, the blood banging in his temples, ready to go for the cross-draw holster under his coat.

Suddenly the figure stood up and went to the light switch, illuminating the entire lecture hall.

"*Está terminado?*" the Guatemalan janitor asked. "Feenish? Feenish, señor?"

*   *   *

At eleven o'clock that night Mario Villalobos was sitting in The House of Misery with the regular cast of losers. Everyone was very worried about him because he stared at the broken mirror. He had a shot of vodka sitting in front of him, untouched.

Since delivering his lecture to the befuddled Spanish-speaking janitor, Mario Villalobos had twice called the home of Noah Fisher with no answer. He had driven to the scientist's house but found both cars gone and the premises deserted.

Suddenly a momentous event occurred in that saloon. Leery took the detective's watery drink away and replaced it with a fresh one. *Free* of charge.

The detective responded only when Cecil Higgins said, "Did ya hear, Mario? That kid smoked it. The Gooned-out Vice Cop. He was found this mornin in bed. Shot himself in the mouth, poor kid."

"Sweet Jesus!" Mario Villalobos groaned. "Is there no end to it? Sweet Jesus."

"I wish I'da bought him a drink," The Bad Czech said.

"I wish I hadn'ta been scared of him," Dilford said.

"I should've tried to talk to him," Jane Wayne said.

It was a very morose night. Mario Villalobos, who had been wrong so many times, began to wonder if he could be wrong again. About all of it. If so, it had not been delta to delta-star, only utter madness.

He got his answer just after eleven o'clock.

The television news caused Mario Villalobos to spill his untouched drink all over the bar. During the recital of local happenings, one of Los Angeles' happy-talk newsreaders, an eye-shadow champ with bangled earrings, worked her eyebrows for all they were worth. And made an announcement that Caltech scientist Noah Fisher had leaped to his death in Pasadena. Overlooking the Rose Bowl. At a place called Suicide Bridge because it had claimed so many other miserable wretches.

After Mario Villalobos spilled his drink and walked shakily from the bar, Leery said, "Goddamn! That's the *last* time I give anybody a free drink! Where does generosity get ya?"

Epilogue

One night in October of 1982, Leery stood behind the bar in The House of Misery resplendent in a brand-new L.A. Dodgers batting helmet, happily sucking his teeth and leering at the assembled cripples and misfits and losers, who had remained after drinking hours for an exceedingly bizarre reason. They were waiting for a telephone call about an event in Sweden.

They were joined by a civilian guest with hair like a cockatoo who drank with The Bad Czech and promised to take the monster cop to the best little whorehouse in Lima, if The Bad Czech could ever rathole enough money from the spousal support to his three ex-wives.

Due to the time difference, it was 4:00 A.M. when the telephone call came. Ignacio Mendoza picked it up, listened, and made an announcement: "The Swede must have believed you, Mario. The Russian did *not* win!"

This brought a roar from the gathered group reminiscent of the one earlier in the year when the Los Angeles Lakers won the championship of professional basketball.

It was exceedingly puzzling to a liquor distributor

who found the flotsam and jetsam when he made an early-morning delivery.

"A celebration?" he said incredulously. "Because a Russian didn't win a Nobel Prize? No wonder detente's almost dead!"

Mario Villalobos looked around at the grinning boozy faces with some satisfaction. He made everybody ecstatic by buying another drink for the house, now *absolutely* finished with a case without evidence which would be officially and forever classified as an unsolved homicide.

When Leery was carrying beer down the bar to Hans and Ludwig, he discovered that Ludwig had skulked up onto Leery's *new* pool table and gone to sleep.

The saloon keeper started to say something, when Ludwig began growling in his sleep. Deep in some canine dream or fantasy, Ludwig began to *moan*.

Leery looked at him in horror, lying there the full length of the new pool table, below the hanging light. There was no mistaking it.

"GODDAMNIT, HANS!" Leery screamed. "LUDWIG'S JIZZING ON THE NEW POOL TABLE!"

Mario Villalobos didn't finish his vodka. He didn't drink so much anymore. He stepped out of the gloom into cold blue moonlight and black shadows, into the fresh smog on Sunset Boulevard. He took in a lungful of noxious fumes and looked up at frosty stars. Like spinning electrons in a black Los Angeles sky.

The last thing he heard from The House of Misery was Leery screaming: *"Achtung,* Ludwig! *Achtung!"*

ABOUT THE AUTHOR

JOSEPH WAMBAUGH, a fourteen-year veteran of the Los Angeles Police Department, is the author of numerous best sellers: *The New Centurions, The Blue Knight, The Choirboys, The Onion Field, The Black Marble, The Glitter Dome, The Delta Star, Lines and Shadows, The Secrets of Harry Bright,* and *Echoes in the Darkness.* He lives near Palm Springs with his wife and children.

RELAX!
SIT DOWN
and Catch Up On Your Reading!

☐	05057	**THE ALCHEMIST** by Ken Goddard	$14.95
		A Bantam Hardcover	
☐	25432	**THE OCTOBER CIRCLE**	$3.95
		by Robert Littell	
☐	24172	**NATHANIEL** by John Saul	$3.95
☐	23336	**GOD PROJECT** by John Saul	$3.95
☐	24607	**LINES AND SHADOWS**	$4.50
		by Joseph Wambaugh	
☐	26217	**THE DELTA STAR**	$4.50
		by Joseph Wambaugh	
☐	26302	**GLITTER DOME**	$4.50
		by Joseph Wambaugh	
☐	24646	**THE LITTLE DRUMMER GIRL**	$4.50
		by John Le Carré	
☐	26705	**SUSPECTS** by William J. Cavnitz	$4.50
☐	26733	**VENDETTA** by Steve Shagan	$4.50
☐	26657	**THE UNWANTED** by John Saul	$4.50
☐	26658	**A GRAND PASSION** by Mary Mackey	$4.50
☐	26572	**110 SHANGHAI ROAD** by	$4.50
		Monica Highland	
☐	26499	**LAST OF THE BREED** by	$4.50
		Louis L'Amour	
☐	26021	**SECRETS OF HARRY BRIGHT** by	$4.50
		Joseph Wambaugh	

Special Offer
Buy a Bantam Book
for only 50¢.

Now you can have Bantam's catalog filled with hundreds of titles plus take advantage of our unique and exciting bonus book offer. A special offer which gives you the opportunity to purchase a Bantam book for only 50¢. Here's how!

By ordering any five books at the regular price per order, you can also choose any other single book listed (up to a $5.95 value) for just 50¢. Some restrictions do apply, but for further details why not send for Bantam's catalog of titles today!

Just send us your name and address and we will send you a catalog!

BANTAM BOOKS, INC.
P.O. Box 1006, South Holland, Ill. 60473

Mr./Mrs./Ms. _____
(please print)

Address _____

City _____ State _____ Zip _____
FC(A)—10/87
Please allow four to six weeks for delivery.